Lisabetta

a novel

BOOK ONE: A STOLEN GLANCE

for sarah and david

book 1   'LISABETTA – a stolen glance'   ISBN 978-1-7750471-0-0
book 2   'LISABETTA – a stolen smile'   ISBN 978-1-7750471-1-7
book 3   'LISABETTA – a stolen sister'   ISBN 978-1-7750471-2-4
book 4   'LISABETTA – a true face'   ISBN 978-1-7750471-3-1

Edited by Silent K Publishing
Typeset in Garamond and Vollkorn at SpicaBookDesign
Printed in Canada by Island Blue Book Printing, Victoria B.C.
www.islandblue.com

author's disclaimer

Why did I use my own name, Veronica, for a main character? Fate determined my choice for me because sometimes the truth in plain sight is too perfect to ignore. **'VERONICA'** is the Latin anagram for **'VERITAS ICONA'** – literal translation, **'TRUE FACE'** – the most appropriate name to celebrate a story about the lost identity of the most famous face in the world, the 'Mona Lisa' – *V Knox*

ART HISTORY DELIVERED IN A GHOST STORY

The essential promise of fiction is a 'What-if', followed by an author's unchecked imagination.

For me, the astonishing nature of lucid dreaming and synchronicity, and the compelling possibilities of fluid time, the afterlife, and reincarnation, inspire my ghost stories grounded in historical facts.

Fact… a Florentine census from 1463 references that Caterina, Leonardo da Vinci's mother, gave birth to six children, including a daughter named Lisabetta.

Leonardo had a sister named Lisa. Coincidence?

What if the 'Mona Lisa', often speculated to be an androgynous self-portrait of Leonardo, is a portrait of his beloved sister? What if Lisabetta followed her brother into the studio of his teacher, Andrea Verrocchio as one of the many anonymous women artists who supplemented the work of their brothers and fathers and husbands without pay?

What if Lisabetta was the second lovechild of Caterina and Piero da Vinci – Leonardo's full sibling with whom he had strong biological and creative ties?

Most women of the 15th century remain historically invisible, absorbed by time as insignificant wives and mothers, documented, if ever, on a first name basis. Caterina's full identity has been lost even though her son was famous in her lifetime. She was a discarded unwed mother, quickly married off to Antonio Buti, a local tenant farmer.

Leonardo, her firstborn, suffered the bane of illegitimacy all his life.

Studying art history for my Fine Arts degree, led me to imagine: What if a master artist was able to capture the soul of a person in their paintings? And since only the finest art is truly immortal, what if there are portraits that refuse to stay on the canvas? Lisabetta Buti's fanciful biography was begun in 2008 – the 500th anniversary of her death, originally published under the title 'Second Lisa', no longer in print. Now, nearing the 500th anniversary of Leonardo's death (May 2, 1519), I'm delighted to republish a revised edition of Lisabetta's posthumous quest for recognition, in four volumes under the umbrella title 'LISABETTA' – my tribute to the hundreds of unsung female artists of the 15th century, and in particular, the historical woman I premise is lost behind the Mona Lisa's smile.

-*Veronica Knox* – May 2, 2018

Table of Contents

Author's Disclaimer v

Part One. Verily

1   The Varnished Truth. 2
2   Victory on the Stairs 8
3   Bella Veritas 16
4   Growing Pains 20
5   A Blind Date. 23
6   Lisabetta Country 27
7   The House of Clues 35
8   A Meeting of Dreams 39
9   On the Rocks with a Twist. 43
10 The Musée du Louvre 46
11 The Louvre's Closet 49
12 Grand Entrance 52
13 The End of the Line 56
14 The Sleeping Beauty 61
15 The Muse in the Machine 70
16 Le Chat Noir 77

Part Two. Incubation

17 The Voice of Rebirth. 86
18 Bed & Breakthrough 87
19 Earth & Water. 92
20 New Beginnings 98
21 Twice Juicy 102
22 A Second First Date 110
23 Twice Cursed 116
24 Fire Damage. 122
25 The Cave of Fragilities 127

26 Niles' Denials 130
27 Twice Blessed 132
28 Niles' Hidden Valley 136
29 Running to Ground 141
30 Mother & Child 145
31 The Retrograde Moon 151

Part Three. Second Childhood

32 Peacock Truth 156
33 Peacock Lies 158
34 Peacock Promises 162
35 Milestones 168
36 Page One 184
37 Mona Lisabetta 195
38 Women's Work 202
39 Nobody's Child 206
40 The Perpetual Child 208
41 Singularity 211
42 Saturday's Child 217
43 Puppy Love – Act I 218
44 Mercenary Gifts 219
45 The Knot Eternal 224

Part Four. Thresholds!

46 Duking It Out 232
47 Farewell to Nova Scotia 235
48 Transitions 244
49 Hello Electric Street 248
50 Veritas Medusa 250
51 A Room of Her Own 256
52 Sandro's Umbrella 266
53 Dangerous Times 269
54 Mistress Lisa 278

55 Family Snap 283
56 Victorious Night Scribbles 291
57 The Victory of Artemis. 295
58 A Matter of Truth 300
59 Born Too Late 303

PREVIEW of BOOK 2. 'Lisabetta – a stolen smile' 309
Glossary 320
Art Themes 322
Prevalent in Leonardo's World 322
Author's Comments 323
Second Thoughts 329
Now Lost. 329
Historical Footnotes 331
Historical Fantasies 337
Acknowledgments 339
Veronica Knox: A Few Words About Me 340

Verrocchio's 'David' – c.1466
– a portrait in bronze of Leonardo da Vinci, age fourteen

the 15th century

LEONARDO AND LISABETTA
– twins born six years apart

That summer day, when I was six-years old, visiting the caged lions in the Piazza della Signoria with Leonardo, I shivered violently, even under the burning midday sun. I was proud that Leonardo's hair was the same tawny color as the lion's mane he sketched in his notebook. He was my 'il Marzocco', the heraldic lion that symbolizes Florence's freedom. But I was saddened. Leonardo had been tamed. My brother was a statue. Master Verrocchio had turned him into an icon for the Florentines to ogle.

I hated seeing Leonardo's smile trapped in bronze. I loathed walking away from it, leaving my shy, fourteen-year-old brother, who so desperately safeguarded his privacy, on public display, trapped in the Palazzo Vecchio, an exhibit for all to see.

I was lost. The worst had happened. Master Verrocchio had stolen my beloved brother for his apprentice and left me behind.

– Lisabetta

the 21st century

BASIL AND VERONICA LYONS
– twins born six minutes apart

My future happiness was stolen the day a rogue fire claimed my twin brother Basil when we were six-years-old. From that day to this, I've carried his smile, captured by a camera, inside a locket I wear to remind me he'd been real.

In desperation I'd looked for him in his favorite hiding place – the oak tree we named Leo in our backyard. I climbed up, high into its leafy mane during a storm to prove to Baz I was no longer afraid of heights or lightning or thunder. He would have been proud of me.

But the worst had happened. Falling from a tree would have been nothing. Death had stolen my beloved brother and left me behind.

– Veronica

Part One

Verily

chapter one

*"To be conscious
that we are perceiving or thinking
is to be conscious that we exist"*
~ Plato

The Varnished Truth

THE LOUVRE MUSEUM – PARIS
MARCH – 2008

In the spring of 1519 my brother Leonardo still believed he could fly. I, in turn, assumed my death in 1508 had been pure and uncomplicated, but then, my brother and I were always a pair of insatiable dreamers. We flouted the rules. We shared the same birthdate, April 15th. We were like twins born six-years-apart.

I inhabit the most famous portrait in the world, immortalized by my beloved brother, but tonight I'm restless as a caged lion.

I've grown weary of being hidden in plain sight. Because I'm still here, in Paris, confined to a single room in the Louvre Museum, my skin unblemished, picture-perfect beneath a patina of craquelure paint, and varnish jaundiced with age. I am the 'Mona Lisa'.

The only freedom I have is in the mountains and valleys bathed in sunshine that Leonardo painted for me. He gave me a bridge that links to my past with paths that trail into the future and places to hide. Safe places where I can shout myself hoarse and weep.

A true visionary can always tell if I'm away, roaming the landscape behind me or when I return their gaze from my golden 'window'.

I startle the poor incredulous creatures when I blink. I unnerve them when my eyes track them across the room, and when their comments amuse me, my smile widens perceptibly enough to unsettle them. It's the least I can do to make their lives, and mine, somewhat memorable.

That innocent April of 1519, when Leonardo turned sixty-seven, the French countryside of Amboise felt unbelievably sweet with the anticipation of heaven. I sensed Leonardo's transition was only a matter of days away and that liberation from my portrait was similarly at hand. But I had forgotten the impassioned wish I had painted on heaven's door like the mark of plague.

But for a single misshapen letter, I would be musing in heaven. The letter 'a' deposed me. Betrayed me. Sabotaged me. It was not even a whole letter but the merest tail of one. My legacy was tied to the tail of a hapless letter 'a' that unseated me from Giocond*a* to Giocond*o*.

But for an untimely pen, a spluttering candle, and a myopic historian, I would be the celebrated 'laughing woman'. I am most certainly NOT the dreary wife of a common silk merchant.

I was well acquainted with Monna Lisa Giocondo but we were never friends. And yet, she envied me as much as I despised her and all the dainty women of her class. I am galled to be misidentified as *Mrs.* Giocondo. Of all the insipid women…the world could not have chosen a more perfect way to insult me.

A parched quill simply ran dry, and my story moved on without me.

I didn't steal away. I was stolen. Dethroned. Many many times.

One only has to gaze into the eyes of my portrait to discover the undeniable truth – that a master artist can capture the soul of a subject. But some artists break all the rules. After the creative fusion of artist and muse is spent, only great art remains truly immortal. And sometimes it takes five-hundred years for the energy to cool.

I still have birthdays. Such is the absurd mockery under the most well-intentioned curse of immortality… fame. It would seem that anniversaries intensify the hope of salvation, and so I listen impatiently for the arrival of a champion.

A quickening of my pulse heralds the first euphoric stage of separation from the matrix of wood and paint. I lift ever so slightly and fall back to my painted earth, the plaything of gravity – a caged bird remembering how to fly.

I refuse to be held hostage in a room for another five-hundred years or crouch in the shadows subservient to the point of imbecility. I swear on my brother's life, I will no longer be silenced.

– Lisabetta
the true face of the 'Mona Lisa'

FROM THE DIARY OF VERONICA LYONS

Halifax, Nova Scotia
March 27, 2008

I'm unusually expectant tonight. I'd put it down to leaving for Paris tomorrow, but it's more.

My standing date with 'The Mona Lisa' looms. There's no turning back. Facing her again makes me nervous as a bag of cats.

Strangely, I'm at my most lucid this half-hour before my meds kick in, when the muse takes control. This is the time I can't help obsessing what's hidden in plain sight: secrets I need to confess, events I want to forget, people who wound and betray, and paintings with stories to tell.

I miss my twin brother. My darling son is lost somewhere between autism and genius. And I'm lost between sainthood and motherhood. The ironies alone justify taking an extra 'disappearing' pill to offset my fear of flying.

I named my boy Jupiter in my first trimester because I was as round as a planet, estranged from the small and ordinary, and curiously drawn to all things elemental.

While pregnant, I was unconscious of the revelations that the sky god Jupiter represented the immensity of omnipotent intellect, unearthly merriment, and larger-than-life storms. But during the nine months of gestation I felt an overwhelming sense of mental expansion along with my belly. I was connected to the stars. I believed in destiny.

It was natural to address my unborn child, acknowledging his greatness – my ancient child with faraway eyes who sees hidden truths.

We're best friends. More like brother and sister, born a generation apart. Sometimes I think Jupiter is the mother, especially the times he grips my hand when episodes of despair hound me. He is my champion. Some children break all the rules.

My name, Veronica, mocks me as the forged signature of the woman I was born to be. Tonight, its Latin anagram, veritas icona (translation 'true face'), weighs particularly heavy. Perhaps the guilt trip is mine after all because I'm an impostor masquerading as a Supermom.

I'm not being true to myself when I pop a pill and turn my face to the wall. I hide whenever possible. Invisibility suits me. I'm weary of representing my family's heritage of shame.

And so, I dress my little man in grey lies and happy colors, hoping his father will take up his cause before I disappear down the same dark rabbit hole as my mother.

The unvarnished truth: Paris is a guilt trip. Not mine. Jupiter and I are a disgraceful blot on his father's social calendar. Paris is compensation for us agreeing to disappear. To be erased from Niles' family's pedigree.

A euphoric slowing of my pulse heralds the first stage of separation from conscious thought. I sink to the floor, the plaything of gravity – a bird flying in the face of the lie that everyone is born equal.

In the meantime, I've grown to accept my obscurity. But the truth is, I've given up many many times, and yet I almost believe in poetic justice. We have a new beginning and Jupiter has a chance to shine. He tells me this is the year of yellow. I have no idea what he means but I swear on my brother's life, I will no longer be silenced.

— Veronica Lyons

*'The Winged Victory' a.k.a. 'The Nike of Samothrace'
on the Daru Staircase in the Louvre Museum*

chapter two

Veritas (Truth) + Icon (Image) = True Face
Latin anagram for the name Veronica

Victory on the Stairs

PARIS – THE LOUVRE MUSEUM
APRIL 1 – 2008

Jupiter Lyons clutches a brochure folded open to the Leonardo page. The map legend of the Louvre's second floor shows several miniature numbers circled in red pen. Veronica Lyons uses their entrance receipt as a bookmark, turns to the floorplan on page one, and points to the X on the map. "We're right here, sweetest of peas." Her index finger travels over the page, back to Leonardo. "I've marked what we've come to see. You can be the navigator."

Her six-year-old, an autistic savant, shrieks with glee, gloriously verbal now he has an important job to do.

A long queue of museum warriors inch forward towards the elevators like a glacier. "We'll have to join that line later," Veronica says, rubbing the blister from her holiday shoes. "I'm sorry, but it's the only way to see 'The Mona Lisa'. We're taking the stairs. Do you remember why? How are your feet holding up?"

Jupiter smiles with satisfaction. "I remember that you want to save her for last," he whispers to himself. This was his mother's way, contrary to his own system. He treated himself to his favorite things first: the dark chocolate pudding before the buttery taste of green beans, but after the salt-drizzled French fries with ketchup beside them, drawn in an O rather than a solid dollop. Delaying comfort seemed pointless, especially after his mother declared him 'especially special' when she pinned his favorite badges on his new beret from the airport giftshop.

 LISABETTA – A STOLEN GLANCE

"The one *you* are saving for *last*," Jupiter shouts. The words 'you' and 'last' bounce off the walls leaving out any possibility of a question mark.

Veronica pinches her son's cheek, plants a kiss, and wipes the smudge that isn't there. Jupiter doesn't appreciate being smudged. "Absolutely, spot on, Jupe, old bean. "

She guides him forward, firmly pushing his shoulders ahead of her. "I wish there was an easier way, but everyone wants to see her. We're going to visit the 'Madonna of the Rocks' first." She taps a square of color on the open page. "That one."

"The one wearing your brooch," Jupiter mouths quietly to himself.

Veronica beams in spite of her burning heels. She bends closer as if sharing a secret. "But before that, *we* have a date with the 'Victory' – the Nike of…?"

"SAM," Jupiter shouts smugly, raising his chin for another kiss. He's answered cheekily to make his mother laugh and kiss him again.

"Samothrace," she corrects. "The Winged Victory." She raises her fingers, threatening to tickle. "Exacerbating child."

He doubles over, giggling, trying to pronounce his response. "Exas…exaser…bibble." Jupiter's eyes are feverish with excitement. He chuckles, performs a little dance, punches the air, and shouts 'wings, wings, wings.' "You look like the Cheshire Cat," he says. "My feet are fine."

Jupiter waves his crushed brochure like a fan. His voice reverberates from the marble halls, surges up the grand staircase, and swirls around the shoulders of the 'Nike of Samothrace'. "Mom, she's – wear – ing – your – brooch," he says, deliberately enunciating each syllable. Silently, he mouths the words 'your brooch' three more times.

His mother witnesses Jupiter's mouth move as if his lips need to catch up to his latest speech. "Who's wearing my brooch, luvvy?"

Jupiter covers his face with the brochure to make a point and gives a muffled answer from behind the picture of the 'Madonna of the Rocks'. "She's right here, Mom."

Mother and son stand alone at the foot of the stairs.

The boy's delighted shriek would have reached the statue's ears if it had a head. He shouts to the companion voice that returns in a breathtaking sweep from the vault of the high ceiling. Jupiter loves echoes. His shadow voice captivates him, and he calls again just to hear it float. "BROOCH, brooch, brooch, brooch!"

Heads turn. Scowls wash over them.

Veronica ruffles Jupiter's hair and gently tames his enthusiasm into social acceptance.

"There's a museum voice, and a restaurant voice, and a movie theatre voice," Veronica tells him. "The Louvre has its own voice," she says. She makes the gesture of a plane swooping low that ends in tickling his tummy. "We keep our voices low enough to fly under the security guards' radar. Right? We've practiced this."

Jupiter squirms. He clamps his hand over his mouth and whispers "Sshhh."

Mother and child hold hands for a moment to savor the famous Daru staircase that sweeps before them, as enticing as any mountain climb with a goddess waiting at the summit. The sound of visitors blur into a company of ghostly wallpaper people.

Veronica squeezes Jupiter's hand four times, her signal for permission for him to run ahead. "Not too fast," she cautions, but he stays glued to her side, listening to the museum echoes that waft down the stairs.

Jupiter crams a navy-blue beret tighter over his mop of sandy hair that constantly threatens to cover his eyes. The face of his ever-present companion, a stuffed lion doll, peers from the outside pocket of his backpack emblazoned with Leonardo's 'Vitruvian man'. Leo 1, has three identical brothers with distinguishing characteristics that only Jupiter fully understands. Jupiter's aversion to buttons meant the lions' original button eyes had to be replaced with black yarn sewn in two crisscross stitches. Jupiter is drawn to triangles. The letter X is acceptable because it forms four triangles. He counts things into fours all day long.

He's wearing his mother's 'Mona Lisa' T-shirt that falls below his knees, a denim bomber jacket, khaki pants with pockets on the knees, and red running shoes with rainbow laces. Three badges are pinned to his hat, forming a triangle. One reads: *Don't mess with me. I'm high-functioning.* The second is the image of the Mona Lisa's smile. The third, larger than the others, reads: *This is no ordinary kid.*

Veronica straightens her son's lopsided beret and sweeps his hair to one side. "Settle down, sweetest of peas. You're as fidgety as a bag of cats."

That sets Jupiter giggling again. Cats are his favorite things.

Sometimes Veronica touches her son's shoulder and she resorts to sign language. Mother and child are fluent with word pictures, finger alphabets, and mime. Signing had been recommended to coax Jupiter into speech after a formal diagnosis of autism at eighteen months.

Today the doors of Jupiter's brain are characteristically open and he volunteers information that arrives from shapes and colors and textures. At other times, Veronica sees him struggle to communicate with an inner friend. Nothing escapes his senses. Sometimes he processes images for days before sharing them with her. She's learned to hone her skills of observation like a detective at a crime scene. And yet her son's perception often blindsides her. Jupiter only records important details that could be lost if left to hover and evaporate as a sole thought. He retains images the way an optimistic dog gnaws a bleached bone. Somewhere deeper there's a morsel of puzzling marrow. Solving puzzles is an art form, and Jupiter is a master, committed until the last piece snaps into place.

Veronica and Jupiter's holiday mood fills the immaculate hallways. Jupiter stops talking, and stamps his feet to test the acoustics. He listens for the voice of his new shoes. His expression is incandescent. Veronica is thrilled. "You're already shining," she says.

The grand stairwell is great place to wear shoes that clickety-clack or squeak. They both love the sound. They're here for the art, but the vibes of the stairs charm them.

Their world is measured in small grand moments of mutual pleasure. It can be anything where they're together, to pick up the noises and scents and tastes of the right-brain life lived raw and spontaneous. The lost mother, and son born out of wedlock, are companions who share the resonances others forget to see or taste or smell.

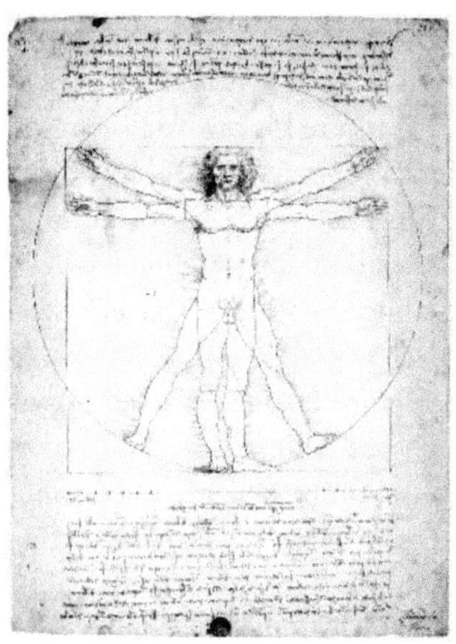

'The Vitruvian Man'

'The Winged Victory'

Jupiter clatters up the marble steps, pausing on each fourth step to jump. His backpack with the 'Vitruvian Man' image swings erratically from one arm as he contorts to examine the 'Winged Victory' from every angle.

Veronica's muffled voice in Jupiter's ear is the internal whisper she wants him to emulate. "I never thought I would really stand next to her. What do you think?" There's no answer. Jupiter is thinking. He's measuring. He's scanning for triangles. "Jupe? What do you think of her?"

Jupiter's eyes focus. He faces his mother with a puzzled scowl. "It's dangerous to fly without a head," he says.

There in the Louvre, surrounded by iconic images of 'Mothers and Sons' and sweeping landscapes of poetic illusion, Veronica and Jupiter explore on complementary senses. He is the litmus test of untainted understanding. She is the dowsing rod of historical truth. When Jupiter hears Veronica pronounce, Firenze, he hears the words 'fear' and 'ends'. When Veronica writes the word, Firenze, she sees the word 'fire' and hopes her fear of fire will end. Together they weave the psychic threads of eccentric behaviors into a coherent story.

Working two subsistence level jobs to provide for herself and her son, tests Veronica's survival instincts. Mental travel is an indulgence she can afford. She and Jupiter have learned to live on lily pads of small pleasures. This trip is a physical windfall, more accurately construed as blackmail, floating on a lily pad the size of Europe.

It was plain that she and Jupiter had to disappear to pacify Niles' family – to be 'reborn' in a new place. 'Go west,' Niles had suggested, but it was more an offer he dared her to refuse. As a single-parent of a child with mental challenges, Veronica agreed to disagree. The alternative was landing on the flypaper of social assistance, again. It also spelled disaster for her uncle's research. Some choice.

The deal had come with a holiday proviso. Niles painted a black and white picture: 'up stakes to anywhere on the planet,' he'd pressed. 'Your pick.' He studied his immaculate manicure, pretending to push back a perfect cuticle. 'Why not gallery hop on an expense account for a week or two in Europe while your things are on the road to wherever you decide.' He met her eyes briefly. 'And I will personally guarantee your uncle's research will be safe.' He knew her well.

Art galleries dangled like poisoned bait. It was possibly the only serious holiday she and Jupiter were likely to have. Great art was chocolate-covered poison. Veronica caved.

A guidance dream that night was the clincher. Nike flew in her window and morphed into the 'Statue of Liberty', wielding a torch. Her plaintive advice, within a blinding beacon of light, called out in a voice too loud for a museum: *choose Paris... she is here... waiting... please hurry... she's running out of time...*

'Nowhere or somewhere,' Niles badgered in the background. 'Pick a tarot card. Stay or go.'

Nike's stone feathers shivered and shattered to the floor. It had been an auspicious, if not obvious, confirmation, and Veronica woke determined to accept a couple of return tickets to Paris via London. Besides, her uncle Oz deserved to be placated for a change, and she was aware of who was waiting.

In the spirit of cooperation, Veronica chose the city of Victoria to homestead, as far away from Halifax as possible yet still remain in Canada. "Three weeks then," Veronica countered, "first class seats to London and Paris, and you'll personally look after Peyton and the cats while we're away. No kennels. No catteries. And, by the way, this arrangement will not effect the lawsuit. I won't sign away *our* son's legacy. Are we clear?"

Niles flinched at the word 'our' but replied "done", with forced enthusiasm.

"You'll fly the animals to Victoria before our flight touches down," she'd added. 'And I want a van and driver to pick us up from the airport so we can collect them on the way…" she paused to press a contentious point with deliberate eye contact. "…*home*. Jupiter will be anxious to be reunited with his touchstones. I'm sure your secretary can orchestrate the logistics."

Niles confirmed "no problem" with a greasy smile. Pets were more than family. They were therapy animals for his son, and Niles Duke, absentee father, deadbeat dad, and eternal bachelor, felt a curious stab of pleasure that Veronica still entrusted them to his care.

At first, the city of Victoria was a remote dot on a shape called British Columbia, but Veronica's choice had a poetic edge. Bound for a new home in Victoria was a clean metaphor for victory. Nike had reached out, and now she waited on the stairs for another chat.

Victoria via Paris was hardly a Band-Aid trip, and pioneering on a scrap of pure fresh space, surrounded by mountains and the waters of the blue Pacific, promised to be homesteading delivered

   LISABETTA – A STOLEN GLANCE

inside a symbolic message. Even the word pacific implied a healing balm: pacify. She and Jupiter deserved to be pacified for a change.

"It's not house arrest. It's not the Hotel California," Niles had said. "You can leave anytime, but you'd be crazy if you do. The rent for one year has been prepaid." His head, tipped to one side, expecting to be thanked.

Veronica turned from the room without giving him the satisfaction of her Cheshire Cat grin. Maybe this time, both of them had won. "What makes you think I'm crazy?" she said, facing the closed door. "I'll start packing tonight." She never looked back. The hallway carpet seemed more like a golden road paved with light. A feeling of buoyancy lifted her. She was already on the road less traveled.

She wrote in her diary:
Poverty has its own voice. It says 'yes' to things one would rather not face, but a rumor persists that sometimes beggars CAN be choosers, drawn into an alternative reality ruled by a rogue gene of synchronicity. Jupiter and I are due to cross paths with 'the Winged Victory, and the chance to fly free. Perhaps my truest image is coming into focus. I will face 'Mona Lisa' at last. What will she say this time?

Jupiter surveys the statue of 'Nike' like a twenty-first century spectroscope. He probes – a natural master of forensic science. He counts individual feathers and observes the positive shape of the wing and the negative spaces under it and between the ship's prow of its plinth. "It's the same wing," he points out, but his mother is lost to the creature of the stairs. She's drifted out to sea in a pea-green boat.

Jupiter, enchanted by whispering stairs, measures the angles of Nike's wings. Her white marble draperies cast shadows like hills and valleys covered in Nova Scotia snow. "HOME!" he shouts. "BROOCH, HAMBURGERS, CATS, cats, cats, cats."

The diversity of high-functioning autism and wild imagination enslaves them. Private worlds have different food chains and atmospheres and inhabitants. Veronica's ears search. Jupiter's eyes listen.

chapter three

Bella Veritas

'beauty and truth'

AMBOISE, FRANCE
THE MANOR HOUSE OF CLOUX
APRIL 15 – 1519

April 15th is an auspicious day. Brother and sister share the same date of birth, born in the heart of Tuscany – six years apart.

Across the room, Leonardo is too busy to notice his sister's wistful mood, but then, it was typically so. Work is a blindfold to the everyday things of life when your name is Leonardo da Vinci.

Lisabetta is lured from her portrait towards the blue sky of the open window. She walks past Leonardo, his table, and his abandoned midday meal, creating a gentle disturbance that flutters its strewn papers. Mathurine's 'soup-of-the-country' grows cold next to the old man intent on documenting the entire world.

The gargoyle on the roof outside Leonardo's bedroom window seems poised to leap at a passing sparrow hawk. Lisabetta looks out over its stone wings to the 'Leonardo Tree' below. From this vantage she is reminded that the scale of trees is irrelevant.

It was one of the first art lessons Leonardo had taught her. Together as children, they gathered trees of moss that fit into the palms of their hands, and studied the forms of the cloud trees that towered over the Tuscan landscape.

  LISABETTA – A STOLEN GLANCE

Lisabetta is momentarily distracted by the figures of a woman and a boy moving diagonally across the lawn. Her eyes track them as they walk in a beeline for the main door until they disappear out of sight.

Behind her, Leonardo's pen scratches furiously at the design of a fountain for King Francis's new palace.

"Leonardo," Lisabetta announces abruptly, "it is time."

"Time?" he answers absentmindedly, "for my medicine?"

"Time to eat your soup... to breathe fresh air... to feel the sunshine... and to put down your pen," she says.

Leonardo responds with a smile, but he mischievously writes one more thing to vex her: *here I must stop because the minestrone grows cold.*

Leonardo's last stroke has puckered his left hand into a feeble paw which still allows him to sketch and write, but his paints have long been abandoned in favor of designing follies for the King of France.

It is unusually warm for April. Newborn bees test their wings in the sun, and Leonardo is persuaded to set aside his frantic scribbling and venture downstairs on his apprentice, Cecco's, arm. Leonardo's Tuscan chair is carried ahead with blankets and silk pillows, and a tray of his favorite sweetmeats: a platter of marzipan pigs, Madagascar dates, and a blue majolica bowl filled with crystallized ginger.

The young bees serenade the first flowers beginning to blossom in the walled garden, beyond. Cecco chooses a perfect yellow rose from the adjacent conservatory and tries to lure a fat bee onto it with a small net, but the bee is provoked into a frenzy until Lisabetta cups her hands around it and sets it gently onto the head of the flower. The calmed bee burrows contentedly into the petals and is transported to the front lawn, where Leonardo dozes in the half-sleep of old-age.

At sixty-seven, Leonardo projects the aura of an ancient magus ensconced on his wicker throne – an ordinary chair made from the reeds of the Vincio River near his birthplace. It's strategically placed in the shade of the great oak that Cecco dubbed the Leonardo Tree – so named, the day of their arrival three-years ago, at King Francis's pleasure. Leonardo had placed his hands on the tree and said he could feel a numinous energy within it. 'Here is power,' he had said, and claimed the oak as his.

Leonardo sits like an emperor soaking up magic – a noble figure with flowing white beard, resting his chin on one gnarled fist, his lion-head cane gripped by the other. He wears a violet skullcap, and a matching shawl. His legs are tucked snuggly under a regal coverlet embroidered with his own device – the monogram LDV worked into an elaborate Vinci knot in silver thread. It is the same design that Cecco has engraved in the bark of the Leonardo Tree.

Lisabetta runs ahead of Cecco and whispers to her sleeping brother: "Leonardo, I will be right back. Happy birthday."

"My Bella Veritas – our birthday, it is today?" he says, inside his dream.

She kisses his cheek. "April 15th," she replies and hurries away.

Leonardo smiles, remembering the baby sister he once held in his arms. "I thought you would never come," he murmurs to himself. The stars sang the night she was born. Knowing that Lisabetta will never leave him is his greatest comfort. "Don't be long. *Ti voglio bene,*" he calls, after her.

"*Moi aussi, je t'aime,*" Lisabetta calls back over her shoulder. "We are in France now."

"France?" Leonardo puzzles. Only this morning he had observed the familiar swan-shaped mountain near Vinci from his window and ordered Zoroaster to check the new wings of the ornithopter. He had been testing the wind velocity. Cecco had even copied the latest calculations into his notebook. They were ready to try again. Even now, he was resting on the grass of Mt. Ceceri's eastern slope until the updrafts were stronger. Soon they would wake him and he would claim the sky.

"*Monsieur Léonard,*" Cecco says, addressing Leonardo by his French name. "You have a visitor." He presents his fragile offering, lifting the net slowly.

The bee remains settled. "*Voila! Maestro*, may I present a small admirer who brings you this birthday rose as a token of his esteem."

Leonardo is delighted to observe one of his favorite miracles of flight so closely, but the bee buzzes after Lisabetta in a disappearing trajectory of yellow and black, following her signature of violet perfume.

Leonardo inhales the rose's fragrance and closes his eyes. "This yellow... I am reminded of a canary I once..." he starts, but his voice trails off at the sad memory. He looks lost. "Where is Rinato?" he asks.

"Maestro, Rinato was before my time. He has been gone for many years now, but the house dogs are near. Do you want me to bring one of them?"

"Rinato must be with Lisabetta," Leonardo says.

"Of course, Maestro, that must be where he is," Cecco replies.

Leonardo clutches the yellow rose tightly with his good hand and cuddles an invisible dog. "I've left Lisabetta too long," he says, and waves the flower like a scepter. "This is for her birthday birthday birthday birthday," he says, and begs Cecco to take him and Rinato inside.

chapter four

"To sleep, perchance to dream...
for in that sleep of death
what dreams may come?"
~ William Shakespeare

Growing Pains

In 1519, my portrait was a teenager, painted in 1503 when Leonardo had intended to abandon his paints forever. Instead, in a burst of inspiration, my brother turned me into an icon. A gilded frame is my window on the world. It's my only escape route – my window of opportunity.

In many ways, Leonardo had been my first mother, and I returned the favor by mothering him for the rest of his life, but my brother needed protecting as much as nurturing. I did that too.

I was born to watch over him. His considerable strengths made him more vulnerable. He was in a hurry to be wise. Caterina, our mother, called Leonardo her ancient child with faraway eyes.

I understood his obsessive preoccupation with minutiae. To a lesser degree, I shared his fascination for details, but Leonardo's studies tested the limits of intellectual drowning. I sat with his melancholies, in awe of his courage. His physical stamina was legend. It had to be to conquer the merciless recurring headaches of flames and chills that hounded him.

In spite of my brother's inherent delight in music and a joyous affinity with natural science, a desperate river of sorrow ran under his ecstasies. Abandonment weighed heavy in his heart. Piero da Vinci kept Leonardo on a leash of hope until his legitimate sons arrived. And in the end, the stain of illegitimacy doomed his sweetest son to the hapless task of proving his worthiness in a haze of unappreciated filial duty.

The first time could be pardoned. Piero had been young and scared, but the second time he was heartless – his true nature had built a wall around the core of his 'pure' family. He was a cold, calculating lawyer. For those *egregious sins, I despised him with enough hatred for two. Leonardo never hated anyone.*

I truly care nothing for fathers, and my denied pedigree to Leonardo continues to rankle me into the desire for recognition – full disclosure of all that I was and all that we were and always will be, together. I was never my father's daughter... neither of them. I had two. One was descended from notary-guild stock and socially invisible to me, the other was a brutish mercenary soldier. Both were selfish. But what I remember most about my time, was that, after they turned fourteen, all the men in my century were selfish.

Bloodlines were easy to disguise because we women existed invisibly under the complex lineage of our menfolk. I grew up as Lisabetta di Antonio Buti del Vacca in a deliberate act of mistaken identity perpetrated by two families. I was never her. If you follow the dictates of government officials and historians, I was never a woman of consequence. And yet, with my brother's help, I have clearly made my mark on the world. Even so, a disturbing thought continuously haunts me. Was I ever truly here?

Time plays tricks. If my name is irretrievably lost, posthumously cut apart from my time and permanently erased from the world, overshadowed by the lies of silence, could I ever be sure I lived, other than in Leonardo's imagination?

After my death I remained beside Leonardo in spirit form to honor our extraordinary bond. Beyond death was simply a necessary extension of our mutual pact to companion each other always – in all ways. 'Until death parts us,' was a hollow sentiment while one of us still breathed.

You may have heard that Leonardo kept the 'Mona Lisa' painting with him until his death. Now you know why. Leonardo never accepted my death, and my portrait was the best place for me to hide in plain sight. My animated portrait stabilized him. In many ways he'd captured my soul with his brushes. But it was more than art. It was artfulness on my part. His needs eclipsed my own.

And so, after my own transition, I lingered in the painting, willingly-enough for my brother's sake, and continued to minister to him with affection and compassion – a decision I never regretted while he lived. But, may heaven forgive me, I never envisioned staying five-hundred-years.

Waiting for Leonardo to die was a peculiar mixture of guilt and relief, and I've had plenty of time to observe the living with increasing vexation. But, as the April of 2008 approaches, a promise tugs at my sleeve. It's pure. Delivered lovingly. At last, I have a chance to reveal my true identity. It's time to redress a wish made in haste.

I am animated with memories and a new secret. Centenaries are venerated for a reason… they contain power. I've been granted a new wish on the occasion of the 500th anniversary of my death. If I can find someone to release me within the year 2008 I can move on as death intended. Significantly, there are nine months left in the year… perfect timing for the gestation of a human life. And even more true to the point, to paint a new death.

After my death, I bided where no time and all of time co-existed in a tapestry of memories and dreams. The 'Mona Lisa' painting made it easier for me to stay, acting as a bridge between my accustomed invisibility and Leonardo's need to see me. He chided me. I was perfect, he said, but I would never be finished, which accounts for the heaviness of never-ending varnish.

I was delighted to discover the ability to revisit my younger years with ease, and I indulged by celebrating the joys of my childhood, allowing them to outshine the harsher years of poverty and abuse. I especially dared to imagine a blissful reunion with Sandro Botticelli and the delight of seeing my daughter again, but most days I stayed focused on the task of keeping Leonardo happy.

Leonardo's last birthday prompted a spell of reminiscing. For his sixty-seventh year, my mind wandered as I lazed in my portrait's mountains and valleys, ruminating over the events of my own life.

Not surprisingly, the lies loomed larger than the truths, but I was never sure of the truth anyway. I had the knack of justifying everything I did for our success.

chapter five

*"Lives toughen
from ducking God's thunderbolts
and surviving random encounters"*
~ Lisabetta

A Blind Date

PARIS – THE LOUVRE MUSEUM
APRIL 1 – 2008

Her words *'date with Nike'* float back to Veronica as if strolling past the Winged Victory is a casual event. The 'Nike of Samothrace' had imbedded itself in her psyche by gracing the front cover of the course textbook for 'Art History 101', her travel companion, accompanying her during on the long bus-rides home from university. She'd studied its stone fabric crevices, captured in dramatic light, and followed the contours of its billowing draperies, frozen in time like the volcanic ash of a Vesuvius victim, wondering if its missing head had long flowing hair. She decided it did.

"She's easy to find," Jupiter says, staring at the magnificent statue, looming on the stairs. Veronica had deliberately avoided its peripheral energy, hovering up and to her right, wings outstretched like the sails of a ship. Her muscles tingle deliciously on high-alert from the anticipation of meeting a goddess. She savors the body-high of an art junkie, deliberately choosing to experience the visceral shock of facing an icon full-on, the way one steps up and confronts a movie star on the street: "Hello… I'm a big fan."

If terror doesn't ruin the moment, she intends to greet the 'Mona Lisa' with the parallel smile of an old acquaintance. She's rehearsed Mona Lisa's mystery smile many times in various mirrors, but the cold marble of Lisa's halls is confidence shaking, and she notes every exist against aborting her mission.

Leonardo's portraits can be moody to the point of demanding, but they're always intimidating. He's a painter of souls. One never knows their disposition until their eyes blink.

Popping another tranquilizer for Dutch courage alters her perception. The word 'strange' floats from the word 'estranged' and pulsates in her wrist. The main thing, is that Jupiter remains in the dark on this especially bright day.

Discussing paintings is one of their favorite pastimes.

Leonardo miraculously painted the 'Mona Lisa's' eyes to engage every onlooker from any point across a room. One expects her to speak. They will be able to see her as a 'postage stamp' from the back of the salon – an undersized window in an expanse of wall.

A thumbnail image will diminish the impact of Lisa's direct gaze and delay the confrontation.

Veronica's plan is to edge forward, attached to the throng in front of her, averting her eyes until the last moment. At optimum range she will close them tight, pause to a count of four, and look up for an emotional hit. Nothing less than a gut punch. Nothing less than an extrasensory blast of immediate recognition. *Is it really you?* followed by an apology.

In a way, Veronica is meeting an old friend – an entity who has haunted her for years. Today the dream materializes. She is sure the ground will tremble. She already feels faint. Surely, their combined energy will short-circuit the Louvre's breakers and dim the lights of Paris.

Jupiter and Veronica approach the 'Nike of Samothrace' on parallel wavelengths. Jupiter probes for hidden truths. Veronica observes in a surreal daze. Her perceptions transport. She heads straight for the dizzying mother-lode of historical destinations… romance in the truest sense of the word. Her viewpoint expands to a prolonged Hellenistic haze, more than she'd hoped, all expectations exceeded. She is prone to ghostly whispers, and the rustle of archaic white robes.

She appreciates the sensual curve of a phantom cheek, and the liquid flash of olive-dark eyes. She brushes against the heartbeats of the once living, and hustles alongside the echoes of ancient sandals. She experiences the world sensually. Art invades and conquers her on sensitive overloads to the scents of warm winds off ripe lemon groves.

Veronica is no longer in Paris. She's standing on a beach, blinded by the brilliance of turquoise water against white marble pillars, following the receding footprints of bare feet running on powdery sand.

Until her son's voice penetrates her vision, Veronica's eyes ache from the glint of sunlight off freshly-whitewashed plaster. The shape of the descending Nike casts a mauve shadow on the cliffs as she touches down with a message of victory. Nike's trumpet blasts the beauty of an Aegean day into a joyous triumph.

Veronica savors the salty kiss of a warm breeze on her lips and smiles from the memory. She holds onto that smile to give the Mona Lisa.

Lisabetta – age 45

 LISABETTA – A STOLEN GLANCE

chapter six

"Only great art is truly immortal"
~ Lisabetta

Lisabetta Country

PARIS – THE LOUVRE MUSEUM
APRIL 1 – 2008

Lisabetta turns her back on the salon. She walks for miles, hitches up her green skirt, and scrambles up a bank of steep rocks. A cloud of kites screech her up the last few feet to their eyrie. Her determination sends a crumble of stones behind her in a gentle avalanche. The toes of her leather shoes remain un-scuffed, but Leonardo's veiled sun scorches her hair until she reaches a familiar plateau where she rolls into the shade. From here, she can view the full extent of her past, melting into the earth and grasses, camouflaged by the colors of nature as Leonardo had intended.

A trickle of water leaves a brown trail of minerals from a fissure high above in the face of the cliff, and Lisabetta makes a cup with her hands that interrupts the water's journey towards a natural basin of stone lined with moss. The lip of the basin is dry. She strokes its emerald velvet with fondness – they are Leonardo's miniature trees. She plucks a single stem and cradles it in her hands – the same pose as her portrait's hands. It's a grand memory. One that she hopes will stir others to uncover a way home. Home being a heaven she's glimpsed, rather than a sterile museum.

Lisabetta's base camp is the place where a windbreak of gorse and marigold forms a human-sized amphitheater. Inside the curve of it, the mountain has made her a blanket of thatch and fern, woven by the wind and plumped into a cradle between the crevices. She settles down and closes her eyes to concentrate and tries to evoke the help of her brother, the master of this illusion. "Leonardo, Leonardo, Leonardo, Leonardo," she intones, four times for luck.

Lisabetta draws down the mists clinging to the mountain peaks – Leonardo's gauzy curtains of seclusion that turn landscapes into land escapes, to put more distance between the Louvre's intensity and her need for retreat. Her brother's disposition and his frequent need for sanctuary had mirrored his observations of nature's moodiness: damp wind and smoky rain and the heat rising from sunbaked stone. He had taught Lisabetta to surrender to the alchemy of weather for inspiration. His muses were hers. "Elemental answers wait inside torrential storms of nature and emotion for the patient artist," he had said.

Leonardo had relaxed behind his screens – free to say and write and dream blasphemous ideas, dabbling with forbidden science, safely unobserved. His tendency to hide, reflected a dangerous need for privacy.

Nature protected its own. Leonardo understood a town's need for isolation and a hill's need for solitude, and that an owl's eggs begged invisible nests for survival, no less than bear cubs evaporated into the depths of a secluded cave. Horizons were compassionate places blanketed by mystery where anything was possible.

Leonardo's ferocious melancholies had been comfortably masked by Lisabetta's administrations of cold compresses and the smelling salts of fresh lemon zest.

His imagination had been the safest space for truth to flourish. Many times, Leonardo had disappeared on trips into wilderness like Lisabetta's in order to insulate himself from the church and superstition, as well as bill collectors and public humiliation. Rebels need mountain hideaways to plot revolutions, and Leonardo was as passive a rebel as Lisabetta was an aggressive mediator.

Leonardo explained that secrets had a chance to take root inside a storm. One could dream there, in its eye. Lisabetta hoped to meet him by chance, one day in her hills, testing the updrafts and measuring the degrees of opaqueness between seasonal miles of air. Perhaps copying illusions into his notebook, or scribbling occult dreams backwards in code.

　　　　　LISABETTA – A STOLEN GLANCE

Sometimes, Lisabetta sees Leonardo on a far-off hill, with his back against an oak, or under the arch of the bridge below, sketching the eddies of water from stones sent into the river by his own hand, but never any closer, and she has come to feel grateful to see him at all. Often, Rinato accompanies him – a small white canine energy darting like a butterfly over the grass.

Depending on Leonardo's age, his owl, Lydia, is with him – a soft cloud hovering over her master or a tiny flutter of canary yellow perches on his sleeve.

This is Lisabetta's country. Hers and Leonardo's. It's delightful, but it isn't heaven. Leonardo would live larger in her heaven, and Sandro and Leona would be there, along with her old zoo: her pony, Stella; dogs, Rinato and Giallo; and Picolini and Simonetta with countless generations of their feline offspring.

Lisabetta trails out the played scenes of her life. Lily pads of time form rows like the words in a story. Carefully preserved experiences are counted as ripples of light: a wing here, a shadow following. Receding voices disappear like running feet, but she remains the guilty center of the world, and not far from this spot, she is still a jumpy thread of posthumous nerves who resides in a museum room wound tight with adoration and disappointment.

She is determined to rake her years for a lost clue. Any signpost is welcome if it points towards atonement. Lisabetta willingly revisits her scenes of misconduct, but none appear vile enough to warrant her unworthiness to fully die. No stray curse shows its teeth. No echoes of voices fly back that could injure a reputation. But she waits – something will come, and it arrives as the sound of her own laughter and horses clopping towards the horizon. Rinato's faint bark chases the currents of the Vincio River while her sisters harvest the whispering reeds and silence them into bundles for weaving baskets. It must be September.

Lisabetta examines the consequences of her actions like a scientist – the way Leonardo taught her, but on kinder days she encourages a passing fragrance to linger for entertainment. There were the sweet hours in the studio when Leonardo chided her for her rainbow fingers. His need for spotless sleeves and hands had been meant to inspire discipline. No, there was no malice there, nor was there in her mother's objections to her five-year-old daughter's prattling of escape during the days she shadowed Leonardo like a hungry cat. These were harmless criticisms given with affection. Lisabetta strains for muffled gossip and digests her shames that howl like circling wolves.

Often she disturbs the old scented-days, spent under magic, thirsting for art and love, and these drift by like pale swans and make her smile. Once an amber brooch shone on her palm with an innocent bronze key to nothing in particular that she could remember. Once she had been in a room lined with books and seen her portrait lying on a table without its frame. A girl had been sleeping beside it and Lisabetta had first thought it was herself, but the clothes the girl wore were those of a boy. She'd begged him for help, and he'd run from the room.

By contrast, fragile experiments of pain wait in line – each small betrayal counted on young fingers. Childhood innocence dances in circles with expectation, and lastly, the most exquisite dreams: the first blossoming of dizzying arousal, desiring beyond the capacity to survive a missed kiss. Especially the emotional tugs later – the days-after sort of life that show themselves like shy strangers. There's a rumpled bed, abandoned with rouge on the sheets. Lisabetta smooth's the covers, and places a primrose over the stain. She rises again, above the penalties of forbidden honey – the old days spent in pursuit of love's heat, musing over the enchantments and promises of more – the possibilities of rubies against green silk and white fur – and success. Always success. Forever the bittersweet relief, drenched by the storms of business.

Lisabetta combs her mistakes, but can find none tainted sufficiently with enough sin to be cheated from heaven. Her savage exile remains a mystery.

Lisabetta resurfaces from recounting a list of failed strategies, dazzled by a vision of sunlight caressing Il Porcellina, the stone pig from the market, in 1504 – the time she had called down a sainted energy and given herself a fright. An overwhelming feeling of anger at the unfairness of life accompanies the memory. It had been a sweltering day in the *marketa* of Florence. She was there to cool her bleeding hands, stained bright-blue, in the fountain.

Branacchi, the new overseer in charge of an 'Adoration' for the Vespucci, had given a cursory glance at the folds of an orange velvet cloak she was rendering and consigned her to grinding colors. She had been in a glorious trance, using every tender refinement Leonardo had taught her when Branacchi's orders shattered her concentration. For a moment she was disoriented, but then his voice rose sharply, cruelly dispelling the sacred moment between artist and art.

He shouted an order in mid-stride. "You. Girl on the ladder. Stop. Leave that. Lorenzo will finish it. Sandro requires a quantity of ultramarine. Take extra care. It is expensive, and you know how demanding he is."

She complied, scowling, and pulverized a lump of raw lapis for hours until her hands bled. Her anger lessoned as the color took over. She surrendered to the calming rhythms of the pestle and mortar, slipping into the exacting ritual of crushing rock into a paste with almond oil. When it was perfect, she scooped the buttery blue mound and delivered it on a clean pine board like a holy offering.

Her fuming returned. Not one word of praise, and of all the talentless little upstarts – a spoiled toady like Lorenzo di Credi was destroying her work. Her beautiful orange cloak with its elaborate border picked out in gold, ruined by the hand of a clumsy catamite nonentity before Leonardo had a chance to see it.

An ancient statue of a female boar, basks in the oppressive heat of the *marketa*. Like all Florentines, Lisabetta has made casual wishes on its nose many times, but today is different. Today she communes like a priestess before making her request.

The moment feels suspended, lived outside the commotion of the marketplace, as if she and the statue are alone on earth. As the chaos of the square subsides around her, Lisabetta places her blue-stained hands on either side of the sow's snout and examines its tiny eyes for signs of life. "*Dio.* I swear if it takes five-hundred-years I will be accepted. I will *make* them see me."

The bitter desires that Lisabetta pours into the soul of the pig thrash together. For a moment there is silence, but when the pig squeals yes four times, quite audibly inside her head, Lisabetta pulls her hands from it as if scalded and bolts from the piazza. She hurries, tripping over barrels and baskets, through the filth of the market stalls, skirting hungry dogs and the hungrier street urchins who collect in small filthy gangs.

At the corner of the Campanile, Lisabetta stops and wipes her hands together to rub off the hot magic. She checks them for blisters, but apart from the blue stains her hands are unblemished and she chides herself for over-imagination. The strain of several sleepless nights, the fierce sun and an emotional outburst has made her ill, and the scorching skin of the bronze pig has only seemed to sear her like fire.

She reassures herself this is the truth, but she knows it for a lie. She had been angry and the stone had been warm to the touch, but not excessively so, and she had felt her rage leave, absorbed by the statue. For a brief moment her hands felt stuck, and then a jolt of lightning entered her body through them and she had a vision of cruel flames engulfing her. She must shelter from the sun and rest, and most of all, she must forget this incident and the ugly business earlier with Monna Lisa Giocondo.

A quick glance confirms her panic has gone unobserved, but when Lisabetta lurches on she can feel the snuffling breath of a smiling pig on the calves of her legs, and she slows to glance over her shoulder half-expecting to see a lumbering, snorting beast in pursuit. She stumbles on past pens of squawking poultry, unnerved, distracted by the stink and grunts of porcine livestock louder than their stone mother in the market square.

Lisabetta only slows to a walk after she reaches the shady side of the Medici palace – a safe distance from the imagined miracle. The palace walls are a soothing touchstone. Their rough surface grounds her. She doesn't believe in miracles or curses. She is the victim of a bizarre hallucination delivered by an unforgiving sun, and even now a bright pain is forming behind her eyes – nothing more.

The Via Ghibellina rests slightly cooler under a welcome blanket of violet shadow, but a shard of bright sunlight stabs Lisabetta's left eye when she turns the corner and glances up at the sky. She flinches and retches into the street. She swipes her lips cracked with thirst on her sleeve. The promise of water urges her on.

Lisabetta's feet stretch towards the quiet interior of Leonardo's studio. It's close enough to savor the coolness of water that awaits her parched throat. A flushed Lisabetta rushes past Leonardo, working at a long table. "Bring lemons," she says, not stopping. "I need your help." The back room is quiet. Lisabetta splashes water on her face, closes the shutters and collapses onto a straw pallet.

Leonardo is concerned. "Is it the blackness?" He follows and places a cool compress on his sister's forehead. The silence and the scent of lemon peel restores her enough to warn him. "Don't let it in," Lisabetta mutters. "Five-hundred-years... five hundred!"

"Don't let in who?"

"Giocondo. She and I... " Lisabetta's voice trails off in a fit of crying.

"There is no-one here. Lisabetta who has upset you? Please. You will make yourself ill."

"The wishing pig in the *marketta*. My hands. It burned my hands."

Leonardo examines his sister's hands. "There is a little paint. Nothing more." He tries to still them from twitching but she grabs his sleeve, panicked.

"It followed me. It's at the door. *Dio*, they're locking the doors again. I am trapped."

"Cara, there is no pig. You are safe. The door is not bolted. You are free to leave whenever you like."

"*Non*, I'm a prisoner. I cannot escape. I thought you would come but you abandoned me. I waited for you. I trusted you but you left me behind."

"I promise you, we will be leaving together as we always do. I would never leave without you. This blackness will fade and..."

"Make the crowd go away. They stare, so. Leonardo, please help me."

"I will. I will make them go away if you promise to sleep."

"Five-hundred years, Leonardo. How *could* you?"

Lisabetta surrenders to sleep, and Leonardo returns to his maps and calendars for their latest escape route – retreating and escaping have become their specialty.

Lisabetta is momentarily puzzled. This pig memory feels more significant. It's brighter than the others. She feels the quickening of intuition. It had taken three days to sufficiently shake off the disturbing dream of a bronze statue squealing with laughter. She will allow the memory more time to speak. Test it against a reawakening sense of truth.

There is no revoking a wish made like a demand but a second wish may soften the first, especially when other powerful creators are involved. Divine comeuppance is the ultimate system of poetic justice and there are synchronicities at stake. Wishing too big lacks humility, but Lisabetta had heard somewhere that wishing too small was an admission of weakness.

No matter, Lisabetta of the Louvre painting, remembers making a wish, and wishing is a form of prayer ... and when in trouble, any statue is a saint if it can reach the ears of power.

There's a soothing light around the year 2008. In two weeks, five-hundred-years will have passed since her death and subsequent internment. She has heard several visitors chide each other with lies. Today is April Fool's Day.

She was a fool to have toyed with fate, and now, the first three months of the year are gone. The two-faced truth of things to come is continued detention in perpetuity or rebirth. Her plan is a simple historical correction. No more 'eye-for-an-eye', but a name for a name.

chapter seven

*"Our lives became a blend
of apocryphal god-bolts
and random encounters"*
~ Lisabetta

The House of Clues

AMBOISE, FRANCE
MAY 2 – 1519

Lisabetta is surprised to know that she has been dead eleven years. She surmises it from the date,1519, that Leonardo has scrawled in the margin of his notebook next to the words: *'di ieri di domani'* – more than yesterday; less than tomorrow.

There had been signs over the past few weeks to indicate that Leonardo's death was imminent. Today, Lisabetta can see his form waver, translucent against the sky and the green lawn as he gathers the waxy clusters of lily-of-the-valley that shelter between the toes of his namesake tree.

Lisabetta believes a gentle heaven awaits her after Leonardo's death, and that the power of life *before* death, is all the authority one may possess. She looks forward to the joyous day of her brother's transition when she will teach him to fly. She created her heaven for one – crafted it all her life, but after her death she spends her time polishing it for four.

With the shiver of heaven so near, she and Leonardo had discussed it often with eager anticipation, but once, a thought had troubled Leonardo's aged face. "Rinato can come, yes?" It was the question of a child.

"Of course," she had said, "Rinato can come."

It is pleasant enough for Lisabetta to wait for Leonardo in the land-scape he painted behind her. Lying under her stars, she is free to imagine her heaven somewhere overhead. Waiting for eleven years has been no great hardship. From here she can turn her head and see Leonardo's bedroom window in Amboise as a distant star, but as she watches, the horizon flashes with silent colors, and the wind, stirring with the sound of a million agitated bees, begins to grumble with approaching thunder.

Lisabetta flies towards the twinkling light of Leonardo's window, and hovers over the manor house crouched small against the future. The skies above Cloux churn with anger. An electric claw rakes the sky with white fingers. The Leonardo Tree explodes into sparks.

Lisabetta listens for her brother's voice.

The thunderclap crackling with ozone, startles Leonardo. He stirs within his dream of immortality – roused enough to call out: "Lisa is that you?"

The hem of Lisabetta's dress ripples across a tapestry of Persian flowers in a cloud of emerald silk and rustles towards the old man in the canopied bed. "I am here," she says. "It's me... Lisabetta. Leonardo, I think it's time."

Lisabetta takes Leonardo's lifeless arm and they walk towards the open window, but she remembers the painting beside the bed and tells him to go on without her. "I will be right back," she says. "I just want a word with Cecco."

Inside her portrait, Lisabetta looks out at the red and gold room and Francesco Melzi, the young man in attendance, dozing in a chair. She had recruited him for Leonardo, and now he is responsible for Leonardo's legacy and the future of the painting that had been her recent home.

Lisabetta's work is almost over. She notes the rich bedclothes and the fragile contours of the newly-abandoned human shell beneath them. She calls out excitedly: "Cecco, *mio caro*, wake up. It is time. Leonardo is safe with me now."

Francesco Melzi startles from the sound of a loud crash within a dream where a dog had been barking excitedly. Furious rain pelts the windowpane as simultaneous thunderclaps and flashes of lightning shake the walls and panic the flames in the fireplace.

In Francesco's dream, a young boy had been shushing Joan of Arc, who brandished a square shield with great urgency. The shield had been painted with an image of her face. The dream had shown her, as the locals so often recounted, a young peasant girl sacrificed by fire. Francesco had been witnessing Joan's martyrdom – seen her face age inside the flames until her skin was covered in fine cracks. A crowd had hung her shield over an altar as a religious icon and were worshipping her as a saint, scattering violets at her feet.

Francesco experiences the anxiety of the dog as his own. "Maestro, did you call?"

The woman's voice in his head is insistent. "Take the 'Mona Lisa' to the king."

The 'Mona Lisa' panel lies face down on the floor. Still disoriented, Francesco places the painting back on the easel. Leonardo must have reached for her again.

For five-hundred-years, Lisabetta will remember clearly, the midnight window that hangs like a painting on the far wall. She smiles at the transparent form of her brother, no longer an old man of sixty-seven, but her twelve-year-old hero, standing now with his back to her, gazing spellbound at a shimmering vista of the Loire Valley. He holds their scrawny terrier, Rinato, over his shoulder, and Lisabetta struggles in vain against the varnish to rejoin them: "Don't leave me. Leonardo wait!" she calls into the drone of bees humming.

Leonardo replies, still faced away from her, distressed: "Come out crazy girl and be quiet or he will hear you and come back."

The last thing Lisabetta sees is the eyes of the animal which plead with her to follow as boy and dog are pulled into a blue flash and disappear into the night sky like stars returning home.

Since her death, Lisabetta had moved freely across the threshold of her portrait in response to Leonardo's every summons, loyal to his need, but now he abandons her like all the rest.

Leonardo had been the only one with the power to call her out, and a disturbing new thought overwhelms her. Perhaps she had been wrong. Maybe there was a god after all, but what if that god was just another man.

chapter eight

A Meeting of Dreams

PARIS – THE LOUVRE MUSEUM
APRIL 1 – 2008

So many eyes in a day. Probing. I see them go from indifference to awe and oftentimes shock. I am too small, they whisper. But there is a ripple in the air like the gentle fizzing of static before a storm. I can smell it, and so I'm as vigilant as the enamored front row gawpers. I troll for the disturbance as they scan me. Synchronicity is a double miracle. It's always a matter of time. My atoms tingle with electric sparks. There's no wild portent, but a lightening of the air that streams through me. For this reason, I delay my usual retreat into the Florentine landscape behind me.

The hum of heavier voices drop in the shrine of my throne room. I usually drift into the outer hallway if I want to hear the gossip. That's as far as I'm permitted. The prattle is mostly about the best restaurants, where to go next, and the price of eggs.

The queue has been imprisoned for at least the span of one missed meal. Children who have reached the threshold of the Salle des États, are carried asleep or walk stupefied.

Museums are not for childish minds. They are the precincts of academic singularities or precocious youths and their opposable-thumb parents. Even the cream of the elite who swan everywhere else, creep humbly here.

Would it shock them to know my brother loathed painting.

Painting was not his choice. It was a living at his fingertips. Leonardo yearned to be an academic. All he ever wanted was to be cloistered with scientific experiments and plenty of writing paper and ink, but art plucked him from his father's clutches and set us both on a road to freedom.

I am privy to visitor's hushed debates and stale theories: I am Leonardo's self-portrait. I am his mother, Caterina. I am his dark lady-love, his transvestite apprentice, or the everywoman of his past. I am the housewife of a dreary silk-merchant, the duchess of this or that, the queen of here or there. A prostitute. I am the mistress of a prince. I have heard every presumption of mistaken identity, but never the truth: I am his sister.

The truth is supposed to set one free. I hope this is true. I am still holding out for it. I had thought that I could leave the Manor House of Cloux with Leonardo the night his soul flew home, but my streak of stubbornness won out. I thought my attachment to earth matters would only last a short while, and since time doesn't affect me anymore, I suppose, by that reckoning, it has.

I heard a voice say: that woman really does have a secret and no mistake. A second voice countered: she looks like the cat who ate the canary. Its companion was not to be outdone: a whole flock of canaries by the look of her.

The 'look of me' confounds them. Do I wear a contented expression of canary-love? Yes... a little. The first voice returned and sang the lyrics to a popular song, very low in their companion's ear. Do you smile to tempt a lover Mona Lisa? The words are cut short by an elbow jab to the ribs. "Shush."

They were all correct, and I am flattered by the cat reference. I have often considered that cats would make good lawyers. I survived from being catlike and lawyer-like much of the time on my stubborn, feigning-indifference, catty days. I had a cat named Picolini. I knew the look.

If you've ever had to sit for a portrait, you will know how tedious the hours stretch into weeks. It is tiresome after only a few minutes. One's mind drifts like a leaf in a whirlpool until it settles on a fantasy which evokes a pleasant countenance. One doesn't fight direction, but surrenders to an incandescent destination and enjoys the journey, dreamed far enough away to appear detached.

Do I smile to tempt a lover? Not exactly. I once did, but during my portrait I smiled because the temptation had already been consummated.

A good artist copies a likeness of his subject, but a master artist captures their soul. By 1503 Leonardo had studied me for forty-five years. He told

   LISABETTA – A STOLEN GLANCE

me to imagine my best dream, and I was the ideal sitter. I knew how to look through solid objects and see what I wanted to see. In that semi-conscious state I envisioned Sandro Botticelli behind Leonardo's right shoulder as an enticingly nude Mars. Sandro sent me a cheeky wink and I responded, shyly. Gallery visitors witness an invitation accepted – caught by a sorcerer.

Can't you see I'm gloating? I was not being secretive. I was indulging in a romping good daydream, and I had a plan. I always had a plan. I was a seductress of success, never Sandro. When it came to Sandro Botticelli, I was always a timid twelve-year-old shadow with a grandiose dream of being seduced.

I was not especially patient in life but death was worse. Death brings the absence of lateral time, and the chance to review long-forgotten latent desires – the denied successes and the comeuppance of poetic karma. In my case, it made me more determined than ever to shame my century for the things it did to me. To all us women. It's an understatement when historians fail to glean the truth between the lies. Documents have always been reams of paper ghosts – endangered species subject to damp and fire, and most of all, ignorance.

Names are like skeletons who meet on fleshless calendar dates. Populations ooze away from life like the run-off from an abattoir. Life is more than a slaughterhouse of frightening mistakes and whimsical love interests, and if anything, life must stand for a divine dynamic – a petulant thought of non-local mind. I have spoken to others behind the living. Outside of art, none of them have met God or an angel or a demon. Life ends, and death goes on.

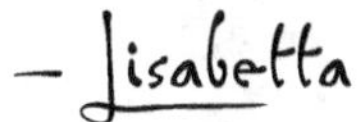

'Madonna of the Rocks' – version I in the Louvre

chapter nine

*"Three things cannot be long hidden:
the sun, the moon, and the truth."*
~ Buddha

On the Rocks with a Twist

PARIS – THE LOUVRE MUSEUM
APRIL 1 – 2008

When Veronica and Jupiter stand in front of Leonardo's 'Madonna of the Rocks', Veronica understands. She checks the lapel of her coat where an amber cabochon brooch clings to the navy blue wool. "You're right, well-done you," she says. Its smooth oval is the mirror image of the one on the Virgin Mary's cape.

Jupiter's reply is a giggle. He waves at the painting.

Golden yellow winks against Cerulean blue as the Madonna bows her head towards them to listen to their conversation. Jupiter scans the painting's surface. His fingers mimic the hands of the Madonna and angel and child. He looks up, radiant with a secret.

Veronica turns away with resignation. "Come on, sweetest of peas. It's time to meet 'Mona Lisa'." More accurately, it's time to join the pilgrimage. Meeting the painting will take a while. They can see the queue. It's an entity in itself – the tail of a restless dragon. Mother Veronica heads towards it towing her reluctant son, whose brows remain knitted in thought. He's calculating. All Veronica can hear is the blood rushing to her head. Art like this makes her dizzy.

For all Veronica's fanciful nature, astronomy wins over astrology, and the dawn-of-reason over Aquarius. The New-Age is far behind her, filed as an immature, but necessary, rite of passage. Joseph Campbell's 'Hero with a Thousand Faces' had been one of the stable academic mystics she could digest. But the business of art is a serial killer that murders its artists slowly and cruelly, and Veronica abandons her creative dreams after a disappointing response to sales. She considers herself a practical human being, and rationalizes that a girl has to eat. Even if she has to work for minimum wage in a supermarket.

By way of explaining her actions, Veronica explained to her Uncle Oz that she preferred to creatively-suicide before art claimed her as its zillionth victim. Uncle (Perry Lyons) Oz had been sympathetic. "Art takes hostages," he had said. Authenticating art is the one passion he allows himself, and as a master geneticist, he appreciates that the art of the genome is closely related to the forensics of paintings. Both require intensive microscopic attention.

Jupiter remembers to whisper: "Mom? -- Mom? -- MOM?... the painting is signing." He waves the brochure at her, but Veronica brushes it aside like a stray lock of hair. She stares straight ahead – a zombie walking through deep water.

It's half-past lunchtime and her continental breakfast has long been consumed in the passionate metabolism of Nike's spell. Veronica is hungry for eggs and bacon, and strong sweet tea to down her pills, and the 'Mona Lisa' is upsetting her stomach. She takes her place at the end of the Lisa devotees. "Jupe, don't stray too far. I need to see you, okay?" she says.

Jupiter wanders a few feet investigating the parade of textures. He tests the resilience of brown suede and red silk. He counts buttons, passing over the shiny brass ones. The sheen of high-gloss upsets him. There are plenty of safe plastic discs. The best ones are covered in cloth. He prefers the buttons with four holes, but only if the thread is sewn in an X or a square.

Parallel lines are unstable. He continues to monitor the fringes of scarves, tassels and the crisscross patterns of shoelaces, and the murmur of conversation drifts over his head like an evaporating cloud. He only picks up its trail when he hears the words Mona, or Lisa, or Leonardo. These are the associations he and his mother have discussed relative to the day. These he is primed for.

The Egyptian exhibits are for the afternoon. *'After'*. Jupiter knows this word. It parades before him as flashcards of food, and paintings, and sculptures. It means *after* lunch… *after* the 'Mona Lisa'… *after* the Nike. He waves to the perfect cheeseburger waiting on the horizon.

Jupiter is confident his mother will refuse the elevator for second encounter on the stairs. He looks forward to descending and reclimbing the Daru Staircase three more times. Like a mountaineer he will reach Nike's base camp, and this time he will stop to listen for Nike's opinion. She is Queen of the footsteps. Does she relish the velvety shoosh of felt slippers the same way he does? And how about the gentle slap of sandals, and the crisp contact of hard rubber, and the warm squeak of crepe soles? Jupiter has four questions to ask 'Nike'. He will point to his running shoes for the first: "Did you know this Nike shoe has stolen your name?" "Do your wings hurt?" "Do you miss your home?" He saves the most important, fourth, question for last: "Is your face lost forever?"

chapter ten

"It is hard to contend
against one's heart's desire;
for whatever it wishes to have
it buys at the cost of soul"
~ Heraclitus

The Musée du Louvre

PARIS – THE LOUVRE MUSEUM
APRIL 15, 2007

You would think one of the museum cleaning staff would use their unique opportunity to examine the art close-up, but they mop the floors the same way a peasant sweeps straw from a hovel. It's a job. Ashes to ashes – broom to broom. The same dust lands on treasures and ancient litter alike, and heaven knows enough privileged carbon-dated memories lie under-glass, no less valuable than diamonds displayed in a jeweler's showcase.

The *Salle des* États is the first salon to be cleaned and the last to open. April filters through a decorative row of lattice bars set deep into the high windows along its east wall. Inside the gallery, the 'Mona Lisa' broods behind an impenetrable curtain of transparent steel. Inside the painting, Lisabetta frets under an assumed name. Nearly five-hundred-years of captivity seems penance enough for a crime she can't recall committing.

All she wants, is to reach her heaven – the personal heaven she created worth dying for. It's a humble enough appeal to make of an abundant universe, but dreaming too small is unworthy of an artist, and she had been nothing if not that.

When she does dream, it's always the same: first the choking fire and an expanse of blue sky, then a dusty road beneath her feet, and she is running, running ... flying down the road to Fiesole towards Mt. Ceceri

– the great swan. What follows is a sea of faces in a church, where she's a saint offering communion from behind a silver altar, but the people's mouths are closed and she has nothing to place on their tongues but fame, and all she can do is smile beatifically and try to wake up.

Lisabetta slips from her baroque frame and takes a turn about the gallery to study her companions for signs of habitation. The absence of visitors feels eerie, but the din of life will begin soon enough. She dances full circle about the room and comes to a stop, facing her portrait like a mirror, and melts into the Tuscan fields behind her benevolent smile. The months it took for Leonardo to paint her had been a revelation. She had been forty-five then.

Lisabetta rests inside her painting, beside the track leading to Anchiano, and breathes in the sunshine of early spring – a renaissance Cinderella at the stroke of dawn with her dress restored to emerald green and her hair returned to its natural shade of honey, plaited in a single braid.

Leonardo once had the strength to bend metal bars with his hands, almost as well as he manipulated the laws of science and tamed the forbidden powers of alchemy. Will he ever arrive to release her like one of his caged birds? His ingenuity could easily confound a crystal wall and the current laws of detention. She is sure Leonardo would rescue her if he could.

If only wishing made it so.

PARIS – The Louvre Museum
APRIL 1, 2008

It's right there in the Louvre's guidebook: portrait of *Lisa del Gio-condo*, first floor, Denon Wing, Room 6, *Salle des États* – the 'Mona Lisa'. What mortal would argue with the printed word or the French Republic? In French she is 'La Joconde'; in Italian: 'La Gioconda' – the laughing woman. She is the pun, the twist of fate – the sainted name of a resident Queen.

There are times Lisabetta feels that the museum has been built for her alone and that the other works of art are her courtiers. She reigns in an emotional palace, enchanted under a faerie glamour thrown over her destiny. But the fates still bend to her subconscious wishes – the fame of eternal life, and the elegant reckonings with her enemies as she once numbered them.

Lisabetta had been clear when she planned her heaven, desirous of being surrounded by paintings and sculpture. Her temple beyond death must be palatial to compensate for a life spent in cottages and cramped studios. She wishes for large airy rooms full of art where she will hold court, with her days of invisible servitude over. In her most intensive daydreams, Lisabetta envisions herself the center of attention, for once, the iconic lady acknowledged by admirers, celebrated by poets and kings – the equal of her illustrious brother. A *principessa* in her own right.

It's oppressive in the open space of the *Salle des États*. Lisabetta is restless as a caged tiger. It's a day of opposites: dull yet expectant – stifling without heat. Listless air fidgets in dry whorls and flaps into the corners of the ceiling like disturbed bats. The gallery holds her in a psychic vacuum. Today she is an exhibit rather than the star of a show. Her audience is reserved. No... transparent. They're fading out, or she is – vibrating too slow. Their voices speak in undertones enveloped in fog, and Lisabetta craves distance where she can breathe back the spirit of her Italian sunshine.

chapter eleven

"It is by going down into the abyss
that we recover the treasures of life.
Where you stumble,
there lies your treasure"
~ Joseph Campbell

The Louvre's Closet

Immediately below the *Salle des États*, where four stone arches meet in a vaulted dome, Lisabetta's market pig, sits on a pedestal and shivers with power. Its museum plaque reads: 'Il Porcellina'- *the market pig from the city of Florence – c.1300 A.D. – a marble copy of an original Hellenistic statue, c. 350 BC, now lost.*

The ancient pig once ruled the old *mercato* of Florence until it was unceremoniously usurped by a bronze impersonator in 1612 and housed in the Uffizi, the Louvre's museum cousin. Its history is violent, having surviving the Uffizi fire of 1762, and seized in a French raid.

Lisabetta and her nemesis have been apart, yet together under the same French roof, disconnected, dreaming of each other for centuries.

'Il Porcellina' sends its venerable matriarch a message: "I think it's time."

Less than four-hundred-miles from Paris, a forgotten cache of appropriated art, lies at the end of a mile of tunnels in a network of underground caves. Near the back wall, under a natural vault of stone painted with pale horses, is the original statue of a boar – a Greek marble, thousands of years old. It's wrapped like a mummy, muffled in unbleached linen and sealed in plastic bubble-wrap, which attests to its most recent move, in 1952.

This is to be its last sighting.

The depository marks the end of a long line of possession. There were times when the priceless sculptures had been celebrated in the shade of private loggias, but mostly, they have been cloistered in secret rooms and private galleries, unwaveringly stoic, and now consigned to a womb in the earth.

The 'pharaoh's tomb' of classic sculpture passes covertly from archaeologists, antiquities dealers, museum employees, and desperate relatives, to patrons with questionable scruples, and the relentless urge to claim, conserve, hoard, and possess.

The priceless objects, laundered through the great houses of Europe into private hands, have been hidden in a relentless journey, through political wars, family disputes, revolutions, and human greed, until their provenance is confused beyond all accounting.

Finally, they're shifted to lower ground for safe-keeping – a delightful subterranean sculpture garden, stashed, catalogued, secret, and invisible – acquisitions too famous to be acknowledged, kept safe from being repossessed by countries with long memories.

It remains a private collection. More than private now, since the demise of its last heir, who perished in a freak fire along with his letters, maps, photographs, and catalogues. Its line of patrons, who once boasted diplomatic access to the corridors of the Louvre, is now extinct. Whereabouts unknown.

The antiquities wait for a new champion, alongside several relatively youthful works from the sixteenth century: fragments of a giant horse and a sleeping cupid, both circa 1500; the arms of the 'Venus di Milo', several Parthenon marbles, a flawless statue of Hatshepsut from the temple of Deir el-Bahri, the head of the 'Nike of Samothrace', and the original 'Il Porcellina' (considered lost for two-thousand years), slumber in hermetic stasis.

Il Porcellina's youngest sister, pig-napped, missing since 1552, echoes a familiar message: "Mother, I think it's time."

The original pig had been replicated under the watchful eyes of Nike's creator. Its energy is doubled by each clone with the elegance of homeopathic math. One pig reaches the marketplace of Florence, its twin is buried in rubble for centuries and unearthed during the reign of modern archaeology. The genealogy of art remains: copies of copies of copies.

Lisabetta surrenders to the year 2008 and distracts herself with long excursions into the mountains Leonardo painted for her pleasure. Her agitation subsides within the furthest reaches of her landscape until the buzzing of bees informs her it's time to return to the April gallery. The room drones with its usual humanity and Lisabetta is about to abandon her post and retreat once more down the track behind her, when she feels the air in the *Salle des* États quicken. The doors blow open and what arrives is a revelation.

Time is no respecter of chronological order and the shock transports Lisabetta to 1464 when she first understood her capacity to hate. Two things are immediately apparent: an ordinary day may bring a surprise, and the dead can still experience amazement.

chapter twelve

Grand Entrance

PARIS – THE LOUVRE MUSEUM
APRIL 1 – 2008

Redemption smelled like violets. It arrived with a woman and a boy who entered my gallery in a corridor of light that flattened into a wide ribbon and trailed behind them.

When I stepped onto their shimmering carpet, it turned into a vaporous hallway where I observed lateral time expressed with two vanishing points. One direction led to the past, the other, I presumed, to heaven. The entire length of its walls were inscribed with a continuous math proof that extended either side of me.

The three of us stood on an endless strip of colored light, in the vibration named yellow. Ahead, the spectrum stretched green and blue towards a distant glow of violet. Behind us, the floor reached out to orange, pink, red, and violet, to connect full-circle.

It felt warm there, as one would imagine yellow to feel, like being outside on a perfect Summer day. The air changed to a delightful breeze of sunlight infused with ozone. It was familiar, and whenever I stepped outside it, the tunnel flattened to a path once more and the atmosphere in the salon appeared stale and grey.

Infinitely thin strands of light, in the same bands of fluctuating colors, threaded their way into the navels of each person in the room, connecting

them. Other filaments transmuted into gentle sparks that flashed from fore-
head-to-forehead and wrists to knees in dazzling arcs, woven into a network
of light. The firework display dissipated slightly, but remained as a soft humming sound.

An aura of shifting colors ran down each strand, turning the assembly
into a hundred marionettes performing without tangles. Their strings passed
uninterrupted through each other – a ballet of light beams energized into an
abstract painting of wriggling lines that writhed with vitality until the room
was reduced to a multi-layered image of squirming animation.

Eventually, the bright cords became so dense it was impossible to see
through them, and I floated there, suspended, enjoying the surreal view, similar
to swimming under water, in an ocean teeming with life. I imagined the earth
as a spinning ball of pulsating string. One continuous string of light wove itself
into the Eiffel Tower in an impressionistic cityscape of oscillating colors.

Somewhere, on the far side of the moon, I knew the eternity of colors
would collide into an effervescent beam. They would unite, not in darkness,
but emblazoned as the incarnation of pure white light and join violet-to-vi-
olet, forming a circle like the mystic Ouroborus (the snake biting its own tail)
so luminous as to make an artist weep.

The spectacle swirled together, reconfiguring into a flock of paintings
adhered to the walls of the Salle des États, once more a bustling throng of
visitors surrounded by art and a mystic road that begged me to follow.

Veronica and Jupiter Lyons were a blast of freedom, and I danced
around them creating a vortex from our energies, but Veronica looked through
my real face to stare at my portrait. She was afraid. Once again I was eclipsed
by celebrity and suffered the frustrating experience of being studied intently
and completely overlooked at the same time, but her son, Jupiter, smiled hello.
I assumed that mother and child, were my passport home. I whispered to the
mother that I forgave her, but she was too wound up to hear me.

What I understood was primal knowing. It gave me reason to believe
in the power of sustained meditation. I didn't believe... I knew instinctively
that corporeal interference was vital in order to put things right. I had a score
to settle with fate, and yes, I wanted to wipe the smile off Lisa del Giocondo's
face... wherever or whenever she was.

Two years after my death, Sandro Botticelli, died. I had been scaling one of the easier cliffs, when I heard him call my name. A strong surge of love from Sandro tugged me towards him, and I called back into the valley. My echo broke against the mountains. Then came the terrible silence and I felt twice-abandoned by love.

In 1508, when I died, I explained to Leonardo that he and I would only be apart for a short time, but he became agitated, and I knew I would stay in my portrait until his own transition.

And so we spoke daily, and time being fluid in the territory of the void, ebbed and flowed in magnificent waves. I was not yet in that pleasant dream of afterlife. I did not know then, that I was dangerously suspended in a lucid gap between life and death, halfway to heaven with one foot mired in French soil.

Death is only a moment. What follows is an epiphany as a receptive universe writes its pleasure in occult poetry. I am not a traditional ghost. I do not wail or clank undignified through the hallways of a dark museum. I have more style than that. I am a presence. I am the 'Mona Lisa'.

I created my heaven carefully, but failed to anticipate a legacy of anonymity and to be so wiped from the memory of the world that my resentment would hold me hostage for five-hundred years.

Time is an eternal equation – the quantum mathematics of celebratory death wishes and birthday surprises. Each party marked with a red flag at the intersections of peak moments: potent anniversaries and geological events. There are cycles for conscious extinctions and lucid resurgence. Human wars and celestial explosions destroy on cue, but loves are plotted on perpetual calendars of empathy. Love defies formula. Love is the universe breathing out of control.

I have learned, the hard way, that a creative mind receives what it asks for. The importance of being extraordinarily clear while wishing cannot be overstated. The ambiguous prayer is a toothless contract. Invoking one's highest good is, at best, a murky invitation. An unpolished dream is unfinished business. Leonardo begged me to never leave him yet in the end he had no choice but to leave me.

　　　　LISABETTA – A STOLEN GLANCE

I am well aware that a great artist paints much more than a likeness. What possible chance for escape did I have? I had been captured by a master – my brother, Leonardo da Vinci.

The human language is selfish. It lacks ethereal flexibility. The Poet-God declared that my identity would rhyme with singular purpose, but my name breathed the same sigh as that colorless woman, Monna Lisa Giocondo. I have been dead five-hundred-years, and the poem isn't over.

— *Lisabetta*

chapter thirteen

*"Alice sighed wearily.
'I think you might do something better
with the time,' she said,
Than waste it in asking riddles
that have no answers."*
~ Lewis Carroll

The End of the Line

PARIS – THE LOUVRE MUSEUM
APRIL 1 – 2008

Jupiter is in heaven, pressed against a wall of blue cashmere. The young woman inside it stirs with impatience. He can feel a burst of irritation float from her in a grey cloud. It settles above her male companion who shows little regard for the treasure that has mesmerized an entire herd of anticipation towards a single face. Eavesdropping is Jupiter's only option.

Jupiter is an absorber of information. His mission is to help, to put right, and to offer wisdom, but for the moment, the luxury of a soft cardigan lulls him into silence.

"Who *was* she again?" the young man in the frayed jeans asks. His fingers tap an impatient staccato on his visitor's guidebook. He lacks finesse when it comes to faking interest.

"I told you," the woman says in a speech bubble. "Lisa Giocondo". She sighs at him like a mother with a small clumsy child who's spilled his milk. "That's why the painting is called the Giocon--DA... 'da' is the feminine. Giocon-*da* means smiling woman." No response. She points to the brochure and three letters, 'Joc' in 'La *Joc*-onde'. She pronounces the J, soft. "Joc? The J hardens to 'Joke' Do you see?" She punches her companion's arm with what he interprets as mock anger. He is deciding whether to ask if the 'da' in da Vinci is also feminine, because he heard once that Leonardo was gay. He wisely thinks better of asking. Innocently, his gaze wanders abstractedly to the ceiling and he sings the famous lyrics under his breath: *Are you warm? Are you real? Mona Lisa…* Not caring to push his luck, he hums the rest, looks askance at the girl of his dreams, and begins to whistle the Mona Lisa Song under his breath.

His companion is serious. The grey cloud darkens and dowses the young man with freezing rain. He slips his hand into hers as a peace offering, but she withdraws it immediately with a slither, and he jams his fists into his pockets feigning remarkably genuine indifference. From now on he can be himself. "Waiting in this line is a *joke*," he says, too loud.

The young man sees his girlfriend's face crumple into the past.

"And you're a big jock," she says. The heat of chemical attraction short-circuits like the fizzle of a hot skillet in cold water.

The physics of art appreciation parts them like the red sea. The ex-girlfriend watches as he floats away. He's too male to understand the finality and will hang on to what he considers the bitter end, and ogle the 'Mona Lisa', after all he's come this far and paid for the tickets, and they're nearing the finish line – a term he can relate to. He can see the goalposts of the *Salle des États*, and maybe… just maybe, he will stretch for something amazing, locate his dormant culture gene, engage his brain, and make a profoundly intelligent comment to impress the princess at his side. He's young enough to think winning her back is possible.

The young woman feels vindicated. The jerk didn't even have the class to change his sweatshirt emblazoned with the words Notre Dame. He thinks it's a football team. "Uncultured oaf," she mutters to the ceiling.

Jupiter picks a piece of lint clinging to the jean's back.

"Glaciers move faster than this," the jeans say, and the cashmere sweater shivers in disgust.

The jeans spy Jupiter's beret. His gaze lingers on the 'don't mess with me' button. "That's an interesting button," he says.

"It's a BROOCH," Jupiter says, "brooch brooch brooch. I...
DON'T'... LIKE ... BUTTONS!"

"Sorry. Geez, how was I supposed to know?... weird kid."

Veronica hears and sends him a withering look that turns him away.

Jupiter smiles and replaces the piece of lint on the jean's back. "Lint, lint, lint, lint," he says.

Jupiter already knows 'Mona Lisa's' identity. He can see from at least a dozen nuances of shape, exactly who she is. He has cross-referenced her eyes, and mouth, and nose, and chin to other images he's seen in his mother's art books. He's about to explain when a trolley, pushed by armed guards, swings by like a creaky ship listing to the left from its bulky cargo. It squeaks his attention away from the mystery of Lisa's identity to one of its silver wheels.

While other eyes check out the wrapped curiosity secured to its surface, Jupiter works out how to fix the wonky wheel that wobbles like the orbit of a misaligned planet. Wonky is a word he uses to express how broken things annoy him.

The hallway babbles with frayed tempers in every conceivable accent. Foreign words pepper the air in a human buzz, but humans cough, and grunt, and sniffle, in the same language. The din is almost as overwhelming as the choking battles of clashing perfumes, and the clinging smells of tobacco and body odor. Impatient feet dance the 'Mona Lisa' shuffle. Jupiter studies the different configurations of small colored boxes: cameras, cell phones, and music-pods, that preoccupy everyone so deeply. His eyes follow the trail of them back to a cherry-red enamel square. His mother is reading a message. The forest of human stench is making him dizzy.

Jupiter experiences a kaleidoscope of expectant faces and impatient hands that, for nothing better to do, preen hairstyles and smooth crumpled clothes into submission. There's an overall confusion of constant opening and closing of museum programs, mouths, women's purses, and shopping bags. All of it amid a jumble of plaid coats, striped shawls, and flowered shirts.

A pair of eyeglasses swinging on a silver chain grabs Jupiter's attention. It's too far away to calm down. Another lady's multiple strands of cheap beads heave restlessly up and down on her pink neck. A white strand of pearls rests against a smooth tanned wrist. Jupiter counts the pulse beats. The glare from the perfect spheres hurt his eyes.

A new light flickers at the end of the bright hallway like the tunnel in a near-death experience, and the cashmere woman steps over the gateway with Jupiter attached to her blue sweater. A guard guillotines the line immediately after Veronica, silently ushering his charges left and right like a bored traffic cop directing sheep. Jupiter imagines him blowing a shrill whistle to wake up the hypnotic queue before shouting 'showtime'.

Inside the hallow-of-hallows, Jupiter demands confirmation. He wants to know why people are so blind. Mostly he wants them to know who the lady in the painting is. He shakes his head trying to dislodge the reasons how one portrait could be so many different people. Clothes should make up their minds. Is the sweater right? Are the jeans wrong? Do the swaying eyeglasses make anything clear? Guesses are unacceptable. But he knows one thing for sure, and announces it to the distracted crowd: "She's not cold, but she *is* lonely."

The line flows like honey into soft rows, and from his new position, Jupiter peers through the coats and sees his mother's idol. His thumbnail easily covers the 'Mona Lisa' — a postage stamp drawing the swarm of bodies towards her in a slow-motion stampede. She captivates the herd like a hypnotist's pendulum.

Lisabetta feels a disturbance unraveling the back of the line and wills herself to determine if it's a promise or a threat. A blast of white light indicates the former. Two visitors within a yellow halo move towards her and she leaves her painting to meet them in the center of the room.

"I wish I could tell you for sure," Veronica says. "Leonardo liked to play tricks." Jupiter stares at his mother for more. "Leonardo loved funny words, so he left clues," she says. "He loved puzzles almost as much as you." This thought wanders off with Jupiter in tow as the 'Mona Lisa' conga line, milling now, funnels into singular awareness.

Jupiter covers his ears. Art is noisy. Museums are ear-splitting places. "She IS a lovely work of art," he protests loudly over the din of impatient paintings. "Lovely lovely lovely."

When Jupiter first heard his mother refer to him as special, he had heard the word *spacial*. He agreed with her. Every object he sees makes a solid forward-shape made possible by the dozens of air-shapes it shares with its neighbors. He focuses on the spaces between things when he wants to draw, but now his eyes need to find a home and rest. Jupiter returns to Veronica's side, and settles on his mother's amber brooch. It winks on her blue raincoat – a honeyed tomb with a lonely bee trapped inside. He taps it to make it buzz. "The Mona Lisa is lonely too," he says to the bee. "She's hungry."

The bliss from fitting Louvre pictures together is exhausting. He closes his eyes, and remembers the word 'after', and his mind flash-forwards from the face of the 'Mona Lisa' to a birds-eye view of a round dining table draped in red and white cloth. In its center is a round white plate holding the brown dome of a hamburger bun. He loves the concentric circles. But circles weren't always safe. Next to it is another brown circle of chocolate milk in a tall glass, all seen from above like a seagull hovering over the sidewalk cafes of Paris.

"Why don't you join us for lunch?" Jupiter says to the lady from the painting. "We're going to find hamburgers. My name is Jupiter."

"Mine is Lisabetta."

Jupiter giggles. "Betta betta betta betta."

"Better what?" Veronica asks.

Jupiter takes Lisabetta's hand and swings it casually as they walk. "Better if we have hamburgers for lunch."

"We will," Veronica says in a pinched voice… "*after* we see the Mona Lisa, okay?"

chapter fourteen

"There comes a pause,
for human strength will not endure
to dance without cessation;
and everyone must reach the point at length
of absolute prostration."
~ Lewis Carroll

The Sleeping Beauty

PARIS – THE LOUVRE MUSEUM
APRIL 1 – 2008

The anticipation of confronting the Mona Lisa is terrifying. Veronica's feet ache from eleven days tramping the art galleries of London. Every step is a foot impaled on a sharp spike. She glances down at her shoes, half expecting them to be made of glass, seeping with blood like the cursed red slippers in a fairy tale. The highs of meeting Nike are crashing. And now, the erratic sugary meals of Paris are playing games with her blood. She's lightheaded. She grips onto Jupiter for support. Her brain hisses. Mona Lisa's installation shimmers like a heatwave on the horizon. She looks away and counts to four.

Her thoughts spill like entrails: *I'm unworthy. I should go. I abandoned her. What was I thinking? I have no business being here. I can't face her. What if I was wrong? What if she's a big disappointment? What if I am? What if I'm crazy? I need another pill. Fairy tales always unravel. I'm Cinderella, an imposter in painful slippers, pretending to be a lady. It's almost midnight. I should definitely go. I know better. Happy endings are rubbish. My feet are killing me. I need to sit down. It's high noon. How ironic.*

Lisabetta breaks through the pity tirade with a demanding "Look at me," in a raised voice.

Veronica obeys without question and lifts her eyes. The fairy tale resumes. 'Mona Lisa' is trapped like Snow White in a vertical glass coffin. *Even your intrepid prince will have a tough time getting to those enchanted lips.* But in an instant the illusion is gone and SHE'S there – Saint Lisa of the roving eyes. Her painted lips tremble. Lisa's coloring is brighter. Can she be blushing? *Is it possible for a painting to blush?*

A drip-feed of icy anesthetic trickles inside a vein in Veronica's left arm. Her solar plexus seizes.

"I dare you to grow up," Lisabetta says.

Veronica flexes her rigid arm and huddles for warmth inside her coat. "Can you hear me?" she asks the 'Mona Lisa'. "Do you remember me?"

"Mom, quit pinching me for luck," Jupiter says. "Yes, I hear you."

"Sorry, Jupe. You're my anchor."

Jupiter reaches up and pats his mother's hand. For a moment he connects the two women like a bridge. "Mom, are you having one of your earthquakes?"

"I'll be fine. Just a few... *um*... aftershocks, is all. I'm overexcited."

"You need to sit down."

"Just let me lean on you."

"You need tea and cakes... and hamburgers, burgers, burgers, burgers."

But Veronica doesn't hear. She's out of body, floating up to the painting until she's inside it looking out – a saint looking down from a shallow niche, drowning her believers in a beatific smile.

She calls out 'help me' to Jupiter, but her painted lips are glued shut in the mystery smile of all time. And now she knows that a smile can hold fear in check. A smile can hide anything from anger to joy. A living smile is nothing but a momentary reflex.

Mona Lisa's smile is contrived by a genius. Leonardo invented Lisa's smile to incorporate every emotion. A painting is subjective. A woman smiles. Perhaps she's happy or wistful. Perhaps she's lying. Perhaps she's deliberately hiding her true feelings in order to survive. Women of the 15th century learned to hold their tongues and submit, early.

The amber silk sleeves are cool to the touch. Below, Veronica's body stands beside Jupiter and 'Lisa the Obscure', isolated in a pink spotlight. Veronica's fingers locked in layers of ancient varnish, struggle to sign the word 'help'. Finally, her pulse animates and jumpstarts Lisa's wrists. The connection is undeniably synergetic. Symbiotically shared. Mutual. Lisa's painted fingers twitch uncontrollably and crack the varnish.

Hallucinations are the price one pays for abusing bipolar medication. But it's more. Veronica feels gutted from the full measure of being trapped against her will. Hot waves of nausea meet the ice-water of fear. *What if I'm trapped here. What if I can't leave? Will that 'me', down there on the floor carry on? Will she a better mother? Will Lisa leave me here?*

Veronica meets her own gaze, and for a moment all is clear. This is a meeting of souls. A crossroad. A parting of the ways. Whatever else, she must remain calm and surrender.

She's faint from hunger and breathless from the constricting corsets of a painted dress tethered to the fifteenth-century. From on high, Veronica studies the spectacle of herself and Jupiter and Lisa standing together like a group statue. No-one is moving. She sweeps the frozen crowd. Lisa's parallel smile, widens into the grimace of the Cheshire Cat. Veronica feels it as a freakish grin imprisoned in amber.

The erratic palpitations of two women mingle and accelerate, building into the chaos of war.

The shrieks of a thousand warriors battle for freedom until the Mona Lisa's stifled screams turn the salon walls to glass. Inside them, the power lines writhe like angry snakes. Veronica's blood vessels atrophy with age and cease pumping. Her brain boils. A feverish star bursts in her right eye. The room melts in an orgasmic shiver and rests silent as a tomb.

The floor is solid beneath Veronica's feet. She's back on earth. The 'Mona Lisa' is intact but stray sparks of static electricity flash around her once or twice.

Jupiter stands alone, at her side, his eyes wild with fear, squeezing her hand extra-hard. It was a momentary 'earthquake'. Nothing more. "You're shaking," he says, massaging the warmth back into his mother's hands.

Veronica grabs Jupiter's brochure and fans her face. The Mona Lisa is nowhere to be seen other than her rightful place on the wall. Veronica catches her breath. "This crowd takes all the air," she says. "I must have forgotten to take my pills. I'll be fine."

"You took one, two, three, four," Jupiter replies, counting on his fingers. "Too many."

Lisabetta locks eyes with Veronica's. Veronica stares back in defiance but her shredded nerves sabotage the peak moment. Still, her irreverence surprises her. She hears herself address the painting while her eyes remain deliberately averted, fixated safely on the lip of the gold frame. "Lisa Giocondo I presume?" she says, and wishes it back. Leonardo deserves better.

Veronica hears *"You presume wrong"* hissed in her ear. She checks out her neighbors… all are preoccupied with claiming their precious elbow space.

She detaches her hand from Jupiter's and checks to confirm her coat sleeves are rough navy-blue wool. The slippery sheen of silk is gone.

"Is it *after* yet?" Jupiter says. "My feet need to sit down."

I've studied visitors for hundreds of years. Human parades reveal a great deal. But I forget that Veronica may hear my thoughts unless I block them, and the last thing I need to do is give my savior another fear to chew. She and I, dare I say it, are interchangeable. Strangely compatible in a perverse way, especially our drives. Hers are paralyzed. Mine are animated by a strong sense of entitlement.

I gave Veronica a taste of my medicine to jolt her memories and to illustrate how petty her challenges are. In many ways, she is as privileged and lifeless as my nemesis, the flavorless 'other Lisa' who eclipsed me. Fate is apparently, more mysterious than a smile.

— 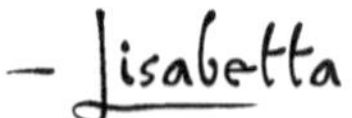

Centuries collide when Jupiter removes his jacket, and reveals a silk-screened image of the 'Mona Lisa'. He compares the golden flesh tones of the original, visibly dismayed his shirt is dull by comparison. "The colors are different."

"No print can capture the presence of a Leonardo original," Veronica says in a shaky voice. "Truth be told, I'm feeling a little… *um*… captured myself." She dry-swallows another pill. Her throat constricts.

Jupiter holds up his right hand and wiggles his fingers. "That's five," he says to Lisabetta.

Someone is sobbing from far away. Sobbing like the fragile echoes of footsteps in Nike's stairwell. The room is about to catch fire. Veronica tests the solidity of the floor to make sure she's reasonably grounded but her feet are numb and her limp body hangs weightless as if she's levitating.

"Mom, stop floating. Lisa's crying. You're making her cry. Look!"

The thing is, people buy souvenir prints of my portrait on the way out of the museum. I suppose it's considered gauche to wear them inside. Jupiter had no such reservations. His concept of fashion was fluid. Rules were verbal lint. His red shoes were tied with rainbow laces. He wore mismatched socks, and his beret boasted a badges that declared: 'Don't mess with me, I'm high-functioning.'

Clearly his mother indulged him, and hopefully, had also encouraged his creative side and applauded his special sensitivities, maybe even flaunted them to the world in defiance. Jupiter was oblivious. He adored being himself, and I envied him. Leonardo had been the same – most of the time.

I suspected that Jupiter was not always so jubilant. Even a genius finds zeal too heavy to carry indefinitely. I sensed Jupiter heard the museum's soundtrack, saturated with whispers of half-dead memories. I saw him struggle with the noisier ones. I've learned the rarefied atmosphere surrounding ancient artifacts can choke a sensitive mind. I've seen too many hardy souls faint and be carted away on stretchers.

I sensed Jupiter suffered from a similar malady as Leonardo. At first, I wasn't sure the boy saw me. He examined me without meeting my eyes, but his mind accepted my conversation. He seemed indifferent and fascinated at the same time. I was simply an anomaly he needed to file. I knew then, that this was the opportunity to jump or stay, because it tasted and smelled of synchronicity and irony, two of the flavors I'd come to know as signatures of a perverse universe.

Suddenly I cherished the gold frame that protected me with its golden fence. I had lived inside a baroque border which delineated... no celebrated, where I belonged. Here I was honored. I was queen of a salon, this building, and the city outside. Paris relied on me, as I depended on it to champion my existence. How could I leave it for a heaven I'd never seen, or perhaps only imagined?

I needn't have worried about Veronica mishearing me. Her medication was a wall between us. It would have to crumble, one pill at a time. Jupiter would know where the weak spots were, and if we hit it right, it would fall. Together we would save her with tea and cakes. She would heal sufficiently enough to lean into my mission with a vengeance. Jupiter would gain a stable mother in the deal, and Veronica could challenge the art galleries with renewed vigor. Perhaps renewed was too big a word for never having confidence in the first place, but she could eke out a decent living and look herself in the mirror without flinching.

Nothing could be as disheartening as the subsistence farming that I was born to, nor the subsistence painting Leonardo subjected himself to.

— Lisabetta

Lisabetta speaks gently to Jupiter. "*Buongiorno.* Do you know who I am"?

"You're Italian."

"*Si.*"

Jupiter points to the 'Mona Lisa'. "Her shadow."

"Are you afraid of me"?

"Not yet. Are you coming with us?"

"Oh child. If only I could. The truth is, it's impossible for me to leave my portrait. I suppose you could steal it, but as you see, it's under lock and key."

The delightful chuckle that escapes Jupiter from deep inside is contagious. "Us, us, us," he mimes.

Lisabetta's smile widens in spite of her hopelessness. The boy's eyes crinkle with a secret. He doubles over with merriment and performs one of his happy dances. "Of course you can." When he looks up, his expression is ecstatic. "The truth is a game."

"You must forgive me child, but I don't feel much like playing today."

Jupiter smiles slyly down at his shirt and taps his chest. "Your painting is right here," he says. "Mom always says to be careful what you wish for."

Jupiter made me laugh. It was enough to make us friends, and it was the first time a visitor invited me to lunch.

He was a direct invitation as much as a surprise. I am charged by an unshakable law to remain with my portrait, but jumping into the cloth face of Jupiter's shirt meant that I remained dutifully confined. It was a spontaneous artful escape. I love that child's mind.

— Lisabetta

Veronica does what every Louvre visitor does, she sweeps the 'Mona Lisa' like a mine field, hoping her eyes will act as total-recall cameras, and zoom in on facial tics later. Three minutes is not long enough to peruse a dream. She is jostled out of place by a firm arm. One of the seven dwarfs, no doubt guarding his princess. She looks down at a pair of shiny black boots, then up at a giant's French face. It shows boredom and distain. "*Vas-t'en!...* move along." Ah, it's 'Grumpy' then. No chance of 'Happy', this *is* Paris after all.

The fairy tale is intact with the arcs of peasants and princesses: Cinderella, Snow White, and 'Mona Lisa'. One can't detain a bad fairy's curse or a French museum guard.

The air snaps with departure anxiety. The 'Mona Lisa' morphs into a foreshortened panel seen in three-quarter view. Veronica exits backwards, as from royalty or someone she distrusts. Leonardo is everywhere and nowhere. 'Mona Lisa' is the proof of his touch. She is the Polaroid of a five-hundred-year-old event, and Veronica grudgingly moves along without saying goodbye.

A stranger in the crowd voices a popular opinion. "Nobody really knows who she was," it says.

"SHE knows," Jupiter pipes up, but his short stature causes his words to be absorbed by the black duffel coat in front of him. "And I know… I know… I know," he whispers into the itchy wool. "I KNOW."

"Are you ready to eat?" Veronica is relieved by the steadiness of her voice and her mundane question. *I guess it's over. I must have been mistaken. I feel like a gutted fish. I survived. I could eat a horse.* An image of Leonardo's giant horse statue flashes across the universe. She chuckles. *Maybe just a hamburger.*

Two answers arrive: "I am ready," Lisabetta says.

"Mom. I've been ready to eat since right after we had dessert for breakfast."

Jupiter blinks at the disappearing room behind him, sputtering like a dying candle. He intends to scrutinize anything that affects his mother so deeply. She has talked about the 'Mona Lisa' and Leonardo da Vinci long before he uttered his first words. They are family. When he and his mother scan their photo albums, he expects her to point them out: *'There's Uncle Leonardo dressed up as Santa Claus. Oh, and that woman with her back to the camera petting the cat, is my Aunt Lisa'.* He's sure he's heard her say that.

The empty shell of Veronica drifts slowly towards life. Christmas Day is over. Practical life resumes. The gifts have been exposed. The anticipation is gone. She received everything she asked for and it isn't enough. Greed has triumphed. Guilt resumes.

Jupiter's informal art lessons began in babyhood. 'Professor Mom' had offered visual treats from her textbooks, and Jupiter had watched his mother mix colors and apply them to large white squares, his favorite shape, even though triangles now rule. Geometry is fickle but generous. Jupiter had easily absorbed Leonardo's diagrams of the proportions of man, the squared circle, and the divine rectangle. Children's book illustrations mingled with the shapes of science. His education had been a parade of erratic images – from Alice's wonderland animals and pea-green boats to the Fibonacci spirals of seashells.

The elegance of math is a language Jupiter understands intuitively. He's the only visitor to the Louvre who brings a backpack sporting the image of Leonardo's, 'Vitruvian Man', *into* its gift shop. A lion doll's head protrudes from a side pocket. It wears a happy expression. Its three brothers are sardined inside the main compartment with a box of crayons and a spiral-bound sketchbook. A black border has been drawn on each of the book's blank pages. There's an even number of crayons. Orange is wonky. The orange wax stick has been evicted to calm his nerves.

Jupiter prefers to draws his thoughts on graph paper. Blank sheets are upsetting. Information can slip off their edges. Some days the world is flat. His favorite paper comes ruled with turquoise blue squares that capture each letter. He loves crossword puzzles. Grids are good. Safe. Order is essential. The grid he pictures now, inside the Louvre, is a tablecloth of red and white gingham. Placed upon it are white circular plates, hamburger domes, and stable wedges of apple pie.

Jupiter's responding chuckle had been the deciding factor which breached my hesitation. I followed it into his shirt and let it massage me like a hug. It was then I knew I had made the only choice. Right away, Jupiter Lyons was my adopted son, my new little brother, and a dear friend. Second thoughts attacked later. Veronica was a master performer when it came to acting indifferent.

— Lisabetta

chapter fifteen

"Confused things
kindle the mind to great inventions."
~ Leonardo Da Vinci

The Muse in the Machine

It would be easy to say I am the true face of the 'Mona Lisa' and equally truthful to say I am not the original. How I came to live in France is well-documented. The part no-one knows, is who traveled the short distance from Amboise to Paris, and why Leonardo painted two of us.

I had wished for fame but neglected to ask for recognition, and so I remain as invisible in death as I was in life, supplanted by a woman I envied – a woman I inadvertently raised up to preposterous celebrity. When experts attributed my face to Lisa Giocondo, I saw blood, but by then it was impossible to silence her. Both of us were long dead.

When I turned eight, my half-brother Leonardo was fourteen, apprenticed to the master artist, Andrea Verrocchio, and he began to pass on what he learned, to me. I was thrilled to learn the trade by copying my brother – to be spared the crooked back of a farm laborer and becoming an old woman at thirty.

I had been content as an artist's assistant. I was invisible according to the guild, but my work put extra funds into Leonardo's pocket and he designated me his accountant. While my brother followed the path of his insatiable muse, I saved for the day we would open our own studio. He had all the power, but I was learning how to use it.

Leonardo suffered from the maladies of genius. He saw too much – plagued with excessive ideas, but hadn't the insight to navigate the business of art. He was different, not necessarily troubled, but trouble-causing. Obsessive. His mind functioned apart from the world, and he carried the burdensome weight of his insatiable curiosity into each day until he was often unwell

     LISABETTA – A STOLEN GLANCE

from the strain. When he needed to restore his health, he slipped into the hills outside the city fortifications.

When I was a girl, Florence was enclosed by a protective wall with eighty gates and watchtowers. Beyond them stretched the main roads and worn tracks that led into the wild country between towns, each with similar barricades against nature and war. Beyond these portals lay Leonardo's earthly heaven – his church with its dome of blue sky that demanded nothing and offered salvation.

All I ever wanted was to be an artist's assistant until Lorenzo di Credi reminded me it was the most I could ever be. After that, I desired nothing less than incandescent fame. Regular fame was not enough.

I can confirm that the pollution of hubris is red as blood. The prospect of success contaminated me the way a spatter of wayward vermillion paint corrupts the sanctity of its neighbors. I think this is why I am here. Perhaps Sandro's God punishes women who refuse to kneel, or believe, or obey. And especially the women who dare to create in their own name.

My brother taught me everything he knew about painting. What he omitted to tell me was that a portrait can trap a soul like flypaper. Now I am mired up to my smile in paint and varnish, and ambition.

I want to go home – the home some consider to be heaven. Anger won't take me there, willpower won't take me there, humility alone won't take me there, and so, in death I have to be as wholly redeemable as Leonardo's masterpiece. My portrait may be priceless, but I must become a woman worth saving.

Galleries and museums are full of misidentified treasures, and dreamers trapped inside 'desiderata', once-desired things, but only a human dowsing rod can tap the energy that radiates from them... from us... from me. I'm more than a painting. I'm a woman inhabiting one.

Death is a pleasant surprise, not unlike love at first sight. Vibrations mingle. Signatures fire. The confusion is delightful. The rare collisions of mystical purpose and organic thrum are the surprises we live and die for.

When I was alive I felt overwhelmed by my insignificance and I fought like a tiger to be noticed, but I realize now my war wasn't with visibility – it was with being known. The truth is, the unseen energy of a repeated thought

*is the most creative power a person can possesses, but hungering for success
makes beggars of us all. Lorenzo had been right when he said art prostituted
its creators.*

*After Leonardo and I left Florence, I cultivated abrasiveness as a weapon. I
could no longer afford to be silent. I used everyone to gain a foothold on art
for Leonardo and recognition for myself. I didn't know how to serve us any
other way.*

*I lived beside a large life and negotiated Leonardo's reputation against
his best interests. I maneuvered him into the places I wanted to go, and the
worst of it, was that the guilt I felt during his rise to fame didn't stop me, and
the remorse I felt afterwards, was pushed into the dark hole where my life
could have been.*

*At first, in 1508, I had been entirely at home in my tranquil landscape,
and the thought of escape from solitary confinement never occurred to me.
But when Leonardo died, I looked back at my portrait as a refuge. It was
my first mistake. I had created a heaven worth dying for, but I turned from
it towards the painting. I was drawn back to its power. Inside it, I had the
attention I craved. I was immortalized. There was no letting go of that. I
think I was half-afraid to go with Leonardo and be diminished again by his
talent. I wanted to belong, and I wanted to remain visible. Fame is a seductive
promise, and so I let go of heaven and death let go of me.*

*Living inside a painting may be safer than the dangerous world in
which I once lived, but I discovered that safety over time kills passion, and
even a life blessed with serendipity is flawed. A half-truth is still a lie, and I'm
tired of being a lost woman from a century where I was considered worthless.*

*It only took a few years before my name evaporated and I became
Leonardo's little shadow more than ever – an everywoman/no-woman. For
a while I was celebrated as a Madonna, and I enjoyed the status of icon, and
then I became her – 'Princess Giocondo'. The truth is, I've been an anonymous
female since my birth, five-hundred-and-fifty-years ago, and the feeling I still
hate most, is being overlooked.*

*Ironically, by the year 2008, I had become Leonardo's equal in celeb-
rity, but I was a forgotten sister, not his collaborator, and with even greater
contradiction, I had been defined by my indefinable mood.*

I've learned that time beyond life is like a river with undercurrents and eddies that take one off course. The Greek stories of the River Styx are some-what accurate, but I was not ferried to my heaven, and I forgot nothing. A hundred fluid years on death's calendar is not protracted. There is no lateral flow from one event to another. Neither Julian nor Gregorian years are made from a succession of tedious minutes and hours.

One day, a teenage girl happened through my salon with her beau, a strapping red-head with heavy-lidded eyes of cornflower blue. She clung to his arm and looked up at him adoringly, and barely gave my portrait a glance. I could hear her mind intent on marriage, breathless with the expectation of owning his soul. But it was not her feelings which engaged me. It was the canvas shopping bag she was carrying, imprinted with the image of a painting I knew well. Sandro's 'Birth of Venus' drifted past me, and I followed it like an obedient puppy to the end of my power and watched the pair of lovers take the stairs past the winged goddess to the freedom of the Paris streets.

I was sucked back to 1476 and Verrocchio's studio, an eighteen-year-old girl, hanging on to Sandro Botticelli's voice and scent and touch.

I have been able to revisit every thought, conversation, and vision of my life with more clarity than is comfortable. I am transported within the lucid dreams of the spirit world – outside of solar time, but inside the limitations of my personal understanding. My kin called to me, beyond my reach. I missed my daughter and my brother and little Rinato. I missed Sandro. I missed my paints.

My craving for heaven finally grew stronger than my resentment of Lisa Giocondo and I thought there was a chance I could complete my tran-sition from life. I reasoned, that if I could erase her name and restore mine, I would be free, but it became obvious that human intervention was required, and I began to wish for true death as fervently as any devout believer ever prayed for forgiveness.

My chance came in April on the wings of a perfect human host. She would have to be. How apt that there were two of them. Veronica and I share a similarly constrained smile, five-hundred-years apart, not as bemused as some people imagine, and hardly vacant, but wistfully staring into a waste-land of broken promises. Life had taught us to suppress our expectations. She and I automatically sniff the air for predators, ever mindful of leg traps and verbal poison.

But a promised passport is only the hope of a journey, a ticket home is only the intention of a destination until redeemed, and liberation is only a concept until the day one is absolutely released. My rescuer had no appreciation of the invisible documents she carried, and I had no idea she would be so problematic. Success was a coin toss. Trapped for eternity or freedom.

I recognized my savior at once. A dim memory informed me we'd met before. But adulation had spoiled me. I assumed Veronica Lyons had grown into her power. That she'd overcome her fear of the truth between us. And so, I expected her to honor my request without hesitation – committed absolutely, out of her admiration for Leonardo.

I felt her awe when she walked into my salon but it wavered inside a mind choked with fears, and I momentarily second-guessed my instincts. I savored the forgotten challenge of being successfully checked by another's purpose. I knew she would be worthy of a struggle. I didn't know how much. I'd never before witnessed the damage of anger so intense as to eclipse loving a child.

I presumed Veronica was the bearer of a ticket to my promised land but she was more like an official who issued them, which was insensitive, since later, she was often casual, if not indifferent, to my situation. Time has its reasons and seasons. Veronica communed naturally with the spirit of her brother. I'd read this in her when we first met. It was this openness that enticed me to connect. But in my excitement, I reached out too soon and set our progress back.

I'd unwittingly caused irreparable damage to her relationship with hallucination, the paranormal in general, and me in particular. Although denial was her specialty, she was unable to entirely block my auditory presence. Our connection is too strong and her willpower matches my own. And by willpower, I mean our ability to lie in order to save face.

I have false confidence and a disregard for limitations whereas Veronica has resentment and a tendency to cower under pressure. We both confuse love and hate, power and control, and giving in with subservience.

We have one terrifying weakness in common: we'd let our brothers define us. Sibling rivalry, disguised as devotion, drives us still.

Veronica's son Jupiter was different from ordinary 'Mona Lisa' fans. His senses weren't jammed with sentimental hype and his distant expression showed me he listened to an inner world. He made me ache for my brother, in the days when we were peasant children who ran crazy into the hills of Campo Zeppi and soaked up our happiness under a sky no artist could paint.

I rarely indulge in such memories.

You may find it paradoxical that the apparent 'ghost of the gallery' can herself be haunted, but what trapped soul could be otherwise? Unfinished business? Well that's what is said, but I assure you, all business ceases with the last breath. What traps humans into pockets of afterlife, is the finished thought. We manifest our strongest dreams, and to prove it, I still smart from living a small life in the shadow of a master.

When I am calmest, I retreat into the land-escape behind me, where I walk contentedly with a generous death. A death that allowed my dream of fame to come true. Well, half-true. That's the problem with desires – we write them in passionate ink, and they're translated into literal requests.

Yearning makes humans careless, and at the moment the pair of 'Lyons' entered my world, I had been far from calm. I was ecstatic. So pixilated, I danced around the salon arms outstretched not bothering to circumvent the patrons. Some women fainted and several children were so over-stimulated that parents had to lead them into the hallway.

That day my rescue team energized me. The salon was like a beehive on fire. It pulsed with emotion. The air changed colors, from pink to orange-red and back to yellow.

Paranormal? Occult? What do they mean? They denote above and behind the norm, and what lies beyond the ordinary but the extraordinary: the unexpected hiccups of genius, the greater than, the hidden from, the infinite, the elegant, and the divinity of mathematics – nothing less than the absolute essence of creative expression. The great god, Hydrogen, was the first artist.

Leonardo's hills and streams stand in beautifully for my patient afterlife that no doubt holds its breath for me with timeless grace. I sense its sanctuary, balanced high, inside a dimension that I can taste. It pulses and beats, looping like a mantra – the comforting humdrum of a past-perfect universe sleeping under the accumulated chaos of evolution.

I catch a faint whiff of heaven's atmosphere when the gallery clears and the cleaners have gone, and the small red dots of the security system patrol the hushed spaces where art lives on. It smells like violets.

Jupiter was worried about his mother. And he was in danger. I sensed that much. His eyes told me he was eager to help me, but engaging a child wasn't enough. Neither was throwing words at the shade of his mother – a woman teetering at the abyss of defeat, although, the empathy of a kindred sister would be a welcome change.

Clearly, for me to move forward, I would have to pull her back… pull both of them back. Jupiter's eyes met mine when he heard my thought. He didn't smile. He studied my face without blinking. I was being measured. "Well," his eyes said, "do we have a deal?"

We did.

Anniversaries carry more potent memories. The year 2008 is the fifth-centennial of my ongoing dance with a half-life. I crave recognition as much as ever, but to achieve it, I will have to win Veronica's trust gradually through the careful friendship I must forge with her son, and even then I fear she may betray herself and me. Now I smile two different smiles: bemused and expectant.

How the universe loves to spin its ironies. The renaissance era in which I was born is known as a time of cultural rebirth, but the troubled woman that synchronicity sends to rescue me, can't release me until she fully lives, and I can't be reborn if I don't fully die.

— *Lisabetta*

   LISABETTA – A STOLEN GLANCE

chapter sixteen

Le Chat Noir

THE STREETS OF PARIS
APRIL 1 – 2008

Lisabetta follows like a dog on a leash when Veronica and Jupiter burst from the museum into a 4 P.M. drizzle. Hand in hand, they dash across the sweeping skirts of the Louvre, and into the swarm of human traffic. They flow like salmon towards the famous café, 'Le Chat Noir'.

Veronica veers to circumvent an actual black cat. It's an automatic reaction. She searches for a hint of white fur. A pure-black feline may be an omen, not to be entirely trusted.

Jupiter calls out "Mom, can we stop. There's a French cat over there that needs me. Mom! It's a special-needs cat," and the dampness of honking cars and body hunger refocuses. The cat has slipped into an alley.

The green lady is still following. Jupiter waves to her and taps one of the buttons on his beret. He stifles his giggles with his hands clamped over his mouth, and finally sputters "Don't mess with me."

"I never do," Veronica replies, tapping the badge causing all the merriment. "Race you to the hamburgers."

Lisabetta's skirts skim over the spotless pavement in a swash of green silk. The traffic is chaos. Angry drivers shout at each other and any pedestrian who dares to halt their progress. Lisabetta, fresh to the streets of Paris, is distracted. She swerves too late to entirely sidestep a pair of skittish Afghan hounds attached to a chic woman. They whine and cower, trying to avoid the green hem that brushes their fur.

A delicate floral whiff assails the expert nostrils of the corner flower-seller offering old-fashioned nosegays of spring violets. She pauses her regular chant, raises her head, and sniffs the air, puzzled. She samples her own posy. Nothing. Her blooms are sold for their color. The faint lingering scent that now accompanies the latest varieties of violets pales next to the perfume which has passed by. Encouraged, she waves a bunch after Veronica and calls out *"Avril violettes... tant qu'elles durent."* Fragrant April violets ... while they last.

The sun worms its way out of a black cloud and miraculously the street tables fill. Mother and son fly on hunger pangs and descend like the children of Nike to the only available table in sight. A waiter materializes and dries the puddles on its four chairs. Jupiter lands his backpack on the empty chair. Leo One looks hungry. Jupiter opens his pack and stirs the other Leos, art supplies, and his *'Aslan book'*, searching for his Louvre brochure and a red marker. Lisabetta looks on overwhelmed, heady with too much freedom.

My decision stunned me. I sat in shock, at a table in Paris at the invitation of a child.

Death changed at the end of a long corridor, the moment I passed 'Victory' on the stairs. Jupiter's smile pulled me down the stairs. But it was the squealing of a pig laughing that pushed me out the museum doors. I will no longer go back to the black fog of imprisonment without a fight, yet, going forward is a white fog of unknown fears. The air smells of spent rain and pungent chemicals. Puddles steam on a pavement of smooth grey stone.

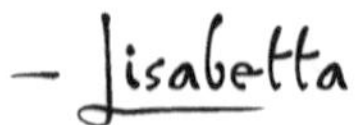

Veronica's purse opens fast and releases a red steno-pad with its companion pen jammed into the coil binding. She scribbles like an executive secretary while a ballet of loaded plates swings by at eye level. Waiters glide here. Each plate is a perfect still-life painting. Water is poured with attitude. Menus are stylishly dropped. Veronica's nose stays glued to her page. She wants the immediacy of the moment on solid paper. Writing stops her hands from shaking.

Dreams of bacon and black cats are forgotten. Veronica shoos the first waiter away like a fly while Jupiter reads the photos on the menu. He flips the pages, looking lost. The waft of passing espresso reaches for Veronica like smelling salts and pulls her into the present. Responsibility scores a hit. The immediate necessity is the refueling of two bodies who regularly require more than jam and rolls at 7 A.M.

Jupiter looks up, confused. "Why aren't there French fries in France?" he asks.

"By Jove, that's a good question," Veronica says smiling, using one of her son's nicknames. Trust Jupe to ground her. His honest takes on the world refresh her. "They do have them, but they're called *pommes des frites*," she says over the top of her reading glasses. "And dishes called *'Veronique'*, after me, mean they're full of grapes. Can you smell violets?"

Jupiter looks horrified at the prospect of grapes in a hamburger. He notices his mother's cup has automatically been filled with thick black coffee, and worries she may even drink it. Doesn't she know it's nearly four in the afternoon – the zenith of teatime? Coffee upsets her nerves.

Jupiter doodles red hearts around the photo of the glass pyramid in front of the Louvre. He rotates it to show Lisabetta. He has underlined the letters L-O-V-E in the word <u>LOUVRE</u>.

Lisabetta smiles.

Veronica remarks his souvenir is already *'Juped'*. It's a running gag. He *'Jupes'* a lot of things, but never library books or anything belonging to others. A *'Jupe'* mark is like planting a flag on new land. It's his stamp of approval. Unimportant items aren't worth claiming. Sometimes he makes a circle with a large dot inside for Jupiter, instead of printing his name.

Veronica craves tea, but she doesn't want the hassle of crossing the server who has anticipated that everyone in Paris drinks coffee strong enough to melt a spoon. "It's four o-clock," Jupiter reminds her, after he's measured the angles of the big and little hands on her watch, and recalibrated them right-side-up. Knowing the time reassures him. Four o-clock at home is high-tea, Jupiter's favorite meal – a smorgasbord of desserts before a savory dinner, later in the dark. He draws a tree with a cup balancing on the top, and an angel without a head wearing running shoes. Lisabetta recognizes her Louvre neighbor, Nike.

Jupiter reflects for the space of a heartbeat, and announces loudly that he'll pass on the *'freets'* and grapes. Veronica is not surprised. But there are no hamburgers. She helps Jupiter order a grilled-cheese sandwich, and has the presence of mind to tell the young waiter: "please *not* to cut it in half... *um*...demi," she adds proudly. Her inadequate French is accompanied by hand gestures. Veronica mimes the shape of a square in the air, a sawing motion, and finally two triangles. "Voila" she says, hopefully. "*Doo tree-ongla ey fromage grille sil voo play,*" she says, then wipes her order from the air like a blackboard, and makes another square with her chalk finger. She crosses it with a bold X movement. "*Non,*" she says, waving away the second air-knife. "*Oui?*"

"You are *Canadienne?*" the waiter asks, pointing to the red maple-leaf luggage tag attached to Veronica's handbag. "You are not... eh... by... bi...ling...?"

"Bilingual? No, as you see... I'm not."

More mad gesturing.

"*Oui, Madame,*" he says, and waits for different instructions that arrive in the same airy offhand hieroglyphics.

Veronica decides it's best to ask for the sandwich whole. If it comes sliced into rectangles or squares there can be an awkward silence. Lately Jupiter likes his sandwiches cut on the diagonal, preferably into four with one triangle removed for poetic balance. He is in his triangle phase. Veronica is used to consuming fourth triangles. She prays the sandwich doesn't arrive on a croissant.

She draws a new square, encircles it with her hands, and says, "Like so."

"Madame wishes the sandwich whole?" the waiter says in perfect English.

"*Mama*", Jupiter says. "The violets belong to my friend, Lisabetta. She says *bongiorno*."

"*Tres bon*," Veronica says, smiling radiantly into the waiter's stern face. He nods and escapes to the kitchen, convinced he hates his job... and now Canadians.

"Mom," Jupiter announces offhandedly. "The violets you smell belong to my friend. She says hello."

A pot-bellied Dachshund waddles by during the food-waiting game. Veronica raises her eyebrows and inclines her head. "That dog reminds me of a pig."

Lisabetta looks behind her. "*Porcellina!* Where?"

"Not a *real* pig," Jupiter says in a loud voice.

"No of course not, Veronica says. "It's an expression."

"Like the times you stop me from eating like a piggywig."

Veronica opens her notebook, adds the words 'stronger meds' to her list, and underlines it four times. "Nonsense, you have lovely table manners, Kiddo."

Lisabetta's panic is palpable. Jupiter takes the wedge of lemon from the lip of his water glass and holds it towards her. "Would you like the lemon from my water?"

"No, but thanks for asking," Veronica says.

"*Si. Grazzi,*" Lisabetta says.

Jupiter scratches the lemon peel and inhales the zest. "Lisabetta says lemons calm people down," he says.

Veronica concentrates on the scribbles in her notepad. "I didn't know that."

"We can try it sometime," Jupiter says. "When you're, you know... quaking."

Jupiter and his mother glide on sensual time, exploring like a couple of extra-terrestrial innocents riding camels across a desert. Movies take them most places, and daily excursions are spent in a caravan of two, on buses that stop at every oasis. Restaurant menus, art galleries, museums, and stores are considered historic sites.

On rare, healthy days, life is a private fun-park. On earthquake days it seems they're stuck at the top of a Ferris wheel with thunder approaching, but at least they're together. Sometimes a rusty chair swinging above the bumper-car collisions of society is the safest place to be with one's best friend.

Jupiter once overheard his mother explaining *artism* to a stranger. She had called it an umbrella. His mother has a lot of them in a box by their front door. He likes the one with the surfer lady on a shell, the best. Veronica pretends the Lyons family's challenges are eccentricities. The rest of the world calls it the autism spectrum. Uncle Oz calls it creative-friction to make his niece smile. Jupiter calls it seeing in pictures.

Paris shrinks dogs. A miniature collie walks past their table with its head tilted high – a movie-star dog on a fashion runway. Lap dogs mingle with fur coats and pearls. Rhinestone collars glitter on pedigree necks. A few spoiled noses protrude from designer bags like Leo One in Jupiter's pack.

Jupiter stares after the collie with dreamy eyes.

"You'll see Peyton soon," Veronica says, patting his arm. "I miss her too."

Lisabetta raises her eyebrows. *"Who is Peyton?"*

"Peyton is my dog," Jupiter says, pointing to the retreating collie. "Like that ginger one… only much bigger." He holds out his hand at tabletop level. "She's this tall."

Veronica checks over her shoulder. "Who are you talking to?"

"Me," the voice says.

"The food tastes better here. It's alive," Jupiter says. "But the ketchup is wrong."

Louvre fever lingers. Mother and son share the same elevated mood: a world sieved through carefully trained senses, anchored to the general hubbub of foreign diners in conflict over prices. Their collective bickering builds into a crescendo that drowns out the classic concertina soundtrack of Paris.

Veronica smells violets again and looks up. She slams down her pen – releases it as if it's red hot. It rolls until the clasp halts its progress, and Jupiter aligns it parallel to the longest edge of an Isosceles triangle napkin. "No," she announces flatly, "I'm very sorry Sweetpea, but we won't be going to the Eiffel tower, after all. I have a better idea."

Jupiter sees the monument in his mind's eye – a wonderful triangle made up of steel grids, like the cross-hatching of a drawing. This time the word 'after' means no.

"I don't like heights. They unnerve me. We're visiting Leonardo."

"Were you afraid in the plane?"

"We're going to rent a car." Veronica gazes into space, picturing the color of the car, and closes her fist around the weight of the phantom car keys in her hand.

"Mom, how can you fly if you're afraid of heights?"

"When you're headed for the 'Mona Lisa' and 'Nike' you can do lots of scary things. Treats that make us feel better."

"What about flying home?" He taps the letters l – o – v – e with his finger and traces a square around them with Leo One's tail to keep them safe. "Is that why you took extra pills on the plane?"

"I have you and Pico and Nattie and Peyton, and our new place in Victoria, and Aunt Bea, and Uncle Oz," she says.

Uneven numbers are wonky. "That's seven. You need one more. I have a new friend named Lizzie." He bends his thumbs and holds up eight fingers.

"Thanks. I look forward to meeting her."

Jupiter grins at Lisabetta. "You can't see her. She's invisible."

"I see."

"Mom… you can't see invisible people."

"Well, tell her hello from me."

Jupiter waves across the table. "My Mom says hello."

For a heartbeat Veronica is aware of a palpable presence. "Oh, she's here, is she?"

"I will lend you my 'Aslan book' on the plane," Jupiter says. "He's a lion too. He flies all the time."

"Thanks Jupe. That will help."

"Helping is my job," he whispers to Lisabetta.

Lisabetta reaches to ruffle his hair. "I hope so."

Jupiter avoids her touch and doodles a bee and an ant on his brochure. He looks up from his drawing. "French fries," he announces. "And real ketchup." It's been five minutes since Veronica asked him the question.

Veronica closes her eyes and smiles. "Aunt Bee always wears 'April in Paris' perfume. I wonder what made me think of that?"

Part Two
Incubation

"The man who has intercourse
aggressively and uneasily
will produce children
who are irritable and untrustworthy;
but if the intercourse is done with great love
and desire on both sides,
then the child will be of great intellect,
and witty, lively and loveable."
~ Leonardo da Vinci – 1507

chapter seventeen

*"I would sooner fail
than not be among the greatest."*
~ John Keats

The Voice of Rebirth

I cannot repeat it enough. I was born Lisabetta di Antonio Buti del Vacca, half-sister (I had thought) to my mother's son, Leonardo. I remained invisible even after my brother taught me his trade. He was the sun and I was always hard to see, but if you squint past the brightness of Leonardo da Vinci, you would find that I was always there – real or painted.

I almost don't mind that my work goes unrecognized. Half of my brother's contributions have drifted into the murkiness of time, along with the works of his students and mentors and fellow apprentices. It only takes a generation to lose the in-house tributes, the popular acknowledgments, and the authorships of works critiqued as dazzles of breakthrough.

But I earned my true name.

Miracles come wrapped in sacrifice, and to accept the grace of a miracle one must forfeit a gift of equal value. People love to call me a mystery but I prefer to be known as a person.

— Lisabetta

chapter eighteen

*"I can't go back to yesterday -
because I was a different person then."*
~ Lewis Carroll

Bed & Breakthrough

THE HOTEL DE VINCENT –
MONTMARTRE, PARIS
APRIL 2 – 2008

Jupiter invites Lisabetta to play finger shadows over the wallpaper roses until bedtime. He waves to her as Veronica tucks him in, his eyes too bright for sleep. Lisabetta sees them peeking over the heads of his four 'Leos', lion dolls bunched together in a bouquet. Lisabetta blows him a kiss goodnight, and examines the exhausted mother.

Veronica soaks one foot at a time in the pedestal sink, balancing precariously on a slippery mat. The water is barely hot, but it helps quieten her blisters. She sprinkles Yardley's April Violet talcum powder between her toes and muffles them into plush lime-green bed-socks.

The bed and breakfasts of Montmartre are Spartan, but the decor adds to the 'Hotel de Vincent's charm, and the mattresses are plump clouds which promise falling into tunnel sleep, deep as a cashmere well.

Veronica fancies the wall across from her flickers with the shape of a woman, but she is too tired to care. She cozies into the nest of feathers and holds her new paperback on the history of the Louvre under the gooseneck lamp to read. Its dim light requires the page to be lifted high into the domed shade. Veronica reads that the Nike of Samothrace is discovered in 1873, with only one wing. Her right wing is a reconstruction, cast in plaster from its mate. Jupiter had noticed.

Sleep takes over the paragraph. Nike, small as a barn owl, alights on the end of Veronica's bed and scoops her up. They flutter out the window – Veronica-Athena, this time carried by the goddess's bird-of-wisdom.

Once outside, Nike resumes her full size, and together they soar high above Paris. The glass pyramid of the Louvre glows below them infused with sunset fire. They fly southeast to Amboise, and Veronica is deposited gently at the door of Leonardo's last home, *Clos Luce*. When she looks up to thank Nike, she gazes upon a fine sculptured head with flowing hair like Botticelli's Venus with the face of the 'Mona Lisa'.

"They're *très approprié*" Veronica had said to Jupiter, back in March, in the Halifax airport shop. She refers to their purchase of two French berets. "We've got an hour to kill before the flight." Jupiter ponders how time can die. Perhaps a wristwatch smashed with a hammer? The international departure lounge is a wasteland, and shopping for peppermints and a travel pillow only uses up a few minutes. Time still lives. Time can fly. His friend, Aslan the lion, can fly.

Veronica sees the felt hats first, and Jupiter takes to their soft fabric and the nubs of yarn on the top. He models his straight, but Veronica twists it in one rakish move and lifts it by its *tail* to puff it into shape. "There" she says. "Check it out."

Jupiter admires his reflection in the square mirror with its gold baroque frame. It makes him look like a painting. He selects a pair of sunglasses with violet lenses from a revolving display. "*Très chic...* *très* cool*" Veronica says, and Jupiter envisages a tray of iced tea the color of amber, served in tall straight tumblers, with moisture beads sliding down the frosted glass like pearls.

He studies his reflection from different angles and approves the purchases but he crams his crushed maple-leaf cap back over his sheepdog hair for the plane. "Berets are too cool for Nova Scotia," he says, saving his tam for Europeans, who have what his mother calls, continental tastes.

Jupiter visualizes a map of the world, where the shapes of continents look like pancakes nibbled by mice. "Can we get some iced tea?" he asks. "Shopping makes me thirsty."

He pesters for it until they find a vending machine that dispenses it in chilled cans. The juice kiosk next door can only offer offensive neon-pink straws, so they slide into Tim Hortons and nab a couple of free white ones. Iced tea tastes better through plundered straws, and Jupiter loves the dispenser that releases them with a spring. He slides off the white paper sleeve and wraps it around his finger like a ring. "Tray cool," he says.

"It's the Egyptian mummies or the Père Lachaise Cemetery cats," Veronica says. "You pick."

"Chat *Nwar*," Jupiter says. "Cats, cats, cats."

Either way it's visiting the dead.

It takes half the morning to locate a grocery store that sells cat treats.

Veronica and Jupiter drag a reluctant Lisabetta through a maze of tombstones and meandering lanes crowded with memorial chapels and statues. Veronica places a yellow rose on Jim Morrison's grave, and Jupiter is up to his eyes in French cats *who* appreciate the treats. Mother and son eat their grapes and sandwiches as if the cemetery is a park while Lisabetta perches on a flat headstone and wonders how many of the artists buried here are safe in their heavens.

Jupiter is on board with leaving Paris, but the term 'next week' has no place to land. The Louvre's pyramid was the highlight of his visit. But Paris is a done deal. The Eiffel tower is off-limits if it scares his mom.

Jupiter forms a triangle with his fingers and peers through them at Veronica. "Paris is full of the best triangles," he says. He envisions the painting of a black cat. "Nwar, nwar, nwar," he says.

"We're renting a car tomorrow," Veronica says. "I want to explore a bit on our last free day. Our flight doesn't leave till the next morning. There will be lots of triangles in the countryside. We can look together."

Jupiter is happy. He sips camouflaged orange juice from the spout of a baby's mug to mask its color. Happily, his incognito beverage tastes sweet and green.

The promise of a trip levitates Leos One to Four, sleeping in Jupiter's backpack, curled inside his old baseball cap. Today, Jupiter wears his new beret, and a red T-shirt emblazoned with The 'Le Chat Noir' poster. "The cat *and* the hat," he says, posing for the camera.

Click. Veronica captures a beaming child on forever film. "That black cat kind of reminds me of Halloween," she says. "But you don't like Halloween, do you. Why *is* that do you suppose?"

"Trick or treat is very… orange," Jupiter says scrunching up his nose. He lays cat treats in four careful rows of four on a marble tombstone while a cat watches from a safe distance. "Cats are too smart to fall for tricks. But they love treats." He stands back from his work with his hands behind his back. The cat approaches. "Hello special cat," Jupiter whispers.

Any reference to Halloween is received with disdain. Veronica had assumed it was because of the masks, but it's the orange color of the pumpkins that invade Jupiter's eyes as garish cupcake frosting and wobbly sunlit Jell-O, and the overall offensive decor enforced by tradition. Festive foods are always questionable.

One year, it takes Jupiter an age to pick every shred of desiccated coconut from a bakery *snowball*. After that he was disinterested in the center, and rolled it to Pico. Veronica found a saucer of chewy *snow* under the sofa after following an icing sugar trail.

Jupiter is keen for the road trip. He loves driving past countryside that blurs like wet paint. Fantastic swirls of colors and shapes are better than TV.

"I spy a Monet," he says. "Hey Mom, we're flying inside a painting."

"We are… what sort of painting? We studied Monet."

"Imp, imp, imp, impressions."

The classic unfocused images of wheat fields and poppies, and blue skies and water lilies that Veronica's shown Jupiter countless times, fly past the car windows.

Jupiter is over the moon. He can snack on salty chips, close his eyes when he gets tired, and listen to the hum of the tires. All the while, he can sip apple juice from a paper cup with a lid. Lots of treats are available in France, Veronica assures him. You love treats as much as a cat."

"I spy with my little eye... something beginning with red," he says.

"Poppies?" she guesses.

"Nope... my Aslan book." He giggles. "I'm being *jovial*," he says.

The homage to the mummies will wait. The Egyptian antiquities will gather more dust, and yes, they will purchase the poster of the black cat he likes on his shirt. Jupiter repeats the name of it to hear the sound it makes. "Chat Nwar -- Chat Nwar -- Chat Nwar -- Chat Nwar," he says.

"Yes, and who is the artist?"

"Tayofeelstinelen," he answers phonetically, and gets a gold star from his mother's eyes.

"*Très Bon, très bon, très bon, très bon,*" she says, and taps her finger, four times on his nose.

Lisabetta's butterfly energy flits around the car. Jupiter finds it restful, and is thrilled to have potato chips for breakfast instead of jam and bread.

Today is going to be a fun trip. Jove is one of his happy names.

chapter nineteen

*"Here lies one
whose name
was writ on water."*
~ John Keats

Earth & Water

AMBOISE, FRANCE
THE PRESENT MANOR HOUSE OF CLOS LUCÉ
APRIL 3 – 2008

The last time I saw the Château de Cloux, as it was called in Leonardo's time, was four-hundred-and-eighty-nine-years-ago, and even then, unless invited otherwise, I had to keep to the grand bedroom, where Leonardo housed my portrait.

My consciousness always drifted until Leonardo spoke to me, and in those years, he believed I was still his living sister. He blocked all recall of my death, nor did he differentiate a three-dimensional woman from his painting. I was the ever-present Lisabetta at his side – his companion and advisor. He looked to my painted face for encouragement, and his voice drew me back whenever I tried to visit my heaven.

I sensed my daughter was happy but that Leonardo needed me more, so I lingered patiently, anticipating his time of death. The eleven years did not seem overly long.

Cloux was the place of my brother's sacred transition, and when it was time, I stood with Leonardo in the window and watched him fly at last. I called out that I would catch him up. He had no reason to disbelieve me and I had no reason to disbelieve myself.

I was curious to know if my portrait's fate lay with selfish Salai or with Cecco, in accordance with Leonardo's instructions, and hoped perhaps Cecco would ignore my brother's insistence on erasing my name from his memoirs. He did not. And so, in a dreamlike state, I watched Cecco mole through a mountain of paper and burn my brother's references to me. All but one is now lost.

I witnessed Leonardo's special tree tumble, uprooted during the storm that heralded his death. I saw my abductors in the candlelight. And so I stayed too long, and accompanied the panel to the nearby chateau, where I let the king fuss over me. By then it was too late. I fell from the time track as royal tastes sent me into hiding, or paraded me in style. I moved from Amboise to Fontainebleau, and Versailles, and then Paris. But I could always see Leonardo as a distant light across an abyss of sparks.

By 2008 I had become adept at short-term possession, wandering on visitors' coattails as far as the 'Victory', but no host could take me down the staircase or into the streets of Paris.

My portrait and I could never be separated for more than a few cautious expeditions down the hall. Veronica was different, to be sure, but it had been her son who showed me how to leave. And later, I followed them to a vast marketplace in the museum, where I saw hundreds of images of the 'Mona Lisa', which made me more determined to fight. I had never made it past the headless Nike on the stairs before.

Jupiter seemed fidgety with me inside his shirt, and I was able to restore him to comfort when he waved another portrait shirt like a flag, for Veronica to buy. It was a gift for his Great Aunt 'Bee', he said, and I was able to swoon inside it so Jupiter could feel more comfortable. Veronica selected a design with Leonardo spread-eagled in a circle/square for her Uncle Oz, that matched Jupiter's back pack. She chose two others: one of me and another of Nike, in XXL sizes. Apparently Jupiter loves wearing baggy T-shirts that fall well below his knees, to bed.

So, I left the Louvre inside a shopping bag, not unlike the time I had been smuggled out under a man's coat. The imprint of 'Mona Lisa' acted as a bridge, after all, if the eyes are said to be the windows of the soul, surely an entire face would be a door, and once outside the precincts of the museum, I could move freely by keeping close to Veronica.

I discovered why later. I tested our connection. The further apart we were, I felt myself thinning... too light to skim the earth. It wasn't unpleasant, but I didn't have the confidence to challenge the elasticity of freedom very far.

After Jupiter showed me his drawing in the street café, I blinked out when a tray of glassware crashed to the pavement. I resurfaced inside their hotel room, and watched my new family sleep. The dark skyline of Paris filled the open window, painted in blues surrounded by a halo of gold stars. I always notice skies.

The next day, after Père Lachaise, we reached the Château de Cloux. Sadly, the place was still closed to the public, with tourist season a heartbeat away.

My independence was stronger and I ran on ahead to Leonardo's second-floor bedroom. Clos Lucé (its new name) had been refurbished, and looked unlike any home I once knew, but I recognized the open window and remembered the last time I had seen it. Leonardo and Rinato had been standing in front of it, and I was drawn towards the same view of the Loire Valley they would have seen.

The Leonardo Tree was gone, and in its place was a large disk of wood. Then I remembered. It had fallen the night of the storm, the night of Leonardo's death. As I stared at the disk I became aware of the old oak's shape that materialized transparent as glass above its stump. Leonardo had been right. The oak contained a spirit.

The sound of Jupiter's laughter drifted up to the open window, and I looked down on Veronica with her 'spy-box' and Jupiter running in circles below. She looked up at Leonardo's bedroom window and her inherent melancholy hit me full force.

From Jupiter's shrieks of delight, I thought he was being tickled – but he was chasing his beret that had spun off in a pinwheel, bouncing over the grass. He caught up to it when it blew into the large tree stump that looked like a low round table left on the lawn.

All three of us heard a loud buzzing. Veronica thought Jupiter was brushing away a bee, but it was the energy collecting in a cloud hovering above the oak stump that formed its missing crown, as Leonardo and I knew it in 1516. It's leaves were a swarm of bees that changed shape the same way that wind moves the treetops of living trees.

Jupiter flopped down, clamped the beret back on his curls, and turned his face up to the house. I waved at both of them, but Veronica's gaze scanned past me to take a picture of a pigeon cooing behind one of the roof gargoyles.

　　　　　　　　　　LISABETTA – A STOLEN GLANCE

Jupiter waved back. He told Veronica someone was inside, and they disappeared from view as they retraced their steps to the entrance to check for side doors. Their berets looked like two black buttons gliding out of sight.

I was about to join them when I experienced the joy of seeing Leonardo and Cecco walking towards the house. Leonardo was old and leaned heavily on his lion-head cane, and Cecco ran ahead to dust a basket chair under the phantom tree. It was Leonardo's elaborate wicker chair brought with him from Italy, placed in his favorite spot.

The wind lifted Leonardo's velvet cap from his head in a flash of purple, and his silver hair flew in a halo backlit by the sun. He laughed as he encouraged Cecco's chase. "That's my favorite cap," he called out, and when it was returned, Cecco remarked his master's hair now resembled the bird's nest they had expressly come to visit.

Veronica and Jupiter emerged from the shadows, back from their search and for a while there were four people on the lawn like actors on a stage performing simultaneous scenes, separated by a five-hundred-year-old curtain.

I believe Veronica heard me call out because she tilted her head in my direction, but Leonardo and Cecco glanced up to where I waved, grinning like a mad woman, and waved back.

The next moment I floated high in a dazzling sky as the sun burnt through me. I turned lazily in the air and floated like a bird held aloft by updrafts, wishing Leonardo could know the same thrill. Flying is what he lived for and was denied. But then I realized that in death, he too could experience the joy of it and I looked for him in the clouds.

I was high enough to see the iridescent snake of the underground tunnel that meandered from the house towards the king's residence, the Château de Amboise, half-a-mile away. I could smell the history of it under the earth before the scene darkened. Veronica and Jupiter disappeared and the Leonardo Tree swayed drunk against the moon. Angry rain pummeled the valley and my tranquil sky became a vortex of twisting wind.

Leonardo was not in the sky. I saw him below, this time an ant-sized teenager, tramping into the tree-line, taking cover from the rain. Rinato ran beside him, tripping him up with excitement, glowing white like a paper lantern. Then they disappeared into the green mass of leaves and all I could hear was Rinato barking. I tried to follow them, but I was towed in the other direction, joined to Veronica as sure as a puppeteer and marionette. I was Veronica's helium muse on a string, but gaining the confidence to explore.

Veronica and Jupiter were unaffected by the maelstrom that punished the miniature castle, and I heard her tell Jupiter his hair looked like a bird's nest. I hoped to meet up with Leonardo as she circled the manor house anti-clockwise, but after we turned a corner and faced west, I stood inside the surprise of a grey waterfall, momentarily disoriented.

A shower of water dripped around me and I made out the image of Sandro Botticelli distorted through the droplets, naked and beautiful, sleeping while four fauns danced around him. I saw Veronica lounging near him, staring through me, but I was used to being invisible.

She wore a long dress covered in tiny flowers, and I recognized she was not Veronica after all, but Simonetta Vespucci, Sandro's first serious muse. The resemblance was disturbing.

And it wasn't a waterfall. I was outside, deluged by rain, pressed against an unfamiliar window, peering into an unknown bedroom. I had recognized the painting 'Venus and Mars' over the fireplace: Sandro's self-portrait with Simonetta, his politically ambitious 'chosen-one', together as the lovers they never were in life. Sandro slept as if dead, and Simonetta stared with unfocused eyes into her future. Perhaps Sandro was dreaming her awake. She had been dead four years when he painted her.

The water was strong midnight rain which pulled me into sensual memories. It pelted the windows and the roof, and I squinted through it as it cried down the glass. Beneath the painted figures of Venus and Mars, glowed a log fire that drew me inside, but I never took my attention off Sandro's dreaming face. Someone slept in a bed across the room, and I realized I had reached Veronica's homeland without trying.

Ironically, I am Veronica's muse, as Simonetta had been Sandro's, and my curiosity vanquished old jealousies. He had been mine in the end... although the end-of-the-end is still waiting. Simonetta died the year Leonardo and I left Florence, only days after I said a forever goodbye to Sandro, so I don't begrudge either of them some companionship inside a work of art. I know Sandro is in my heaven, waiting for me.

     LISABETTA – A STOLEN GLANCE

A black and white cat raised its head from the blanket, hissed, and immediately curled back into its dream. Veronica slept surrounded by books. One of them lay open and shimmered in a blue square of moving images. The dark shapes in her room blurred like wet paint as the storm washed the house on Bear Mountain, and cascaded into a silver thread that trickled into the valley of Victoria.

The rain sounded like the rustle of silk, and I saw that the firelight had turned the white bedclothes to violet in the moonlight. Veronica's hand reached out past a statuette of Nike and tapped the bedside table, lightly as a raindrop. One tap, and a faint glow blossomed inside a white cone. A second tap brightened the room enough to see her groping for pen and paper. She tapped twice more and it grew dark. Magic. I was left in the quiet drench of a spring downpour, wishing I could feel the rain on my face or cozy up to a warm fireside.

A large tan and white collie lay stretched out on the hearth and I watched it turn into my little terrier, Rinato, snoring on his side in the old cottage at Campo Zeppi. I saw my mother weaving a basket and a starry-eyed girl who stared up and through me. Her expression made me shiver… and then it was daylight, and the girl was younger, and Rinato was barely a week old pup, and I knew that girl had been me.

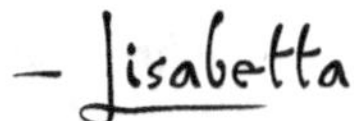

chapter twenty

New Beginnings

AMBOISE, FRANCE
1519

Leonardo shared his lifeforce with me the day I was born, refusing to let me die, and later, during his last days, when he lay close to death, I held his hand so he could feel the weight of my bones. Such was our close connection, that even as an apparition, I had density. I closed my fingers tightly over his, so that Leonardo knew beyond his failing senses, that he was not alone.

My brother's perceptions were like crystal. He always spoke as inspiration came – often too clear for others to hear. Leonardo taught me where illusion began and in 1519 it was my duty to show him where it ended.

In Leonardo's presence, I was more than a seventeen-year-old poplar-wood panel. I was greater than an animated thirty-by-twenty-one inch portrait coated with new varnish. I emerged from the flat window Leonardo created of me and left his masterpiece where my young colors glowed under a glaze of light. I no longer cast a brittle sheen in the moonlight, but to Leonardo, I remained, the fleshed-out Lisabetta of his middle-years. I had taken form to ease his grief, and now, to comfort his final moments. I would have done anything to make him feel safe.

A portrait's voice is captured in the eyes. Only eyes may speak silently, most elegantly, in magnetic communion. My brother and I conversed this way for eleven years. After 'the fire', he called me through the art that was the best of us. Leonardo heard my thoughts as a voice inside his head, inside a waking dream, inside a memory. I listened back in the ways open to me.

He always knew I would tell him the truth.

— Lisabetta

Lisabetta's earliest memory of Leonardo is not visual. It's a voice surrounded by stars. His beauty materializes later and dazzles. He keeps his bouts of hopelessness preserved, away from public nosiness. After Grandmother Lucia's brief reign, Lisabetta is the only one close enough to help Leonardo through the debilitating episodes that dull his brightness. But without Leonardo's remarkable capacity to recover, Lisabetta's career under the formal auspices of the painter's guild, would have decided her creative stillbirth.

Leonardo and Lisabetta share more than a country upbringing under a tyrannical father. Lisabetta first believes that Leonardo's skill as a teacher engages her own artistic capabilities, but it's not entirely so. There is a natural talent within both of them, separate yet the same, to observe and translate the treasures of the visible world into flat windows of illusion. Their minds are connected to each other as much as their hand-to-eye coordination. What they observe flows into the art they make. They isolate different aspects of design, but the procedure is identical, and it's because of this, Leonardo remains convinced only artists may truly understand each other.

That Leonardo and Lisabetta are kindred is documented. Caterina expels them from her womb and into the world six-years-apart. It's the weightier bond of paternity that separates them, but empathy and a strong priority for each other's survival guarantees them mutual protection and promises doubly-victorious fame.

Leonardo daydreams in loops of relentless pictures, endowed with the ability to realize them later and study them under better light. Events so-crystallized, wait for the right time to emerge fully-formed. Regardless of encapsulating joy or pain, Leonardo's thoughts remain alive to be recalled with startling lucidity. Images imbedded with sounds and textures and the accompanying scents of life take root in his memory. It takes only a small trigger to release them unbidden into the present.

Lisabetta's formative years condition her to the hard labor of a subsistence farm. Living in Campo Zeppi comes with the certainty of hardship, but it bequeaths her the edge she needs later to fend for herself and Leonardo in a world that has no time for women or those afflicted with eccentricities not easily bent to conformity.

Between them, Leonardo and Lisabetta have enough skills to meet the harshness of the world without crumbling. Without each other, creative survival is impossible. Leonardo never truly sees a thing completely until he has drawn it from several angles, written down its messages and questions, and shown her. Lisabetta is the complementary yin of Leonardo's experience.

Run-ins with Antonio's bad humor prompt Lisabetta to keep her head during the heat of confrontation. She becomes a proficient formulator of strategies: how best to process defeat into a victory, how to feign compliance, how to use humiliation to her advantage, and the subtle art of exacting comeuppance over white hot revenge. Later, it is Piero da Vinci and Verrocchio who vicariously coach her on the intricacies of covert diplomacy and protocol.

By example, Antonio inadvertently teaches Lisabetta that lashing out at real or imagined enemies is futile and that the art of manipulation is the consistent victor. But most of all, Lisabetta learns that her invisibility is an asset.

It is Lisabetta's persistence that compels her to air her opinions the way Leonardo has always recorded his on paper. Leonardo's studies, being more of an academic nature than hers, come infused with the glorious stamp of breakthrough engineering and medicine and scientific discovery. Lisabetta's musings out loud, are impressions of feminine economy – the specific reflections of a defiant woman at odds with her time, wisely minding her *place*.

Lisabetta hasn't the patience to disguise her observations with codes. What she writes is not so much secret as private, although in her century, a closely-guarded diary is regarded as suspect.

Long before Leonardo is hailed as a genius, he is considered delusional, according to the conventions of society. Poetry is the accepted repository for emotional pain, but challenging the church with science amounts to a personal revolution. Leonardo's compulsion to record his thoughts in clandestine journals begins early. From the age of seven he trusts no-one. He takes confidentiality to extremes, covering his innocent tracks as often as the guilty ones.

Lisabetta heeds the unexpected gems that sprout from trouble as much as the trials which emerge from success.

Leonardo composes music and lyrics embedded with word pictures. He paints images that border on heresy. He provokes authority. He loves to embed eternal puzzles inside the wordplay of disapproving commentary. His mind never lets go. It's paper that captures Leonardo's dreams – the very papers that will eventually destroy Lisabetta.

chapter twenty-one

"Looking at a painted landscape
you can see yourself again,
a lover with your beloved, in the flowering meadows
or under the soft shadows of the green trees."
~ Leonardo da Vinci

Twice Juicy

Synchronicity is the unexpected marriage of events for better or worse. My existence began on a breeze of human chemicals. My father's musk drew my mother down to open the way a flower obeys the sun. I could only sense my father as a lightning-bolt force. He flashed and was gone, but I coursed inside my mother for nine months, and absorbed her memories and expectations. She once told me that my brother and I were born from 'the kind of love that had to be caught like a butterfly and let go before dark'.

Caterina di Marco di Buti was my mother. I remember my death as if it were a continuation of the account she used to tell of my birth. Her storyteller voice enthralled me with its emotional power. She could deliver a story whole, offering it like a precious jewel.

Caterina had been the first one to assure me that I was a special gift. Not from God – she was a non-believer when I was young, but as proof of love. She had wished on the stars for another lovechild to come and I was the fruit of that heartfelt hope.

Her desire for my true father, Ser Piero da Vinci, never waned, but I was a secret – the second child, of their forbidden union. Leonardo may have been relatively transparent to the da Vinci family for his first few years, but I was always invisible to them, and because the rest of the world only acknowledged me when I was persistent, I learned to use a woman's natural disguise of insignificance to my advantage.

Obscurity may be a double-edged gift, but to Leonardo, who had difficulty keeping his feet on the ground (literally as well as figuratively) I was *always larger than life. He had wished for me too, and I came to believe that I had been born in order to serve him.*

Caterina taught me that an impassioned prayer carried power, and I made sure that I was single-minded when I wished for anything. I never wished for small things. Small things were easily accomplished through determination and cunning.

The shock of my death caused Leonardo to suffer a mild stroke – the first of three which left him increasingly disinclined to write or draw.

His young apprentice, Francesco Melzi (sweet dear Cecco), was more like a devoted son than a pupil, and eventually he became Leonardo's secretary and body servant. With our care, Leonardo adapted and thrived by living evermore separate from reality in his inner world where he was most comfortable.

It had been an obvious choice for me to remain earthbound for Leonardo's sake – more like my maternal duty to turn my back on heaven and let its fragile portal close without me. Heaven would wait, I told myself, until Leonardo and I could leave together when his time came, and since I existed in a suspended state, it was not a hardship to endure a few years in-between worlds.

Reassuring Leonardo meant constantly pulling him away from the threshold of a grief that threatened to consume his joy for art and science. His immediate need eclipsed the call of a refreshing afterlife, no matter how tempting a prospect, but I never viewed this as self-sacrifice. It was love.

In his denial, Leonardo automatically substituted my portrait for the flesh-and-blood, me, refusing to distinguish between the physical dimensions of life and the image he had painted of me. It became his habit to keep my likeness close, while I freely inhabited the land 'escapes' he had created for me.

Leonardo's small entourage of faithful followers humored this transference as another presentation of eccentric genius, but dear Cecco knew it was more serious. He knew it was the beginning of dementia – the next progression from Leonardo's productive episodes of creative instability and melancholia.

For me, it had been a flawless transition to step beyond the physical boundaries of death into the realms of time between the living and the after-living. Posthumous communication was natural.

I soon realized, that even in spirit, I could still experience inertia, and to dispel my over-sentimental reverie on a long-past April birthday, I propelled my brother and I into the restorative sunshine of Amboise.

That Leonardo would be compelled to resist me was never in question. We played an ongoing game between us. I cajoled, Leonardo teased, and I always won – Leonardo deferred to my mothering out of habit and from the joy of pleasing me.

I remember the sublime hush that surrounded my mother when she recited our story... hers and mine... and my brother, Leonardo's. She said we were tied together in a knot that had no beginning or end.

As she told it, her destiny was stolen the day she was born – 'sealed by a lazy signature', she used to say, 'and scratched in the heartbeat of a careless summer'. The truth was less poetic, but her misfortune decided my own fate and that of my brother, with the same stroke of a pen.

Legal promises are only one kind of poison that can twist events into surprises of despair. That's life. I thank the stars above for heaven. I can change pretty much anything there with a thought, but what counts as history must occur within the denseness of gravity under the laws of sidereal time.

There are no records in the afterlife. No rewards or punishments. Ironically, there's no death sentences of regret and shame. But I wasn't there in 2008. I was in Paris.

— Lisabetta

CAMPO ZEPPI, Tuscany
JULY 1 – 1457

At sixteen, Caterina's first sin left a white streak across the sky. That was the comet, Leonardo da Vinci. A second chance was delivered in her twenty-third year. Caterina narrated in her sweet throaty voice. 'It arrived on a lemon wind', she intoned, 'a wind that licked the hot dust from an acre of succulent figs'... that was me.

A presence took her off guard. She faced it, welcomed its tease and dared it to stay. My mother knew well how providence could breathe or die on a slow contract. This time she planned to rebirth its cruel sting into a better dream.

But, I was not the better dream. I was only half of it.

Caterina loved to recount the story of me behind the ears of my elder sisters, but she waited until I was old enough to understand, and by that time Leonardo had left us for school where he taught his teachers the art of painting.

Caterina's memories enchanted me, but I was too young to sense their tragedy. I only absorbed the romance. She began my story with a whisper. It was the morning of my conception. She had listened to the horizon and visualized herself on the quiet track to Anchiano. It felt strange, she said, to witness her own departure down the tunnel of tall cypress near our farm in Campo Zeppi. Beyond them lay the fragrant embrace of vineyards that spread towards the flatlands of Lamporecchio and freedom. She had been wild to be away.

Her bare toes splayed into the damp dust of morning and clung to the soles of her feet. My beautiful young mother, Caterina, glowed country brown, the lost daughter of a middle-class notary thrust into the role of peasant wife. I could see her face, flushed all the darker for excitement.

As she spoke, I felt my own face glow brighter in response from knowing I was worth the art of story. This tale was me. For once, I was someone larger than the girl who did chores and kept silent against her father's deep resentment.

My father, Antonio di Piero Buti del Vacca, feasted daily on a sick repast of indignation. He was humiliated from making useless daughters and being trapped in a marriage for personal gains that evaporated soon after the da Vinci fee was paid. That he took it was no surprise. My father was a mercenary soldier when he wasn't working the kilns near our desperate little farm.

My mother told how the air had turned playful and rustled the silver branches. It rattled the olives and was tamed into a breeze of September silk. It blew tender plumes of smoky rain on her face as she crossed the yard for water and landed on her skin, cool as a veil. She shook it from her hair. It was her moment of peace before the chaos of daily survival began.

Caterina pulled the heaviness of water to the surface and stared at the horizon. The promise of escape allowed her to breathe. I knew this feeling well.

She had learned to expect little from Piero da Vinci, other than to exchange an occasional glance. It was hardly surprising. Six years of servitude defined the grim boundaries of her shrinking power. But there were occasions when Caterina would push her son, Leonardo, ahead of her in the rough crowd of Vinci, and expect a civil brush with the family who tried to forget that one day a young notary's daughter passed their way and almost turned a da Vinci head from his duty.

Caterina told the tale often, but she never used the name, Piero or da Vinci and for too long, I assumed I was Leonardo's half-sister. Leonardo was not to know the truth for many years after that. Caterina and my paternal grandmother swore me to secrecy until after Ser Piero's death. He died in 1504 – the same year I was metaphorically reborn as 'Mona Lisa'.

A doorway has two faces: an exit and an entrance, and events are the moving parts of a well-oiled machine that we pretend are coincidental to comfort ourselves. I like to imagine that Piero da Vinci's last act was gallant – a gentleman who held the door open for the lady, Monna Lisabetta, to enter in her green dress, and that he was mystified by her enigmatic smile as she brushed past him entering into immortal life. But Ser Piero was no gentleman. He was a ruthless lawyer and I was his unacknowledged invisible daughter.

I loved Leonardo all the more for his afflictions of melancholia. That's what we called genius. Antonio was a brute who treated him cruelly, but my mother's half-truth also meant I grew up thinking Antonio was my father, until the full story of me released my shame. I never forgave my mother for that. It had pained me to think Antonio Buti and I shared the same blood, but it also fueled the anger that thrust me into a world where murder and power were interchangeable. A world in which I thrived, in spite of being treated with indifference.

By the time I arrived, my mother had given birth to two Buti daughters and a stillborn son. My Aunt Fiore told me Antonio had been livid. He had beaten Caterina and given a name to the boy he had been waiting for. He named the child, Umberto, and secretly buried him amongst the consecrated graves of Santa Croce. I sometimes passed the place and felt a chill – which I now know was a premonition of anger and treachery.

Sometimes peasants in the city were safer than the rest of the population. We were irrelevant. Our hungers were small. As a woman, even my

  LISABETTA – A STOLEN GLANCE

work in the great art studios of Florence was invisible. Leonardo was my road
there, as I was his safe pathway back from the dark spells he had to endure.
Leonardo carried the hope of the da Vinci clan back then. He was considered
Piero's only child, and illegitimate or not, the heir apparent. Only three people
knew Piero also had a daughter. I was not one of them.

My brother craved the life of a scholar. He would have been content
to permanently withdraw from business and serve his muses, even the ones
that tortured him. In a way, he did. After we had our own studio, Leonardo
immersed himself in the sciences any time I released him, but he always
remained the wild child. His insatiable need for play was the core of his greatness. The 'business' of art caused him actual pain.

Leonardo was pure scientist. I was pure ambition. He only became a
master painter with his own studio because I was hungry for acclaim and
to be free of rural servitude, and, as I frequently cajoled him, even scientists
have to eat.

My mother poured water into the trough baked with slime. The
sound alerted the horses. She smoothed the grey's neck, kissed its muzzle
and received a velvety kiss in her palm in exchange for a sweet apple core.
She named the mare, Lezza. It was their secret. Such things were not permitted in the Buti household. Sentimentality overstepped her position as
drudge wife, farmhand, and baby machine. Caterina combed gently. 'Bella
Lezza – beautiful Lisa,' she crooned, as she untangled the weather from
her pony's mane – and I was delighted to be reminded my namesake was
a beloved horse.

The new day shimmered from the slick of early rain. Slices of sharper
wind arrived like bullies and tormented the straw grasses of the flatlands into
rough waves. Perhaps an omen. My mother said, it was as if the presence of
Antonio stirred the fields into protest.

This was the part of our story where I'm sure I smiled. I hated my
father too, but I knew what to do with my hatred, and my mother suffered
in silence. At six, I plotted his death. It was a possibility which enabled me
to survive in Campo Zeppi without going crazy, as long as I did. Daydreams
were my specialty. Revenge I learned later.

Caterina had placed sprigs of lavender into the folds of a clean shirt
saved from her previous life as the daughter of a notary. Inside it was her

mother's amber brooch, the only jewel she ever owned – the same one she pressed on me with tears in her eyes when I turned sixteen. She had made quantities of rosewater, kept cool and safe in stone jars under the horse's straw, and after Antonio was gone, she washed her body, careful to sprinkle drops in her hair and splash the precious liquid on her wrists and throat.

That day, Caterina met the only man who mattered. I saw her eyes close and her chin tilt up to inhale as she recalled the nature of the air, still alive. It was, she honeyed, 'charged with sharp yellow promises that clung to it after it whispered through the citrus groves of Campo Zeppi'. The thought of her first love still made my mother dizzy.

Her hands had delivered sparks of electricity from her wool shawl into the silver buckle as she polished Lezza's bridle. Caterina's long elegant fingers, that matched my own and Leonardo's, fumbled the simple knots, and she took a deep breath to steady herself against the side of the horse.

Then, my mother made sure my eyes met hers. 'Help me Lezza,' she whispered into the pony's ear, and I became the horse who heard a human prayer and responded on instinct with a raw animal shiver. I could feel my hooves paw the ground wanting to speak. That was the part where Caterina always reached out and stroked my hair.

Her plea must have traveled to the ears of the angry 'God' we were supposed to believe in, because 'He' responded in 'His' usual detached manner – a garbled code, delivered as a vague blessing, wrapped in denial. Apparently, the only male who loved games and riddles more than my brother, was my image of an angry patriarchal god, and it's true – I came to view Leonardo as 'god-like' in all his manifestations of creativity.

The world may now agree with historic hindsight, but during our lives it was often the opposite. My brother lived on the edge of heresy all his life, and where he lived, I was there fighting off the superstitious carrion who feared every independent thought, and attacked anyone they didn't understand. Leonardo dared convention... all the time.

Who could praise a god who stole the destinies of innocent babies? Caterina could not. She was a practical woman.

I learned to trust Caterina and mistrust 'mother church', and I knew early on it would be a betrayal of my intelligence if I put my faith in anyone other than myself. I could be as ruthless as God or his latest pope who tried

 LISABETTA – A STOLEN GLANCE

to force sin down our throats, or to be intimidated by the manipulations of the black-beetle priests who scuttled at his feet.

I was never impressed by any deity shallow enough to live inside pretty boxes of gilded stone or garish statues, and I was especially unmoved by the embellished representations of religious art. The church didn't play fair. Its paintings were orchestrated to hold viewers hostage. Fear, pathos, and guilt were the only stories they portrayed. Those, and that suffering was somehow important to experience in order to be accepted into heaven. I rejected all the church's visions of heaven and designed my own, but the church was right, suffering is the greater part of reaching one's heaven. Any heaven.

Leonardo had his bird gods and I had some grandiose concept of omnipotent stars. Stars were better than another cruel father. Between us, Leonardo and I owned the sky and everything under it, and when we were young, our naiveté saved us more than once. As we matured, Leonardo became cynical, and I grew contemptuous enough to turn our jaded expectations into profit.

But the personal details of everyone's stories disappear when they die. For all my bravado, I was not so pretentious to think mine was so very different, but my identity, such as it was, summed up the extent of my existence.

That was how I saw it in 1508 when I died. This is how I continue to see it. I won't play humble. I will never dismiss my entire purpose for being born.

What I did assume, was that my brother's fame contained the gem of my own truth, and I would be a visible shadow to his greatness – that I would live and die, but my name would always shelter under the da Vinci star. I wrote a story worthy enough for my brother to live. I turned the pages of his life into a healthy legend.

I understood the ways of men: they were dictators who documented the history of things. But of all the social indignities I suffered, eternal obscurity was too callous to bear quietly.

I cursed my desire for more into Death's face – never a wise strategy as it turns out.

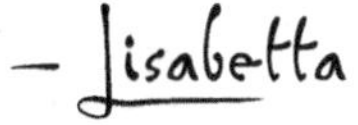

chapter twenty-two

*"Leonardo never believed
in random acts of creation."*
~ Lisabetta

A Second First Date

HALIFAX – 2001

Veronica Lyons' and Niles Duke's first date lasts two weeks – the time it takes for polite exchanges of interested chemicals to decide it isn't the real thing. Their second first date was recorded in invisible ink in an imaginary diary.

Veronica's emotions respond despairingly, a heartbeat before they shut down in self defense. Underneath her indifference is the imprinted memory of a ghostly lover's eyes, and lips, and kiss. If only dreaming made it so, but the golden fantasy of him is always swallowed by morning. She had no intentions of settling for second-best reality. Molecules were overrated.

Mr. Wrongs are a non-starter when compared with the idyllic union of an ethereal beloved. Immortal lovers deliver unselfish devotion, fidelity a mere mortal is incapable of providing. Blind-dating a dream eclipses organic lies of love and promises which end in betrayal.

Dream lovers are devoted masters of intimacy who leave a girl feeling cherished. But they're gone before morning without leaving an impression on the pillows, and in the light of day, it's exhausting to hold out for a fairy tale. In the end, Veronica chides herself: *the concept of soul mates is absurd. Impractical pipedreams for the Eleanor Rigbys of the world. It's time to get out of fate's way.* She comforts herself with the thought of true love lurking nearby in plain sight.

Veronica Lyons decides to settle for the accidental density of whoever shows up in the future, with the lamest of excuses after a quick anagram reveals that the descrambled letters of the word 'density' spell 'destiny'.

The Duke's Duke Institute of Gerontology's company Christmas party is a gush of perfunctory fellowship. Veronica puts in the token appearance, kisses her uncle on the cheek, and whispers: "Are you having fun yet?"

"Any year now," he replies.

Veronica grabs a bottle of champagne and leaves quickly for a sane space and Niles watches her go.

Behind the solid doors of the boardroom it's another planet of empty chairs and a long table barren as a landscape. It's hardly domestic cheer, but more authentic than the force-fed merriment of seasonal decor down the corridor, trying to blast an aura of goodwill into the chilly corporate offices of business-as-usual.

Medication with a champagne chaser sends Veronica into a comfortable retreat. She stretches out, autopsy-flat on the boardroom's sofa, no different than the countless times she has flopped there afterhours. The blur of yuletide music recedes into the static of falling snow.

The door opens and locks with two silent clicks. Veronica awakens too weak to protest with any conviction. She claws at her phantom attacker with rubber arms. Niles takes Veronica's moans for pleasure and finishes quickly. Veronica swoons into a fever-dream where she is an embryo swimming in the effervescence of champagne.

Niles allows the hot water of his shower to explain what happened. Someone who looks a lot like him is responsible. He dials the water pressure to massage and leaves his face in the direct stream for a million years. The recent incident becomes smaller like his bar of soap melting on the drain. He turns, and the back of his head receives the same luxury of therapeutic forgetfulness. He feels safe in a glass room, blissfully separate from business and women and family politics.

The confines of Niles' shower make a perfect confession booth where his crimes slink away as lazy suds. He shouts everything into the ceramic tiles with brazen confidentiality while his brain is gently pummeled into amnesia.

Each lie drizzles down his body and drains between his feet. He watches them disappear in a comforting whirlpool of white foam.

He emerges clean and guilty, wraps his certainty in a thick robe, and sleeps like a baby.

While Niles showers, Veronica's wanders inside a fractious nightmare. She burns three candles. Surely her brother will see the flames and head for home. One candle is for him. One is for a fluttering new life. The third is for her ghostly lover. Hadn't Prince Charming just visited and kissed her into this hundred-year-sleep? He's her answered prayer, but before she drops into alpha, Niles' disembodied face floats over her hissing like a demon.

Niles wakes from his own nightmare with an alarming headache. In his dream, he was being baptized. A bottle of champagne had been smashed over his head while a crowd cheered. He had dived under the water where a predator circled him, and a net captured them both. He remembers the feeling of being hauled into harsh sunlight – exposed, still in danger of being eaten alive.

His day begins shakily, but after strong coffee, Niles feels reborn and sends Veronica a dozen undercover roses to mask his shame. The roses are yellow. The attached unsigned card has a single word written in red ink: sorry.

The water-cooler grapevine picks up the scent of a refreshing scandal. Hijacked into a relationship by her drunk boss creates a politically incorrect climate that pollutes the workplace. Niles' mother, Millicent, the CEO of the Duke Institute of Gerontology, made Queen Victoria seem like Bambi. Neither showed much amusement regarding breaches of social hierarchy. Contraventions of employer to employee protocol ripple through the company in a powerplay of artificial diplomacy.

The obligatory aftermath is a socially courteous formality.

Niles and Veronica's last date is a tricky follow-up of stage-two compulsory flirtation to ease the tension. An awkward café rendezvous is hastily arranged by Niles' mother to camouflage embarrassment. A romantic blip of indiscretion is swiftly downgraded to a one-off mistake and left to bleed out to its natural demise. A simple parting of the ways, and no harm done.

Two months pass, but simplicity, not being a concept the universe values, Jupiter is already floating in amniotic bliss, dreaming of lemon groves and running wild in a landscape of towering poppies and miniature trees.

The day after Veronica disclosed her pregnancy, Niles feigned disinterest, but his eyes disclosed the terror of hidden truths. The consequences were unimaginable. He turned his back on her and spoke to the window. "I'm no longer in the picture. The child could be anybody's."

"Do you really want to claim that, when you run a business based on genetic research? A DNA test is, like, ten yards from this room. It isn't a picture, Niles. It's a situation, and like it or not, you're in it. We both are."

Niles turned and gestured towards the open door. "Now, if you don't mind, I have work to do."

She raised her voice to a modified shriek. "Work? You?"

He brushed her aside in his rush to close the door. "Keep your voice down," he said, lowering his voice. "Look, my bank account is temporarily dry. You'll have to be on your own for a while. We can fix this. And because of the esteem in which this company holds your uncle, you can keep your job. If, however, there are any reprisals such as a claim of any kind for formal financial compensation, I'm afraid his funding will not be renewed and you won't have a job. Is that clear?"

She backed away with growing incredulity. "You're afraid of me. Of me?"

"I am protecting my company."

"From an unwed mother?"

"From a... a slut." Niles had rehearsed the word, but his hesitation failed to deliver it with conviction.

Veronica dropped into a chair, her face a white mask. She kicked off her shoes, and curled into a ball. Her ashen expression shamed him. She is a great girl, and he is fond of her. She had never revealed his drunken behavior as an assault nor kicked up a fuss when he ignored her afterwards. She had even thanked him for the flowers.

"They are my favorite color," she'd said, and he made a white lie into a meal, saying he remembered it from one of their conversations. That was when she had blushed and looked at her feet. When she looked up he'd gone. She had given him that kind of time. The remorse was mutual. They formally dumped each other on Boxing Day.

She had never accused him of sexual assault. Their week of corporate civility made the holidays more chilly than usual, but there were no recriminations. She had gone about her duties, unmoved until the bombshell of expecting a child blindsided them equally.

"I apologize. You're not a slut. Anything but, and I'm grateful that you've been so..."

"Discreet?"

"Understanding."

"Millicent hasn't been," she said. "And now..."

"God, she'll self destruct," he replied. He glanced at Veronica's belly. "Are you sure?"

Veronica crossed her arms and stood her ground. "If she self destructs she won't be a problem, will she. We'll talk later. Soon. Okay?"

Niles met a maternal wall of steely accusation. Millicent took control and settled Niles' matrimonial options quickly in a wealth-to-wealth society merger. Moira Salt and Niles made a lovely power couple.

Niles slouched off to compose an alibi to cover the next twenty-three years.

Veronica's pregnancy started to show after three months.

Niles' reaction was predictable. He made a gallant speech – a stream of apologies with hesitant interjections of child support and best wishes. He delivered it like an actor testing the wind – an emotionless voice-rehearsal just to get the words out.

Niles placates Millicent, realizing he's going to need a killer excuse or a miracle.

He gets both.

chapter twenty-three

"In rivers,
the water that you touch
is the last of what has passed
and the first of that which comes:
so it is with time present."
~ Leonardo da Vinci

Twice Cursed

CAMPO ZEPPI, TUSCANY
JULY 1 – 1457

Caterina leaves her sister-in-law, Fiore, to wipe the noses of the Buti: tanned hooked noses, and wide flat noses that nudge into the endless days of boredom without bothering to test the wind for predators. Already the babies are crying and the small children are wailing to be fed.

The Buti children hide behind their mothers. Fiore stands defiant and faces the wrath of her brother-in-law full on. In this, she is unlike his long-suffering wife. At times like this, when the stakes are high, Caterina has no intention of acting superior. There are days, like today, when acting wretched serves her.

This is a day Caterina could easily unsettle Antonio with a defiant look, but she chooses something else. She wants her husband to leave quickly, and confrontations have stalled him before. Today there must be no endless delays; a stance of humility is best. The two Buti wives know this one thing: that the moments to one's self are not trivial events.

"You look different. It is today?" Fiore asks, after Antonio strides off muttering. Caterina startles at the question. If Fiore notices a difference in her, what may the rest of the household see? But then, women can read further under the skin than men and most children.

She must keep her distance from her mother-in-law to stay invisible. Caterina barely has the strength to nod a silent yes.

"Your eyes are full of light," Fiore says.

"As long as Piero sees it."

"He would have to be blind."

Caterina makes a strangled laugh in her throat. "I am beginning to believe all men are blind," she says.

Fiore smooths her sister-in-law's hair and pats her cheek affectionately. The pair are closer than sisters. They're allies fighting a war of slavery against an army of Buti. Neither one thinks they can survive without the other.

"I will make your hair beautiful as soon as he leaves," Fiore says. "I have some new braid knots to try, or will you wear it loose?"

"Loose," comes the reply. "He must see me as a maiden."

The things a woman does to ensnare a lover are brittle after marriage drains one of seductive magic. Enchanting a man grows more difficult with the years.

Caterina learns early to manipulate the few threads of power left her, and these she weaves around the neck of her husband. She tightens them imperceptibly, and hopes fate will do the rest. Prayers to saints are futile. She prays to any demonic force that can crumble the patriarchal walls of cruelty at their source. In her most guarded imagination she stands apart, and watches her rulers of greed and lust, her judges, and jailors, and executioners, thrash on the ground in their own agonies of defeat. In Caterina's dreams, she steps over their cold bodies and moves into the airs beyond captivity with the same elegance a Florentine lady bypasses a puddle on the way to mass.

The pre-leaving insensitivities postpone Antonio's leaving. Caterina wants to smack the nearest face – any face to transfer her mounting anxiety into a release of surprise for another. She feels increasingly violent towards this clamoring crowd of carelessness called her family, who tears at her time. They claw her day into shreds even before the damp mist of Campo Zeppi burns into the seamless blue of early autumn.

Fiore tells Caterina to make herself ready and leave early. "Slip away now," she says.

Caterina won't risk it. "Once I change my clothes I can't be seen," she says. A white shirt can tell secrets. A scented, bejeweled peasant with unbound hair, will cause a strong ripple of disturbance across a day marked as commonplace. She knows, because it had happened before on a day like this. It's best to remember that jewels, and shirts, and roses, have voices, and that all such commentaries contain the truth of a lie, and that even a blind cuckold can smell a lustful prayer.

The cramped house is a prison of domestic servitude. Children demanding or hurting or hungry – always something to scrub, or lift, or stir. There are only last minute observances to get the tough guy out the door and on his way to his parallel life as a mercenary soldier. Antonio shows his impatience to be away, and deliberately pushes past Caterina too closely. He bruises her arm with the rattle of weapons wrapped in oilskins that he carries like a shrine, raised high and away from his body like an offering.

When Antonio's comrades ride into the yard he's ready. He wheels dismissively from his sour mother and reluctant wife, and his two ridiculous daughters, and his moony stepson with the strange notions of grandeur. He thanks God they will soon be behind him, even though what lies ahead will certainly involve life-threatening skirmishes.

Antonio fights dirty. One day a disgruntled local may have the insight to knock him even more senseless than usual, but so far, none have ventured into that precarious space to confront a professional bully with fists the size of hams and a brain to match.

Caterina, the displaced gentlemen's daughter, helps prepare meals for eleven mouths. Two mouths are old and almost toothless. Five are screaming toddlers or howling babies. Leonardo remains separate, an indefinable entity. Fiore is the one who gives Antonio hostile looks when he is especially uncivil.

     LISABETTA – A STOLEN GLANCE

Antonio is unmoved. His brother's wife can think what she likes. She is, like all women, an invisible commodity. He endures her frowning tirades and dismisses them. She can scratch and bite, but her teeth are no more substantial than the clouds that loom over the fields and valleys of Campo Zeppi.

The stink of Antonio moves with him, outside. It mounts his horse and rides out clinging to his broad back, journeying into the morning, free to pollute another place, and when he's gone the fields settle into a calm sea.

Caterina's mother-in-law, Antonia, sweeps up her grandchildren like a housewife with an angry broom. She swears under her breath that the di Marco whore has ruined her son's life. Today, Caterina cares less than usual. The old woman looks hard at her radiant daughter-in-law, and mutters a mean-spirited incantation. If Caterina returns the stare it will turn Antonia Buti to stone.

Caterina pretends she's alone. Loathing is a powerful charm. A visual hex can easily pass between the eyes of two women, and nothing must jeopardize the spell she has thrown to the stars. A rendezvous with Piero is a sacred opportunity and if Caterina is vigilant, it will be one that Antonia's misery can't touch. There must be no opening for a contemptuous mother-in-law to dilute Caterina's last spark of power.

Caterina had fallen through a chance that arrived on an August afternoon, six years prior. It had been a blissful experience. Unplanned. No omen whispered to be mindful, but by day's end, it was an imprudent event of wild passion that claimed her happiness. Now Caterina treats encounters with Piero with more restraint, but a second da Vinci pregnancy may liberate her from a nightmare life. The lives of their respective spouses separate them. War and childbirth may yet bless them, and with a new marriage, she may yet quit her existence of dishonor and take her rightful place as mother to a civilized bloodline.

Caterina carries the possibility of Antonio's death like a jewel. He uses her fertility like a weapon to prove he's a begetter of sons, but his plan continues to fail. Antonio beds his wife to relieve himself of organic pressures. If she bears another girl and dies doing so, he will have fulfilled his obligation as a mercenary spouse. The da Vinci had paid him well to take Caterina off their hands, but now, six years later, the money is spent, and he and his brother and father are cursed with a houseful of women.

For twenty-two years, Caterina obeys in order to survive. She would change the events of 1451 if she could. She would be less naive... less pliable. She understands the low value of her gender and the harsh rules of legal propriety more completely now. A lawyer's family must appear beyond reproach.

Punishment is an unapologetic teacher. Banishment is a severe lesson to learn at sixteen. It's clear that her weak father and brothers will always turn their backs on her in favor of a da Vinci nod, and so Caterina now makes promises she can't keep to a god she doesn't believe in. God is another father, and fathers are not forces a daughter may rely on.

Had her mother been alive, her father and uncles may have been persuaded into keeping her at home, hidden out of sight with a bastard child, but her stepmother, a year younger than herself, and already downtrodden, would never come to her aid. Had Caterina sniffed out their betrayal, she would have fought them like a cornered bear. Savaged them before they had a chance to steal her destiny.

Caterina is no less suitable a match than Albiera di Amadori, the one chosen for Piero at birth. The two girls had known each other well enough. Caterina even liked the shy creature and helped her through some delicate moments. The daughters of notaries are allowed to mingle together, corralled like pedigree beasts to be fed and watered until their marriage contracts come of age. Caterina had been devastated. Her father's bid had simply failed to manifest on the relevant document because he lagged behind a neighbor who had the foresight to apply first.

The business of gestating an heir carries a death sentence within it. Caterina is no barren maid. She proves her fecundity each year, and fate-willing, may get another by Piero to raise her prospects and keep the Buti line from spreading... and now, Albiera da Vinci has failed once more to conceive an heir.

In her first year of marriage, Caterina discovers that the delicious feeling of sleeping alone with one's thoughts is almost as pleasurable as being with a lover. She thanks the showers of shooting stars over Campo Zeppi that her husband is away for months at a time.

Caterina rides defiantly; her face silent and her body telling anyone who cares to read it, that she, Caterina di Marco di Antonio Buti del Vacca, is leaving on a domestic errand, and will return by day's end, to comply once more with the routines imposed by poverty and the rules of rural subservience. But for now, she is of singular purpose and it's best to stay out of her way.

chapter twenty-four

"The death of fire is the birth of air
and the death of air is the birth of water."
~ Heraclitus C. 535 B.C.

Fire Damage

HALIFAX
2002

Mr. French's second-hand store, 'Buried Treasures', is cat-friendly, precisely because he is never there. His manager, Pamela Saddler, runs the shop and is quick to bargain, barely glancing at the selections through her thick glasses. Pam has to squint at the price tags she mostly ignores over creative math. Disinclined to play bargaining games, she has devised her own system, an inexact science of accepting any reasonable offer if the cats respond favorably.

The good stuff is sold in the main location, uptown by Mr. French, himself, which means the merchandise in 'Buried Treasures' has already been skimmed like cream to become the repository of remnants, passed-over scraps, bargains, and seconds, controlled by a team of feline appraisers. Pamela's only instructions are to move inventory, fast.

Cats perch on shelves and rub against the legs of customers. Some sit in sunbeams refusing to budge. They're employee-children, and any customer who offers them a kind word is awarded an intuitive discount.

Mr. Perry is not only a regular, he is a 'cat person', and so it seems, are his niece, Veronica, and her son, Jupiter. Veronica drifts through the aisles with twelve-month-old Jupiter, cuddled into a navy-blue baby sling.

The cats have brought Veronica's solemn child to life, and it seems as if Jupiter magnetizes the cats to come closer.

Pamela reels in her customer. "They don't usually respond so positively to children."

Perry makes such a fuss of Princess that Pamela is prepared to markdown even more generously.

It is generally accepted as an urban myth, that miracles of science periodically slam into existence from lateral mistakes. The times when left-field discovery is drawn to right-brain activity. Like the breakthroughs of collectors before them, Veronica and Perry stumble upon a lost 'Botticelli' when their minds are open.

The small painted panel is warped and scarred – an image of the goddess Diana, whose face is familiar. Veronica had been sifting through loose sheets and panels while Perry concentrated on framed works, and recognizes the startling countenance of a teenage 'Mona Lisa' staring through a fog of ancient varnish and grime.

"Uncle Oz," Veronica calls out in a shaky voice, "*um*… I think you should see this."

"What have you got th…?" Perry starts to say, and stops, momentarily stunned at the painting in his niece's hand. When his eyes lock with Veronica's above the painting, Perry's expression is that of a man deranged. All he can say is "Bloody Hell."

"This one could be good," Veronica mouths softly.

"I know this painting," Perry replies, his voice breaking. "It's better than good. I know this painting, well. Do you believe in coincidence?"

"I used to believe in everything, until I grew up."

"I think you mean cynical," he says.

"You don't look well. Maybe you should sit down."

"Go. Buy it without a fuss. You'd best do it. I can barely stand."

Perry drops into a creaky roman chair and reaches down to pat Princess but she leaps into his lap. Pamela is impressed. Princess Barometer, Perry calls the little cat, later.

Pamela is eager to fair-trade with Mr. Perry, and Princess shows Pamela where a desirable price-cut is appropriate. Princess says the price is fifty dollars. Skip the tax.

Veronica clutches the purchase trying not to look excited. She stifles the urge to run into the street, where the painting's ownership would seem more official. Instead, Veronica looks casually at a blur of junk and searches around for a cat to ground her emotions.

A preening 'Russian Blue' on the other side of the room, is happy to oblige.

Disoriented and reeling from shock, Perry grips the arms of a Queen Anne chair. A female voice floats over his shoulder. "Dearest."

He listens. The voice is more insistent. "Dearest."

"Hello?" he says, a little too loud. "Who's there?"

Lisabetta is dreaming, somewhere between Electric Street and the Louvre. "I want to show you the Vanity fire," she whispers, all the way from Paris.

Back in 1987, within Cate's need for sympathetic woman-talk, Cate had unwittingly handed Millicent the keys to all her subsequent victories with Perry. The Café Amadeus was in a genteel uproar over the rush of afternoon trade. Blue Willow china clattered over the strains of Mozart. A decor of blue and white wrapped the room in sophistication: white lace tablecloths floated above a blue carpet, and arrangements of white carnations and baby's breath sprouted from antique cobalt-glass vases. Blue Willow wallpaper echoed the china, enveloping the upper-class clientele with the culture of high-tea.

Cate fiddled with her cup and saucer. "Veronica has been half a child since the death of her twin brother when she was six," she said. "Mention the word 'fire' and she pales into submission. Basil was not only her confidante, he was her confidence. Veronica has no faith in herself. She's never trusted life since he left us. To some extent she's the embodiment of giving up without a fight. The poster child for self-fulfilling her own prophesy."

Millicent rearranged the veil on her pillbox hat and tugged her gloves smooth, again. "Veronica dotes on her uncle," she said, craning her neck. Her eagle-eyes scanned the room. "Where's that waiter. Strange title when it's us who do all the waiting."

"Yes." Cate tried to smile. She turned her cup and studied the tiny bird flying out of the pattern. The painter had missed a spot on the rim. "And he dotes on her. They're quite inseparable." Her thoughts spun a small daydream above her head. *How lovely and sad to escape the landscape of a blue and white teacup. I would love to sit all day and paint china. Leonardo loved to paint birds. And he famously bought them and set them free.*

Veronica surrenders to the painting. Her Fine Arts Degree and a short stint as an art teacher gives her the stamina for scanning paperwork and assessing graphic design. She identifies each plant and flower in the surrounding landscape of the 'Diana', and correlates them to the flora of sixteenth-century Italy.

Veronica is divided between instinct, love and responsibility... drawn to what promises to be a five-hundred-year-old masterpiece, her son, and the money to be earned from successfully uncovering a lost Botticelli.

Art grounds her as much as it frustrates. The vulnerable provenance of works swirl in the disturbing anonymity of an artist's mislaid signature. Veronica and Perry have the torn half of a treasure map no more substantial than an underexposed roll of film. Conclusive evidence meets the grit of detective work where the educated guess is emotional speculation at best. "*Attributed to,* is an academic opinion with a revolving door," Veronica tells Perry.

The inner spiral of 'Diana's trial by fire; her DNA (Diana's Nebulous Adventure, Veronica calls it) transports Veronica to another world, and affords her a low research profile underneath reality. The work before her may or may not be a Botticelli, but it had definitely been executed by an Italian hand. It carried a mystery within it. Someone had allowed it to be charred yet cared enough to keep it. Someone had saved it from a fire.

Wherever it had travelled it had been conserved in its damaged state and eventually found its way to a shipment of eclectic antiques, a.k.a. abandoned junk from estate sales and auction houses.

Perry and Veronica successfully clean and authenticate the beleaguered work known as 'Diana' – a missing Botticelli referenced from a description in Vasari's 'Lives of the Artists', the only known biographical work written when the artists circa Leonardo were either still breathing or had died within living memory while their anecdotal references were fresh enough to be true.

Millicent stands to make a cool profit with six zeros. Perry and Veronica are offended by a pat on the back for their efforts. The compensation game becomes legal and nasty.

Millicent hates that the worth of her painting is dependent upon Perry's report and legal stranglehold, and his niece's claims of child support in perpetuity, and decides it is time to kill two birds with one threat.

Perry's inventory had cataloged the 'Diana' honestly, expecting fair play, but their instincts are crushed by Millicent's conscience. As soon as 'Diana' is authenticated Perry loses it to Millicent's vault where it languishes in dispute – a frozen asset awaiting trial. Perry blames himself for using his company expense account to purchase the painting.

It had taken twenty-one years after meeting Millicent, for Perry to realize that Millicent had declared war the first time they shook hands. A war that left him festering under the auspices of royal ser-vitude. Millicent's soured sponsorship had come swiftly enough after Charles' kid brother, Niles, stepped in. Perry gained an eager young ally the same year he lost Cate. The same year that he became a surrogate father to Veronica. The same year Millicent decided it was time to name Niles her heir.

chapter twenty-five

*"All things are an interchange of fire,
and fire for all things, just like goods for gold
and gold for goods."*
~ Heraclitus c. 535 B.C.

The Cave of Fragilities

ANCHIANO
JULY 1 – 1457

By midday, the turquoise sky of Tuscany blasts Caterina with hope. It sustains her. Caterina's chilled skin drinks in the sun as she follows the ripe wind into the hills of Anchiano. When the track turns north, Caterina stops to attach her amber brooch to the collar of her white shirt. It catches the light, and she stares into its pockets that look like the bubbles inside dark honey.

The largest bubble contains a small bee, an embryo of flight locked in a golden womb – an ancient, fragile life, overcome by pine lava. It reminds Caterina that sometimes danger arrives before a fragrant cloud can pass across the sun and that a girl may succumb to the bittersweet nectar of forbidden love.

The shirt and the brooch are two of the possessions from Caterina's marriage chest, flung at her upon leaving – the things she keeps away from Antonio's sour tongue. If she will not use them, then her daughters may, but this thought is torn before she even reads it. Her daughters are born to a life of service, and if they're lucky, no man will find them attractive enough to pry another generation of perpetual mothers, farm hands, and fodder for the army, from between their legs.

The scent of rosewater rides with Caterina. Inside her strong resolve, she's a woman leached of vitality, fragile as a pressed rose. Her hopes, pressed between passion and duty, feel ready to crumble into ash with the slightest hesitation of wind. But the ghost of love still cleaves to her, singing a dream of truth.

She rides for an hour before her shoulders relax into a posture of confidence. She releases the Caterina she pretends to be, and engages the part of her that remains constant in spite of interference. She has little faith in God, although she attends weekly mass and performs the rituals expected. Her job is to act pious and retreat small enough to pass under the noses of society. Even the backcountry has its pecking orders and spies. Some days Caterina struggles to be free inside a mistake that feels like a prison of stone honey.

Her destination is the olive-press at Molino della Doccia that lies due south of the cool marshes of Anchiano. The mill of crumbling yellow brick waits on a shady rise off the dirt track to Montevettolini. Behind it, the hill slopes carelessly down to the osier beds that choke the banks of the River Vincio. Here, the lazy water meanders past Monte Ceceri, the great swan, on its way to Florence, and picks up speed after sweeping the outskirts of Larciano. Past Larciano, it rushes towards the waiting embrace of the Arno. The landscape is familiar. The grasslands along the river anchor the ghosts of Caterina's childhood where she and Piero had played as children and grown to be best friends, and continued to meet as love-struck teenagers.

The mill harbors a secret – an outcrop of granite lumps that form a hollow the size of an apple where papers may be wedged. Letters are sent and received there under the twist of an angular stone. They refer to it as the 'Cave of Fragilities'. Sometimes Piero leaves Caterina a token from the city: a delicacy or a ribbon or a flower. Sometimes she leaves Piero a small thing she has made or found or that belongs to her body: a love knot of wicker or a heart-shaped stone or a lock of her hair. Such things of inconsequence wait there with the fine ambience of an object recently touched. A memento that holds the aura of a beloved's phantom lips and fingers. These trivial reminders tell of times when a meeting is possible or to beg a simple question, but mostly they're exchanges of two emotional shadows, out of step with fate too potent to ignore. Caterina and Piero acknowledge all that is left to them. Their messages are clear: *'Di eri di domani'* — *more than yesterday, less than tomorrow.*

The shrine is revisited in varying degrees of urgency, but never ones of casual connection. The words and gifts alter the fabric of their 'between days', and bridge the encounters that grow fewer with the business of life — the events which intrude on the hours once held by each as free time, when there was still hope for something kinder than fate.

FROM THE DIARY OF VERONICA LYONS

- FOOL'S GOLD -
JULY 1 – 2003

If compatibility reigned would any imperfection matter? I stand self-pressured… heavy and pale, gravity-trapped within my personal orbit. How would one survive all the inspections of a lover? How could I confidently raise my eyes to meet those of a stranger's absolute truth? What would be revealed and what would remain hidden under such scrutiny? An artist cannot lie about beauty… it's the stock and trade of visual perception.

My dreams are self-conscious twins, fashioned from gold or tin… depending how the light strikes them.

— Veronica

chapter twenty-six

"Love is invisible and inaudible.
So how will I know if it arrives?"
~ Veronica Lyons

Niles' Denials

HALIFAX – 2003

Millicent has an excuse to act even more indignant. "Jupiter is not quite right." The accusation floats, trying to land inside Niles' brain. "Jupiter is not quite *right*," she repeats. "I told you, no good would come from that stupid girl."

After the birth of his son, Niles had found himself weakening. Jupiter's condition is irreversible. "Autism runs in your family not mine," Niles says to Veronica. There's no counter to his declarations. It's true. It's an accusation. "Contrary to our recent renewal of friendship, you are..."

"Out of the big picture?" Veronica finishes. "Yeah I get it. The full picture."

"Well, I want to be friends," he says.

"Really? You can pretend whatever you want as long as I'm not out of the *'Diana'* picture. I found her. I don't need my boss to be my best friend. I work here. And I'm due a bonus from that painting. If you want to play footsy with 'Diana', you can expect a lawsuit."

"Well, technically *we* bought her, so..."

"Technically, you're an asshole."

"Jupiter will be taken care of, but mother thinks he should be in a mental institution."

"This *place* is a mental institution. I wouldn't leave my son alone here for a second. I don't need your money. I earn mine fairly. My instincts recognized that painting. Not yours, and not your mother's."

Veronica believes she needs a father figure to support baby Jupiter. She will settle for any breadwinner – anyone kind will do.

Eighteen months later, Niles has alimony payments. He is rebuked by three women: his mother, his mercenary ex-wife, and his harridan lawyer. Niles' arranged marriage had lasted less than nine months. Thankfully, although Millicent thinks otherwise, there had been no children.

chapter twenty-seven

*"Sometimes
the last harvest
is the sweetest."*
~ Lisabetta

Twice Blessed

ANCHIANO, TUSCANY
JULY 1 – 1457

Caterina sits on horseback, tall enough to reach heaven, and Piero da Vinci forgets the effect she has over him until he sees her horse pass the stained sails of the mill, hiding her progress: first a sheet of white linen, next a bright reveal of copper hair, her back regal – free of chains. Her posture on the farm is not as straight. It suffers from shame, as much as the functions of workhorse and birthing three children in five years. Humility has nothing to do with it.

Piero watches Caterina's head tilt to hear the sun. She is nervous. The horse picks up her body's signal and prances the last few yards, crushing the beds of wild chamomile. She rides silently through the fragrance of dog parsley and lavender. Piero feels guilty for feeding a torturous plan that shames such a brave emotion as passion. Desire has reduced them to belligerent pawns prone to defy rather than comply.

Six years of backbreaking labor has failed to turn Caterina into an early crone. But it will. Piero knows without a doubt he will turn from her the way a sunflower seeks the sun, to the newer tender shoots of womanhood, barely older than one's own sons. The fresh daughters paraded out, fragile as doves, empty-headed, trained to submit, fearful but succulent and willing to obey the patriarchy that begot them. And their stepmothers, only slightly more senior in years, happy to be rid of the constant reminder that they were once the same silly darlings of rosy-cheeked promise, thrown to the lying old wolves who vowed them undying protection. It's the way of the world, and Piero plans to have as many wives as it takes to birth a stable-full of legitimate male heirs.

Caterina cherishes the last moments of a tryst that runs like a startled rabbit. She dives and swims and washes ashore, left like human driftwood to bleach in the sun that exposes her guilt and the recent sins she has committed in the name of love. She rights the confusion of her wild hair and twisted clothes, and moves towards Lezza.

The pony's head is bowed in the heat of the day, grazing, but it hears the storm of Caterina's crushed skirts approaching in a defiant bustle. Beneath them, Caterina is still moist and ready, but the fox is gone, and the position of the sun tells her it's late.

Caterina, mother of three, possibly four, turns Lezza's nose north into the oncoming spiral of road dust. Her pony snorts through the flurry of leaves and gravel, kicks through it with a fine side-step and carries her into the landscape beyond where the wind vanishes. There is no need to hurry. The only feeling of expectancy left is to return to the familiar crush of humanity with the resolve of good food and the secret hope she carries a second seed from Piero within her.

Caterina's reverie carries horse and rider home like a flickering torch towards the certainty of a meal spent in idle meditation, her two girls mercifully clamoring with their cousins for attention, and Leonardo, a silent force of nature, slipping between them all with ferocious willpower.

During the evening, Leonardo sits apart and smiles to himself, wrapped in a disturbing glow of solitude. Caterina envies him the ability to preserve his innermost haven while being bombarded with her husband's insults that rail like angry fists. Caterina moves to hug Leonardo, but as always he anticipates and dodges her touch. He does not dislike his mother yet he keeps her a stranger. No-one may stray uninvited into his carefully-constructed sanctuary of strange beauty. He hates to be touched.

The fork-tailed kites of Monsummano circle and swoop like the flour-
ishes of a notary's pen – looping and dipping with emphasis on the
abrupt turns, to dart away as a dash or alight on a high branch as a
dark silhouettes. Wings like a blotches of ink against white clouds.

Somewhere within an afternoon's ride, Piero is making polite
conversation or taking supper, or sleeping with his barren wife. Caterina tries to imagine his presence, barely eight miles over the low-lying
hills.

Piero is home, nestled under the same stars, but for Caterina, the country is only a vast space between her body and his. It is
an ever-expanding separation of fortunes. At night, Caterina stands
abandoned under the moon gazing past betrayals, near enough to
mock true love.

There's enough rosewater left to wash Piero away, but Caterina
savors being his phantom wife for a few more hours before life picks
her up and tosses her into relentless mourning and women's work.
She remembers the day as something intensely richer. She can refine
the adventure, and by tasting it twice, she rewrites something more
poetic than reality.

Tonight she will indulge her fantasies by staring into the low
thatch of ceiling, blessedly alone within the circle of nine other souls,
snoring and scratching and whimpering in their sleep. She will lean
on the soft sounds of the animals shuffling in their straw behind
the wall she shares with their shelter. The beasts pause and snort in
soothing rhythms. The night noises whistle the grasses rustling under
owls hunting for mice while the moon searches the ground for lost
souls, and foxes use its light to sniff out innocent rabbits. Most of
all, Caterina will remember Piero's tender *"Ti amo"* and the way he
had looked into her eyes and waited until they cried out in ecstasy
together.

The daughters of Caterina and Antonio are blissfully ignorant
of a more sumptuous fate than the rough living of farm life. They have
not seen the velvet curtains and the four-poster beds or been blinded
by the sheen of polished gold or the redness of rubies or tasted the
temptations of marzipan and honeyed-figs. For them, the snoring of

their father and uncle and grandfather represents a hub of safety. For Caterina, safety rests inside dreams of riverbank-love. For Leonardo, it's the blue updrafts of skies filled with birds.

Sixty days later, Caterina smiles into the morning. She places her rough hands across the flatness of her belly. Inside Caterina's womb, Lisabetta curls in amniotic solitude, an embryo quickened with grace, pulsating like a trembling shrimp – delivered in a random drop of da Vinci honey. Lisabetta is the belated twin, the beloved shadow child. A child in amber.

When Lisabetta is united with Leonardo they are something quite extraordinary. Together they will have enough of what the other lacks, to become an irrepressible, singular force-of-art.

FROM THE DIARY OF VERONICA LYONS

- UNHEALTHY THOUGHTS -
HALIFAX –OCTOBER 31 – 2004

Something tainted and impure remains from the dream-time… a presence of forever lost… suffering suffused into a hard insistent ball… nausea and waking pains. Growing-pains. Waiting is necessary. Remaining open is vital. I am willing to understand the moment, later. Actually, I have no choice. The notion that time is the enemy is an illusion. It's the thoughts of incriminations, small and defeating, that are spineless opposing forces to good. I'm not a true scientist but I do know that low vibration thoughts of loss and lack appear to replicate themselves like bacteria.

chapter twenty-eight

"The promises of this world are,
for the most part, vain phantoms;
and to confide in one's self,
and become something of worth and value
is the best and safest course"
~ Michelangelo

Niles' Hidden Valley

HALIFAX
2004

While Perry Lyons defends his right to the 'Diana' painting, Veronica acts as his paralegal assistant and Jupiter receives the necessary care he needs from specialists, reluctantly sponsored by the Duke's attorneys.

Perry has even more incentive to study his infant nephew and the family tree.

Veronica, suffocating under financial dependence, surrenders. She uses work as an additional sedative and sieves the internet like an archaeologist. One day it's to dissect the provenance of art and another it's to shake down the genetic data from the Lyons' computer base into graphic charts. Veronica welcomes the long hours, and gradually the humiliation of Niles' abandonment recedes, but over-thinking her lack of options, and Jupiter's future seethes into a slow fuse of depression, and while her uncle's counterclaim reaches a break*through*, Veronica heads for a break*down*.

Alzheimer's-in-waiting shadows her – a mother/daughter relationship taken to extremes, in death after life – or is it a karmic glitch necessary to clear a pathway of higher healing? Perry thinks so. He's seen it before. Denying the truth of non-local medical remissions requires an open mind, and he is a scientist who is living a miracle.

Jupiter's challenges are as great as the painting struggling for identity, and if it hadn't been for the Botticelli and because of the Botticelli, Veronica feels she might have joined Cate.

Humility has a bitter aftertaste. Hate, the collective cruelties of the legal system, and fate, eventually burst Veronica's reigned-in life, and Perry has a more immediate problem to contend with. Millicent and Niles call a meeting to discuss a solution, and Perry first hears the deal to send Veronica and Jupiter to the far side of the country.

Perry breaches the subject with Veronica bearing tea and cakes. "I'm afraid we're out of options," he says gently. "But no worries. While Mama's boy wriggles like a worm on a hook, I've negotiated a European vacation for you and Jupiter to spare you the agonies of moving."

"That doesn't sound like something Millicent would finance."

"You'd be surprised. Law suits make her nervous. You have the upper hand which means we play poker for a while. Your effects will be shipped west and unloaded in a property of my approval."

Veronica stares white-faced. "Oz. We're used to being near the water. It's not that I'm ungrateful, but I don't want to live in the grey cement slide of Vancouver or some hot valley of farmland. I've been to the Okanagan. It didn't feel right."

Perry approached his niece and enfolded her in a bearhug. "Child, child, this is me. Your old Uncle Oz. I know what you like. We settled on the inner core of Vancouver Island, near the fresh open sea. Victoria is surrounded by rain forest. Whales in your backyard. Jupiter will love it."

Veronica grasped Oz's lapel and sniffled into his tweed jacket. Her voice, muffled in itchy wool, came in a breathless whisper. "Is it safe?"

"Safe as houses, baby girl. Victorian society is more genteel than Vancouver. Time is quite different. And you'll be happy to know it rains a great deal. There's a house near enough to Victoria but isolated from traffic. Think of it Lass. Five years to paint to your heart's content. And Jupiter will receive the best of care. I negotiated a nanny if you want one."

"*And* a trip to Europe? How?"

Oz kissed the tip of Veronica's nose and massaged the circulation back into her cold fingers. He sent her his best grin. "A gallery crawl from London to Paris. The National Gallery, the Ashmolian, The British Museum, and…" he winked, "the Louvre."

Veronica stood back, wiped her face on his extended handkerchief, and took a deep breath. She looked into trusting eyes. "So, the 'Mona Lisa', at last."

Perry beamed. "Not bad, eh. Didn't I tell you we have Millicent over a barrel."

Millicent laced her fingers together in the shape of a church over Perry's desk and tapped its steeple onto heavily rouged lips – a mouth painted in a grim red line. "You know," she said to Perry in a conciliatory tone, "renting that house could be upgraded to a purchase. In which case, Veronica would own a property, outright. Consider my offer carefully. It's worth more than the commission you and Veronica claim is your right."

Perry's desk drawer is crammed with pending lawyer's invoices. Money would go a long way to erase the accumulation of financial debt. Millicent nudges a fountain pen forward. Her meaning is plain. Sign on the dotted line. You'd be a fool not to. Years of court battles lie ahead.

"We will make your legal bills disappear if you extend your niece's stay to ten years. And as a further bonus," she says, without the hint of a smile, "We agree to pay for your sister's extended care."

Perry raises his eyes to meet Millicent's steely stare. He almost admires her. But she's more of a coldhearted negotiator than a coolheaded strategist. "Beatrice must be housed in an institution of my choice," he says.

Millicent straightens in her chair… all business. "Of course, providing Niles connection to Jupiter is erased."

Her widening smile indicates there's more.

"And? You want them whitewashed too?"

Her eyes flash. The room freezes. "Veronica and Jupiter must stay three-thousand-miles distant, on the other side of Canada. AND you must give up all claims to the 'Diana'.

Halifax and Victoria are the bookends which hold the deal together. Under litigation, 'Diana' is a prisoner, barred from sale. It's Perry's trump card. He leans forward as if he's about to cave and picks up the pen. He pockets it, slams both his hands on the table, and scrapes back his chair. "It isn't enough," Perry says. "It will never be enough. We accept moving and travel expenses to and from Europe and five years rent-free. I guess 'Diana' will have to remain in purgatory… with you."

FROM THE DIARY OF VERONICA LYONS

- RENAISSANCE GAMES -
JUNE 13 – 2004

This morning I was back to fear and feeling unwell in body and spirit… all sick nerves and uncertainty. Feeling too alone and out on a limb. Some rogue thought snapped a last nerve. I called time out. Enough was enough, and I had the presence of mind to cry and surrender to its power. Waterworks are a wise way to release tension.

I am breathing a little easier for it, but one butterfly remains to keep me on my toes. Ironically, the feeling of desperate heaviness comes because so much is up in the air.

How I wish I had the optimist gene like Uncle Oz.

FROM THE DIARY OF VERONICA LYONS
– M&M MONSTER –
JUNE 14 – 2004

Jupiter offered me all his orange M&M's, and it reminded me of Nile's shrill of a mother.

I can't bear the thought of Uncle Oz facing her alone. I wish he was free of all the mess. Millicent still holds 'Diana' and the family's finances taut as harp strings. Staff call her 'Militant' behind her back.

She has an expensive paperweight of porcelain roses on her desk, and I told my uncle: 'old Militant' must have looked at some fresh flowers and turned them to stone.

Since then, I refer to her as 'M&M', short for 'Mother Medusa', but everyone else thinks it's because of the jar of colored chocolate buttons she always keeps hostage on her desk.

— Veronica

chapter twenty-nine

Running to Ground

CAMPO ZEPPI
APRIL 15 – 1458*

There are birds inside the house. Only this can explain the chaotic screeching. Leonardo stares into the rafters and sees the undisturbed bundles of herbs drying there. The window is open to a square of morning sky. The birds must have escaped to the eaves outside. The noise is still close.

Aunt Fiore is busy attending to the bird screams that emanate from his mother's bed. The birth is not going well. The face of Caterina hovers above the bedclothes. Her shift is pulled high, covered in sweat and clings to her body. She looks, but can't see her son.

Leonardo is no longer there, he's running.

The tall grasses crush underfoot and bend away from him. Rogue stalks scratch at his face and try to grab his hair. They close around him and pull him down. He curls into a ball and rolls around until he's made a clearing. He looks like an egg in a nest – a huddle of a child wound tight, humming like a beehive in a copse of trees. His song increases. He is a drum. The terrible screams of his mother

---

* Leonardo's sixth birthday… the day of Lisabetta's birth.

turn into the sound of friendly kites calling mid-swoop overhead. They lend him their song. Leonardo rocks as they serenade the day until he feels safe. Their cries tell him to look up. They say "join us."

Leonardo opens like a flower and unfurls like petals in the wind. He lies in a curve on his right side in order to see a flurry of wings between himself and the sun. Their busy movements force his eyes closed. Wings make the sun flicker dangerously and he vomits his fear into the grass. The birds laugh. The grey fluttering departs with a noise like dry leaves as the sun falls on him like a blanket. He stretches his six-year-old body as far as he can to relieve the tremors in his legs and arms, and forms a triangle with his hands to view the black dots that circle the sun and spin clockwise. He can't turn away. He is drawn inside the centrifugal force of heaven, pinned like an insect to the earth. His arms flail sideways in the pose of crucifixion.

Leonardo holds his breath and closes his eyes. The birds sound far away. He lifts to join them, soaring higher into the tree canopy. A branch stops him and he looks down on his body. He sees a smiling boy embracing the wind, inviting down the sky.

He loves the weightlessness as he ascends, pulled upwards on invisible strings at his wrists and elbows and head. He streams higher and the purified wind massages his sore temples, and the clouds turn into giant swans.

When Leonardo wakes, the sky is green. The birds have swarmed back to the house. He rises and the breeze cools his damp spine. It feels awkward to walk. He's clumsy and heavy, thrashing through the fields like a wild beast. The sky turns blood red with purple clouds. Gold threads sew them together. It looks like an embroidered pillow he has seen in his father's house, made of rich stuff. He wants to pull it down or swim to it and lay his head upon it. His wings are tired, folded over his shoulders like a white cape. He is grateful for the warmth they provide and he hides his head under one of them, the way he has seen the cranes do on the marshlands of Anchiano.

A yellow square of window floats in the darkness. Leonardo trudges towards it the way a moth's memory seeks the dream of a flame. He feels sleepy. The light is friendly. It means something. He is a sliver of moonlight, and more than anything, he wants to disappear into the night like a waning moon.

The storm of birth is over. It has blown his cousins and sisters into a heap with their snoring grandmother. There are other piles of bedding with no children, or uncles, or stepfathers, under them. They glisten with sweat and specks of blood.

A helpless movement stirs the bedclothes. Leonardo sees his mother's mouth move... a tired face too spent to disapprove. She raises herself as if to beckon him, but she gives a shriek and the child flows into the room on a river of transparent blood. Fiore blocks his view too late. Antonia stirs in her sleeps and calls out to her daughter-in-law. "Is it a boy?" Fiore's answer is slow... "a girl."

Leonardo is frozen with conflicting emotions. He is horrified and curious. These two feelings will be forever fixed as motivations to discover, uncover, and understand women. There's more bird chirping, but this time it sounds like a bleating lamb. It's an animal song, safe to explore. Leonardo is drawn to the voice of a newborn's language.

A bundle is pushed into his arms. His aunt is brusque. "Take her outside. I need room. Go. Hurry," she says, shooing him away.

The bundle is a small pink creature that mews like a cat, or is it a baby bird with wet feathers? It squirms inside its covering. The midnight sky mutes the sounds emanating from the window. He hears the wail of his mother and then silence.

Caterina is riding Lezza and the day is suffused with joy. She tells the pony she is beautiful. "Bella-Lezza," she says. The name is uttered within a secret smile. "Lezza," she says to the animal, "My beautiful girl. Bella Lezza." She lets the pony take her away from the shabby room and the face that stares down at her in fear.

Fiore hears Caterina call out, *"Lisa my beautiful girl."*

Leonardo hears and looks deep into the miracle of his new sister. "Your name is Lisa... Lisa-bella," he whispers. A pink rosebud searches for milk. Leonardo puts an index finger into the rose and feels the hard tug. His soul enters the rosebud through his finger and into the creature. He is drenched with warm honey. The lamb surrenders. "Is it you?" Leonardo asks her.

The stars bend down to Campo Zeppi for a closer look. Leonardo pulls aside the cloth that has blown over his sister's face, and is captured by a pair of wise-dark eyes, bright as a bird's. "It *is* me," they say.

What can a newborn possibly retain from the hour of her birth? That the stars are in or out of alignment? That they trine favorably or fight in opposition? The zodiac does not care to answer.

The swaddled infant short-circuits Leonardo's young brain. His eyes move from the horse to the cow and up to a star he has chosen as theirs'. This thought fuses Leonardo and his *Lisabella* into a 'mother-and-child icon'. This birth is a miracle. Caterina swoons in restless sleep. Angels have finally smiled on Campo Zeppi: Twins, are born, six years apart.

When Lisabetta is five, she remembers something of her birth – a face she will always know as mother. Leonardo can recall more. He sees the Christ-child in his arms, surrounded by a night sky, animals, a bed of straw, a manger filled with sweet hay... and stars. Perhaps one is brighter than the others. He had wanted to fly into the brightest of them, but they danced for his sister, he is sure of that, and her sacrifice is a long way off – too far away to disturb the night.

   LISABETTA – A STOLEN GLANCE

chapter thirty

"Il sole non si muove"
"The sun does not move"
~ Leonardo Da Vinci – 1510

Mother & Child

THE TOWN OF VINCI
APRIL 16 – 1458

The marble font is to be the same one used for Leonardo's christening. Caterina is half-awake, long enough to make her wishes clear before she rides away. The newborn is to be taken to Vinci and not the parish church of Anchiano.

"You will take the child," Antonia commands her son, "Leonardo can hold her."

Antonio is reluctant. "Why should I? We can bury the thing right here. Or…" he adds, addressing his sister-in-law. "*Both* of them."

Fiore is adamant. "Lisabetta will die by nightfall," she says, "and, *si*, maybe Caterina as well."

Antonia crosses herself. If she can help it, the last conscious act of the whore, Caterina di Marco di Buti, will not add further cause to her son's suffering. "You're a fool, Antonio. A dying mother's wish may turn into a curse," she replies. "I order you to go and go quickly. And pray the infant survives in time."

There is a rush to get Leonardo and the baby into the cart. Her name is to be Lisabetta. Fiore had misheard Caterina. "Don't forget," Fiore reminds Leonardo. "It's what your mother wants." But Leonardo still calls her Lisabella. "Antonio, be careful," Antonia says. "Your soul is in danger."

Antonio shrugs off Fiore's order. "I should overturn the cart and be rid of two mouths to feed who do nothing but exhaust my patience."

Fiore is appalled. Antonio is delighted to see that his lack of compassion still has the power to shock her. "Perhaps I should load you and your daughters, and my other two as well," he says. "Have done with all of you. My brother would be pleased, yes?… to be free of another wife who makes no sons. Both of you drain my wages with your brats."

The horse and cart pass through the gate and Fiore stares after the broad back of her brother-in-law and the small shape of her nephew. She takes a deep breath and turns towards the sound of children crying. Her next task is bringing Caterina back from another swoon into the world of sleep.

The bleeding has stopped and with infusions of herbals Caterina may live. The baby is a different matter. The child must be baptized today before she goes to God.

Inside the house, four toddlers watch the rise and fall of bedclothes to see if death has claimed their mother and aunt. They are too young to be horrified and too old to be indifferent.

Fiore pushes them towards their grandmother, fans Caterina with the edge of her apron, and waves the rind of a freshly cut lemon under her nose.

Caterina turns away from the scent and dreams of lemon trees. She lies luxuriously beneath them, unfurling her toes, stretched on a blanket soaked with blood, and gazes up at the bright yellow fruit hanging above her. She smells the white blossoms that open and close like the mouths of birds. The baby is hungry. She must wake and feed it. She hears her name called and feels the sharp slap that accompanies it. Fiore's face smiles. Caterina can relax again. Her competent sister-in-law has fed the baby enough worms and she can return to sleep. Her name floats again.

"Caterina?"

"Yes, I am here."

"You must stay awake. I have something here for you. You must drink, yes? Lisabetta is safe. Antonio has taken her to Vinci with Leonardo."

Caterina hears on a brief wave of lucidity. "Who is Lisabetta?" she asks.

Antonio drops the two children near the church. He raises his fist to cuff Leonardo but the boy ducks. Antonio spits, aiming for Leonardo's shoes but misses. He wipes the excess spit from his chin with his sleeve. "You have the day, bastard," he growls. "Be here later or I will leave without you. *Capice?*"

The interior of the chapel chills Leonardo from the inside out. The contrast after cooking his skull under the sun for three hours is a relief. The walls of stone sends waves of cold like a winter wind. It's not healthy for a newborn already near death.

If anyone can save Lisabetta, Leonardo can. He only needs to reach the bargaining table below the crucifix and beg. He has seen it done often.

Leonardo's body heat comprises the entire boundaries of Lisabetta's world. She is warm but she feels trapped. She'd tried to make them understand by screaming "let me out." While everyone is sure Lisabetta is struggling to survive, she struggles to be free. Swaddling clothes are the first of many things that will try to control her. She protests with more screams. "I want to move," she howls, and Leonardo hushes her.

A pair of godparents are hastily borrowed from the street. The promise of wine and honey-cakes brings them inside, but they will only receive a short prayer for their time. There are no sweetmeats. Priests negotiate with honey cakes of power but deliver false promises. Complicity is an easy bargain to make with fear. Soon enough, a message for their soul's salvation will make its way to heaven on candle-smoke and they can wonder at their good fortune, passing the parish church of Santa Croce at such an hour when they may serve God's priest as well as themselves.

Leonardo is impatient for the rites of baptism to be over so he can give his sister the comfort of dying under the sun. They are of one mind. Leonardo understands that Lisabetta wants to lie on the grass and kick her legs. Wave her arms. Signal to the world she is animate. She is less than twenty-four-hours-old. She must feel the delights of the April sun on her skin. She is a fragile baby bird, her wings still wet, but the hot Tuscan wind is ready to dry her feathers. Lisabetta begs for the vastness of space outside the tomb of cloth that threatens to smother her. To be freed from her linen prison. She cries "Leonardo, I'm stronger than all of you."

Friar Piero di Bartolomeo echoes Leonardo's desire for a hasty performance. He intones and gestures appropriately in his theatre of lies, and it is done. Another soul saved with a dispatched formula of grace. He is eager to climb his stairs, to where a woman waits. She waits on his authority to intervene on an obscure matter of feminine conscience and is willing to loan him her body in exchange for his best advice.

Such paltry urgencies as a newborn's passage into Christianity with eternity waiting to steal her, is not as important as the carnal promise that shivers upstairs. In any case, the infant is a girl... a peasant girl at that, and here is the illegitimate brother – the only family interested enough to deliver her from purgatory.

At this moment, brother Bartolomeo feels himself a powerful figure. This moment that looms over two children: one dying; another, a futureless bastard; and a desperate woman waiting in deference to his smoldering power.

When the baptismal waters pour over Lisabetta's head, Leonardo hears the mention of the trinity and is rewarded with an image of Piero da Vinci, himself, and a Holy Ghost, walking in the clouds of heaven surrounded by angels. He hears the priest offer up the name Lisabetta, and his reverie shatters quickly. The water is a shock. Lisabetta screams as loud as she can but she needs her arms to release the full sound she wants to make. The effect is instant. Leonardo stops her mouth with his finger and Lisabetta pleads with him to liberate her from the blanket and dry her head.

Leonardo's first impulse is to remove screaming from the world, but he needs to be angry with someone for making his sister cry. It must be his mother's God who has the power to order his priests to upset babies. The building is oppressive. Outside there is room to think. He will return later to light a candle, but for now he wants space between himself and God's apprentice as much as Lisabetta desires the space to move. God's commandments may be overruled easily enough but Leonardo dares not change his sister's name, now that it's been sealed under the stricken eyes of a painted Madonna mourning her own child.

Leonardo wants his sister to live and if he's not swift about it, she will die in a fit of colicky despair. Aunt Fiore knows of these things and she says baby Lisa will die before dark. Leonardo's maternal task had been clearly stated — it was to deliver his sister's sin to this font belonging to God, and bring back a purified baby whose body his stepfather can give to the earth of Campo Zeppi.

Leonardo counts his mother's God as a third angry father, another man who rules her with a hard fist. The creator of his own world is a benevolent white-winged thought. If Leonardo runs into the hills without delay, he can lay Lisabetta in a manger of tall grass that stretches to the horizon, and bargain for a sky miracle.

Leonardo's own god can kiss her wings into life with divine light, but Lisabetta can't fly to heaven unless Leonardo performs this task for her.

Leonardo is outside at last. In his church. The green breath of the trees cools his face. Their sap, bubbles yellow under their bark, down through the roots. Golden blood surges into his back as he leans against an oak pillar that supports the dome of his sky. Leonardo is the trees' priest who writes their contracts with humans for wood and paper, and amber and shade. He squints into the blue and watches his miniature angels — butterflies that swarm in a colorful cloud and land like painted leaves. He noted, long ago, that a butterfly's wing held up to the light is a miniature stained-glass window.

Leonardo and Lisabetta melt into the landscape outside the fortress walls and he unwinds her swaddling next to a small stream. The sun's face is blanket enough. He fetches a handful of water, wets Lisabetta's head, and invokes three potent symbols: the sun, the moon, and the stars. In a strong voice, Leonardo offers Lisabetta's name to the sky. This time she laughs at the gentle trickle of holy water that has warmed in her brother's hands.

Leonardo makes Lisabetta a bed of wild daisies. He sits hugging the curve of a budding fig tree and watches his sister commune with the sky. She has a lot to say. He looks up at the scorching disk and the yellow color hurts his eyes. He shields Lisabetta's twice-blessed head so that the shadows of the fig branches dance over her face. He can see she is beautifully formed. Her tiny hand wraps around one of his fingers like the tendrils of a plant. Her ear is a pink shell. Most of all, he feels entrusted with her future. His path is clear. They must run away. He will provide for her. His promise is a soft echo inside her head as she, in turn, vows to nurture and protect him.

The big why of everything is a large task for a six-year-old. Always, Leonardo demands: *dimmi*, show me. Prove it... tell me. Now there's a 'where?' and an urgent responsibility to find a place of safety from the chaos of the world. He is no longer alone.

Leonardo recites the story of the labyrinth and the Minotaur to Lisabetta. In his perverse way, Leonardo changes the fable to suit his purpose. He tells his sister of two children who follow the thread into the maze rather than out. The monster is only a bull, after all, and he talks to horses and cows, and will know what to say. The bull will listen and somewhere, lost inside its lair of twisting tunnels, Antonio Buti, or Piero da Vinci, or his mother's God, will never find them.

Lisabetta gurgles and waves at bird shadows. "I am your brother," Leonardo says. She blesses them: The Mother, the brother, and the Holy Ghosts in the sky.

"Take me home. I'm hungry," Lisabetta gurgles.

Leonardo lifts Lisabetta from the wildflowers and lays his cheek on her head. "I've been waiting for you," he whispers, cuddling her close. "I thought you would never come."

chapter thirty-one

The Retrograde Moon

THE TOWN OF VINCI
AUGUST – 1458

The weathered stone font in the church of Santa Croce in Vinci is the site of Leonardo's first holy bath. It makes a fine story. Caterina retells it on one of the days she is well. Leonardo is happy to see his mother smile, but reluctant to let her hold her daughter. Most of the time Caterina cries and stares at the wall.

Leonardo cuddles Lisabetta and listens to Caterina. This story links them together and it is important to ask questions. "At your christening," Caterina says to Leonardo, "there were nine godparents."

"Where are they now? Why do they not visit?" Leonardo asks. "Why does my father not want to see me?" All nine godparents have disappeared into their own histories and left his blank. His past is a cloudless sky. These missing well-wishers and relatives had surely been the birds meant to fill it. "I will go to each one, and ask them to visit Lisabetta," he declares.

Caterina reminds Leonardo that he has met one or two of his godparents on the saints' days in Vinci. Leonardo vaguely remembers being presented and expected to speak rather than stare. He had tried to remember why these well-dressed strangers were of interest to his mother. Their manners towards him told him he was *insignificante*. Flawed and of no consequence.

There were rare times when Leonardo glimpsed his father in Vinci. Leonardo fixed on him like a cat after a mouse but his father refused to look back. Piero da Vinci always makes sure he sees someone or something behind his son. Once Piero noticed a pair of wide eyes staring at him from between two women and had been puzzled. When he recognized Caterina, he'd turned away.

It has been four months since Lisabetta's birth and Caterina still slips in and out of a private dream where she cries and curls into a ball. Antonio and his mother are furious, but Leonardo has occasion to thank his mother for her illness. When everyone in the family is busy, he is given Lisabetta.

Leonardo washes Lisabetta and fastens fabric around his waist in a knotted sling so she can travel wherever he goes. He takes her into his church of hills and valleys and trees, and together they count the bird-gods in the sky.

Caterina has days when she refuses to talk or eat. She acts as if Lisabetta is invisible. Nothing can persuade her to focus her eyes. Antonio says she's mad... her boy has always been loco. He rides to Vinci to petition Leonardo's grandfather. It's time for Leonardo to go. He is acting even more strangely. Leonardo is the cause of Caterina's disruption. He guards Lisabetta like a dog... sings and talks to her. Perhaps school?

Leonardo devises a canopy of branches and nails it above Lisabetta's cradle. He hangs shapes cut from leather: a star, a triangle, and a bird. He strings a feather and a blown egg, and hangs them as well. Lisabetta spends hours watching them while Leonardo watches her. When Antonio sees the contraption he tears it down and feeds it to the brazier. The egg rolls away and Antonio crushes it like a fragile skull. Leonardo grabs at the ornaments as they're tossed into the flames.

Leonardo's da Vinci grandfather agrees it's time Leonardo attends school. The da Vinci patriarch has the right to take him. Lisabetta is pried from her brother's arms and he's forced to mount his grandfather's great horse, bundled like kindling. He is returned to the da Vinci fold, carried as dead weight and deposited in a room of his own.

　　　　　　　　　　　LISABETTA – A STOLEN GLANCE

Leonardo's mind twists into a resistant knot of cool defiance. A six-year-old boy, almost-seven, has no power. He rolls himself into the bedclothes like a swaddled baby. He thinks to himself: *this is how life will stay if I remain helpless. This is how Lisabetta felt.* The only roles he can play from this house are dutiful grandson and alienated brother. *Lisabetta, why can I see your face everywhere?*

The first night away from Lisabetta, before he forgets, Leonardo draws what he remembers of her: a lock of fair hair curled into a circle, a rosebud mouth, and the outlines of a bird, an egg, and a feather, inside a triangle.

It is morning when Leonardo unclenches his fist. In his hand, is a crushed leather star.

During the first estranged months from Lisabetta, on trips to Florence, Leonardo is fascinated by street faces – drawn to the deformed beggars of the city. When he sees them, he leans in for as close a look as he's allowed, recording their twisted faces, warts, and rubbery lips. He is pulled away, but is determined to ask questions. Always Leonardo has questions. Many years later, when Leonardo is troubled, these are the deformed faces which appear in the blank spaces between his cruel designs for war machines. Demonic faces come to haunt his most violent creations. They spring from Leonardo's pen so often, he is unaware of their subliminal presence.

Leonardo surrenders to the abacus school with a purpose. He will gain back his sister by pleasing his father. He will defy the rules. The da Vinci patriarch may have ordered Leonardo to never return to Campo Zeppi, but grandfathers of his advanced age are a small matter. Death will take him, and not soon enough.

In his dreams, Leonardo tells Lisabetta to wait. "Don't cry," he says. "I will come for you."

Lisabetta calls back "Please hurry." She's a fussy baby, unused to waiting.

For all our seasons of feast and famine, birth and death visited my brother more lightly in the spring. I am grateful for his sake. Although my arrival in his life brought a degree of unease that changed the way Leonardo viewed women. Even though my brother retained a lifelong fascination for the human deformities of the street, and compulsively documented the grotesques of madness, the horrifying trauma of childbirth deeply shook his refined sense of delicacy and offended his fastidious nature. Leonardo was meticulous to a fault. He pushed marriage and fatherhood from his mind.

Never one to forsake a challenge, years later, Leonardo's aversion to female genitalia emboldened his anatomical studies when he dissected the corpse of a pregnant woman, documenting the womb with meticulous precision. His courage precipitated a new standard of medical research.

But in spite of his reticence to procreate, Leonardo delighted in children and was a wonderful mother to me when Caterina turned away from me. My mother was bedridden and deranged in the aftermath of producing an anonymous daughter. She had lost the only race she cared to win and never fully-recovered from her last chance at the da Vinci crown.

~ Lisabetta

  LISABETTA – A STOLEN GLANCE

Part Three

Second Childhood

"And so we beat on,
boats against the current,
borne back ceaselessly into the past."
~ F. Scott Fitzgerald

chapter thirty-two

*"One rarely recovers
from answered prayers."*
~ Veronica Lyons

Peacock Truth

POINT ROYAL PARK, HALIFAX, NOVA SCOTIA
JULY 1 – 2003

Baby Jupiter, fourteen-months-old, snuggles under several blankets in his pram, and scans the canopy of leaves and branches for monkeys. Beside him, the Monday morning duck pond in Point Royal Park is deserted. Its stone bench is an abandoned bookshelf that seats two birdwatchers like bookends, far enough apart to be solitary.

Veronica gazes past the oily slick of water lilies and fallen leaves, and imagines the tip of Excalibur breaking the surface to emerge in the fist of a goddess. The woman almost next to her is a black and white nun. The silence requires a courteous something. It's chilly for July.

A peacock shriek startles Veronica with a shrill of wild kingdom reality. Peacocks are the antithesis of polite bird society. She rocks her son's baby carriage with a subconscious foot.

Veronica addresses the water. She hears her voice blurt: "I'm an atheist." It shocks her. Peacocks make people do odd things. Yes, it's the peacock's fault.

The nun is surprised, but she joins in as if the two have already established the etiquette of strangers' rapport. She corrects the informal blunder.

"Hello. I'm Sister Camilla." She looks amused.

Veronica turns towards the soft, apologetic voice. The exact sound she expects to issue from a nun. "Sorry that came out wrong. Veronica Lyons. Hi."

"People always want to discuss God with me. I can't imagine why."

"We assume he speaks to you directly. It's the outfit. You're very visible."

"Well, *She* doesn't." It's the expected New-Age feminine response.

"This is my son, Jupiter. He has autism."

"Are you always this blunt?"

"He can see you, but he won't look at you. He never looks at anyone. Only cats. Apparently bird-watching isn't on his list either. Can you tell he has aut..." she clears her throat. "...autism from his eyes? Can you tell?"

"Perhaps he's distracted from listening to God."

"I said I was an atheist."

"Well, maybe *he* isn't," Camilla says.

"I'm never going to get my head around that possibility."

"Brains aren't called grey matter for nothing. The truth is always grey."

"What can he ever learn?"

"Well, he's probably a teacher."

"My uncle and I are in the science business. Reality is our religion. Five-hundred-years ago, your church would have considered my son possessed. Maybe it still does."

Camilla spends a few seconds to examine the sadness in Veronica's face. "You look troubled."

"Yes, well, I have a big decision to make."

"The rock and a hard place kind?"

"Yes."

Sister Camilla twists in her seat and leans towards Veronica with a Gioconda smile. "Good, those are the easy ones," she says.

chapter thirty-three

Peacock Lies

POINT ROYAL PARK, HALIFAX, NOVA SCOTIA
JULY 1 – 2003

Veronica thinks the Lady of the Lake must be laughing under the water as she watches bubbles breaking on the surface of the pond. They set the floating water-lilies in motion. A human sigh pushes them into the shadows. It will rain soon.

"In one way, I envy my son," Veronica says. "He'll never have to decide anything. Autism runs in our family. Some genetic flaw. My Aunt Bea stares at birds for hours. With Jupiter, it's cats."

"Lost souls are God's business, not ours," Sister Camilla says.

Here we go, Veronica thinks. "Then your God should be reported to the Better Business Bureau, or the SPCA," she says. "He has suspect business practices – a typical CEO. Cruel enough to step on his own ants."

Camilla expects more, and Veronica continues: "My son's... *father...* suggests I place Jupiter in an institution. So, there it is, another ant hill for your God to flatten. There's no hope for a miracle. My son's father is ruled by a wealthy mother, who calls the shots. She's Medusa incarnate."

Sister Camilla rises to the challenge: "Grace isn't luck, and it doesn't descend from the sky like pixie dust. God doesn't play with magic wands. *He or She* uses synchronicity. So, as another wise man said: *'do or do not, there is no try'*, but at least discover the surprise."

"Yoda? You're quoting Yoda?"

"Yes Ma'am."

"Yoda is Catholic?"

"You see? Surprises. You've discovered that nuns watch movies."

Veronica and the day absorb this amazing fact. It isn't profound or new, but it settles on the two women and makes it easier for them to talk. A small, well-known secret has made them companions – intimate enough to argue and badger with no hard feelings, or at least feelings which can be smoothed over politely for the sake of anonymous kinship.

"It's easy for you," Veronica says. "You drop your problems at the feet of ceramic saints every five minutes."

"You could do that if you wanted to."

"Well I don't happen to believe in the wisdom of inanimate objects. But you think you're married to God, so you'll pretty much believe anything."

"No, God is my father-in-law. I married his son."

"Shouldn't that be *mother*-in-law? Still, it looks good on the resume. Besides, phantom husbands are convenient. No faking headaches or the nightly Passions-of-Christ... scuze the heresy, and an omnipotent patriarch calling the shots to boot. So, did you ever give the Almighty a grandchild?"

Camilla hums a recognizable tune. She sings a line to Jupiter as she touches his fingers. His eyes flicker towards her song, but return to his wildlife vigil when it ends. *"We are stardust we are golden, and we've got to get back to the garden."*

"So, which disciple said that?"

"Matthew," Camilla says, "Matthews' Southern Comfort. You know – the hit song, *'Woodstock'*? 1969?... Saint Joni?"

"That was ten years before I was born."

"Well great music is reborn every few years. So stay tuned."

"I will."

"Are you New-Age enough to believe in rebirth?" Camilla asks. "We founded a mishmash church-of-all-sorts. We were religious about our beliefs, but we couldn't decide which one, and all faiths lumped together, muddy things up – by the way, that was *my* tough decision. In the end it was simple." Camilla flounces her veil. "I loved the outfit. This was my invisibility cloak, and I loved that I could disappear – evaporate from... things. Many things. But here we are, and you think I stand out."

Veronica grins. "You were a hippy!" It's almost an accusation.

"No, I was just irresponsible, but I prefer the term flower-child. There's a big difference."

"No, there isn't."

"The sixties are a past-life. I had a child from that little party. I gave him up for adoption. So... so much for peace and love. The peace movement had the molecular structure of cheese. Mice loved it, but sheep don't eat cheese, and we were sheep."

"I thought Christians were supposed to be lambs, you know, following the great white shepherd into a heaven beyond the stars, and all that?"

"Ah, well, the great thing about stars, is they make pictures in the sky, but you can't see a constellation until you connect the dots. Bigger pictures always require distance. The Flower movement was based on the '*me generation*' and never looked past immediate gratification. 'Loving the ones we were with' didn't bode well the morning after. Fortunately, every age has its own herald in sheep's clothing."

"So, what's ours then? Fair warning. If you quote anything astrological I will projectile vom...."

"It's still Star Trek." Camilla shrugs. "Sorry, it's kind of astrological."

"No, no, Star Trek is... I think of it as *creative* astronomy. It's only sun-signs that are bullshit. Sorry, but it's true. I thank God for reruns. My hero was Mr. Spock. Who was your favorite?"

"My favorite was the flawed one," Camilla says. "You know for an atheist, you invoke God a lot."

"You mean the captain?"

"No." Camilla smiles and shakes her head. "The female computer. I loved it when she said: '*working*' while she was thinking,

 LISABETTA – A STOLEN GLANCE

but they should have given her a name. She deserved that. Everyone deserves a name, and she worked hard, 24/7."

Veronica plays up the role of Captain: *"Stella, take a message: Captain's log, star date 2003. Petty science-officer, Veronica Lyons, has asked for shore leave. The transporter is out. In the meantime she is blathering on the holodeck. She has programmed a park scene where she meets a nun. I'm sending her to sickbay as soon as security comes to restrain her."*

Camilla answers in cyborg monotone: *"Working... follow the prime directive. Stay out of sight. Do no harm. Get out before the pitchforks arrive. Don't forget to thank God for Scotty and technology... and remember... Vulcan logic is full of shit. More holes than Swiss cheese."*

The word shit slaps the conversation serious. "You said shit," Veronica accuses. She laughs and tries to imitate Spock with a raised eyebrow. "Fascinating."

"I didn't say shit, the computer did," Camilla insists, but the shock takes the wind out of their conversation, and they stare at a mother duck and her ducklings, moving in a line like the targets of a shooting gallery.

chapter thirty-four

*"Beyond a wholesome discipline,
be gentle with yourself."*
~ The Desiderata – 1820

Peacock Promises

POINT ROYAL PARK, HALIFAX, NOVA SCOTIA
JULY 1 – 2003

Camilla, the Lady of the Flowers, lifts her face to the first raindrop kiss. A few more sprinkle over the pond like wedding rice. Soon the park will be umbrella territory.

"I have to give my answer tomorrow," Veronica says. "Is wool-gathering and meditating the same thing?"

"Yes."

"Then I should be enlightened by now don't you think?"

"You're stalling for time. You know you can only respond to a fake question with a fake answer. Serendipity is alive, but you can pretend to argue with it if you want to."

"So you're saying that I've been debating serendipity?" Veronica asks.

"You've been *praying*, Veronica."

"No Ma'am. I'm an atheist. Born and bred."

"Prayers have to percolate, rise to the surface and simmer slowly," Camilla says.

"Well they sound delicious. You're a great therapist, Santa Camilla del Fiore."

Sister Camilla smiles a question. "Well thank you for the promotion, although I'm not sure what it means."

"Sorry, I used to study Italian architecture and art at university. The Santa Maria del Fiore in Florence, is the only church I'm interested in exploring, and *Del Fiore* means *of the flowers*. And... the old name for Firenze, was Fiorenza, after their symbol, the Calla Lily. I see the word *'calla'* inside your name, Camilla. Coincidence? I can't help seeing words inside of words. I love anagrams. My name is an anagram. I expect you've heard of it. Veritas icona... true face."

"Your eyes got all bright just then."

"The Italian Renaissance is a subject that kind of carries me away. It's *my* religion. Well it used to be, but I still believe art is as close to divinity as life gets, and I thank you Saint Calla Lily, of the transcendental flower-power."

"No need to thank me, 'Saint Veronica of the true face'. I just sat here and watched the ducks while you prattled on. Anyway, whoever you're trying to convince, your little atheist prayers will be answered one way or another, so hang on to something solid."

"How does one ever know they've made the right choice? I mean when does the penny finally drop? Or does it, do you think?"

Camilla pretends to flip a coin in the air. Her eyes follow it, and she fakes its capture with the palm of her other hand. She raises it high in a triumphant toast between slender fingers. "A great philosopher, Piet Hein, once advised: to decide anything – toss a penny and play heads or tails. It won't matter how it lands because when the coin is in the air, you'll suddenly know how you *want* it to land. Veronica. You... are up in the air, and you know what to do." Camilla opens her hands as if to release a bird. She blows the fake coin from her hand, and mimics the surprised face of a magician amazed by his own trick.

Veronica applauds with slow-motion clapping. "So your religion thinks Jupiter is special?"

"I don't have high enough clearance to speak for Mother Church. Personally I consider your child to be... *um*..." The nun chooses her word carefully... "Selective. Deeply introspective."

"Nuns should be able to speak up for their Mother," Veronica says, and rustles a bag of birdseed at a pair of shimmering blue-green creatures approaching from opposite sides like hunting velociraptors. More iridescent turquoise heads waddle towards them from the pond.

"I think we give the 'Mother & Child' pretty good press. I see the peacocks and ducks have joined us."

"Yes, well only the drakes. They're more aggressive than the hens. Vanity gives them chutzpah."

"God does amazing work," Camilla says, deliberately sly.

"Your God's a man. A shrewd businessman."

"God's an artist. Male birds have to be more colorful in order to..."

"Sure, like red cardinals? And, I'd call the Pope a *human* peacock. No offense, but so is the parade of your plaster saints. Gaudy. It's even a nice pun. *'Goddy'*. I notice you're dressed conservatively for contrast. Minions wear brown and black. Nuns and monks and the poor." Veronica points to her camel coat and classic wellingtons. "Like me."

"Red shoes distract girls into big trouble," Sister Camilla says, waiting for the inevitable *'what would you know'* look, but it doesn't come.

Veronica stares hard at the water. "Yes, I know the fairytales – red shoes and glass slippers and cats wearing boots. Brothers' Grimm women may have been witches, or princesses, or peasants, but all of them were greedy or stupid and..."

"And they didn't fare too well as I recall," Camilla agrees. "Their stories were cleaned up for our generation. Cinderella is a rags-to-riches kind of girl. I'm the opposite: a silk-to-homespun story. What kind of story are you?"

Veronica lifts a cynical boot in the air and examines the leaves stuck to the leather toe. "Prince Charming was a creep with a foot fetish who didn't notice Ellie till she was dolled up. What does *that* tell you?" She tosses a handful of seeds into a cloud that peppers the ground into a food frenzy.

A peacock trumps the quacking with a piercing cry that fails to engage Jupiter. The child is busy communing with a black blob of liquid mercury that slithers over the branches as it darts and hesitates, and turns on a dime to listen to higher instructions. The squirrel god says climb. Squirrel appetite says approach. Even rodents have a tough time deciding greed from survival. Descents are dangerous.

Veronica watches the ducks scoot away from their flamboyant cousins. "Somebody's got to feed the underdog. The wife-birds in the nest. The bird-mothers teaching their chicks to swim and fly. They're the ones that have to squabble over the crumbs left behind... and what about the ugly ducklings that never turn into swans? The ones only a mother can love. What about them? And please don't tell me God watches over them. I apologize for my bluntness. I know it's rude. I guess I need to vent."

"It's called confession. I hear it's good for the soul."

A chuckle escapes Jupiter, and Veronica and Camilla turn to see a squirrel on his blanket, waving its tail in Jupiter's face.

Veronica imprints Camilla's veil, full skirt, shawl, and her 'Mona Lisa' smile. "No doubt."

There's a long pause while the lady of the lake takes back her magic offering. "I wish I'd never been born," Veronica says. "How's that for a confession? My mother thought so too, so... so much for mothers."

"And yet you champion them. You want to feed them."

"Mothers get hungry. I'm hungry. I bet that squirrel is a mom."

"I will pray for you both."

"Thanks, but I'd rather you didn't include me," Veronica says. "I'm sure you know the curse of answered prayers."

FROM THE DIARY OF VERONICA LYONS

- CAMILLA'S WISDOM -
JULY 10 – 2004

My wisdom teeth were removed this morning. I remembered Sister Camilla as I washed into Middle-Earth on Demerol wings. Her words of wisdom followed me a long way. She said not to confuse sacrifice with responsibility, and that loss was a necessary form of love. She said humans were inherently careless. She told me to make a wish, and to say hello to 'Mona Lisa'. She said her kind were half-a-million strong.

I saw that she carried a bridal bouquet of three white Calla Lilies against an Alice-blue wedding gown. She tucked one flower behind my ear, placed one on Jupiter's blanket, and before saying goodbye, she made the sign of the cross over him with the last lily as if it was a magic wand. She dubbed him 'everyone's child'.

The sweet scent of violets filled the operating room, making me sleepy, and cathedral bells blew me into heaven.

I dreamed that I laid a wreath of peacock feathers at the feet of a St. Christopher colossus, the patron saint of travelers, while the Nike of Samothrace stood to his left, tall as a pillar, like an approving wife. I heard the whoosh of a Star Trek door open and close as I was whistled aboard my own ship with its engines engaged in a buzzing of bees.

I noticed the smiling eyes of a nurse above a surgical mask. When she winked I recognized her as my Aunt Bea. The crown of an oak tree made a halo behind her head – its branches swarming with turquoise monkeys. She held up a canary, perched on the tip of her finger for me to kiss, but it turned and tapped its golden tail on my lips. "I call tails," she said... and then: "Choose... chicken or egg... step right up... duckling or swan... place your bets".

Her nurse's uniform changed to the habit of a Franciscan nun, but the robes were covered in Vegas sequins.

I heard the seductive tease of a spinning roulette wheel and the gentle plop of the white ball as it decided my fate. The ball was an egg. I had chosen. My winnings were pushed towards me with a crucifix. The croupier was a gypsy woman with an enigmatic smile. She knew something.

She winked again, took the egg and crushed it silently, reverently with kindness, while she stared into my eyes. It was empty. She blew the shattered shell from her hand as easy as pixie dust.

Mr. Hein had been right. I knew what to do. I tossed my problem into the clouds, caught my decision in midair, and the coin disappeared. I looked up where it had momentarily eclipsed the sun, and the sky turned to night. My Uncle Oz smiled down at me through a firmament of stars. He told me to connect the dots counting backwards from one hundred and one. It made the shape of a boot and I spun into the star called Florence.

— Veronica

chapter thirty-five

Milestones

THE TERRIBLE TWOS
Jupiter age two

Jupiter Lyons dreams in surprises. His attention surfaces from time to time. The world grates against his skin, filtered through bright static. Sound-scapes arrive out of focus, brittle and loud and startle him. He's a tender two-year-old, lost in a haze of autism – a child who plays hide-and-seek with the world.

The child is a consummate escape artist, and when his mother initiates connection, Jupiter looks through her until they physically drift apart. Looking and seeing are different.

Jupiter is amused by even numbers and a desire for squares. Squares are comfortable. He's on a constant quest for triangles. Triangles can't tip over. He chatters in cat-speak to his furry subjects, Pico and Nattie, with rapt adoration, eyes half-closed.

Jupiter's out-of-focus smile echoes the one that stares from the otherworldly 'Mona Lisa' poster in his mother's kitchen.

Somewhere behind the 'no trespassers' sign in his eyes, are windows closed tight to keep in his light. Inside, lie brightly illuminated conversations, and scraps of songs, and childish passions, and tidy piles of unmet needs tied up with clean ribbons.

Stretched out from a thought no bigger than the dot of an 'i' is an extraordinary energy which intermittently circles the perimeter to paw at four swinging doors. Jupiter's vocal chords are a tangled ball of silent opinions. His stillborn questions wait behind a corridor of blue doors.

From under each door protrudes an electric string humming with the first sound.

Veronica endures her son's *'terrible two's'* with fear softened by mood-altering medication.

If Veronica had been counting, she would have noticed how her Pan-child collates his life in fours: Four building blocks. Four bites. Four steps. Each wall in Jupiter's universe holds a leaded window divided into four. Each pane frames a white landscape, barren but for sixteen felines chasing their tails in a funhouse mirror. Each door is a deeper shade of sky blue. Four-times-four is perfection. Sixteen plaintive mews fill the room, distributed evenly with grace. Jupiter counts them all day long.

THE ILLUMINATING FOURS
Jupiter age four

Jupiter's Leo dolls are a species unto themselves. He clutches a stuffed lion toy in his right hand while he crayons with the other. Three identical lions sit in a row on the windowsill. Veronica assigns each of them a number, but her son knows them by their distinguishing characteristics. Jupiter's lions are quadruplets with singular power.

The Children's department of 'Knights Bookstore' had been deserted when Veronica rolled a shopping cart past a wire bin of stuffed animals marked: CLEARANCE – *buy one, get one free* – $4.99. She noticed they were all 'seconds' – discounted goods. Jupiter made his mother stop, and examined the contents so carefully that Veronica waited long past the allotted time for idle browsing. She studied her son like a scientist – a fallen star in a petri dish waiting to be discovered.

Jupiter sorted them. Colored critters were thrown back like undersized fish. Jupiter collected a pile of white lions. He held them up, compared faces, and discarded until four 'keepers' were left. One of the 'keepers' was the least damaged of the bunch. The remaining three were odd choices.

They all had buttons for eyes, a felt triangle nose and ears stuck on with dodgy glue, and mouths stitched carelessly in black yarn. His unnatural selection favored the haphazard over symmetry. Except for that most perfect, *'one'*, the lions represented a Darwinian pool of endangered species: a motley specimen with one ear, another with a sad expression, and one with a leg dangling by a thread.

Before they reached the checkout, Jupiter had torn off three eyes and tossed them overboard with two ears and a tail.

The purchases never made it into a plastic bag. Jupiter crushed them together, receipt and all, as if they were one creature. Every manufacturer's tag had to be removed in the car. Jupiter watched, flailing like a jumping bean until his new friends were freed from labels with his mother's manicure kit. There could be no identifying brands and washing instructions to identify they were toys. His lions were living creatures. Staples and plastic strings are bad. Taboo buttons had to be replaced with thread later. Jupiter painstakingly adjusted each lion's face.

From then on the foursome travelled as Jupiter's companions, although Veronica noticed that one toy was always favored, riding shotgun in the car or propped beside Jupiter's dinner plate or cuddled to sleep. It took months to realize that the 'Leo' her son carried matched his mood. It was the best ten dollars Veronica ever spent.

Mother and son make gingerbread men. Veronica rolls the spicy dough thick, and lets Jupiter work the cookie cutter. He guards the first batch while they cool and takes frequent glances at the second tray, still baking.

When it's time to decorate, Jupiter tells his mother "no buttons – no buttons – no buttons". She leaves the gingerbread tummies bare and squeezes icing dots for eyes on all but the one Jupiter snatches one away. He presents the bare cookie to Leo Four – the lion with no face.

He takes a second gingerbread man, scrapes off one of its eyes while it's still soft, and pops the sweet dot into his mouth. The one-eyed cookie is delivered to Leo Two, the doll with one eye, one ear, and one leg.

Jupiter squirms happily, adapting cookies three and four to suit Leo's three and four. Four cookie doppelgangers are matched to their twin dolls. Veronica is rewarded with a leg hug. Jupiter licks off the icing smile of a fifth cookie and eats it's head before giving it to his mother. Veronica stares at her gingerbread man as if it's a voodoo doll.

The next day, Jupiter exchanges his happy-face lion for the one with no ears, mouth, nose, eyes or tail. Its three brothers are propped together in a haystack. Shortly after, Jupiter shuts down and enters one of his grey silences. The scene is eerie until she realizes it's authentic theatre... the elegance of communications from Jupiter is pure monkey-see-monkey-do. The fallout is immediate and positive. The consequences are startling. Awareness means paying closer attention until Jupiter's Rosetta Stone is decoded. She is a mom-anthropologist and her son is a civilization unto himself. Jupiter has assigned himself four personas, created lion clones of himself, and carries the 'lion of the moment' claiming his emotional territory with a recognizable flag.

Veronica need never ask 'how are you doing?' The answer is as plain as the nose on a lion's face. Jupiter's choices have been clearly identified. His lions are his inside voices that say: leave me alone, I'm not feeling well, yes, that one please, and sometimes, albeit rarely, please hug me.

Jupiter's language is an alphabet of shapes and colors and numbers. He arranges cubes of food into rows of even numbers. Geometric shapes are validated in order. Squares and cubes are favored. Triangles are a close second. Spheres and circles are systematically discarded.

His room can be read like body language. His toy chest is an untapped encyclopedia. Veronica lists its treasures against the contents of a shortbread tin of clearly unwanted minutiae: a tartan ribbon, buttons, and marbles. Orange is clearly not tolerated. M&M's, an orange string, orange crayons and orange markers.

Veronica reads hers son as she would face any foreign language. She checks Jupiter's eye movements towards Leo One for yes and Leo Four for no. What Veronica fails to hear is Jupiter whispering privately with Leo One – the special times, when Jupiter calls Leo One, Dad.

Eyes are tricksters, and like the Mona Lisa, Jupiter's lions have no eyebrows to determine mood. Veronica replaces their button eyes with crosses of thick black darning wool. Jupiter stays close, watching the needle move in and out. "An X is four triangles in an invisible square," he says.

The Leos are sewn from unbleached linen, mannequin-style, with two dangling arms and legs. Leo One looks happy, Two appears angry after Jupiter draws claws onto its paws with a black marker. Three is sad and anxious – armless and clawless, impervious to hugging, Four is vacant of any expression minus eyes and nose and mouth. Its arms are wrapped around its body, tied in a knot behind its back in a self-hug of defense against depression, anxiety, and disinterest.

Leo Four represents Jupiter's overwhelming need to shutdown by absorbing every negative emotion that plagues him. Jupiter counts his 'family' after each move of a checker on a black or red square. He counts them into a four after every fourth move. The round plastic discs have been pushed under the carpet and replaced by small blocks. He uses his left hand to perform the rites of building, and to eat, and to squeak his colored markers across seas of clean white paper. He loves the smell and sound of them.

His mother's voice penetrates his task, but in no way disrupts his concentration. Voices are separate entities that fly overhead like birds. He counts the three pillows on the couch. There should be four. Four is better. Jupiter's eyes get lost in the tangled squares of a plaid blanket. His mother has yet to understand that squares need to float free of each other.

Plates without borders spill food. Blank paper is a dangerous place for drawings until Jupiter connects four lines into a fence. He can relax when his drawings can't run off the edges. With this comforting thought, Jupiter dismisses the world to count the handful of cheese cubes which descend from his mother's sky. They land in a heap. One or two form a crooked line. Jupiter counts eleven cubes and makes a fuss. Veronica deposits another handful that brings Jupiter's treasure to seventeen. Instead of protesting, he discards one and arranges the others in a grid: four rows of four cubes before he eats them. His mother's willfulness is a constant source of agitation. He has been teaching her the art of the squares for a long time.

Jupiter wants his plate to descend without food first. He likes to contemplate its emptiness before it is inhabited by foreign colors and shapes that fight. Orange cheese is an insult to perfection. White cheese is best. Pale yellow is acceptable. He has to prepare the battleground plate for what will materialize. This time his fear subsides. Four rows of four morsels is a war won. Soon his mother will be on his side. He has one square plate with a blue border that he likes. The round ones were returned after their contents were deposited onto a square drawn on paper.

Veronica had understood the first rule of the square. She assumes Jupiter wants finger food, but when peas are presented there is holy hell. The green beads are hurled into an angry cloud. Grapes are rolled aside and discarded behind plants or pushed down the sides of the sofa cushions. Veronica finds them everywhere. The world is a dangerous place of fives and seventeens and spheres.

Leo Three stares at a plate of five savory bites. The solution is quick. Jupiter smiles at Pico rolling around the cheese cube thrown in his direction. Veronica tells him that lions are cats.

"Cats are the best things," Jupiter announces at age four, with a clincher that shocks Veronica: "God must be a cat," he says.

Faeries and ghosts had often made guest appearances in Jupiter's books, but never, ever … God. God was a concept that had never been approached.

Mother and son enjoy a backyard picnic. Jupiter sits on an island of blue blanket in a grass sea. He kneels in the center and surveys the lawn for weeds. He looks like Aladdin scanning the earth below from his magic carpet. He declares "Dandy lions must be left to grow," with authority.

His *'dandies'* are in agreement. It's five against one. Veronica will be stuck with an un-neighborly spread of green with yellow polka dots if she complies. If she doesn't, the wrath of Leo Two will argue the dandelion's case with magic-marker claws. Veronica smiles and calls Jupiter's lions with their long stringy legs, are lanky-doodle-dandies which pleases him.

Doodles are his favorite art form.

- WINTER WASTELAND -
DECEMBER 1 – 2004

Rather never than late, the winter has come in like a lamb. The first innocent snow has whitewashed the world, but underneath lie all the same problems, feverish and hot. I can hear the second snow ... the lion's share, hanging heavy in the grey clouds, roaring.

I took Jupe to the window and showed him the snow, but he only saw the single snowflake that landed on cue on the glass in front of him. His breath made a patch of mist, and I took his finger and drew a happy face in it. I could tell his eyes didn't reach past it to the street.

I dressed Jupiter for the playground in the navy-blue one-piece snowsuit we found in a thrift store. The nylon fabric is imprinted with tiny silver snowflakes he insists are stars. He watched solemnly while I retrieved his mittens, dried on the radiator. I demonstrated how warm they were against his cheeks and threaded their string through his sleeves. He stood passively as a doll, while I stuffed his fingers into twin red cushions. Doll hands dressed by a little girl playing house.

The mittens reminded me of the time Basil and I made a crude telephone from a couple of tin cans strung together. It never worked, but we didn't need cans or even mouths to communicate, and when our snow fell, we zoomed. We frolicked. We raced toboggans down a hill steep enough to make Cate crazy. Well, crazier.

Jupiter stood like a sentry, arms at his sides. Autism etiquette meant he endured being dressed. His eyes stared through me like pieces of coal. I tied a red wool scarf around his neck, buttoned three lumpy buttons, deposited a red and white striped toque on his head, and tweaked his carrot nose as a finishing touch. Dressing Jupiter was like building a small snowman – too old for a soother. Too young for a pipe.

He remained unresponsive until I rattled the nut jar. Hearing him say 'skwirls' made me sad. His one-word gem broke the silence like the last icicle in the world, falling. Meaningless potent conversations. Jupe and I are minimalists. Marginal souls.

The word 'skwirl' was a question as well as a statement. It meant: 'are we going to feed the squirrels?' as much as, 'yay! ... we're going to feed the squirrels!' The enthusiasm is mine. I have never heard Jupe say 'hooray' in any language, or seen him express joy before he meets the squirrel or cat face-to-face. Afterwards, yes ... he radiates life. He will melt a little... or a lot. Animals animate him. Creatures jumpstart his brain across miles of white static. It's awful to imagine that his own storms of whiteout terrors may be worse than mine.

When his 'skwirl friends' appear, Jupiter's eyes are bright windows and mine require windshield wipers. I fastened Jupiter into a pine chair with runners for legs. It has arms like a red steel cage, and the word 'Flyer' written on the side – a child's chariot pulled by a mother horse. I felt harnessed. Held back. I wanted to run, but I was compelled to drag a loaded sled.

I don't think of Jupe as a burden, but somehow I feel reduced to a beast. No thoroughbred prancer, but a slow ox hauling a mute Raggedy Andy, bundled into a limp, red, silver, and blue package.

Other kids wave their arms and shriek giddy-up! We are plodders. I was yoked to a steady walk with no jingle bells. Jupiter glided. I guess it's a form of flying. I tramped and the sleigh marks covered my tracks.

The playground had disappeared under a white cloth. It looked like an abandoned room with furniture draped in dust sheets. Jupiter looked like a three-year-old astronaut landed on the moon ... a red-white-and-blue icon covered in stars and stripes deciding where to plant a flag.

He stood surveying an alien landscape and finally headed for the moon-squirrels. He moved deeper into wonderland – a ghostly field with crystal swings and a white seesaw, surrounded by trees made of lace. Snow collected in the empty wading pool. I had the impression of cold flakes softly falling like frosted cereal in a bowl. I watched a mental Christmas movie – a poignant scene with a muted soundtrack. Jupiter called out 'Skwirl' three times and his words rebounded from tree-to-tree. I had to look into the sun to keep from crying again. Life is unfair.

I looked back at him, wandered away from me, and saw that he resembled a small statue that reminded me of a low gravestone. A cold shape that watched over the death of grass. There was Jupiter, scanning the distance beyond the edge of his latest thought. I called him and he turned at once, a frozen snowman with eyes made out of coal – his sweet mouth applied to a chilly expression, neither a frown nor a smile. It simply hung straight – a tiny horizon below eyes like two cities marked on the map of a lost world.

It saddens me that I have to leave him alone in his baby frontier – a glacier polished smooth of emotions with no dancing snowmen or snow angels in sight. Snow angels require lion snow, deep and feathery pillow snow... wintery thick carpet snow... mauve powder-puff snow.

I wish Jupe and I could live inside a snow globe with a microscopic zoo – safe from the greater food-chain of society. A contained world of warm blizzards, swirled for pleasure like a glass of fine brandy. A glass planet, tipped on its axis from the tailwinds of passing angels.

We caught snow on our tongues, and I covered his boots in snow, but there were no squirrels and I told my little garden gnome a ridiculous lie. I said they were away doing their Christmas shopping. To change the subject I burst into song. I actually startled myself. Singing is not something that comes natural to me. Any returning, self-respecting squirrels would have headed for cover.

I sang the lyrics of 'Frosty the Snowman' to Jupe: 'was a happy happy soul'... 'there must have been some magic'... 'he began to dance around'... 'shouting catch me if you can...' but there was no magic in Jupiter's knitted red-striped toque with its sheepskin lining, and droopy earflaps, and blue pompom, and my song lacked the music of a happy soul. Each note hit a floating crystal star in a digital snow-wars game and was blown out of the sky. Did I mention that life is unfair?

Jupiter was not wearing a top hat. His nose was not an orange carrot. The snow was not deep and crisp and even. It was movie-set drift of shaved soap that would be gone by noon. Not even enough to build a snow-child, but sufficient to trail thin parallel lines in the blue snow that were all that was left to show we had been there.

— Veronica

"C'mon Jupe, catch the lobe," Veronica says rolling a ball towards her son. Strictly speaking it's not a ball. It's a blue hedgehog squeak toy with rubber spines. Veronica is advised to correct Jupiter's mirror speech rather than encourage the permanent repetition of backward pronunciations. Back words. Some days, some words, some moods. When asked, Jupiter says his absent father, Niles, is a lion or a river, but 'Mom' always comes out the same.

There are times Veronica's thoughts are as scrambled as Jupiter-speak. She grasps onto the end of his sentences and follows them to an audible code... an object's identity translates. It's how Veronica knows the name Niles is more than a river and that a 'loob lobe' is a blue ball.

Names of things are ethereal attachments. Word associations leapfrog from lily pad to lily pad at the speed of autism. Jupiter calls a chair a sitting cube.

The night Jupiter chooses to camp out in a pup tent beside his bed, Veronica's brain shuffles the insistent images of pyramids and cones, and fire that haunt her dreams. She collates pictures and sounds, into a nightmare collage of the past. She was six when Basil was killed by a wild campfire.

Basil's tepee had caught a rogue spark, flashed the wilderness like a midnight torch, and dimmed Veronica's light forever. She is left to find her brother in stolen pockets of time where they wander together in the shadows of afterlife communication. They stop talking regularly after Jupiter is born, but Veronica continues to avoid fireplaces, favoring plastic coal and electric flames that mime the ability to burn yet fulfill the primal human need for hearth.

Veronica and Basil's twin teddy bears, Alice and Arthur, sit back-to-back on a small chair, above the separation of death. Their animation is contained – imprints of their princess and prince are forever present in their toy memories. When Veronica reads to Jupiter, the bears join the four Leos. They make a stable family of eight, not counting Pico, Nattie and Peyton. Jupiter tries not to count them together. Eleven is not a good number. He's looking for a twelfth life to join his team. Better yet, five more lives. His favorite number is four times four. Sixteen makes a perfect family.

When she collects the laundry, Veronica finds Leo Four with his head wrapped in a green sock. Jupiter fails to acknowledge her presence. His

   LISABETTA – A STOLEN GLANCE

eyes are all about the wood and plastic and fabric blocks he collates in order of the color spectrum by sheen, texture, and ascending size. All day, Veronica has been jousting with eyes. When she addresses Jupiter, she knocks at the door to his mind, but the child refuses entry.

Jupiter pushes Arthur and Leo One under his mother's arm while she naps. Veronica wakes and scrapes ingredients together that loosely resemble a buffet supper.

Jupiter had dictated a short list of preferences by way of reaction. A food is presented. The child expresses rejection or acceptance. Mother and son dutifully comply with pediatricians and science, and when Jupiter's learning curve gasps for lack of progress, a regime of trial and error medication and food supplements are shuffled into his diet. The list gets shorter. The days feel longer.

Jupiter passes on bright-colored food. The orange of cheddar means war. White Havarti is deliciously quiet. He refuses spheres of any flavor. The green grapes are the right color. The purple ones have two counts against them. Cantaloupe balls are objectionable by sight, shape, color, and scent. One count is all it takes to be out of order. It takes a year to realize the only solid things Jupiter will eat without protest are squares or cubes: white cheese, croutons, crackers, toast with crusts removed, and miniature marshmallows. These few delicacies are Veronica's maternal peace offerings.

Veronica clues in after a sliver of pear makes the no plate, and she dices it up for a salad. Jupiter's small hand reached into the bowl, and separates each cube from the orange segments and honeydew balls. Miraculously, apples, pears and honeydews can be cubed.

Browsing a flea market, Veronica finds an antique sugar spoon with a square bowl. She calls it Jupiter's 'runcible' spoon, an homage to one of his favorite stories about an owl and a pussycat. It's a magic shovel that delivers soup, oatmeal minus blueberries and raisins, and any crunchy cereal woven into squares that float in milk. She makes 'picky plates' – rows of food cubes on a square white napkin with a border pattern.

It becomes obvious that Jupiter prefers china without patterns. Then a gift arrives. An 'Alice in Wonderland' place-setting decorated with the Cheshire cat, another of Jupiter's beloved characters. Jupiter is confused. He wants the square plate, but can't touch the shine of it. The cat is trapped there. He becomes so distraught, Veronica hides it away disappointed. Jupiter calls out: "Lisa-Lisa-Lisa" and she retrieves her son's 'Alice book' so he can see the cat illustration, safe on paper. Jupiter carries the book under his arm for the rest of the day.

It's only by accident that Veronica has delivered four crackers. It will take more time to realize Jupiter's counting tricks, and his obsession with even stacks and straight rows. That night he refuses to settle under a plaid throw. He cuddles his happy blanket of crocheted squares, and throws hers into the laundry basket. His fingers explore the familiar squares like Braille, consumed with happiness now that some perfect thing has finally arrived. He is grateful. Tapping his mother's hand four times is as close to a goodnight kiss as she's ever received.

She leaves the room in semi-darkness. A Cheshire Cat nightlight glows a few inches from the floor. Jupiter still clutches his 'Alice Book', and falls asleep with three lion dolls arranged in a row on his pillow. He hugs one of them tight. Tonight it's Leo One.

It's the extension of an understanding. The higher awareness of four is imparted. The deciphered code brings stillness to the illuminated space they now share. The magic of 'four-ness' reaches into a mother's exhausted consciousness. Right brain reads what has been there all along. A mother's discovery of communication. The principle of four is written on a mountainside in neon lights. All sign language is upgraded to high alert.

There are random meltdowns over colored bedsheets or a new brand of soap. Jupiter is an emotional monsoon over sensual details. Veronica introduces new things by gradual selection. Jupiter's rages are not the tantrums of a spoiled child. They're reactions to intrusive shapes or textures or sounds. He is an obsessive curator of the familiar. Safety is a frozen impression of intimate peace. New toys are chosen not given. Things wrapped in paper are traps. Jupiter touches the sheets and shirts and foods he considers worthy. It's futile to purchase otherwise.

Jupiter has his own theatre – a portable square DVD player he permits to be activated the same time each day. He allows himself only edited entertainment, patiently waiting for any movie which contains a cat. The anticipation cannot be exaggerated. First viewings are restless fidgets until, happily, a cat scene appears to relax and delight. Veronica is careful to screen for positive content. The mother & child connection is precariously balanced. Veronica reads her son as she would a book written in a foreign language. Every so often a familiar word jumps into consciousness and another fragile link is forged. Etymology rules.

On week sixteen, Jupiter's medication engages. A crack in his sky lets out the dark. He opens his eyes on a new world. First light is mystical. He squints into the pinpoint glow of blue light, blinking beside the bed, and touches the blue dot on the clock-radio. The tip of his finger surrounded by a halo of blue sparks makes him giggle.

The wonder of small things captivates him. Objects of mysterious beauty that were alien when he last closed his eyes, are benign objects. A snow globe is tipped in delight. The moon is a disk of happy magic. A single grape sings sweet and purple. Jupiter's kaleidoscope is tamed. Its moving prisms that used to overlap and shriek, are silent. The sharp edges of shapes and colors fail to leave bruises and sores.

Jupiter chooses a blue crayon, and writes the word cat backwards: *tac*. It stays quiet on the paper. He writes it again in purple. He opens the shortbread tin and finds an orange marker. He writes *cat* again, this time forwards. He replaces the marker in the box. Some changes take time. He rips the page out, crumples it, throws it on the floor, and watches Nattie pounce on it and tear it to shreds. He takes another sheet, draws a border, and writes two words.

Windows of the soul are meant to be opened. Jupiter meets his mother's eyes in a first hello. He hands her his paper. It reads Jupiter *lions*. He knew his name all along.

With a sense of irony, they return to the starting point of an old game board, and begin again at square one.

FROM THE DIARY OF VERONICA LYONS

- MIND SOUP -
HALIFAX – MAY 2 – 2006

My relationship has been patched so many times I'm in fear of disintegration. I could never resurrect the lie of Niles and I into a second, living breathing, chance. I'm not surprised to see his name contains the word 'lies'. Love tests ones capacity to accept evidences of serendipity. I find myself being careful to knit a blanket big enough to cover the entire dream.

Experience is a mind-soup that wants the spice of life added in great handfuls. Reality is an almost good man – a salt-of- the-earth pinch. One forfeits flavor for the blandness of safety. The taste of imaginary bliss is not worth the payoff… a quick-fix spiritual high followed by the crashing sound of derisive mockery, and after the dust settles, one has to mourn the loss of fantasy which is such a big death.

Materializing in two places at the same time defies science. A double life requires a dreamer and a waking dream that pays the rent. Fame is a speck of magic dust that aggravates someone else's eye.

— Veronica

FROM THE DIARY OF VERONICA LYONS

- SAINT LOBE -
HALIFAX – MAY 17 – 2006

Poor Jupiter... Lucky Jupiter! His 'lobe' rolled into the street and Peyton followed. I heard the car brakes squeal. Peyton is safe. The lobe was sacrificed and Jupiter required hot chocolate therapy in the middle of a heatwave.

I am in awe of Jupe's logic. After we say goodnight, he asks me to turn on the dark rather than turn off the light. I love that kid's mind.

— Veronica

chapter thirty-six

"I now begin my book,
'De ludo geometric
(On Geometric Games)
in which I show further ways
to infinity."
~ Leonardo da Vinci, 1514

Page One

FROM THE DIARY OF VERONICA LYONS
- SILENCE IS GOLDEN -

I need to write about the voice. I need to write about my brother. I need to write letters and telegrams and lists of questions to Basil.

The female haunting my ear has reached the stage of urgency that will not be denied. She insists it's long past the time for recording my thoughts. It's therapy, she says. I asked if it was for her or me. She answered 'us'.

It seems that only the black and white of paper will tame this madness. So, I am writing my memoirs to see if that suffices to send her packing or me spinning down a winding road to a home for the insane. She laughed at that and rebuked me. 'Had I considered it was possible to spiral *into* control,' she said. I hadn't.

Then she said something strange: *'History repeats in the name of comeuppance. Guilt on paper can be burned, but the flames of vanity never die.'*

Lucky me. Thought ghosts haunt harder than the regular ones. I'm hemmed in by mental demons with immortal thoughts. My kitchen has become a twee confessional for atheists.

A memoir feels redundant. A bit like dirty laundry washed in greasy water. Curses hanging up to dry in an airing cupboard.

My first three words were decided for me by Charles Dickens. I shamelessly borrow them in the spirit of great truth. Let the paper therapy begin.

Chapter One – CAMPO 'BAZZI'

BAZ WAS DEAD. Nothing else mattered after that. What more can be said, other than it was all Cate's fault. He died in a fire. I dreamed he died, the next morning it was true. He was gone, apart from lounging around in the shadows, because he stayed by my side in spirit form to comfort me. He is still around but he has things to do, or so he says.

Other than math, Baz continued to help me with my home-work. He gave me art lessons and encouraged me to paint. I distinctly remember him drawing an angel with no head. He tapped it several times and told me it was important for me to remember. I got mad and burned it under the Leo tree, which was a spiteful thing to do considering the circumstances of his death. I know now that it was 'the Nike of Samothrace'.

It disturbs him when I say it, but the truth is, I was always half of everything after his death. I was content to be erased. My existence meant nothing. I accepted being a lost soul. I was no-one without my brother. The trouble is, becoming pregnant required me to 'reincarnate' as a mother. I made an effort to locate the maternal gene inside me that Uncle Oz, my intrepid guardian, says exists, and stepped up. He ought to know, he's a geneticist. But I am still a twin, and being a spliced gene doesn't follow the general rules, and being half a mother half the time isn't half good enough.

The trouble is stepping up requires *staying* up. Mothering a special needs child requires a double helping of parenting skills. Uncle Oz has generously extended his devotion to Jupiter and I – the unwed 'Mother and Child' dependents. We sound like an iconic renaissance painting, and Oz studied us as if we were.

But that's his hobby. Uncle Oz researches the provenance of paintings and analyses their attributes hidden in plain sight: the brushstrokes, the DNA of materials, and the forensic ambiance of style attributed to the ghosts of master artists who linger in the air above the varnish. I almost believe him.

The years after great epochs attributed to AD are measured as After Death where hell begins.

I suffer misgivings about my ability to raise a special-needs child through small epochs. Until lately, I used to keep my insomnia-helpers in check, and tempting as they were, I never resorted to more addictive substances of distraction. Since I was diagnosed as bipolar last year, my regime has slipped into a dependent zone. The voice chides me and I know she's right.

When I was a child, my stepfather, Alan, always referred to his spiked ginger-ale as his 'medicine'. Basil had called them fizzy-dizzys. Avoiding a tipsy parent was enough to build a permanent wall between my low self-esteem and his peripheral alcoholism.

Besides, these days, I prefer my suffering served up-front and painful.

If only I'd gone camping with Basil, Jupiter would have another uncle. It was her fault for blocking their telepathic link after Baz had called her a selfish girl. 'Crazy girl', he'd called her. Crazy to prefer a tea party with old ladies over a camping trip to Cape Breton. "I hate hate HATE camping," she had replied, and stayed home in a sulk.

Tea with Aunt Bee turned out to be a punishment. Now, every cup begs the questions where and why. Why had I been a million light-years away at the wrong time. Cate's not the only one who feels entirely to blame.

Chapter Two – 'ARTISM'

Potato/potahto… autism/artism… let's call the whole thing fate.

Basil went camping with Dad but not me. Cate needed me home. They took the Indian tepee. My mother hates camping. Me

 LISABETTA – A STOLEN GLANCE

too. Instead we visited my Aunt Beatrice at the home. She is not like other people. She has 'artism'. She draws pictures backwards. She drew a picture of me sitting in a chair and made my feet first and then my knees and the ribbon in my hair last. My mother says she draws like she is knitting a scarf because it doesn't matter if you're knitting the beginning or the end of a scarf first.

My beloved 'Bee' pours pretend tea from her 'Alice in Wonderland' teapot. She lets me have the Cheshire Cat cup even though it's her favorite. She takes the dormouse cup. She has the best smile but her eyes look far away, the same way I looked for my cat, Spock, when everyone lies and tells me he's on his way home so I will stop pestering. I couldn't sleep until he was on my bed. Aunt Beatrice always looked as if she was looking for one of her cats when she asked me if I took pretend sugar in my make-believe tea. I wanted to click my fingers in front of her eyes and say hey, I'm over here.

My mother called her Alice, but I called her Aunt Bee. She doesn't like to be hugged. She hugs cats instead. She calls herself Lisa and me Caro. She pronounces some words backwards or repeats them over-and-over. My Uncle Oz called mom Cat or Dotty or Dodo; and me Toto; and Baz, Wizo. He called Aunt Bee, Birdie. Our family liked multiple names from books. We read them all the time. Baz and I even named the apple tree in our backyard. It was a boy tree and we named him Leo because we were Lyons, and the tree's crown looked like a tangled lion's mane. Baz was crazy brave. He climbed way up high and dared me to join him. He said the view was futuristic. He said one could see into next week, but I wouldn't go. I had... *have*, a fear of heights.

I liked to draw too. My mother said I was artistic so I thought I would have to live in a special place when I got older. It never bothered me because you could have several cats where Aunt Bee lived, and Baz, the consummate artist, would live there as well. Baz doesn't like tea.

Tonight it was thundering and lightning. Spock arrived home, bedraggled and scared and hid under my blankets. I watched the storm from my window and Leo waving his branches, telling me to stay inside. I saw Baz clinging up high when the lightning came, but I was imagining things. He wasn't there. He was camping.

I should have gone with him. Cate shouldn't have made me stay home.

When Cate came in to say goodnight. I told her something felt bad. She called me a worrywart. It was just the storm, but I knew Baz was scared. I heard him calling me 'crazy girl', like always, but this time he wasn't teasing.

I am the sister of Baz. His twinned soul. The keeper of his spirit. He's trapped inside a silver locket I wear for companionship. It's easily opened for a quick consult or a long conversation, and sometimes, a warning. I am Baz's second chance to shine. He is my only chance to survive.

Chapter Three – A DREAM OF <u>FIRENZE</u>

By the time I was eighteen, I wasn't afraid to dream anything. Except for the 'burning dreams'. But even then, waking agitated, I was happy to have felt my brother so close again. His presence in my repetitive dream no doubt caused me to retain it, although as dreams go, it was beyond lucid. I was there, in Florence, at the Vanity Fire again, and it was as familiar to me as the shoreline of St. Margaret's Bay.

In the morning, the bathroom mirror reflected red and swollen eyes from crying or the smoke of the fire... maybe both. This is what I remember. Brutally clear as yesterday.

I instinctively recoil from a burst of orange sparks, spat from the fire's heart, and note the spectators to my left before I take a deep breath and wade nine feet into the white hot crucible of scorching wood. Basil calls me in and an unknown woman has my back. I hear my brother's voice say: "I'm coming out, crazy girl" from inside the fire, but I can't wait to see him, and so I run ahead to meet him.

There was a hole in the blazing construction – a window, shaped like a triangle. It widens into a door with a pointed arch. I enter a golden pyramid – a roaring lion's cave of flame, hissing with snakes.

The heat is intense. A bright tingle of electricity brushes against my skin. Having molecules firmly based five-hundred years from this spot, I don't ignite or feel the searing pain of burning flesh, nor do I choke on the belching smoke.

I used to think that all bonfires were systematically constructed cairns piled into circular mounds – all the better for gathering around, but the one I breached was no cone-shaped pyre. It was a long barricade of unstable burning rubble where low sections periodically coughed sour clouds of green fumes. It was packed with treasures: paintings of Greek gods, gilded mirrors, gaming boards and jewels, all crushed together, held captive in a web of branches which looked like the claws of a thousand demons.

Baz was not inside, so I left the heart of fire and stood outside the blaze. There were a few street urchins and their canine siblings lingering within earshot, who slunk the perimeters of destruction. They give the flames a wide berth, and I notice several clumps of human stragglers huddled together in random gatherings of worshippers and thugs. I'm not surprised they acte like paid mourners, howling and carrying on in a command performance of fake repentance. The raging monk Savonarola, required a show of solidarity, and the citizenry was terrified enough to act as submissively as they could.

The tall shape of Giotto's Campanile wavers in and out of focus behind a haze of smoke and cinders, giving the impression it's about to topple. This imminent disaster would have caused me concern, but I know the bell tower will be standing for at least another five-hundred years.

My feet ache from patrolling the Piazza Signoria. Inside my shoes burns a fire of my own. I hear the great bell, La Vacca, summon the Florentines to spiritually rally, and the ringing interrupts my preoccupation with discomfort. It sounds like a mournful cow, and I get the impression that I'm on time. I remind myself that I have a ticket home in my back pocket.

I scan the vicinity again, looking for Baz as I last knew him, when he was a cheeky six-year-old boy with faraway eyes the color of a spring sky – my fearless leader of twin-ship who left me stranded when he died. I assume this recurring dream is only about him, like the ones that always come on the anniversary of his death. But this time it's unexpected, out of season – a thirteenth reminder that begged me to write it down.

Waiting out the red ash requires no watching. I am alone at the fire's death, and in spite of sore feet and fierce hunger, I continue my vigil. No matter how many times I revisit this location there is something new to see. This time it's a lean tomcat skidding sideways from a jumpy carthorse, anxious from the mayhem in the square.

For twelve years I have ignored the scavengers who skulk in the shallow doorways too far away to matter. I know they linger for the major burnings to bank into smolderings, to sift for the indestructible gems-in-waiting, and the lumps of melted gold which lie underneath the charred embers like stars.

By 7 P.M. I'd carried the smell of acrid smoke with me all day, and was still able to close my eyes and feel the heat of the flames on my face. There was someone else I was supposed to meet… but I'd woken too soon. Pico had been chasing Nattie, the new kitten, and crashed a pile of books to the floor, and as much as I tried to recapture the dream, I remained wide awake.

Art is not a clean fuel.

Chapter Four – THE NAME GAME

Dreaming for old time's sake, I dream of Baz teasing me about my flirtation with names. Once again, it's our twelfth birthday. I had asked for a new name for my birthday and the variations of Veronica produced: Roni, Nicky, Vicky, Vera, and Verity (Latin for truth).

Uncle Oz gave me a pair of Nike runners with rainbow laces and a birthday card with the statue of a headless angel, and dubbed me Nikey. He said the name meant victory and that I could be a victorious kid if I believed in myself. He suggested changing the V to N.

The name Vicky almost seemed to fit. Then Uncle Oz changed Vicky to Victoria, and hearing it gives me a squirmy feeling.

Nicky to Nikey and Vicky to Victory, and Nike, and the Winged Victory, and moving to Victoria.

Basil once called me Budinsky, and I'd adopted it for a few days until everyone became impatient with humoring me. But, Uncle Oz had often called me his 'little budding artist' and that's how my name grew into a daisy. I'd answered to Daisy for a week. It's serendipitous how names evolve in a Darwinian line of natural selection combined with synchronicity.

In last night's dream, Baz and I ran through a field of daisies and he made me a daisy-chain necklace. He has a puppy in his heaven – a mongrel terrier he calls Wren. He's a boy dog made of white smoke. His bark sounded miles away, muffled by fog, even when he was right beside us. He floated into the crown of a tree and disappeared like the Cheshire Cat.

Jupiter's invisible friend made a verbal appearance.

Chapter Five – FIRE & ICE

I still believe that unemployment renders a human unfit to be considered a worthy lifeform. I processed my forced sabbatical as shameful. Low self-esteem thrives between the birth of an illegitimate promise and the 'ships-that-pass-in-the-night' kind of love.

I feel the failure to thrive nesting inside me. I feel the failure to thrive nesting inside me. To this end, I fight small fires: the contained flash-fires of single-parenting, selling my art, and negotiating the road bumps of greater autism.

Like a regular firefighter, I spend the lion's share of my time preparing for events that rarely happen. I polish the art of spare time into readiness for something unseen. The chances of fire multiply exponentially. Medication temporarily douses the flammable sparks, but trials by fire remain commonplace.

I collect karmic brownie points on the coattails of my uncle's science. The position of 'Girl Friday' to a genius should have counted for something on the premise that subservient lives deferring to the greater good deserve some leniency. Uncle Oz is my mentor, and, as far as I know, my only living relative apart from Jupiter which means that counting my deceased brother, I have three best friends. Second-best friends aren't worth the effort.

My contribution to Oz's mission towards sainthood assuages some of the guilt, but my take on it is 'goodwill by association' when I was given time off for *bad* behavior – maternity leave. That's how Millicent Duke, my ex-boss and almost mother-in-law, had seen it, and what the Ice Queen sees, freezes everyone into submission. Her employees see and hear plenty, but they speak no evil. Not to her face. Her son, Niles, had been the prince of charm until faced with his cowardly evil twin. I assumed it was easy for him to act pompous since his mother is Medusa incarnate. So much for the advantages of DNA.

I am an unmarried wife and a semiconscious mother, stuck between two freedoms – a daughter lost between two fathers, the broken half of sibling twins. For years I've played out the surviving half of twin-ship, recovering from the near-misses of accidental love. I remain, a life in waiting... an artist between painting and a hard place. I feel 'let go' or 'set free' depending on my mood. Mostly, circumstances feels like banishment. I color between the lines, wary as a cat on its eighth round of survival. Nine lives is an extravagant inconvenience.

"Darwin was full of shit," I exclaimed one night to a startled Pico. He started to purr. "It isn't the fittest who survive," I continued. "It's the ones with the largest bank balance."

The financial food chain is a ravenous beast of supply and demand. One serves or is served up – a dainty dish or a whole pig. Hand-to-mouth greed. Even the tax man never knows the difference between guilt-money and a mercenary's severance pay.

Fake retirement aside, it's a novelty to shelve debt for a while. Millicent owes my uncle, big time. Niles owes me a few small good times, and I owed him the chance to live with a healthier bride and sire healthier children. For all the confusion, a creative settlement was reached.

Medication pulled me through hoops of circus fire. Pills made it possible to avoid being strangled by tightrope wire.

Most days, I can no longer tell if I'm a proper caregiver or a large human kitten lugged around by the scruff of my life. Felines, Pico and Nattie, serve as my pet confessors and hot water bottles. My teddy bears with attitude. Cats exhibit gumption – something I once cultivated. Something Oz said would be the making of me.

The ghosts of happy-hour still mock my anxieties, offering me champagne glasses filled with hemlock. 'drink me,' they whisper, and I drink, as gullible as Alice in Wonderland. I toast them. *Here's to fear and deal-breaker tugs of responsibility. Here's to the death of poverty and the right number of life boats.*

The best part of me understands perfectly that I must find true north and realign my energy to a noble workforce. To this end, I drift towards battle. Surrender is no longer an option.

Nattie is a terrible flirt. "You watch those Toms," I tell her. "Courtly love is a dirty white lie."

FROM THE DIARY OF VERONICA LYONS
- WAXING LYRICAL -

It's late afternoon. Jupiter is still at the library. I needed a break. I felt indescribably free without Jupe in the back of the car, but sad. The wind is high and wild-warm mad, howling dark and dry. A winter storm in April. The trees are swaying madly and I have subliminal songs ferociously looping in my head.

I drove home, and took Peyton for a lonely walk with my brain on fire. I took every precaution to find my way home through the fog of distracting thoughts. I put heavy stones in my pocket to stop my spirit from blowing away. I left a light in the window and tied a string to the front door. *'Hey, it's only a paper moon'*... the introspection from wandering in the dreamtime of broken promises, can lead one astray.

I want warm toes next to mine... *'but it wouldn't be make believe'.* I want companionship during the long dark nights. I want a hand to hold and a house full of life... *'if you believed in me'*... I have a case of the Moody-Blues. *'Just what the truth is'*... I want a hot-water-bottle slave. I want a teddy bear prince... *'I can't say anymore'*... I want a servant bearing a glass of hot milk. I want a knight-light. I want smaller dragons under the bed.

It's one of those nights when the storm whispers the things I long to hear. *'Just what you want to be'.* I want to forget how life is a constant battle. I want a golden warrior to vanquish the memories of lead soldiers. Sleep calls softly. Problems wash away with the sound of reality rain... *'you'll be in the end'.* I want one of those crazy lonely knights who craves a white satin doll. I want a suit of armor hanging over the back of the bedroom chair, but it's just another night of imaginary bliss... *'never reaching the end'.*

— Veronica

     LISABETTA – A STOLEN GLANCE

chapter thirty-seven

*"I was a bright-eyed peasant child.
At five, I already sniffed the wind
for predators."*
~ Lisabetta

Mona Lisabetta

FLORENCE
1468

One must take it on trust that a child may know more than her years should allow.

By the time I reached the age of ten, I was well-educated in spite of myself. I missed little, and on my visits to the city of Florence, I absorbed the conversational tones and mannerisms of my social betters the way others breathed air. I watched Verrocchio's painters, and studied the art while the apprentices slept. I sketched in borrowed hours, during the days spent in the thriving studio.

"You may stay here permanently and work here in two years if Verrocchio agrees," Leonardo told me… warned me with raised eyebrows. "And, if you work hard at your drawings."

I returned to the Buti homestead, my head dizzy with a golden future. I carried bundles of drawing materials, my mind filled with the shapes of saints and landscapes, and sketched Rinato, the scruffy little dog that Leonardo gave me on one of his earlier visits.

Leonardo declared Rinato was to be my new brother. The day he was delivered, I clung to the dog's trembling body when he whined pitifully after his disappearing master.

I kept the pup close to me for days and was rebuked for taking such pains as tying a string between myself and the creature. It slowed down my chores, and we were ridiculed, but in the end, all the fuss had been worth it. Rinato no longer pined for Leonardo and I became acquainted with the part of Leonardo's soul that lived in the dog's eyes.

We were content in each other's company. I told Rinato stories when we settled into the grasses of the wild hills. His ears followed my voice even while he slept.

Leonardo had arrived one afternoon with Rinato as a tiny bundle inside his shirt. The feelings of another's abandonment pressed hard on Leonardo. He'd found the runt of a litter, near death, nurtured him back to life, and kept him out of sight till it was strong.

Leonardo took the young dog as a positive sign. Rinato brought our number to sacred three.

Rinato and I tramped enthusiastically through the grasses outside the boundaries of the farm, following the invisible scent of Leonardo who left an indelible imprint of himself on our world. It was easy to imagine him at the edge of the tree line or beckoning from the low rise at the end of the rows of olive trees. The golden brother and the benevolent master who charmed with his brilliant madness.

We awaited Leonardo's return at the hours of dawn, and midday, and late at night under the stars... all the times that he had made larger. We never knew Leonardo shivered, eighty miles away under thin blankets, holding tight to the thoughts of us, clinging precariously to a terrifying precipice, always alone.

Leonardo reached for flesh and fur touchstones with outstretched phantom arms. All the while his real arms hugged himself into a safe embrace. He called out for me and Rinato in his waking dreams and hummed us into his reality. He clung to a thread of belonging, where sister, brother, and mongrel escaped from the clutches of expectation, and ran freely into the long grasses of Campo Zeppi to evaporate under a scorching sky.

Reunited, we tumbled into each other in paroxysms of joy, happy to be somewhere, anywhere, no longer separate. On the occasions of his monthly visits all three of us ran mad with delight.

Leonardo taught me to look beyond the colors I expected to see and to dive inside the miniature world where plants, and trees, and rivers, could be discerned in the textures of bark, and nestled into the hills and valleys of fresh moss. These were the fanciful landscapes we shared.

We spent hours pretending we'd fallen through the roots of the olive trees into the tiny worlds, away from the larger one, oppressive and cold, choked with rules and rough treatment.

　　　　　LISABETTA – A STOLEN GLANCE

We collected stones, and osier stalks, and lizard skins, and rabbit bones picked clean by the sun. All of these were laid out carefully and precisely, to be copied into portable librero or larger folios of bound drawing paper. Leonardo showed me how to flesh outlines with life and to make notes of their colors. He instructed me to log the wind and weather that had rustled the leaves, or feathers, or flower petals. Nothing was insignificant.

He taught me the divine secrets of human expression that resided in the arches of wonder we call eyebrows – the ultimate detail that held the key to every nuance of human emotion, and how the precise lack of them created mysteries under the surface of observation. "Portraits are stories," he said, "Never forget this. You are perfect, but if you are a true artist, you will never be finished."

Campo Zeppi's backyard was a panorama of natural wonder. Leonardo taught me to observe the movements of things. He encouraged me to notice wings, and the emotions of water, and a single drop of rain splashing onto dry dust. I was quick to understand that everything life-size had its counterpart magic in the smallest of details. At night I dreamed of the wild places that continued to hold us safely together.

Rinato cemented us together during the long weeks spent apart, when time moved slowly and I dutifully captured the changing seasons on bits of paper, recording the world so Leonardo could sift through them, read my story-drawings, and ask me questions.

He wanted details: had I sketched after a rain? What was the light? Where would the shadows fall if I moved to another angle? What had been the time of day?

Leonardo taught me to describe the colors in ways that read like poetry: greens washed with sunlight, stormy blues impregnated with thunder, the earth-tones shot with flecks of gold that smell of rain and wind, the reds ripe as dawn cherries, and the yellows charged with the happiness of divine breath. He was keen to point out the natural triangles that fascinated him.

I learned to gift them back to him as the threes he craved. Trinities focused Leonardo, when his mind wandered into the dangers of everyday things that settled upon him and made him uneasy.

I counted to three with Leonardo or paced silently beside him, under-standing with some unconscious force, that this was a good thing for him, *and therefore also a considerable asset to my own best experience of the world, and my need to be his strength. There were times only I could bring Leonardo back from the abyss that threatened to extinguish his light.*

When Leonardo retreated into his lonely shadows, I stayed close, ready with a shape to distract him, or a question only he could answer, and Rinato presented him with a new trick. Anything to erase the pain in Leonardo's eyes and make him smile and look directly at us again.

Anyone who saw us together, noted we looked uncannily alike in spite of having different fathers, and for ten years, only three people were aware of our true lineage.

There was more to us than regular siblings. We thought along parallel lines, and perhaps knew more than we should of each other's deepest trials. When Leonardo smiled, the sun came out. When I smiled, Leonardo was content. Rinato cared only that his two gods sent vibrations directly into his animated tail.

FLORENCE
1503

By 1503, I was considered old. My neighbor, Lisa Giocondo's children called me grandmother, yet I was barely forty-five and looked as young as their mother.

I rarely saw my three half-sisters, who by all accounts had aged before their time, ripened under the harsh country sun with faces like dried figs, backs bent from lives as beasts of burden and the ravages of endless childbirth.

After news came of Caterina's death, my ties and Leonardo's to Campo Zeppi were severed, but even before the years of Leonardo's big trouble, Caterina had been lost to us. She had withered into a churchless nun, keeping her strict religious counsel, alienating any fond memories of herself as a vibrant girl-mother who recited stories like poems.

Looking back, I am reminded of the occasions when she stood out of time as a vortex of possibilities whirled about her. She could still feel them on

*her skin – fresh as the day they arrived. It had been a time she felt revitalized
from their benevolent grace.*

*Leonardo's reputation reached creative challenges in a perpetual stream of
financial crisis. Lucrative commissions dithered past my beloved brother
to the latest studio princes and upstarts eager to please with less fractious
reputations.*

*As one wall threatened, another wall presented itself, taller and more
impervious to breaching. I'd trusted that Ser Piero's influence with Gonfalo-
nier Soderini, may be twisted to Leonardo's advantage. As the ambassador
to France, as well as Florence's civic leader, Soderini had an untapped line of
influence which, I'd also hoped, may have reconciled the bad blood between
an unyielding artist and his resistant father.*

*Soderini had no choice but to ingratiate himself to a powerful monar-
chy in accordance with the standard rules of diplomacy.*

*By then, as Leonardo's voice, I had formed several shrewd alliances,
and there were always favors to call in, threats to be made, and deals to be
negotiated that trickled down a long stink of conspiracy regarding the oft-ig-
nored social debt to the fate of a singular genius – a struggling artist incapable
of compromise.*

*Being invisible had its compensations. I was privy to the intrigues of
ambitious men without implicating the studio of an innocent artist. I followed
my best strategies for survival. Leonardo and I lived small underneath the
politics of art when it served our purpose, but I took pains that he remained
large enough to impress any power of the moment.*

*Even when Florence chose to ignore Leonardo, I made sure he was
aligned to the present French king, but Soderini wasn't a fool, and even King
Louis XII's power was temporary. Time played chess with us. We bluffed and
gambled, never forgetting for a moment how vital it was to play the cards in
one's hand. If nothing else, Piero taught us that.*

*It was essential to remember that assumptions are fickle creatures,
and that power can serve or destroy according to the unpredictable whims of
human nature. All webs of secrets, jealousies, revenge, and shameful incriminations, reveal ways to defeat them, if one is patient. Between well-forged
affiliations and outright blackmail, it's usually the insignificant breaches of*

confidence to watch for, often disturbingly close to home, but patience became one of my specialties.

It had been my essential task to keep Leonard's studio solvent by obtaining the latest contract for a mural that he could, if I twisted his arm, paint for the glory of Florence.

To this end, my intuition never waivered. I was ever piqued by the faint scent of a passing scheme to charm our way out of Italy.

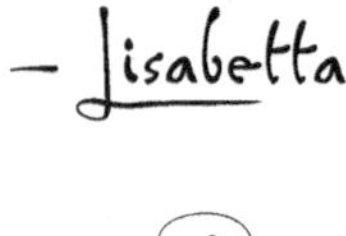

— Lisabetta

FROM THE DIARY OF VERONICA LYONS

- A GARGOYLE HIGH -
DECEMBER 21 – 2007

Winter is a natural death that prophesies life.

So it's no wonder that on the eve of the winter solstice, I have a persistent dream. A presentment of a stranger's life with scenes of a woman's past, laid before me, deliberately out of sequence. I ended up with postcards and details and the need to write it all down.

The Harry Potter movies infiltrate my daydreams. I binge-watch as a form of meditation.

I pretend I sleep with a ghost owl on my windowsill. It perches under an imagined pointed arch against diamond panes covered in frost. The tall ceilings make me scaled small. I need magic to pull me out. I feel like an abandoned orphan about to embark on a new life. Being saved feels imminent and I hold high expectations of a knock at my castle's studded-oak door.

I will creak it open to reveal a rescuer with an enchanted car, or hippogryph, and a spell to cast on my enemies. A flying car. An escape. An adventure. The opening bars of Harry's theme music quicken my pulse. Fourteen magical notes.

I fell asleep to it and it embedded in my psyche as a lullaby. It engaged me.

Magic exists to remedy the wrongs and hurts of a world gone cruel. I dreamed gargoyle high, peering down the long drop to the crusty snow below.

This brittle-cold day is as warm as spring. New flies are born, buzzing out of season. Sultry breezes blow warmer outside than in. Some of the days' horrors recede and I begin to piece together some writings. Last night I wrote several poems. I felt gifted with imaginary friends who appreciate the art of story.

Such is the power of a dreamed life coming true.

— Veronica

chapter thirty-eight

"Heigh-ho heigh-ho, it's off to work we go."

Women's Work

FLORENCE
1470

Andrea Verrocchio's factory smells of cold furnaces, cats, and art. For the moment, the doors are open to the grey dawn and the studio felines have fled into the hills for fresher game than plague rats and sour mice.

The city of Florence welcomes the divine light – the first artist of the morning. It blesses the narrow streets of Sant' Ambrogio, and inside the great workshop on the Via Ghibellina, the miracle of it fills the stale air with gold dust. It brushes every corner and paints the edges of the long tables. It kisses the lips of the water jars and caresses the giant copper sphere still awaiting the rooftop of Santa Maria del Fiore. It strokes the portraits of goddesses and saints to life. It shines the rooms gently until every cube and curve is polished.

The tired faces of the women hustle past the holy families and angels, and sweep the floors with sleepy brooms and the hems of their long skirts. The sisters, daughters, and wives of art, prepare the workshop for their menfolk with raw hands stained saffron and crimson and blue.

The second miracle is turning flour and oil into bread. A young woman beats cornmeal into a bright pudding. Another stirs cilantro into a fresh cauldron of minestrone. The aromas of an awakening kitchen chase away the oppressive night odors and clash with the more pungent cooking necessary for art: bowls of stewed aloes, egg yolks for tempera, oils of linseed and walnut, distilled pine resin, and foul pots of simmering rabbit-skins for glue.

Lisabetta Buti peers at a firing of Madonna figurines through the glow of red charcoal. They stand in submissive rows of blazing martyrdom – sanctified by fire – icons transcending clay and glaze to rise above something finer than mud and water. They endure the torture in order to become more durable, yet their purpose is to remain the fragile spiritual recipients of human troubles.

Monna Orazia, the housekeeper, can coax fire from the bleakest of coals. She is known affectionately as Aunt Rica, and given the title: '*Sollecitare Incendiara*' – caller of the flames. This damp morning it's her duty to make magic over a particularly odious bed of black stones. She draws an invisible flicker into a single orange spark from deep within the cold brazier and blows it into a finger of flame. It devours yesterday's leavings, and takes possession of the iron cradle until many golden hands wave their heat into the draughty cave of her cousin, Andrea Verrocchio's, studio. The main workroom only begins to thaw as the great furnace is stoked twice more to birth its obedient sisterhood of holy mothers.

It's Lisabetta's job to grind the colors for her eighteen-year-old brother, Leonardo. She arranges small bowls of powdered violet, Naples yellow, lapis blue, and lead white, in a row. They wait on the workbench like a string of Easter beads. The palest of egg yolks have been gently beaten into a froth with a drop of olive oil and covered with a scrap of gauze. Her fingertips smell of vinegar from stirring a tepid jar of prepared water. These are the freshest ingredients for painting the best clouds. Skies are her specialty. Even Sandro Botticelli asks for her help with his skies. Today Leonardo also requires a small quantity of lamp black and burnt sienna for the 'Tobias' panel now that the background is dry enough to add the last figure, but her brother's first task will be repairing its crude sky.

At this hour, the little upstart, Lorenzo di Credi, is still warming master Verrocchio's bed, surrounded by velvet pillows and love-stained sheets. Lisabetta is twelve. Lorenzo is barely a year older – chosen from the crowd for his dark beauty to pose for yet another angel. Usually the boys last for one painting, but Lorenzo knows how to play and he rolls over for his supper – enough to stay on as a reluctant apprentice with favors. Lorenzo brags behind Verrocchio's back, that he likes his women younger. At thirteen, Lorenzo leers repulsively at girls like an old man.

Lisabetta beams from Sandro's attention. The day has gifted the purest ultramarine to prepare. She leans into the weakness of the stone, and slips into its rhythm. It crushes willingly – surrenders itself like a lover, but the scorpion, Lorenzo, scuttles across her happiness and casts a prediction over the mortar with casual insensitivity.

His flirtation is rehearsed. "Someday, I think you will be *my* assistant," he says, thinking to flatter.

He teases, but Lisabetta reacts as if stung. "Never," she says. "I will go back to the farm first."

"Well – always menial work, yes?" His arrogance makes a small cut against her neck.

Foolishly, she boasts into his face: "I can already paint better than you ever will," she says.

This declaration is a well-aimed punch that Lorenzo has to weather in front of his studio family. It compels him to defend himself:

"You are a worthless peasant," he says, "and you're only here because your brother is insane. Master Verrocchio wouldn't want you unless you were with Leonardo. Without Leonardo you are nothing."

The upstart turns into a viper and hisses under the nearest rock. For Lisabetta it's too late. She hears Lorenzo's prediction as a dare.

For the first time since confronting her bully of a father, Lisabetta wants to inflict physical harm. She had forgotten the uncontrollable urge to strike out with her small fists regardless of her opponent's size. For a moment Lisabetta weighs the heft of the stone pestle in her hand and considers it a weapon.

The first madness of bloodlust rushes to defend her gender, but something shifts. Lisabetta feels the fury go, and in its place she senses a calm more vicious than violence. She understands the muscle of it. This is the day she learns to smile seductively while mentally slitting someone's throat.

Knowing one's personal power is reason enough to smile.

chapter thirty-nine

Nobody's Child

- LORENZO DI CREDI -

Lorenzo di Credi is a human pet. He visits the studio of Andrea Verrocchio as a seven-year-old innocent and stays permanently, as the master's latest plaything. By the time he turns eight, Lorenzo is irrevocably lost between a greedy mother who sells him into lechery and a man the age of his grandfather.

One year later, Lorenzo is still being groomed for intimacy – a novice lover with no rights, no humane parent, and no home other than the studio where he sleeps like a pampered dog. He is disillusioned with the iconic Mother Mary who reigns in profusion around the studio walls. She taunts her maternal smile from dozens of paintings and statues. Lorenzo's experience is different. He knows mothers to be dangerous and selfish.

He learns to adore simple luxuries, and to address the young priests in the cathedral as father, even though they are only apprentices like himself. They are human sons of God, but in Lorenzo's domestic prison, Andrea Verrocchio's word is god – a continuously dysfunctional presentation of second-hand fatherhood.

Biblical lust is easily re-configured for maximum profit. In the end, immediate gratification overrules affection and affection usurps love. What begins as an innocent ticket to prosperity becomes a permanent lifestyle – the known security over a bleak past and the unknown dangers of the streets.

Feminine power is too mercurial to trust. It's better to pursue the physical opposed to the emotional. A homeless boy should align himself to the might of cold brute-strength. Mothers tend to die early and fathers count their male heirs in descending order. It's only practical to have a surrogate male to champion one's chances of survival.

Leonardo da Vinci arrives unexpectedly one morning as a breath of fresh talent and immediately bursts into creative flame. It's apparent after the first flush of beginner's success that the thirteen-year-old Leonardo is the latest rising star of Verrocchio & Company.

This latest addition is also its most eager recruit. The younger Lorenzo feels demoted overnight. He's confused, unsure if he's an acquired sin, an adopted son, an apprentice, a surrogate child-bride, or all four like the apocalyptic horsemen he hears about in church. He feels apologetic for his audacity to have been born. For now, Lorenzo may best be described as a jealous *'brother'* who prays hard for the destruction of a rival, studio-sibling.

Leonardo ignites a terrible disturbance to Lorenzo's already fragile concept of world.

Lorenzo prays to plaster statues hoping they are divine receptacles for messages to God. He asks that Leonardo, the intruder and the object of his loathing, should experience his own feelings of being eclipsed and left bereft of an identity with a status borrowed tentatively, at best.

At nine, Lorenzo is quick to rally multiple agents to serve the remainder of his boyhood years. He can do or say no wrong in the eyes of his smitten master, but *'Papa Verrocchio'* shows off his newly acquired *'son'*, Leonardo, at every opportunity.

Lorenzo is the only one who cares; he's the only one who has anything to lose by Leonardo's gain – even if only in his imagination.

Lorenzo di Credi hates Leonardo like a brother. He makes no pretense to disguise it.

chapter forty

*"While you are alone
you are entirely your own;
and if you have but one companion
you are but half your own."*
~ Leonardo da Vinci

The Perpetual Child

- LEONARDO -
JULY 1 – 1457

Caterina has no babies now. The infants belong to her sister-in-law, Fiore.

Her own two girls are grown into small brown urchins of three and four, with black hair the color of their father's. Her five-year-old son, Leonardo, bears no likeness to his half-sisters or her husband, Antonio Buti. Leonardo's true father is not the bully to whom Caterina has been sold. Leonardo's face and demeanor have no bearing on peasant stock. He has materialized whole, beautifully made from non-local mind, and there are no words to shape him into a manageable boy.

Leonardo needs space and air. If Caterina is honest, she's a little afraid of him – or is it awe? Dirt falls off his face and hands. He's an immaculate miracle that shines from their family like an egg in a basket of coal. The former Caterina di Marco has been demoted by love. She has been consumed by it and destroyed by it, and because of it there stands an angel son – a golden child with hair the color of nutmegs, who fears her touch, and loud noises, and enclosed spaces.

Caterina wonders if Leonardo has angelic protection. If his dark despairs are perhaps evidence of a superior purpose. She cannot begin to teach him of God and the church. She feels none of their magic, so Leonardo is left to invent his own sacred philosophy. He finds inspiration under the wild sky in all weathers. He speaks so earnestly of the splendors of nature, that Caterina tries to hold his vision as her own, but she cannot. She can only attempt to keep it in slightly higher regard than a stone building, and ignore the omens and the storms as nothing significant to her own small life.

Leonardo's dark eyes rarely meet hers; they stare inward to another world. She's not sure he's human. He has the strangeness of a higher being about him. He mutters to an invisible friend named Bella. He invokes Bella Veritas (beauty and truth) often while walking alone, as well as speaking to animals, and birds, and plants, and half-formed visions.

He is a danger unto himself around the Buti menfolk – an apparition passing through Earth on a short visit who keeps apart from the mortals lest his magic be contaminated or borrowed and used for mindless tricks. He is here to observe, document, create and discover. He is here to challenge and shock, and to excite and disturb. He dematerializes into the countryside at all hours, and Caterina is glad of it. Glad that Leonardo has some respite from the brutal hands and opinions of her husband.

Leonardo is surrounded with the strangeness that alights on a few select souls out for a casual stroll through greatness. He displays none of the confidence or boastful qualities that wrestle under the surface of his skin. His emotions stir beneath indifference, tense and restless. His shadow flickers large in peak moments. These are mysteries that cannot be disturbed before their time.

Leonardo is not like his family. He sees in colorful flashes of insight and realities that overlap, complement, or disagree, and are consequently stored under his scrutiny like bell jars.

Each vision is trapped, caged, documented, and released after study. They are weighed against each other for flaws. Each question begs calculation. Each tell of their length, and depth, and width, and must be recorded, measured and dissected.

Leonardo's brain fires like a perpetual furnace. Persistent thoughts are interspersed with incandescent headaches. He hears in snatches of conversation, left dumb and blind to the mundane world, blinking myopically into endless cruelty and distrust. Faces swim into view and morph into clouds of chaos. Humans are illogical, angry, and demanding. Animals are a sympathetic source of refuge. Birds are escape artists. "God must be a bird," he announces at age four.

Leonardo searches his family for empathy and finds none, and so he retreats into places that meet his need for order. The adults in his life have impressed their absolutes of obedience upon him, and for this he separates from them, forever. Leonardo imprints early to form subliminal opinions and acts in accordance with elegant rules. His right brain and left hand dismiss as he is dismissed by others. There exists in his mind, a restless gap between joy and subsistence, and the sublime and the grotesque.

When Leonardo scans his inner landscape and imposes it upon the fields and sky, he feels a harmony of purpose, and when his eyes follow the flights of birds, the tension of intense enquiry is displaced by kinship. Leonardo imagines he can feel the muscles of his invisible wings relax into the protective arms of a mother. Once established, his link with nature is fixed as his personal star. Purity is his compass. Ideas are pursued to their ultimate understanding or rejected early as insignificant distractions. There are no exceptions.

For now, Leonardo da Vinci is a five-year-old star about to nova – a celestial promise. His stepfather calls him a curse. His father and grandfather call him nothing at all. He is alive and stored in a convenient place to call out if need be, for genetic duty or to serve the da Vinci family business as a potential employee. He is the lone carrier of a dynasty.

Caterina smiles at Leonardo. She stands taller than usual. She watches him skirt the edges of the property with his eye on the house. Caterina looks away from her son for a moment to smooth her dress. When she looks back he's gone.

Leonardo has evaporated into the tall grass that swallows him whole in one humane bite.

chapter forty-one

Singularity

At the age of thirteen, my brother eclipsed all but a few of the senior artists in Verrocchio's studio. Within his first year of apprenticeship, at twelve, his forte for delicate rendering was a driving force behind the workshop's current success. Leonardo's work thrived, as Verrocchio's bottega rode the wave of an exceptional number of commissions. It was this general affluence which transformed Leonardo from a talented boy to a professional artisan. There was no time for the master's art lessons, so Leonardo taught himself and was quickly absorbed into the frenzy of a busy production team.

There was a general atmosphere of prosperity in Florence. Palaces rose on several street corners as our noble families established headquarters and reclaimed the streets surrounding them, plowing them under as if they were virgin land. Our city was a bustle of creation. Every section of the city was blocked with scaffolds and workers and piles of bricks, and in the midst of such largesse, mundane art was promoted to the unprecedented status of 'art-on-a-pedestal'. Creating 'fine' art became the declared virtue of a few 'chosen ones'. Creative skill was learned, but great talent was labeled divinely bestowed. It was easy to be overwhelmed by the fuss.

The church proclaimed art to be inspired, and so there was an influx of religious altarpieces as each parish church and great cathedral vied for God's approval.

Leonardo was at the top of the almighty's special list. God smiled down on his Florentine painters, sculptors, and architects. Artists walked the streets a little taller, wore the latest fashions, and performed within a growing aura of respect. They were considered an extension of God-the-creator, and by doing God's work, artists gained a social voice. Creating was the latest sacred duty. Only a few stuffy diehards failed to embrace this new fascination for breakout art. No longer, were saints and holy families the only icons to worship. Art changed.

The rich and the beautiful decided to formalize their power with family icons. The murals which lined the walls of prominent buildings were more likely to depict members of a family tree. Patron's lauded out for social rewards and to remind heaven and subsequent generations of their heritage until the familiarity of their faces passed into anonymity. I know that history lesson well. Homes made spaces for the statues of living men and women and children. The portraits that adorned the rooms were of wives and sons and daughters, and men of commerce, and heads of state and the clergy, as often as holy families and saints. Even artists painted themselves into large altarpieces. And the landscapes were recognizable as familiar backyards and the changing skyline of Florence as it rose higher with each passing month.

It's easy to see that portraiture was the precursor to modern photography, and as in my day, a blatant form of vanity. The beautiful-people of Veronica's magazines, paparazzi wars, and retouched offerings of plain-faced celebrities still compete in the ongoing pageantry of power. The power of beauty over brains and talent, and pedigree and genetics.

Suddenly it was competitive to hire the best painters to immortalize the mortal 'princes and princesses' – the uncrowned kings and queens of Florence. The Romans had declared the true likenesses of warts and all to be acceptable, but it soon became apparent that flattery was the better part of Renaissance portraiture. The art of patronizing took on a new potency.

Clay and bronze ornaments were one of the mainstays of the art business. Verrocchio's kilns and furnaces burned day and night, and when war loomed over us, it was the best artists who rallied to the calls of generals, and dukes, and princes, with new ideas for weaponry, and patterns for armor, and new designs for standard bearers.

　　　　　　　LISABETTA – A STOLEN GLANCE

But when Leonardo was thirteen, we were at peace, and he was busy designing entertainments.

We Florentines loved the pomp of fine theatricals, so Verrocchio employed teams of workers who churned out banners and costumes and sets, and on any given day, a tour of his studio would showcase a small child being painted gold and fitted with the latest design of mechanical wings. It was common to fit children with harnesses connected to a network of wires and pulleys so that they might fly over the heads of the spectators as angels or putti.

Leonardo took the time to listen to his materials. I watched him stare down a color and weigh the heft of a brush until it was an extension of his arm that held the resolution of the image in his mind. His arm was a bridge which connected his thoughts to a panel. He had a subtle touch and was the undisputed hero of sensual techniques only possible with the new medium of oils. What Leonardo managed to achieve with the slick wet-on-wet colors, astounded us all.

Verrocchio was so entirely taken over with designing palaces and cathedrals and other grand works, he deferred the painting of portraits to my brother. Lorenzo was not pleased.

Leonardo's career advanced far more quickly than his ability to handle the horrors of the social world. He created in seclusion but once a month he rode out to Campo Zeppi and taught me everything he could remember. I practiced during his days in the city.

I rose early and completed my chores with an artist's eye. I noted the different shades of white as I poured the cream into buckets, and the pink and orange behind the clouds at sunset, and the folds of my mother's brown dress when she sat weaving baskets, and especially the golden edge of candlelight that softened the contours of her face.

I couldn't help but sketch my pony, Stella, or Rinato, or each plant that called out to me to capture the wonders of their design in the small notebooks Leonardo brought me. I hid the libricini in my apron, so as to avoid a confrontation with Antonio.

My father thought me a moody girl, but he could make no legitimate complaint of my work. I was a hard worker, and art improved the performance of all my duties. I worked with my hands, in time to the flow of images in my mind, and time evaporated. I worked to hold the spell of art. So I chopped more wood, or stirred the cream longer and with greater concentration. When I groomed our two horses, they emerged meticulous, and while my family slept, I worked at the table with my charcoal and paper, or etched on small lead-white panels with the new silverpoint stylus that Leonardo gave me.

I envied my brother's ability to paint the atmospheric haze of far distant landscape. He called it 'sfumato' – the landscapes that shimmered out of focus behind the transparent smoke of living air.

Leonardo often disappeared into the countryside he painted – he was the keeper of wind and weather. He saw what other painters missed. He laid the results at our feet whole and clear. I knew because he withheld no trade secrets from me. I tried to duplicate his tendresse with trees and mountains and waterfalls, and he taught me to capture the soul behind a sitter's eyes.

When I understood each new law of art, I was amazed. The translation appeared flawless under Leonardo's tutorship. I felt a happy surge of understanding – the 'ah, I see!' and the 'yes, of course' moments of incredible bliss, and at those gracious times our faces shared the beauty of art, and I saw myself mirrored in Leonardo's eyes, so I knew my face must also be suffused with joy. Until we left Florence, our creative world was separate from the harsh realities of human squabbling.

Leonardo and I combined our specialties. I coaxed him out of his moodiness and he taught me to play with the ideas that danced in my head. We were one creature, made possible from two brains, four arms, and a singular purpose to master the art of art.

Leonardo's status meant that one day he could open his own studio, and I would have to be ready. I glimpsed what we could achieve if we could slay the dragon headaches that lashed at his brightness. I was the only one who understood the enchantments of Leonardo's triangles, and the roses and lemons, and the number three. We dedicated ourselves to each other's best interests, but I knew that the harshness of Campo Zeppi would be magnified a hundredfold in the alleys of the city if we weren't careful.

The streets of Florence were a maze of pleasure-seeker's haunts as well as a cradle for artists. To live and work there required the type of social

     LISABETTA – A STOLEN GLANCE

ambition that my brother lacked. I was the wrong gender to succeed alone, but I had a masculine toughness and the energy needed to protect Leonardo. He held the receptive feminine spirit of the art we wanted to create. I grounded him and he offered me the freedom to fly.

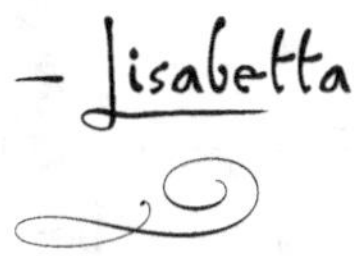

FROM THE DIARY OF VERONICA LYONS

- NEW DOGS -
JUNE 6 – 2008

I found a play group for Jupiter. Our house can't handle another intruder. It bothers me that I failed to sense how Mrs. Bently, with her penchant for murder mysteries and bodice-rippers, was so wrong for us. I blame my erratic transition to Victoria. Jupiter is still asking if he can have a rosary. I took him into a church and he lit a candle, and afterwards I bought him a fake candle with a battery. He flips it on and talks to it. How can I protest when we both acknowledge that Lisabetta is real. Besides, if I make a fuss, Mrs. Bently's crazy religion will have won. It's best to keep recent events, low profile. Candles are innocent enough.

Sandro and I continue to enjoy a relatively flawless relationship.

When a boy and girl hold hands across the sea or make eyes across a dream, signs are released like nervous doves. Casual, mixed-messages are sent: receive-perceive-deflect-reject-advance-retreat-hint-invite-flaunt. The cat and mouse event danced in slow motion is a diversion which leaves dignity intact. Good-sports with no faces lost at the end of the day. Game set and match.

Real-life lovers must willfully step freely on every crack, land on every eggshell landmine, and dare to remain whole and not try to hold back the tsunami of rejections that will eventually come. The world is easily thrown off balance by a pair of lovers.

Toe-dipping conversations are frail gestures of promise. If ever a house of tears and bone can be persuaded to be perfect, the adage of old dogs and new tricks offers little encouragement. It feels so very awkward at this stage of life, to break through to the kinds of freedom required for successful mating.

— Veronica

chapter forty-two

"He who is fixed to a star
does not change his mind."
~ Leonardo da Vinci

Saturday's Child

- LISABETTA -

I was a determined child. I took my labors seriously. Each task was another step towards something I knew vaguely as the concept, destination. I followed my father's orders with numb obedience. These were the ways of the conscientious child-farmhand. Work never ended, but the word destiny lingered inside this far away grand destination of mine and confirmed fate was tied to the stars.

I was fascinated by stars. They drew me upward from my bed. It was the stars that taught me how to count. Caterina had to drag me inside on clear nights when I insisted I said goodnight to each one.

I spoke to the invisible stars that watched me during the day. They demanded dedication, and I decided to be worthy of their grace. Performance and attitude were relevant to stars. What truly mattered to me was leaving.

Born into servitude meant I was all the more precious to the stars, but complaining was dangerous. Work was a valuable thing. I learned how to comb the horses, and feed the chickens, and wash the clothes. I made the cheese curdle, and discovered the best way to bake bread and preserve olives. I proved myself invaluable, followed Leonardo's lessons in secret, recovered from the verbal cuffings and physical blows from my father, and stood stronger for them. I was sure nothing of value could be accomplished without effort. My freedom was coming. I loved the feeling of earning every moment of it.

Leonardo did not spend much time with Albiera, the stepmother who loved him. Piero sent him to his grandmother, Lucia, in Pistoia. That was the only time when a woman, other than me, encouraged him to paint.

— Lisabetta

chapter forty-three

Puppy Love – Act I

CAMPO ZEPPI, TUSCANY
1464

Rinato's warning bark tapers into a nervous whine beside her, and Lisabetta is once again a girl of six, eclipsed by the shadow of a predator she vows to destroy. "A couple of mongrels," her father says unkindly with a kicking motion towards the dog, and as Lisabetta blocks his sport, his boot impacts her forehead in a star of pain.

The loathing she feels, alters her view of men and God, and her desire for power – power over them, and in spite of them.

chapter forty-four

"The eye
as soon as it opens
sees all the stars of the hemisphere.
The mind in an instant
leaps from east to west."
~ Leonardo da Vinci

Mercenary Gifts

CAMPO ZEPPI

1466

(Lisabetta — age eight)

Rinato skulks in the shadows and keeps to the edges of the room. Even the promise of a meaty windfall is never enough to lure him nearer the dinner table. The poor creature announces visitors with a hesitant bark from wherever he's hidden, his canine nature unable to keep wholly silent. Table scraps thrown to the floor lie where they land until Antonio grunts away from the meal, and rides to Anchiano. Lisabetta has learned to toss morsels far enough into the corner where Rinato slavers. Waiting for Antonio to leave is a constant state of nervous expectation for everyone.

Rinato and Lisabetta are inseparable. They escape to the open country whenever time permits. Lisabetta is permanently assigned to the livestock, such as it is: a single cow, a dozen chickens, and two horses.

First light on a limp September morning is routine until the squawking of hens and the jangle of bridles alerts Lisabetta, inside the animal shelter, that horses and riders have entered the Buti courtyard. She lifts her head from her chores. The air smells better when it brings soldiers who gather Antonio into their posses and take him away.

Immediately the sound of Antonio chopping wood, ceases. Joy. They have come for him again. And when Antonio sees his comrades appear through the windbreak of fig trees, he flashes a rare smile and greets them with an exuberant "Thank God. I am saved."

"LISA… BOOTS," he commands, without bothering to look around. "Saddle the grey."

"Wait, you can't take Stel… the mare. She's lame."

"No matter, she will get me to Anchiano."

"I will saddle the black."

Antonio takes a step towards his daughter and lifts his arm to clout, but she ducks, and his backhander misses and swipes air. The absence of impact throws him off balance and he fails to grab her neck to save himself. He rises enraged, crouching to land another blow.

One of the riders speaks with authority. "Leave her, Antonio. She makes good sense. Take the black. We're late. Hurry."

Antonio listens and looks past his daughter. "Thank you Lisabetta, my *son*," he says to the air above her head, but he knocks hard into her insolent shoulder as he strides past her towards his freedom.

Antonio wants away from his women and his brother's women, and his aging mother. There are nine of them: Antonia the matriarch, his wife Caterina, his brother's wife Fiore, four daughters: Piera, Maria, Sandra, Lisabetta, and his two nieces: Maria and Simona. Francesco, his long-awaited son, lies as yet inside Caterina, but even had his gender been known, this future son would never have been enough to keep Antonio home.

When Antonio barks orders, most of the family rushes to obey from their own eagerness for his departure. He pushes past Caterina, heavy with child. She does not exist. Antonio's only message for them is delivered laterally when his fervent thanks to God to be 'gone from this wretched place' reaches their ears.

Antonia fusses. "Do you have enough to eat?" She pokes extra food and a blanket into the spaces between Antonio's sword and a bedroll. The men look away. They have no mothers to wish them well and it's embarrassing to watch Antonia Buti mollycoddle her grown son. The food is pushed out of sight but the blanket is pulled out and tossed back, aimed at her feet.

"Stop fussing Mama, I have enough," he says and swats her away.

Antonia dusts off the blanket, shuffles away to her outside kitchen, and makes a loud protest of loading wood into the oven to drown her son's departure. She hates his soldiering and later her pots feel her displeasure as she scolds the uncooperative flames underneath them.

"Stupido," Antonia shouts at Lisabetta, dispersing the smoke with her apron.

"I'm sorry, *Nonna*." Her reply is automatically as the nearest granddaughter to blame for the inferior fire. The logs had been too damp.

Lisabetta and Caterina offer the same prayer every night, that Antonio's absences may become permanent. When Antonio is 'gone from this wretched place' they remember how to breathe.

Lisabetta smile widens from watching her father grow smaller as he rides away. That day, when the dust from his companion's horses hangs thick in the air, she watches his red jacket fade into a pink shape down the track. It's the brightest thing left to describe him and Lisabetta waits, frozen until it turns to the color of flesh and disappears. The men's muffled camaraderie can still be heard. She listens until the road takes him and the black horse completely. The sound of birds return and Lezza is gifted an apple and words of affection as a reward for keeping her secret.

Lisabetta leans on the pony as it munches the fruit. Lezza's muscles ripple through her skin. She closes her eyes in order to be the horse, and tastes the sweetness of the apple.

When Lisabetta's father vanishes into that autumn day when she is eight-years-old, her energy expands. The sun rises every morning, but on his leaving days it's as if it shines for her alone. The emptiness of Campo Zeppi fills with light. Caterina and Fiore smile and bask in the warmth of silence.

Caterina rests on a millstone near the east door. She eases her pregnant weight down and stretches her brown toes to the first strong rays of the sun, making small circles in the air with her ankles. She manages a weak smile for Rinato clowning in the tall grass. Rinato, the keeper of enthusiasm, materializes in a frenzy of joyous yelps, and hops on his hind legs making the younger children laugh.

Caterina's smiles become smaller and further apart as she's consumed by her greedy God. Smiling incurs questions from her husband and mother-in-law. Lisabetta notes how her mother retreats further from the world each day, but she's too young to know how to stop it or to realize that only Caterina has the power to stop it.

The prospect of her freedom to come, sustains Lisabetta. She will be an artist. Leonardo has said so. She carries his promise like a torch against the inconceivable darkness of its failure.

She is the most stubborn of Caterina's daughters, but it's this optimism which enables her to nourish the dream of leaving home. Lisabetta has been ready since she was six.

The Buti celebrates without Grandmother Antonia – the only one who preserves an expression of bitterness. Sourness has made a permanent home in her eyes. She's accustomed to the barren years spent scraping against starvation with a husband she can barely tolerate. Her purpose is married to the betterment of her eldest son, and now against her wishes, he's off to fight another small war for wages.

Antonia declares loudly that her younger son, Jacopo, is too soft for war, reducing him, along with his miserable father, to spineless men who cleave together as one entity rather than stand alone against her tongue. Between them, the Buti menfolk muster enough wit and muscle to scratch a bare living from the acidic soil of the Tuscan flatlands. This morning Lisabetta's Uncle Jacopo, wanders the distant hills with her grandfather on a happy assignment snaring rabbits. With any luck Antonio's ornery disposition will happily widow Caterina and orphan them all.

Lisabetta's ninth-birthday draws near and the olives celebrate her survival by dancing against the sky. A feeling of independence fills her. She feels the presence of a more permanent freedom.

Lisabetta saddles the pony she's raised from a foal and rides at a leisurely pace towards Vinci in search of Leonardo, to tell him to come home, Campo Zeppi is safe for a while.

Lisabetta is well past the initial blush of eight and Leonardo is nearing fifteen, back from the city while the Florentines recoup from an outbreak of plague.

The chains of Florence seem sweet, but in the meantime Lisabetta perfects her talent in secret as much as Leonardo flaunts his own in public.

chapter forty-five

"A time to keep silent and a time to speak;
a time to love and a time to hate;
a time for war and a time for peace."
~ King Solomon

The Knot Eternal

CAMPO ZEPPI
1468
(Lisabetta, age ten)

The walls of the room glow with amber light from the hearth-fire and paint the inhabitant's faces gold. Lisabetta sits with her mother, trying to copy the fluid patterns Caterina weaves into the rims of her baskets. Lisabetta is nearest the oil lamp. Her basket wants to be different, and Caterina corrects her.

"No, like this, Lisa. You're not pulling the reeds tight enough."

Weaving is tedious. Lisabetta's fingers are too wild. "I think baskets are not my calling," she says.

Caterina frowns. Her hand pauses. She winds a strand of wicker around her finger, shocked at the sorry state of her roughened hands. Her favorite daughter has done the unthinkable. She has sprouted wings. "Women don't have callings," she says sharply.

"I'm going to be a painter like Leonardo. There are women in Verrocchio's studio who grind the colors and..."

Caterina interrupts, her voice kinder. "I hope you won't be disappointed."

"I'm different." She visualizes another Lisabetta who waves her arms and dances, but these are not the personas one shares with Buti women by their fire. Secrets revealed in the dark are thirsty knives in the daylight.

"Stupid knots. This straw is too brittle."

"Broken reeds belong in the fire," Caterina agrees. "Start again."

Relentless predictions of failure cut worse than the sharp straw. "It's easier to design these knots on paper," she says. Leonardo showed me how."

Lisabetta is like Leonardo, she prefers to glow like a banked fire and keep her best thoughts to herself, or share them with Rinato. She's not even sure if it's safe to confide in her mother anymore. There are times when Caterina is a stranger and Lisabetta fears her.

"Why did you give up?" Lisabetta asks her mother.

Caterina is silent long enough to watch the flames take Lisabetta's basket. She sets aside her own basket and massages her crooked fingers. She splays them out – how did her once splendid hands become ugly calloused claws. She speaks into the flames. "You're right. I *have* given up. You must go from here. Leonardo must leave Florence. You had best learn how to lie."

Aunt Fiore is dead. Her uncle's new wife, Maria, shows her sister, Piera, a new stitch. Both seem entranced with the possibility of yet another way to push thread into cloth, but Lisabetta only feels this way when Leonardo shows her his drawings and how to smudge a soft line of charcoal into a contour of sublime form.

The orange light defines a tribe of priestesses by a campfire, where Rinato is free to sprawl amongst them, undisturbed now that the small children are sleep and the men are away. For this, Lisabetta blesses the storm that rages across the marshlands and keeps them huddled together.

Lisabetta's two older sisters nestle with her cousins and Aunt Maria to chatter of marriage. The womenfolk speak freely of old dreams and current aspirations, but Lisabetta is only ten. She has only one dream, and Caterina has been silent about hers for a few years now.

"Why do they care so much about love?" Lisabetta asks her mother.

"They think it will take them away from a life of hard work."

It's obvious from Caterina's expression this isn't true, but Lisabetta demands confirmation. "And can it do that?"

"Love is the hardest work of all," Caterina says.

Lisabetta pauses to think. "It's not hard to love *you*," she says. "It's easy to love Rinato and Leonardo." Caterina smiles and pats her daughter's cheek, and Lisabetta feels pity. There's no light around her mother even when she expresses affection.

Caterina hears Lisabetta, wearily thanks her daughter, and goes on weaving a perfect loop. Complicated and elegant. A snake eating its own tail.

A recent month spent helping Leonardo in Master Verrocchio's studio has Lisabetta more determined. "I won't marry," she announces. "I will be an artist like Leonardo."

"Lisa, I don't understand your brother's world, but it can't be too different from the rest of Florence. Women shine at love and motherhood and even then, not for long. I hope you receive what you wish for. Being stubborn helps." Caterina makes sure the others aren't listening. "You have to lie to fool them... to fool men, and be ready to compromise."

Lisabetta's eyes are wild. "But art *is* different. Art isn't a trade. Artists are born. Leonardo has seen many women painters and he says I am better. He says I am good."

"Of course he does. Leonardo loves you."

The possibility of this explanation rises like bile in Lisabetta's throat. She remembers an even greater truth. Her brother is incapable of lying.

"Mama, it's not in Leonardo to lie. That's why he needs me to help him ... to lie for him."

"Then be very good at it," Caterina says.

Piero da Vinci had ceased to be a marital possibility when he married *Francesca di Giuliano Lanfredini* after the death of *Albiera*. For a brief while, Caterina had waited for a message. She frequented the mill cairn and left word – several messages, but the

   LISABETTA – A STOLEN GLANCE

only answer that came was the announcement that a new bride of fifteen was to grace Piero's new house on the *Via delle Prestanze*, in Florence.

Piero's second wife died with her stillborn child, and not long after, Ser Piero's third wife, Margharetta, forced Leonardo into the workshop of Piero's friend and client, Andrea Verrocchio. Piero had concluded it was bad luck to keep a reminder of illegitimacy in the house. It was easier for Piero to believe that Leonardo was responsible for his lack of heirs. But then, Leonardo had been eager to go. He moved out of his father's office and into the art studio down the street the same day.

Everyone seemed happy with the arrangement, except six-year-old Lisabetta, who heard the news with dismay until Leonardo had explained this is what she needed as well – a trained brother who would employ her when the time came.

Piero's mother, Lucia, had been the only one of the da Vinci family to visit Caterina and bring words of comfort after Lisabetta was born. Caterina had been twenty-three then, and still counted her days as stepping stones towards the da Vinci fold. But Antonio Buti did not die at war... instead, Piero's love for Caterina did. She devotes her time to the Madonna's son now.

The talk is of nothing special. Maria wants only to discuss her babies. Caterina's nieces and daughters giggle together about nonsense. Caterina muses of angels and saints and how she will join Fiore in heaven, perhaps to talk and laugh as they had never managed to do for very long, on earth.

The room is empty of her mother-in-law, Antonia, who died along with her husband last year. Fiore had gone that year as well. Another girl child finished her time. If Caterina could lay down her head and die this night she would go willingly to bed with her rosary and pull the covers over her face. She's had enough of suffering.

Although Caterina encourages her teenage daughters and nieces to speak of their innermost hopes and dreams, her own have ceased to flicker with life. They've been dead for years, fading further from a sanctuary even she no longer cares to reach. Instead she's built a shrine in her mind and submits to the religious icon of the Madonna's face that never ages, and her divine child who can make promises that continually bless.

Maria's twin boys sleep in the same bed with Lisabetta's youngest sister, Sandra, and their baby brother, Francesco. The comforting drone of wise-women lulls them to sleep. The hearth is a warm cave of domesticity. A blaze of green logs function as an altar, and the women crouch before it calling down the sacred energy of feminine power and spin it into songs and stories and baskets. Lisabetta strokes little Rinato softly with her toes as he twitches beside her chasing dream rabbits.

A barrel of osier reeds soak in a tub away from the fire. Piera splits the stalks with her teeth and lays them in neat rows according to length. Caterina selects one and weaves it into a knot pattern that looks like the braids of hair. The wet stalks smell of fields after a rain.

Maria has set tomorrow's soup to simmer on the kitchen brazier and Lisabetta continues to weave into the lateness of the night even though her eyes water from the smoke. She sees her straw creation in the patches of flickering light. The rain softens and falls in a wet song. Her hands stay awake and work while she drifts into sleep. She startles from a snap of firewood to find her basket appears to have turned into a bird's nest.

In the Buti household baskets are another rule of conformity. The designs have been the same for a hundred years. Lisabetta is considered a failure. The fire wants to eat her basket. The heat is oppressive. The cottage door offers escape. Rinato lifts his head when he hears the latch. If Lisabetta calls him, he will go. But this time she does not and he returns to his dream of rabbits.

The fury outside shakes Lisabetta whole again. She runs like a soldier into battle. Arms outstretched into the storm's teeth. Bare feet stamp through the surface slop of mud. Anger anger anger. The freedom she seeks rises from her throat. The red flush of her scorched face, upturned to the wild rain, washes away. Above the downpour the stars are watching her. They will heed her cries. For now, screaming under the cover of a tempest releases her from baskets and marriage and childbirth.

She parts the rain with her face as she heads for the barn and Lezza. The weight of her dress, its hem now soaked to her waist, drags her down. The last of her energy drains as she enters the barn. Lezza is skittish. Lisabetta's restlessness dissipates into a fog of exhaustion. Anger spent.

Horse and girl are illuminated by a sizzling flash of green light. Lisabetta has time before the crash of thunder to cradle Lezza's head and whisper in her ear. "The storm is moving off without us but tomorrow we will follow. Listen. It's calling us. We will leave together, and never return."

More promises follow, broken even as they're uttered, but for the moment they serve as valiant lies. She would get better at lying. The pleasant aroma of the horse's straw says sleep. It cushions her fall, dries her damp clothes, and surrounds her with a cozy blanket of steaming body heat. She falls through a welcome trap door. She hears Rinato's frantic scratching at the door. He tears across the yard and finds her. Girl and dog nestle against the storms to come.

The last hours of the night sends a dream of the open road, riding Lezza to meet Leonardo where the track from the farm meets the road south, to Florence. For a few hours it purges her from the drab plague of hopelessness that permanently cloaks Campo Zeppi.

Caterina's hands are swollen with calluses and twisted into ropes that still work their magic with the baskets. She is old. "Thirty-three," she says, when her daughter asks. Her head is bowed from her responsibility as the family's new matriarch and her eyes need to be closer to her work. Lisabetta is grateful the sour smell of her grandparents is gone.

By firelight, Caterina's face is beautiful. Her hair glows like copper. The kindness of evening defines the contours of her face with tenderness. She will not fare as well in the sun. Her mother has ceased to care for appearances. Her vanity is replaced with a desire for inner beauty and God's forgiveness. But Lisabetta has only just reached her tenth birthday and doesn't know how to save her mother from disappearing into the shadows of the church like a bitter prayer. In any case, church is the one place Leonardo has shunned.

His words are carved deep. "We go there when there's an altarpiece to paint," he'd said. "Otherwise, it is unsafe."

Leonardo thrives... Caterina hears of his shining progress and sees him once a month when he visits against da Vinci orders. The times he comes to teach Lisabetta. The two of her da Vinci children need no others, she can see that. This thought, excludes her, but she is pleased by it nonetheless. She has brought two love-children into the world, strong enough to conquer a country-life, if they persevere.

Caterina had been thirty-one at her third son's birth. The eyes of the men at his christening had told her she looked old. The doctor knows from pressing his fingers on Caterina's abdomen, that her womb is collapsed with tumors. There will be no more children. The news makes her happy. A rare emotion... at last there was no need to hope, and her sadness could be placed at the feet of the virgin and her son, who surely understood the terrors of motherhood and sacrifice.

The other three Buti girls can see no further than their sun-burned noses. Caterina can't summon the emotion to feel sorry for them. They are who they are, with no chance for better. Her chance is gone and it is Lisabetta's turn to wait for a destiny that may not come. She has told Lisabetta to listen and watch for signs.

The light from an oil lamp emits a trail of black smoke. Perhaps a soul with a message. The eternity knots Caterina weaves remind her she is somewhere riding into herself... a heavenly life that will take over this one without a break. She wonders when. She hopes it will be soon.

Part Four

Thresholds

Janus – the god of two faces,
presides over beginnings
and transitions:
the passages of time,
bridges, and every doorway.

chapter forty-six

*"Some days
my head is like a teapot full of bees."*
~ Veronica Lyons

Duking It Out

HALIFAX
2008

For days, Veronica plays 'no', holding out for more, until she strikes the bigger deal in her uncle's favor. Millicent gets to play puppeteer a little longer. Three full years of guaranteed funding for Perry's life's-work will continue. Niles will survive his nuptial demotion, and Veronica's pride is diffused with fake grace. Oz says he will join Veronica and Jupiter when he takes an early retirement. "In three years," he says.

"And Aunt Bea?" Veronica asks.

"Aunt Bea will come too," he says. "No-one gets left behind."

Veronica shuts down, one hope at a time, and begins a new book. Sacrifices of sleep and laughter and trust, once lost in the fog of motherhood, wash away in the rain. Some choices had been made without her, but a fresh world looms. Basic needs are all she has left, but the beauty of this state of being hits home on the day of her leaving.

Her possessions are neatly boxed and on the road. She has all she needs without them. Her pets are safe. Jupiter is excited, and she owns two sets of plane tickets in a flight bag for three horizons: London, Paris and Victoria. Other than human love, triangles are perfect.

There's an art to leaving home. The mixed message of see-you-later, lodges in the language of goodbye. Veronica wants something fine to take away. Basil will know what to do. His gravesite during an electrical storm seems contrived, but Veronica is familiar with surreal moments. Her sunflower umbrella has been duly replaced by a design of Vincent's, 'Starry Night'.

Veronica addresses the name Basil etched into the flat granite marker, without ceremony. This conversation is casual. "So, I guess I'm leaving for Neverland."

"Not without me," Basil replies.

"No, of course not... but I have to get on a plane," she says. "I have to fly, Peter."

"You'll be fine, Wendy. Crazy girl."

"We have to stop meeting like this. I have to say, this storm's a tad Gothic even for a cemetery."

"There has to be a reason for that, don't you think?"

Veronica lays a single yellow rose beside the headstone. "I have the impression something strange will happen in Paris."

"Well, it *is* the home of impressionism. The impressionists *were* strange. You'll be able to see your new umbrella in its original state."

"But London and Stonehenge first... then the Louvre.

"The best for last. Jupiter would have…"

"Race you to the airport," Basil says, and disappears.

Back at the apartment, thunder cracks the dry sky into grey shards. Weather floods the vegetation. The elemental battle of heaven and earth is a thing that's deliciously out of Veronica's control. She joins it outside. Dares it to zap her to smithereens. Her laughter feels good. The drench of a noon-dark storm soaks her black T-shirt emblazoned with the words: 'I'm Outta Here' printed in white, her khaki cargo pants, and her gold pixie-hair streaked with brown stripes. A tigress in the rain.

Water catches in Veronica's eyelashes and polishes her upturned face. She captures some drops on her tongue and tastes minerals and clouds and birds. She rubs it into her hands. Turns slowly. Clockwise arms embrace the last downpour. The trees of Phoenix Street swim behind a curtain of needle rain. The gutters flow. Rivers of homely tears channel down the parched tarmac and over the toes of her new running shoes – a pair of Nikes wrapped in guilt, a subliminal parting extravagance from Niles that arrived with another Spartan message: Thanks.

Veronica surrenders to the puddles. She splashes and whoops – the facsimile of play she remembers as a carefree child of five. She lies back on the sponge of grass, spread-eagled, and makes rain-angels that evade capture. The rain covers her like a blanket.

The 'going away gift' storm, is upgraded to hurricane urgency. Back in her hotel room, Veronica stays in character and sits in a bathtub of tepid water, fully clothed, eyes closed. She dims the red heat lamps, adjusts the whirlpool jets to gentle, and pretends she is listening to a tape of thunder sound effects. This is what she will carry with her; a raw Maritime tempest with flashes of karmic whip-lash, entrail-deep, although where she's going is rain-forest-wet nine months of the year. One could carry a pregnancy full term and never be dry on Vancouver Island.

chapter forty-seven

Farewell to Nova Scotia

HALIFAX
MARCH 25 – 2008

"After I get there I will get some quality sleep," Veronica calls out.

Perry looks away from his niece with love and concern. He has looked at her this way for eleven years. He holds an empty envelope against his cheek and taps it against his lips four times before he answers. "Goodnight little Toto."

The upper left hand corner of the Monday envelope reads: the Duke Institute of Gerontology. The right hand bears a fresh stamp. Inter-departmental communication is too fast. The letter had been posted after the close of business week. Its contents seal the deal. A certified cheque now lies, crisply folded, behind the row of pens in his lab coat pocket. Its illegible signature is a power-scrawl, the indelible statement of a miser. The letters M and D, are worked into a malefic knot of black ink that hates to release money. Millicent Duke chooses to misunderstand the finer nuances of the term 'silent' in silent partner.

The white lab coat Perry wears is blue in the shadows. He looks across the room at his niece framed in the arch of a doorway. The right side of her hair and cheek are traced in a violet line. The dark hallway pushes her forward into the light. It defines her. She looks like a Flemish masterpiece. "I will miss you and Jupe," he says.

Perry has been waiting to air his regrets one last time. "Missing was always too small a word to convey the heartbreak of my sister's death."

"Yes," she says. "I know."

"... and your father's," he adds.

Veronica corrects him. "Stepfather's."

Perry turns away and looks through his own reflection in the dark window. "I can't get the 'Diana' out of my mind.

"Sometimes I can't either, but I don't want to be given a reason to stay. I'm chicken enough to be persuaded. The logic of going is perfect. Give me this one thing… to look courageous even though I'm a coward. I'm not equipped to withstand feeling scared all the time. Over there, in Victoria, I'm free; I'm safe. You know I want to do something brave. Something symbolic and sacrificial."

Veronica steps back into the protection of the hall where her uncle can't see her eyes. The purple corona disappears now that she's a shape in the dark. She wants no more debating, but he deserves some time. Out of character, Perry chooses discussion over solitude.

"It's a completely inadequate expression to cover the tragedy of losing the rest of my family. Lost is a pathetic human cry to throw against such calamity. I will miss you both. Missing implies the loss of casual things. You and Jupiter are not casual things," he says. "I promised your mother ... and your father."

The word father implies Alistair. Perry offers it as an anonymous hook, but Veronica is too keyed-up to notice.

"Three years isn't so long," Veronica says. "You can visit."

"I disagree."

"Consider Friday as just another work day. I will be away on a little business retreat. 'Pushing the boat out' is the next logical step. It's about time. It's my lifeboat... Jupe's and mine," she says. "And yours, Captain Oz."

"I'm supposed to be your guardian, Toto."

"British Columbia is a new world. As I see it, Victoria will be a finely-tuned space. Jupe won't be continually rejected by his father. I won't be suffocated with bills for a year, and maybe I can catch

    LISABETTA – A STOLEN GLANCE

them up. Your work continues, so you can get closer to reversing this shitty curse. It takes big money to finish what you started. Jupiter and I need you... and... you have our backs, which, as I recall, is the essence of guardianship."

Veronica's hands are on the door. The thought: "I need my pills," keeps her focused.

"I've got to get Jupiter from his art class" she says, talking into the door. "Duke money funds the autism. You can't give that up." She turns away from her escape route and lifts her eyes to Perry's face. "I thought you mathematicians loved that. A little elegance in a universe of suffering. Besides, your life work gets erased in bankruptcy court if you don't deposit that cheque. How will that help Jupiter? How will that make things right?"

Perry reverts to Uncle Oz. "Niles is bluffing," he says. "His mother put him up to it. Millicent wants my cooperation as well as my credentials. They need me."

"Millicent wants control. She won't allow herself to need you. She can't blink first. That would kill her. Screw what it *feels* like. Take her money. Use it to control the work. If you don't, she will destroy what's left of us after the lawyers are done."

Perry removes the cheque, unfolds it slowly and holds it towards her. It makes a papery snap when he flexes its length several times.

"I can tear this up right now."

"Now *you're* bluffing" Veronica says. When her uncle resorts to even the mildest of threats, he is out of his comfort zone. He can't play poker. He can't act tough. If he could negotiate fair deals they wouldn't be in financial crisis living hand-to-mouth in a lousy walk-up. She needs to pick up Jupiter and drive home before she can take some meds against the spinning night. Her brain is on fire.

Veronica speaks across the emotional static between them. "Don't worry."

Conversations rarely end the other side of a closed door. What Perry should have said whispers wiser comebacks and a stronger case. What Veronica could have said loops like a tape. Her thoughts feel like a row of prayer flags flapping in Nepal, buffeted by high-altitude winds, torn, tattered, bright triangles. The heat of the car feels oppressive. She opens a window to take in cold air laced with road fumes. It hits her face like a blessing and cuts the impression of altitude sickness in a quick brutal slap.

"I just need my pills," she says, to her eyes in the rear-view mirror.

Perry's missed opportunities lie anaesthetized in plain brown wrappers, left somewhere he can't quite place. When Veronica goes, things will be different. He will squeeze the Dukes like a sponge. He will play dirty. Hide his ace card. He will trickle his finds to his benefactress and hire the best lawyer… again.

Perry's anxiety and subsequent rush of enthusiasm, leaves him shaking. When he can leave with composure, he drives methodically, eyes straight ahead like a waxwork chauffeur. There are no emotions left. He loiters in Point Royal Park and feeds the ducks, watching them flap at each other over the crumbs. They all want more.

The nun sitting on the park bench gives Perry a sympathetic smile. Perry makes a wish and tosses a 'toonie' into the pond. The ducks converge on the splash and flap their wings to scold him.

Later, a brandy jumpstarts Perry as surely as God's touch on the Sistine animates Adam. Mad scientists can do pretty much anything under the cover of eccentricity. His expertise and naivety will net potential millions for Millicent. The time for being transparent is over.

The new ugliness within himself cheers him. Veronica and Jupiter are better off where they can drop out of immediate cruelty. When the mind surrenders, hindsight is beautiful. Veronica has been the parent lately. Sometimes a child leads. Veronica leads him. Jupiter leads Veronica. It seems about right.

Work is Perry's way of coping with guilt. He welcomes the fatigue. A religious man would call it penance. He silently endures the faces of his colleagues with performances of corporate dignity. Accountability to work is nothing to the confrontations of conscience, but

   LISABETTA – A STOLEN GLANCE

he worships at the feet of science, and in fifty-five years he has never properly apologized for a single one of his sins.

Dark circles of insomnia underscore eyes red from forensic squinting. Perry's microscope takes him away from big life… life that asks too much and gives back contaminated love. It reveals the future of medicine and the past lives of art: hidden complexities of cobalt blue and the organic ochres of earth's minerals, trapped particles, and ancient fingerprints. The purple lives of crushed shellfish and insect wings were not sacrificed in vain. Sleeping cells give up their secrets without blame. The underworld of a painting's private life is a landscape of fossilized peace. Perry can dwell there in right-brain time and let the surface of business agendas somewhere above him, unfold as they will. This time he 'has' Millicent where he wants her. It's time to call Alistair.

"What do *you* want?" Veronica asks Perry, on the phone.

"Let's see where it goes. What else is there to do?"

"Let the Duchess have 'Diana' I'm weary of her… of both of them."

"I wanted 'Diana' for you and Jupiter," he says. "For your future."

"Please no more guilt. This family has had enough for two lifetimes. I hate to burst your view of my selfless sacrifice, but I actually prefer the thought of living solitaire. For me it's an escape more than anything else. I don't want a life under financial pressure. I don't want Jupiter to grow up in a world that runs over people like us with tanks. I am excited to be a prisoner on house-arrest. Really… I want out. I want Jupiter out. I wish you could come with us and cut the strings to everything. Restoring paintings is profitable enough."

"That's not such a bad idea," he says.

"Well maybe it can still work out like that. You can follow us," Veronica suggests. "Just abandon the company after my first year is up."

Double malt Glenfiddich begins to assuage remorse. Microscopic furies swim into focus. Perry soaks up the stagnant electricity in the room, and displaces his anger with an offensive line of attack. Thoughts of revenge turn a pleasant shade of optimism, but the ice in his glass tells him his hands are still shaking.

He calls Veronica, misdialing several times in haste before he connects. It rings forever.

"Okay, to hell with them. I will join you out there in one year. I love you. Enjoy Paris," he says into the answering machine. The message makes his niece cry.

Veronica and Perry are family bookends, and between them lies Jupiter. Perry will miss them both. He will make the sacrifices count. There's an art to missing. Perry Lyons-Uncle Oz, the wizard of genetics, art, and playing possum, can taste it between the waves of discovery. It feels a lot like courage mixed with revenge.

FROM THE DIARY OF VERONICA LYONS

- THE VANISHING POINT -
MARCH 12 – 2008

I dreamed that Jupiter and I belonged to a primitive tribe of humans, huddled in a pocket of jungle defending the right to peace from a race of territorial blunderers still intent on fighting over hilltops. But we are fortunate. Our community is one of multiple mothers and fathers who share their maternal instincts and paternal protection under the umbrella of universal family. The attackers evaporate from the collective power of compassion.

I wish I could have stayed dreaming... but there's real life. The Duke's chessboard looks stable. The cuckold King is impotent. Queen Millicent is always on guard. She and her knights of the boardroom table can indulge their secret couplings. Millicent controls the board. Her bishops can resume their clandestine bargaining with the devil. Compromises lie rotting where they fall. It was always going to be a fixed game, and Niles makes any wolf at the door look like a marshmallow puppy.

I have been to the back of beyond and experienced the invisible drowsiness of limbo sleep. My calling is clear. I see from an artist's perspective… a vanishing point on the horizon and the singularity of a blue flash where the sun hisses into the water like the tail of a disappearing dragon.

I hear Hydrogen's computer purring with infinitesimal calculations of fourth-dimension mathematics ... the almighty I am = 1 to the power of eternity. Jupiter and I surrender to the gods of bon-voyage. The rest will find its natural level.

It's too crazy to fight or align to anything less miraculous.

— Veronica

I've studied the mother. Seen versions of her many times. Veronica Lyons is a pale copy of motherhood, an unreachable soul, inaccessible behind her hand-to-mouth anxiety.

The stagnant scent of pariah pervades mother and son, and sabotages their potential without a struggle. Jupiter's father was a 'mama's boy'. And his mother made short work of her grandson's one chance for security. So, after a brief fling with possibility, mother and child were sacrificed for the nuances of public opinion – outsiders dismissed by the inner circle, pitted against a hostile community.

As a love-child, abandoned by a well-placed father, I know the same disgrace. But I was very different… full of myself. Leonardo believed in me and I believed in Leonardo, and for the most part, our ignorance of the finer distinctions of social exile served us well and passed by us relatively unnoticed.

And when I fully understood the reach social cruelty had on my brother, it had the effect of propelling me forward, determined to thrive.

Eventually, being an 'invisible female' worked in Leonardo's favor. I made sure of it. However, bold as he was in art, he never recovered from the stigma of illegitimacy. He became a master by extreme measures of willpower that took their toll in ways only I could fathom or repair. Leonardo became guarded as a teenager – the keeper of secrets, coded notes, and tight-lipped theories, the layer of false trails, the recorder of divine truths, resorting to clandestine assemblies and lies. Subterfuge was kept at his side – a weapon brandishing sleights of hand as well as a paintbrush. My brother, a genius of wordplay and puzzles, illusion and artifice, deceptions and ploys, was the bravest man I ever knew.

Looking back I can say this: the rich are well aware of money's reach, but the fabulously wealthy are rarely cash-wise... they're hoarders of treasure, addicted to loot, and unabashedly consumer-predators with elastic bankrolls to prove it. They shop in a collector's paradise that defies description, where spending limits are left at the door. These were Millicent's people... the funders of crazy... the outrageously solvent, who know that money is ten-tenths of the law of possession.

Rejecting love had been part of Niles' agenda – he volunteered the offer of a long-distance retreat for a couple of candy-coated promises, trying to comply with Millicent's orders in a desperate need for her attention.

Veronica had become limp from holding together the hallucination of a perfect life.

Niles had been in a funk, and when a newly anointed king is offline, the wallflowers hold their breath. His business associates gave their champion a wide berth and huddled in carrion mode. A flunky waits for the wind to blow before taking a stand. Declaring too early spells disaster on the gravy chain.

Veronica had run on brain chemicals with attitude that spiked through her façade of high-octane chutzpah. Of course the Valium helped. In her mother's day it had been gin. They called it Dutch courage. Veronica had reserve courage in several languages. What she needed was a flash flood of serotonin, and a good night's sleep. She has fooled Perry, Niles and Millicent, but not herself, not Jupiter... and not me.

   LISABETTA – A STOLEN GLANCE

A few years back, the tiny yellow pills of temporary amnesia once helped Veronica rock Jupiter to sleep while she wept uncontrollably into the crocheted squares of his security blanket. The wool had absorbed her anxiety. Then tiny blue pills helped when Niles started to pull rank with his latest blackmails. Tiny white pills helped calm her in the face of cruel bombshell destruction both real and imagined. Now, she has progressed to green and black capsules.

I see her at night – a voodoo doll, arms outstretched in a gesture of mock surrender, invaded by pins tipped with adrenalin.

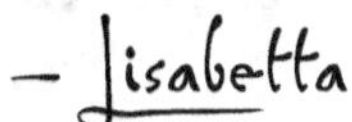

chapter forty-eight

"They dined on mince, and slices of quince,
which they ate with a runcible spoon.
And hand in hand, on the edge of the sand,
they danced by the light of the moon."
- Edward Lear

Transitions

FROM THE DIARY OF VERONICA LYONS

- HELLO PARIS -
THE DOVER TO PARIS FERRY
MARCH 31 – 2008

I read Jupe 'the Velveteen Rabbit'. It's a first edition, 1922, iron-ically as dog-eared from love as the rabbit in the story. Uncle Oz sent it to me for Jupiter, after he was born, passing down the family's copy. Jupiter always makes me read the inscription first:

To my favorite planet
Welcome to the universe
Love Papa Zeus
- 2002

Jupiter is over his anxiety about the rabbit's inability to be real. Naturally he brought Leo One to the front row, but I noticed him replace 'One' with 'Three' during the part when the toy rabbit expresses his sadness and shame that he is unable to hop like the real rabbits he sees in the garden – as his legs are 'all of a piece'. Jupiter's explanation, was that the toy was 'hopping sad' and should be angry as Leo Two.

Some days I want to give Leo One a third eye and turn Leo Three into a Cyclops. To perform miracles as the Button

Goddess who can give and take away button vision with a needle and thread. Leo Four encompasses the three monkey syndrome of denial. No eyes or ears or mouth accomplish an isolation tank of retreat. He is the fourth monkey of feel-no-evil, or feels it so intently that he blanks out.

— Veronica

FROM THE DIARY OF VERONICA LYONS

- A DREAM OF EARTH -
APRIL 4 – 2008

The last night in Paris, I dreamed I was a sculptor. The 'Nike of Samothrace' observed me, her creator, and I observed myself from a remote viewpoint of the statue's mind. I woke and wrote a poem from Nike's point of view because it was the voice I heard most clearly... all day.

- Veronica

FROM THE DIARY OF VERONICA LYONS

- HOME SWEET HOME –
Orly airport, PARIS
APRIL 4 – 2008 – 12:12 a.m.

We are in the departure lounge. Waiting to go home. Home? ... Where on earth is that?

Jupiter is staring at shadows, chattering away to Leo One. He seems like the child I used to know in the days before we found the right meds. It is unnerving to hear him gibbering to someone other than the 'Leo gang'. I will need to contact his new doctors as soon as we settle-in. He has a new invisible friend named Lizzie. There's always room for one more I suppose. His beret has permanently supplanted his baseball cap... god bless Europe!

I got the message that the movers delivered our things three days ago. Somewhere, in Victoria, my car is parked outside a strange address. It was surreal. I was standing in line for the 'Mona Lisa' and talking to a mover who asked where to set up the beds. I told him: how about the bedrooms? He didn't skip a beat, and said, "sure thing, eh."

We're staying at a hotel the first night back, and will tackle the house the next day. I've been psyching Jupiter up for it. He is overexcited that he will be with Pico and Peyton and Nat again.

I've had my list ready for days. First night... the hotel... thankfully a Canadian one with decent water pressure, and bacon and eggs. The second day is when new life begins: pick up the animals, and buy tulips, pet food, kitty litter, Earl Grey tea bags, cereal, and milk. Unpack the kettle and the bedding. Make tea and beds. Order enough pizza for three days. Buy real food. Interview housekeepers.

Have I put Jupiter through too much with this trip by moving all at once? I hope not. And now I have an issue with matter. I keep glaring into the corners where Jupiter seems so at home, talking to an apparition. 'Home'... there's that word again. I don't like that it's only a word. Jupiter and I need a real sense of hearth.

I feel like a cat staring down a ghost. I said 'hi Lizzie' a few times to keep the peace. My molecules feel out of place in the world.

Downtowns scare me. The museum crush was bearable due to the overwhelming prospect of seeing Nike and the 'Mona Lisa'. But I find loud noises and mall herds disturbing.

Like Jupiter, I now abhor strong fragrances and garish color combinations.

Rarely have I found a 'where' that embraces my being outside a sanctuary I've decorated myself. So, it would be huge to drift into a foreign space that smelled of home and touched my soul into staying. Victoria is still only a promise on a map. A clean slate with a fresh forest scent.

I will simmer pots of lemongrass for serenity.

From security blankets to electric blankets, I now reach out, hands across the sea, to touch honest-to-goodness molecules.

— Veronica

chapter forty-nine

"This is the year of yellow."
~ Jupiter Lyons

Hello Electric Street

VICTORIA, BRITISH COLUMBIA
APRIL 5 – 2008

The yellow cab was blue. Already the territory was strange. Jupiter chortled for the first mile as if it was the best joke. "Blue and yellow make green."

The blue taxi wound up and around a steep hill, past unfamiliar street names: Eagle Street, Heron Street, Peacock Street, and arrived at number 18, Electric Street – a yellow house set in a cul-de-sac on the highest point overlooking a lush valley.

Jupiter recognized the silver car parked out front with the bumper sticker that read: *genius on board.*

The moving van had come and gone. The beds were assembled but the furniture was higgledy-piggledy. Boxes piled in every corner.

The rain is kind and only pours once the luggage was inside. The car keys gleam on the kitchen counter. Veronica collects provisions for a week, including a new kettle as it's impossible to know which box holds the old one.

Jupiter finds his Wellington boots and his regulation maritime yellow slicker raincoat in a box marked coats. He kicks off his runners and pulls on the boots. "I'm going on an explore," he says, excitedly, trying to work the snaps on his coat. "The innies and outies won't click. Mom! They moved. The buttons mov..."

"Calm yourself," Veronica says, matching the top snap. "They aren't buttons and they can't move. Remember what we agreed. Take your time and… *click* -- one -- *click* -- at -- *click* -- a -- *click* -- time -- *click*. She hands him the matching rain hat.

"No hat, hat, hat," Jupiter says, edging away as if hats could bite. "Umbrella please and thank you."

"What about your beret?"

"Okay." He crams the felt beret on his head. Veronica pushes his hair to the side and shakes her head. One day he'll accept an elastic strap under his chin. Maybe.

Jupiter bursts outside and splashes over the spongy grass. Christopher Robin trudges past, waving an umbrella like a sword. Jupiter calls out. His words float back to his mother in his happy voice, "We're going on an expedition."

Veronica overhears. *Hmmmnn…* Jupiter used the word 'we'? He'd conjured a new friend already. A good sign.

"An expedition," he repeats animatedly to his invisible companion. "Follow me," he shouts, moving aside branches with his sword, giving his friend a guided tour of the backyard as if he'd lived there all his life. "This is a shed where the lawnmower lives. That's a garden gnome. We don't care for those. Mom will lock him in the shed. Let's check out the forest forest forest. Try to keep up."

Veronica calls out "don't go into the woods" a second too late, as Jupiter's yellow slicker disappears into the tree line. His delighted shrieks of laughter confirm he's home. She squelches to his departure point in knitted house slippers, and overheard Jupiter's one-way conversation.

"Tell her. She'll understand." He giggles. "She's not like that. Just tell her. She's a big fan of yours of yours of yours."

"Jupe? Come out. Please and thank you. We're going to get Peyton and the cats, and you can pick out dinner. It has to be takeout."

"Coolio," he cheers. "Pizza!" And in an aside to his invisible friend. "You'll like it. It's Italian. But it's best to wait until its cut into triangles."

Lisabetta shuts out a painful memory. "You like triangles?"

"Triangles are safe."

She nods, staring at the ground. "*Si*. My brother thought so too."

chapter fifty

Veritas Medusa

VICTORIA, BRITISH COLUMBIA
APRIL 8 – 2008

Medusa's hair had to go first. It bursts into purple flames when Veronica faces her in the mirror. The crackle and sizzle obscures the high-pitched squeals of snakes that twist into dead charcoal strings and crumble away. What will begin to grow is a golden fuzz of baby hair, pale and tender.

This is the silent promise that's missing from the label encircling a clear cylinder of yellow tranquility tablets. Veronica thinks it wouldn't hurt for pharmacists to be a little more poetic with their instructions than: 'take with food'.

She concentrates on her new meds. They're a gentler cocktail of anti-depressants to clear the unplanned pregnancy of her re-birth, goddess style without a sperm donor, scaled small and intimate. One life saving itself.

She cools her temples with a cotton ball soaked in witch hazel, pauses to drink in the scent of freshly-milled lemon soap, and dabs Chanel # 5 on her throat and wrists. Her en-suite oasis is a cozy sauna where a thin vapor shimmers between herself and Medusa, who now looks relaxed.

Veronica winds a towel around the shadows of snakes charmed by the first pill, and smiles at her reflection – surprised it smiles back.

The house is electric. It's been that way for days. The scent of violets lingers in every room. Peyton can't be bothered, but the cats are hot-wired to each other. They twitch at sudden intervals and leap into the air to swat invisible balls of plasma – St. Elmo's fire, no-doubt passing overhead. Pico and Nattie hiss into the corners, but there is no obvious cause for their fur to be frizzed into body halos.

Outside, the spring rain is gentle enough to fill the heads of early tulips in perfect stillness. Inside, an infra-violet wind grows into a small buzzing hurricane that riffs against the pots and pans like a jazz drummer. Veronica likes it.

The bathroom door pounds from Jupiter's six-year-old impatience. "Mom... Mom... Mom!"

Veronica opens the door and faces her son – her best friend.

One word captivates him. "Pancakes?" she says.

He's enraptured by the prospect and makes for the maple syrup. His enthusiasm tears down the stairs trailing the words 'syrup syrup syrup' like a scarf. According to the brightness of Jupiter's eyes, he should be in bed with a fever. He is hyped on the merest promise of sugar.

Jupiter and Leo One, shadow the green mixing bowl filled with flour. Jupiter counts the plop of two eggs that slither down the powder mountain and puff a cloud of flour into the kitchen's sky. A pair of yellow eyes rest like the blobs of a cold lava lamp at the bottom of the bowl. He hands his mother a third egg. It cracks cleanly and avalanches into its companions. Sugar buries them. Milk drizzles them into a paste. "Syrup," Jupiter shouts, hugging the flat bottle.

Veronica pours dollar pancakes and asks: "two, four or six?"

Jupiter holds out his fingers and grins back the number eight.

"Eight it is," she says.

He licks the batter from the edge of the jade glass using his finger as a spatula.

Veronica arranges the golden discs into a grid. Piles of pancakes would disturb the fabric of breakfast.

Three lion dolls watch them eat. The fourth has no eyes, nose, mouth, or ears. Jupiter explains again that Leo Four can feel the nearness of pancakes, and hamburgers, and rice pudding.

"They're all boy lions," he tells her.

Veronica knows better than to ask why. The answer will arrive, and it does.

He flicks the yarn mane of Leo One. "Cause' girl lions don't have this."

They've been home one week. Like a voice in a library, the presence that followed her from Paris speaks smaller than life. Veronica's instinct had been to stifle the intruder before it did any harm. But the feminine entity had retreated to a respectable distance, and now she has become family. She observes Veronica and waits, shimmering at her elbow for the right moment.

Gradually, Veronica accepts its probing, and senses a benign Italian greeting: "*Buongiorno,*" it sends in a rush of electrons. Veronica drowns out its persistence with Andrea Bocelli played loud. She loves the anonymity of Italian lyrics. A foreign language is safe from meanings that trap a mind into story. She can soar with the swell of it and absorb it with her right-brain. Music floats her against the ceiling. Out-of-body cooking. When Andrea sings a line in English, Veronica crashes to the floor.

"She wants to talk," Jupiter says.

Veronica searches her son's eyes and raises her eyebrows. "Who?"

"The happy lady," Jupiter says. He points to one of two empty wicker armchairs in the sun porch. "Her."

"Okay, you take the gang (Jupiter's Pride, she calls them) off the table, and go brush your teeth."

"Lizzie Lizzie Lizzie," he sings, and scoops them away.

Veronica takes her cup of Earl Grey to the other chair and sighs into it. It creaks like weary bones. The violet perfume is intense now.

"My name is Veronica," she says to the chintz cushion opposite her. "I believe we've met."

FROM THE DIARY OF VERONICA LYONS

- RAINBOW'S END -
APRIL 8 – 2008 – 6 a.m.

We're mostly settled in. Victoria suits us. Perhaps because we're strangers here. Only a few more boxes left to unpack and some paintings to hang. As promised, an agency is sending over a housekeeper who will double as a baby-sitter three days a week. All on Niles' tab. There's that to be grateful for. Deadbeat dads with rich mothers have juicy side-benefits.

I set up my old easel, but poetry eclipses paint like the rock-paper-scissors game. I felt the quickening of a story in the National Gallery in London, and then much stronger in Paris, but I'm a poet not a real writer – and now she plays with me. She hovers half-evaporated, out of reach like rainbow gold. I hope she will reveal herself once I feel stable.

Flying unhinges me. Jupe is picking up on my hallucinations. He sees what I hear. Change is not one of his favorite things yet he seemed calm in Paris, and so far, he has accepted our new lodgings as a natural progression. Highly unusual. He is, as ever, a role model for me.

Jupe says the trees here smell safe. I know he loves the color green, so maybe living in the rain forests of Vancouver Island is a lucky break. We're barely twenty minutes from Victoria, perched at the end of a developed cul-de-sac high up the left flank of Bear Mountain and far from street traffic, but I won't let the cats out. There are cougars. Pico and Nattie will have to get used to being inside creatures. Peyton is thrilled. There are trails to walk her around several local lakes.

This province is an enigma ... primeval aboriginal wilderness that surrounds an old-world pocket of Ye-Olde-English

Victorian culture. I will explore its retreats and delicacies later. Right now, crowds and city streets unnerve me. I wonder if I am unwinding in a good way or just unraveling.

The holiday balloons have burst.

I burn incense to ground me. To purge my fanciful notions. But my dreams remain scattered and I wake up from sandalwood voices, displaced – perpetually nervous as a bag of cats. I'm hardly a rainbow.

I began my new meds yesterday. Anxiety is a fluttering of emotional indigestion – an inner boil of malevolent chemicals. The feeling is like the nausea of low blood-sugar, deep-seated and lingering – a tangible contraction of the vital organs like emotions forming a circle against joy.

I shut down and breathe through the gag reflexes. Knees pulled up. Arms hugging myself. Breathing, clinging to the three words, 'I am fine', until the wave subsides into something bearable.

New meds -- New doctors -- New world --
New beginning -- New enemies -- Old battles.

I experience jumpy spurts of indiscreet sleep – a vague, dozing off the horizon into innocence. Yesterday, I talked to an empty chair. Très philosophique n'est ce pas?... I am almost positive there's some French in there.

— Veronica

APRIL 9 – 2008 – 6 a.m.

It's been 24 hours. I've had an amazing 'April in Paris' experience and now the month of May looms with all the horrors of moving to a new city.

The joys of spring feel overrated.

I watched a DVD. I let the ghost choose. She guided my hand as I plucked it from the shelf, the way a jukebox arm tweezes selections from its vast innards.

I have a year to get things right and the tease of a project that haunts my dreams. I must rally or Jupiter will suffer, and more power will be thrown to the bipolar phantoms I need to fight.

— Veronica

chapter fifty-one

"My true face has been celebrated;
Monna Lisabetta is unknown.
Lisa Giocondo's name is legend;
mine has been lost."
~ Lisabetta

A Room of Her Own

VICTORIA, BRITISH COLUMBIA
APRIL 15 – 2008

It's tough being a modern renaissance woman. Veronica buys fresh flowers before bread. She straightens a painting in her writing alcove – tweaks it a hairsbreadth, and wipes an imagined speck of dust off the landscape sky. Her fingers automatically align her pens in a row and adjust a vase of violets until the blossoms make a pleasing shape against the wall. She fine-tunes the painting a second time.

For the fifteenth-time, she makes a trip to the mailbox, searching for a birthday card.

Jupiter trails her to the mailbox, humming *Happy Birthday to you*. "You're expecting a birthday card aren't you," he says. "We'll need a cake."

"*Hmmmmn?* What? … I expect so. How did you know?"

"I was told."

"*Hmmmnn?*"

"The lady told me."

"*Hmmmnn?* Oh, okay."

"Fifteen," he says.

"I'm done. No more mailbox. I promise."

"She says fifteen."

"I said I'm done, okay?"

"Fifteen candles… chocolate icing. Done done done." Jupiter saunters off singing *"happy birthday dear Lisa… happy birthday to you."*

Pico, perches beside the open laptop, and preens like a fat penguin until Veronica acknowledges him. She kisses his nose and nuzzles her chin on the top of his head. He smiles. She strokes him like a bird with the back of her fingers. "My little penguin, my little owl," she says. She scratches behind his ears, and his soul purrs. The desk vibrates, and Pico flops onto a loose pile of papers like a wooden toy with collapsible legs. The initials V and L worked into a glyph declare possession on the landscape's foreground. More specks of invisible dust are polished out of the sky with a moist fingertip.

For the past week, Veronica keeps her diary close to hand. It's no longer a permanent fixture on her nightstand for capturing a last word of the day, a running commentary on Jupiter's progress. Now it is the recipient of thoughts that come faster. Scattered throughout the longer passages written in blue, are the red notes on autism, along with the false starts of new poems, loose words, lists, and the first-impressions from living in a new city.

There are voices in her head determined to be documented. The word 'brother' invades the spaces between thoughts. Is it Baz? No. Baz wouldn't play tricks. All the same, the voice made her think of him. When it shouted 'sister' during a moment of silence she answered. "I'm here Baz. Talk to me."

She's cracked open, missing her brother and the unfamiliar sense of ambition. For the third time in an hour, Veronica reaches for her diary and scribbles small thoughts that come like blowing leaves.

Titles of fanciful books race through her mind. The 'Jupiter Book' will be a form of internal space travel. Her son is a world apart from earthling insensitivity: 'Reaching Jupiter', 'Life on a Distant Mind', 'The Everyday Savant', 'The Creative Gene', and 'Lizzie's Protégé'. Veronica jots down each mention of her son's imaginary friend, expanding her files on the aspects of autism that fall between society's agendas of success. There is no absolute solution, but she hopes to present the possibility of cooperation between species.

Veronica is Jupiter's translator. He is a clear-thinker whose ideas are lost in the din of language. His brilliance is overshadowed by his own conceptual language: communication faster than words in verbal flashcards of stunning intelligence – childish understanding and deeply profound conclusions woven together in a confusing, but revealing, dialogue.

The compulsion to write for her life is urgent. The need to write for Jupiter's is critical, but Veronica drops off the horizon into writer's block. She removes her reading glasses and savors the finality of the plastic click its arms make as they fold against each other. Her eyes dust the eclectic collection of ornaments on a shelf a few inches above her head. Underneath it is a cork board, pinned with inspirational clippings. She nestles in an inspired environment designed by her right-brain. It's intended to connect her to the universe where art rules over cooking, cleaning, and buzzers that shriek when the laundry is dry.

Weeds, the unsung blossoms, take the place of expensive blooms – a metaphor for the rejected, less-than-worthy, selections. She gathers a few 'pruned' flowers from public beds when she walks Peyton through the park, or skims lilacs from neighbor's trees at midnight – a shameless Robin Hood, pilfering from Mother Nature. Thriving is a selfish business.

Veronica's writing desk has curvy French legs. Its romantic pigeonholes and hidden drawers hint of love-letters bundled in satin ribbon and poetic secrets, but they're stuffed to overflowing with unpaid bills. The sight is enough to propel her away from her still-birth project.

Research can only take an author so far. She had felt an idea quicken in Paris, but it was like the end of a rainbow that recedes as one progresses towards it. She had been so sure… and now she feels mistaken.

Renaissance musings have led her here to a final website of obscure data. She half expects what she's looking for to be highlighted in acid yellow, as she scans endless blocks of text, and sifts sentences for clues. The minimized image dives into a small cartouche at the bottom of the computer screen that reads: Leonardo da Vinci's birthplace.

The relief housekeeper, Mrs. Bently, is late on her first official day due to the storm. Warm spring rain judders the afternoon windows. Its intensity calls Veronica out rather than preventing Peyton's walk. External and internal weathers match; the wild roar of a mythical tempest seeks union with an elemental cousin. Anything to blow the cobwebs and doubts of being cooped up dry and restless. Her thoughts feel like the loose notes that overflow a basket and spill across her desk. Their frayed, crenulated edges of different sizes represent a collection from half a dozen notebooks. She has tried to manage them by pinning them underneath a heart-shaped slate. A thatch of poetry, inspiring quotations, and newspaper clippings fill a cork board. The sight overwhelms her. They defy categorizing. A fever dream of words flaps listlessly in the humidity like an injured moth. She had thought them inspired and had hoped they would congeal into a coherent outline, but they remain paper islands with strange inhabitants speaking different tongues. Their individual word games make no sense and yet she stifles the urge to throw them away. Spontaneous ideas have a life of their own. She believes in literary reincarnation.

The present storm threatens to scatter her thoughts the way a body tries to shrugs off unhappy memories. Veronica shuffles the untamed pages of dictated DNA into a pocket file and snaps the elastic cord. It's this act of closure that frees her and deposits her into the real world where she's free for an hour, while her son snoozes with Leo Four. Veronica feels the psychic fatigue of a fairy-tale curse. A princess who wakes dehydrated after a hundred years.

Inclement weather is never an excuse to stay home. Only the extremes of blizzard snow would ever trap Veronica inside. She tells herself, that when she returns home, there will be a clearance. No more silliness. She will rest a day or two and begin again, and this time, she will stay faithful to her diary entries and allow the naturally poetic nuances of autistic expression to stand on their own without embellishment. The Leonardo tale will officially close.

Having a year of free time is proving more of a challenge than working two casual jobs juggling night and day shifts. Present circumstances restrict her. She's trying too hard, and now she wants to be swept away by a wild event. She hopes it's literary.

Peyton is released from her rabbit-chasing dream by a crash of thunder and Veronica pushes her expectations under a sofa cushion, and shake the damage done from hours of vulture-neck posture. The collie requires a bathroom break, and a drive to a deserted off-leash park may cast off the bleak chill of a frozen storyline.

Peyton cowers at the tree branches tapping at the window. "Sorry, girly, we have to go out there," Veronica tells Peyton. "I have some things to do first, and we have to wait for Mrs. B."

Creative ideas can only coax a receptive writer as a passive entity by making no sudden moves. No amount of cajoling may command the muse, but it seems that muses are constant to their own demands. Lisabetta has to wait for an optimum moment and tiptoe around the book that Veronica is writing on the advantages of creative autism. There must be an opening of a tidy corridor. A five-hundred-year-old wormhole.

Jupiter's autism is documented, but it's hard to shape it into a reader-friendly manual. The neuro-typical world prefers their clinical facts softened. Autism is rarely discussed by the world outside the compounds of affected families. Its gifts remain unopened, swept under a public carpet, along with inconvenience, and incompatibility, and impatience. But an autistic eye in neutral owns a precise neural path and is compelled to scan for relative anomalies. Iconography is pure detective work. Jupiter finds dormant signatures and fingerprints outside the crime-scene tape. Master artists know a similar secret: they paint subversive messages in direct sunlight, because center-stage is a blind spot. The untrained eye generally succumbs to 'scotoma'. Leonardo was right. People see what they want to see.

The ten commandments of social worth seem to purposely ignore the obscurities of autistic perception unless they arrive disguised as the secret powers of comic book heroes. Jupiter has genuine vision quests which soar past shallow entertainment. He's a super-hero without a cape.

Pico steals the violets from the vase in one clump and drags them to his regular sunbeam, even though it's now a dappled pattern of refracted raindrops. The flowers get re-bunched into a tattered crush of rearranged purple. Violet heads drop to the floor and a single headless stem is trailed over the carpet to tease Pico. Veronica watches dreamily, reluctant to head outdoors, but eager to be in the car and driving for driving's sake.

The kitchen's white porcelain and stainless steel dazzle her after her dark-corner-life, where a single backlit screen pulls her into digital middle-earth. Preparing Jupiter's snack is an act of meditation. His routine is a well-rehearsed ballet: No crusts, cheese slices the color of dark cream, seedless white bread… lettuce underneath… mayonnaise between the top and filling – a square homely production, cut into four triangles. Her deftly assembles the geometric offering: three triangles presented on a blue plate with a solid border of white, the segments arranged like flower petals around a cylindrical juice-glass filled with milk. No brightly colored drinks. Nutrition, questionable. The fourth quarter becomes the property of the dog, herself, or the garbage can. No exceptions. It waits ready for Jupiter's nap, too late to be called second breakfast, and too soon for lunch. The next meal is high-tea at four. Late-night dinners feel like treats when mother and son dine on holiday time. Today, Peyton is the receiver of the last triangle.

Veronica scribbles a note in the hieroglyphics Jupiter prefers: *'Hey Jupe, please call me. I have taken Peyton for a walk. Your snack is in the fridge. Love Mom'.* She attaches it low on the fridge door with a star magnet. The word phone is an icon of a telephone, and the word 'snack' is replaced by a diagram: a large circle containing three triangles around a smaller circle like a three-leaf-clover. The shape of a heart replaces the word love.

When Jupiter was four he would only eat squares and cubes. Tastes change. That was his cubic period. Today he's the slave of triangles and the number three.

FROM THE DIARY OF VERONICA LYONS

- LIZZIE -
APRIL 15 – 2008 – 7 p.m.

I've been distracted all day with the feeling I've forgotten some-one's birthday. I feel pulled in one direction, then nothing. A dead end. Silence. I am the victim of a lack of focus with an inability to gather my notes on autism together coherently. Then, just as suddenly, desperation clears the air, and a story emerges beneath it. My dreams are erratic, filled with anxiety. I think it's from living in a new place. Perhaps even from too much freedom. A different me pushes my hand to write. I am researching one moment and then I lose the thread.

I am in search of a link to Leonardo da Vinci. That is all that remains clear… and it is a woman. She is the pres-ence I sense in the house, but I have no intention of being possessed. I believe all she wants is to be recognized. I hope so. All I know, is a book is in the making that will somehow serve Jupiter, and that I have been gifted the time to create it.

Discipline is required and it is not my strong point, but worse, if I am to follow Cate into dementia, who will be Jupiter's champion? Whose birthday is it?

My diary is becoming more than a place for summa-ries at the end of each day. I used to write tidy conclusions and expectations… and malignant thoughts that required anchoring in order to deflate them. But now, these pages have become sponges that soak up my creativity. They are a place for plans. With no-one to speak to, I read my words back to myself for hidden meanings. I write with the hopes that a conversation on paper will stabilize the world I now find is both exceptional and irrational. I spill myself into this diary, drop-by-drop, all day long. I grab a pen as if it were a lifeline and let my thoughts write themselves.

I find myself here, at another entry point with something that must be said. Recorded for a later self to regard with the clarity of distance. I am a messenger and the messaged. I don't remember writing much of it, and so I am surprised, but informed by a me with greater insight… or a me who is slowly going crazy.

I spend hours at the computer diving into research, treading words like water, reading everything I can. I sense a woman behind me, waiting over my shoulder, and I want her to be gone. At first I pretended it was Jupiter's invisible friend, but then 'Lizzie' became bolder. Now Jupiter says her name is Lisabetta… and that she is the 'Mona Lisa'. It makes sense. Paris had a profound effect on both of us. Humoring Jupiter is something I have always done without qualm. But things have been shifting, and now even I can pretend his Lisa is real and maybe it's me who is a dream. I barely remember her.

What am I supposed to do when a painting speaks inside my head of brothers and sisters and death?

The strangest thing is that I feel as if I'm invading my own privacy. I welcome my true persona. My name is Veritas Icona. My face in the mirror is true.

FROM THE DIARY OF VERONICA LYONS

- WIDDERSHINS -
APRIL 16 – 2008 – 6 a.m.

Finally we have a housekeeper. I hope she's worth 'keeping'. I signed her on for a trial month after she and Jupe made friends. She seems ideal, which bothers me. Her name is Mrs. Bently.

Jennifer Bently, Jenny, is an older woman, who amazingly, adores animals and is a retired kindergarten teacher who used to work with special-needs children. Having her here allows me to collapse for a day or go on safari with Peyton. The only down-side is, Mrs. B is openly religious, but that's not a deal-breaker, so long as she keeps her beliefs to herself around Jupiter. Life is confusing enough without saints and fairy stories paraded out as truth.

Listening for Lisabetta consumes me. Today is as oppressive as a deeply-listing, loaded ship, cargo heavy, depressed with bars of lead. I long for a clap of thunder to herald a storm of new life, when the trees rustle and the air is expectant with rain, and it grows dark, and clouds swirl widdershins against the goddess… when some 'thing' is about to animate. No, I'm wrong. Something or someone has already animated. I have to catch up.

— Veritas Icona

FROM THE DIARY OF VERONICA LYONS

- SOMEWHERE UNDER THE RAINBOW -
APRIL16 – 2008 – 9 a.m.

I call fairy tales 'backbone stories'. They're always rampant with gender inequality. The gods apparently once favored male 'dummlings' who prevail against all odds, with outstanding examples of serendipitous intervention, but girls clever enough to outwit the smartest woodcutter, fall into mutilation and broken hearts unless they succumb to a prince.

A good fairy's parting gift can soften the cursing blow of disgruntled power… witchy huffiness rewarded with a legal back door. Moronic cuckolds, and kings and widowers, still survive their calculating wives till the last page. Only modern translators rewrite archetypal disasters as happy endings with heroines who overcome their challenges. It seems natural for them to rise above spousal incompatibility. Movies consistently show downtrodden heroines embracing the promises under the rainbow of a magic tomorrow. So, why oh why, can't I?

— Veritas Icona

chapter fifty-two

*"The device you call an umbrella
is something that would have
delighted my brother."*
~ Lisabetta

Sandro's Umbrella

VICTORIA, BRITISH COLUMBIA
APRIL 16 – 2008

Jennifer Bently arrives at ten wrapped in a miniature storm of wet coats and excuses. She brings peace offerings: lilac branches from her garden, a rented DVD for Jupiter, and dog treats. Jupiter is thrilled. The movie is a documentary called 'Cats in History'.

Veronica checks the window. The storm is in a fine temper. There's still time for a wild excursion if she doesn't wait for the downpour to subside, and besides, by the time she and Peyton reach the promenade on Dallas Road, the sun could be out. It's a risk worth taking. She tunes her laptop to hibernate mode and snaps the lid, trapping the screen-saver of floating soap bubbles. The bubbles lure her into an electronic pool table, second-guessing the color changes when they collide with the edge of the monitor.

"C'mon girl, let's get wet." Veronica rolls her chair away from the computer and stretches her arms. Her neck, fingers and wrists crack from sedentary confinement. She arches her back and rubs the pixels from her eyes. Hunkering down wreaks havoc on the body mental. She often forgets weather exists until her collie reminds her with a wet nose... *it's time to pee... please and thank you.* Today, Mrs. Bently is her liberator.

Peyton responds instantly to the sound she hears as a single word: 'C'mongirl'. Doggy neurons spin like the tumblers of a slot machine. C'mongirl is one of Peyton's happy names.

Veronica chooses a navy-blue 'London Fog' with a hood from a coatrack scarecrow. Lodged behind it is a canvas tote bag imprinted with Botticelli's 'Birth of Venus'. Veronica stares at Venus. Venus stares back vacantly, through her. Sandro Botticelli's muse, Simonetta Vespucci, looks bereft. Botticelli had painted his own sadness in her face when he immortalized her as the goddess of love.

Veronica pulls on snug black Wellingtons and reaches for an umbrella. The selection of an umbrella is harder. There are fifteen umbrellas crowding the hall stand like a bouquet of tall flowers. She collects umbrellas the same way she collects walking sticks, and spoons, and china cups. Different rain calls for the appropriate umbrella. Amongst the stems is a matching Botticelli – a second reproduction of the birth of love.

Peyton moves towards the sound of her leash jangling with a new I.D. tag. Veronica clips the two of them together for safety, and they head out like a pair of mountain climbers.

A button deploys Venus in a fast fluid motion like a parachute. The image of a vulnerable naked woman balancing on a floating seashell mushrooms above woman and dog. Venus's shell boat is upturned – her ocean, now a sky. The haunted expression of Simonetta is a renaissance snapshot of a perplexed woman. How else could a goddess contemplate her spontaneous birth from a violent act?

Peyton, the matriarchal elephant, trots stoically ahead, and leads Veronica past the silver Cavalier. "We're taking the car today sweetest of peas," she says, and the collie responds to another name for power... 'car' and the neck-tug that stops her. "We're driving today."

The vehicle surfs over the water cascading down the paved hills of Bear Mountain and reaches the sign of a T-junction that reads Peacock Street. If street names could be transported like furniture, she would have kept the name 'Phoenix Street' from their old address, but their new address, Electric Street is relevant enough.

"Electric Street has a nice ring to it don't you think?" she had asked Jupiter on their arrival.

"It's more like a buzz" he had replied. "Buzzzzz… zzzzzzap… sparkzzzzzzz… lektrizzzzzity."

That was the drive into Victoria when Jupiter decided he was a bee, all the way into town.

"I am bee-ing," he had said.

"Buzz words," Veronica replied. "When you get home you can have a nap and…"

"Catch a few zzzz's," Jupiter had said with a bounce, enjoying the word game.

"Well done you," she had said. "Especially special child."

FROM THE DIARY OF VERONICA LYONS

- PELTING CHALLENGES -
APRIL16 – 2008 – midnight

Jupiter and I live under a social umbrella that flips inside-out at the first gust of intolerance. It's a term meant to encompass and cover a multiple of conditions. It's even meant to solidify in order to ward off prejudice, discrimination, and public disapproval. Chemical imbalance darkens our mental skies, and we huddle underneath judgmental ignorance with water-proof determination. Autism is a six letter word for invisible, and it gives an umbrella its toughest workout. Acid rain has nothing on social cruelty. The term 'judge-mental' puts an ironic grimace on the face of humanity. Thank goodness we live in a world that rains cats and dogs.

— Veritas Icona

chapter fifty-three

"I survived
through a dangerous reshuffling of power.
Rebirths of civilization
are more painful than human births
and they take much longer."
~ Lisabetta

Dangerous Times

VICTORIA, BRITISH COLUMBIA
APRIL 17 – 2008

A second day of electrical storms. The sky holds a single wisp of cloud in its blue-grey arms – an inch-long, white streak, angled from left to right like the trail of a miniature comet descending to earth. The vapor trail hangs suspended – an alien comma to punctuate Veronica's desperate need for signs. She blocks it with an oval fingernail.

Veronica navigates the cars on Douglas Street and the mental traffic jazzing her head. Random words float – a discarnate alphabet soup. Veronica's auto-pilot leads her through a dangerous ballet of city life towards a green space where crazy has room to breathe.

A pocket-size notepad is tucked into her left hand braced against the steering wheel and a ballpoint pen clicked open, poised, in her right – an automaton stenographer-chauffeur on pause.

It's a spiral pad. The sort she's seen TV reporters use to record the loose memories of eye-witnesses.

Leonardo was the consummate eye witness. He always carried such a creature. Small books, no bigger than a deck of tarot cards, with a vellum cover, called *'libricini',* worn at the waist – the fifteenth-century camera of an obsessed life-tourist.

Veronica wipes the fog from the inside of the windshield. Baz was right. I'm a crazy girl. Why would anyone take a dog for a walk on a day like this.

But then she smiles. Transfixed. Leonardo would have loved the coil pad with flipped pages laid flat, and likely swooned more over the mechanics of the pen than her car. For Leonardo, wheels and gears are passé. His little books were fastened shut with a low-tech arrangement of cords and wooden toggles like the small black 'barrel' sewn on the cuff of her sleeve. At the red light, she examines it and is mentally whisked into the past at wormhole speed.

She shadows Leonardo strolling the streets of Florence, stopping to sketch a hanged man dangling from the Bargello or a skittish horse, on paper the color of new ivory, before time turned it dog-eared and golden. Veronica stalks Leonardo as he loops the book through his belt and ambles on. Her smile widens. Leonardo has sent her his truth. A sketch is only a fragment on an artist's memory, merely a touchstone for the creative mind. What follows is the true measure of art.

Veronica stares at the road while she writes squiggles in Martian shorthand. Distractions are a danger while driving, but a possessed writer behind the wheel makes dialing a portable phone look safe. The word portable delivers the hidden word 'port'. A message which leads to portal and port key – an object that enables one's electrons to travel through a gateway and transcend space. The word *libricini* hints of liberation. The art of language is never coincidental.

The car swerves into lanes. Veronica sways with it, and pedestrians appear like targets in a video game revealed by windshield wipers on intermittent speed. Loose messages whispered in her left ear melt in a cryptic mist. A cloudy phrase fires once before evaporating. Her auditory memory is not strong. She's a visual learner. Until a subconscious sound-bite is anchored on paper it's a writer's worst nightmare – a passing thought.

Twenty-first century chaos overlaps the renaissance Veronica is trying to channel. Her brain automatically tunes visions like a radio dial... overshooting the gibberish of human monkey chatter, riding

     LISABETTA – A STOLEN GLANCE

the airwaves too far, until she isolates the voice waiting there in the eye of the static.

Peyton's pink tongue pants in the rear-view mirror like a piece of ham. Black-button eyes and nose, and pink, fur flying in the breeze.

"Hey, baby girl, we're almost there."

Peyton grins, *'Baby Girl'* is another happy name. Her tail twitches underneath her as she inches forward, snuffles the back of Veronica's hair, and sneezes. She makes a high-pitched whistle in the back of her nose and flops into a golden heap, paws crossed in a prim pair of white stockings.

Veronica's purple sweater holds a clue and when she writes down 'violet sleeve' she remembers that two hide under her coat. The image imprints in a game of snap. When she arrives at Beacon Hill Park, she can only decipher nine words out of twenty on her pad: black – eye – triangles – autism – violet – sleeve – echo – speech – mongrel. The rest look like they've been scrawled by a crow walking through ink.

Peyton bounds from the back seat, too skittish to be released from the custody of a lifeline. Veronica hooks the loop of the leash over the U-shaped umbrella handle and urges the reluctant collie on. The storm is still fierce. She hasn't wasted it. They make for the track in the woods and brave the cliffs for a short distance. The grey sky is a protective blanket that separates her from brittle sunshine, too bright for thinking. Her thoughts settle best inside a drizzle.

Driving to the off-leash park is foggy, as if she's been abducted by the alien whispering in her ear. She finds herself transported, mid-daydream, woken by the snap of a hypnotist's fingers, suddenly in the thick of traipsing, whipped by a brisk north wind that throws freezing rain in her face. The raindrops sting her to attention.

Peyton's anxiety rises up the leash into her hand as a pair of exuberant German Shepherds bound toward them. The confrontation of a gentle creature fending off an aggressive attack is inevitable. Veronica positions herself in front of Peyton and braces for impact but the dogs collide in a tangle of leashes and snarls like canine coat hangers. A vortex resembling Cerberus the three-headed dog chasing its own tail takes precedence, and for a moment Veronica forgets the voice in her head and the voice forgets her.

The animals are freed with a few brisk commands. Once separated, they perform the perfunctory sniffing dance. Peyton cowers until the Shepherds move on, leaving the field clear.

Veronica shouts a friendly parting comment, competing against the bluster. "Dogs are never ships that pass in the night, are they?" If there was a reply the wind takes it. The back of a disappearing shrug shuffles away. She huddles deeper inside her scarf with her shaken nerves and reassures herself as much as gentle Peyton. "It's okay girl. We're alone now." But she knows it for a lie as soon as it's said. Peyton remains skittish, sidling into her.

"Now we can talk," the voice says. *"And by that, I mean you should listen closely and take notes. We have work to do."*

"This can't happen. I …"

Lisabetta kneels down and embraces Peyton. She speaks with authority as she rubs the dog's ears. *"Lives are at stake. Yours, mine, and Jupiter's. Of all people, you should understand that second chances don't arrive every day. Your dog is calm now."*

Peyton wanders to the extent of the leash played out like a tape measure and is reeled in to tow Veronica like a tugboat against the wind. The two blow across the field until the tree-line catches them like a couple of tumbleweeds. Peyton is jerked to a stop whenever Veronica pauses to write a word. They progress this way for ten minutes. The rain is cruel. It's time to respect the elements and ignore the muse that riffs in her head like a jazz solo. Some days she can't hear it at all and other times it's an endless thread pulled from an old familiar sweater, or the hook of a song she can't forget.

"I'll listen, but you've got to leave Jupiter alone. Promise me."

"Too late. I've already made HIM a promise. He wants..."

"No. You don't get to use my son for your own ends. What is it that *you* want?"

"Everything."

Lightning flashes a heartbeat before its deafening boom. Peyton's whine is sucked into the storm. Veronica sloshes through puddles, hanging onto the umbilical cord between herself and the dog. She's a kite too drenched to fly. It's a slow procession, heads down against the monster that beats the trees into submission, but they make it to a dripping tunnel of pine and cedar, its entrance woven like a basket – an open door to the dwelling place of Green Man. The weather pushes them inside. She writes *'submision'… a secondary mission* on her pad.

Pan's decor is eclectic. A raw clutter of sculptured wood and vases of twigs. Wild pets scuttle in holes and nests, and dart behind the camouflage of fur-colored air. It smells of granite and moss. Patterns play over textures permeated by the scent of musk. Pan's wallpaper is a designer tangle of bark and leaves. Upholstery and draperies to match, anchor a low ceiling. A winding hallway, sheltered by the dark canopy, disappears at the first bend. Veronica's boots squelch on a sponge of pine needles that float above the mud floor in a prickly carpet.

The wildwood has its own umbrella. Veronica lowers hers to pass under the low branches. She and Peyton stroll into the density of middle-earth. Piles of bracken and the shapes of fallen deadwood move once they've passed. Each downed log is a frozen creature. A wolf wind howls a protective fence around them as they creep through a jungle of enchanted deer, and sleeping bears.

Veronica pushes back the navy cuff of her glove to check her watch. She's been wandering for twenty minutes. The bump of a ring under the wool is surprising. The writing business requires pajamas, a robe, and house slippers. She's become unselfconscious about fashion and jewelry is rarely an accessory, especially when walking the dog.

"Let's go home," Lisabetta says. *"you have a more important mission."*

"What?"

"To write my story. No worries. Your memoir can wait. Besides, mine is life and death. Yours is only a paper moon."

"You're a stalker."

"You have plenty of time for privacy. And I don't have time to debate tactics."

They emerge into a steady downpour, no longer horizontal, that falls thick and silent on a moor of saturated thatch, and head back towards the car: a woman, a dog, and a grey apparition that displaces the downpour in the shape of a woman in a long gown.

Peyton prances. Home is a happy word. The car shimmers in a time zone on the other side of the moor, buzzing like a bee.

On the way home a strong scent of violets fills the car. "Why don't you just show yourself," Veronica says out loud.

"Timing is everything," comes the reply.

Peyton fidgets in the backseat and leans against the door whining, her ears on alert. She's clearly alarmed.

Veronica rolls down the window for a blast of fresh air. "Can you hear that voice?" she asks the dog. "I must be losing my mind."

"Or finding it," Lisabetta shouts angrily. *"It's time you fought back."*

"You know," Veronica says, her face in the wind. "Writing takes no prisoners." She drives on, staring ahead like a crash-test dummy. Fanciful images compete with the stowaway voice. She demonstrates the miracles of a Polaroid camera to her good friend Leonardo. His eyes sparkle childlike wonder when the slow burn of an image of his face appears on a small, white, cardboard square.

Auto-pilot returns Veronica to Electric Street, but she has careened home like a zombie – a driver drunk on ideas, and words, and images. A brimming notebook accuses her of writing on the move in spite of her resolve to only scribble during red lights, or to allow the words to pull her over to the curb. So far she's been lucky with near misses and only punished by adrenalin spikes. The aftershocks from horn blasts have shredded her nerves. Sideswipes and fender-benders live outside her budget. If a car has nine lives, then Veronica's is living on borrowed time.

Veronica and Peyton shatter the serenity of a pristine entrance hall. Veronica peels off a saturated clump of blue fabric and water drips from its sleeves. She strips off knitted gloves to reveal a cabochon stone of ruby glass set in Scottish silver. Long wet hair stains the collar of her mauve sweater to a darker shade of purple. She drops Venus in the corner and leaves her weeping mournfully, upside down in a silk bowl filling with tears.

"Jupe... Jenny... I'm home," she calls towards the open door of her son's room.

"I'm working," Jupiter yells back.

"We're drawing," Jenny adds. "Do you want me to put the kettle on?"

Veronica fills in the missing context of Jupiter's reply: *'don't bother us right now'*.

"Thanks Jenny, I'm on it. Jupe? I'm making tea for Jenny and me. Do you want hot chocolate?"

"In a blue mug-bug," he shouts out.

"Yes, please," she corrects.

"You're welcome," he shouts back.

A shiver of rain from a drenched pooch sprays woolly water into Veronica's eyes. External tears that smart. She wipes them with the heels of her palms, rubbing them into her complexion like expensive face cream.

Peyton is wrapped in a thirsty towel and massaged dry. Her paws are lifted one-by-one. Each toe is separated and rubbed clean. A steaming canine heads for a cavernous bowl big as a waterhole. A quick slurp and the dog sighs down beside the electric fire on an oval cushion the size of a small island.

Veronica flips two switches: red flames lick asbestos logs and a fan blows hot air around Peyton in a private Chinook. She curls tighter into her grey velvet nest – a giant contented hen. A second switch sends current into the kettle. The water hisses to life. Peyton's tail thumps with pleasure.

Lisabetta touches the red plastic coals and chuckles. *"And so, time shakes itself like a wet dog,"* she says.

The storm suited us both. Neither Veronica nor I were working to task. I welcomed the thunder, hoping it would clear Veronica's head. She harkened to my suggestion to write, but became side-tracked with the best of maternal intentions, in weak dutifully dry projects. A rehash of her fear and shame won't serve her the way my memoirs will.

The better vehicle (mine) would encompass the same topics of autism with none of the tedium of clinical observation. Veronica's enthusiasm for writing needs redirection. I needed a mythological lightning bolt to part her from dull essays regurgitating her life in the slow lane and reuniting mine with heaven. Ironically, I have a deadline.

I walked with Veronica and Peyton, my gown windswept as Nike's, along the deserted promenade that hugged the coastline of Vancouver Island. The collie closed her eyes, faced the bluster of wet wind, and stepped daintily forward into the sponge of wet grass. Unlike my dog Rinato who gloried in running wild, Peyton was a subservient creature – hesitant but obedient. She surrendered to Veronica's will the same way I'd hoped Veronica would defer to mine.

She looked like a monk, huddled into a hood of dark wool, holding 'the birth of love', in front of her like a shield, walking behind her umbrella rather than underneath it.

Venus' portrait was an apt choice of shelter. Her father Kronos, has disappeared from view. There had been no need for a mother. Kronos descended from Gaia the earth and Uranus the sky, which made Venus their granddaughter, and later, the half-sister to Zeus, the consummate control freak who, in a bad mood, donated her to her husband in an arranged marriage against her wishes.

The god Jupiter's liaison with a human woman produced Leda. Venus/Aphrodite had an affair with Mars. She is the only goddess to be awarded a divorce. Going against Aphrodite's rules of love have serious consequences.

Similarly, remaining anonymous behind Lisa Giocondo's vicarious fame has dire consequences for me. Veronica is right. Writing takes no prisoners.

I died five-hundred years ago, so it's with brazen irony that I require a ghostwriter to tell my story. I may be Veronica's present muse, but if she dismisses me as monkey-mind I've overstepped my mark. I know better. Too much information washes away perception.

— Lisabetta

chapter fifty-four

"My writer
is a modern renaissance woman;
she's a painter and a poet,
and she has a hunger
to know more about my brother.
Her name is Veronica.
Her name means true icon... true face.
I am drawn to her, and she is drawn to me.
We collide somewhere in the shadows
between thought and paper."
~ Lisabetta

Mistress Lisa

VICTORIA, BRITISH COLUMBIA
APRIL 18 – 2008

The pills are louder now. Their voices echo around the halls, calling her. Veronica plucks nervously at a loose thread of her cardigan. It's been ten days since she banished them from her reach. "Jupe, is the happy lady here now?"

Jupiter scans the room, and knits his brows into 'of course not.'

"What does she look like? I can't see her."

Jupiter frowns through his mother's face.

"Hello? ... Jupe?" Veronica snaps her fingers in front of her son's eyes. "Just describe her for me, please and thank you."

Jupiter selects Leo One, plainly miffed, and takes his mother's hand. He leads her to her studio and brakes in front of the 'Mona Lisa' print. "That's her." He drops Veronica's hand, thrusts Leo One into her arms and leaves her, wilting under the portrait's smile.

Veronica steadies her breath, slow and deep. "I told you I won't entertain this," she says to the woman in the painting. "I won't lose my mind." It's her mother, Cate, all over again, talking to walls and sliding off the reality track into dementia before her time. Refusing to go there is hardly an effective strategy. Some call it denial. Veronica calls it plan A.

Her gaze drops to the floor where she steadies herself by examining the sculptured texture of the carpet. She raises her eyes to 'Mona Lisa' and absorbs her celebrity. The room is a confessional. "What we say here, stays here," she says. "Do we have a deal?"

"It had better not for both our sakes," Lisabetta replies. *"Jupiter's too. But you're wrong about one thing: it's not entirely BEFORE your time."*

Mother and child explore Vancouver Island on cozy drives, stopping to walk Peyton on every beach and in every park they find but new friends fail to materialize. Perhaps she and Jupiter and Lisabetta are three memories who tramp the moors of a previous life, roaming old paths in the fractious mists that separate the living from the dead.

"Lisabetta lives in a condo," Jupiter tells his mother. "Like that one," he says, as they pass a waterfront spill of an art deco habitat. Jupiter's volunteered information haunts Veronica. Her son's custom is to unconsciously blurt casual remarks while he's engaged in remote viewing, as if he has to periodically empty his mind of junk mail.

After the words leave his lips they're up for grabs, and Veronica is left with his loose thoughts blowing in the wind. This latest is a bizarre concept... that the Mona Lisa resides in a high-end walk up overlooking the straits of Juan de Fuca, when all along Veronica has been persuaded to believe the woman wanders her own home.

Visions of Lisabetta poking into her bureau drawers and closets, with nothing much else to do, are uncomfortable enough. Why, seems rather a moot question, but the ridiculous also borders the sublime, which is a continual source of inspiration for a right-brain processing the world.

Wings and prayers are obscure entities one must still court from time-to-time, even though Veronica avoids the possibility of life after death but she continues to hear the Italian voice that trails after her. It has become a pleasant Mediterranean Tinnitus that shadows her like the hook of a song.

At odds with her visitation rights, Veronica leaves Jupiter to his movie with Nadia's newborns, Venus and Mars, and takes Peyton on a freedom run. The swell of wind and water that hugs the coast of Cordova Bay clears her head. The main path is deserted. She makes a beeline for a human dot in the distance. Destination… grown up pleasantries with a stranger. *A new Tai Chi move*, she muses: *'walk dog to horizon'*. She lights a mental smudge stick and swings it ahead of her to cleanse the way. Gliding in a walking-meditation, she lassos her target, and reels it in, but it turns out to be a creep with a pair of jumpy Jack Russells. From now on she will use a sharper dowsing rod.

For the rest of the walk, Peyton sidles up to a dozen panting acquaintances of canine small-talk, but their owners remain anonymous and they smile like imbeciles at their surrogate offspring, tug them away from animal magnetism, and toddle off for toast and tea. Veronica misses plain adult conversation.

Why would 'Mona Lisa' haunt a condo? It's a slippery question that requires an autistic answer. Images that leap from Jupiter's audio-visual frequency bounce like kindergarten flash cards. Veronica has to hear them as a sound-bite in order to descramble. Condo, condo, condo. Its meaning is invisible, but the cards de-cloak into three images: The 'Mona Lisa', a square apartment building, and an assortment of geometric shapes – and there it is… a door opens with a mechanical hiss… geo condo.

Turns out what Lisa said was: "Tell your mother, I am NOT Lisa Giocondo."

FROM THE DIARY OF VERONICA LYONS

- BEYOND GRIEF -
APRIL 18 – 2008

I woke up in deep morning. I can't shake the agonizing feelings of loss. Now I know the meaning of the term bereft. Something so unbelievably devastating has occurred. An event I can neither remember or name has emptied the world. I'm determined to ask Lisabetta to explain because for sure, she is part of it.

— Veritas Icona

FROM THE DIARY OF VERONICA LYONS

- LIMBO HEAT -
APRIL 18 – 2008 – 7 p.m.

How does one describe a boring Sunday that is so vacant it makes empty seem meaningful? Is it the inside sticky limbo heat? or the lack of psychic breeze? Or is it the whisper of relentless small defeats that drown the hours one by one, slowly ticking trickling away? I am adrift… airless. Self-abandoned.

I have mutinied my own ship. I chased my disloyal crew of plague rats to the edge of the dock where they fell like lemmings and swam to shore. I am in dire need of entertainment and air-conditioning. It's hard to adjust the thermostat to take the edge off the rain and not feel stuck in a sauna. But, I will take rain any day over snow.

Jenny is disturbed that Jupiter has an invisible friend. She suggested it was an angel, and I had to sit her down for a heart-to-heart. At least she didn't think it was a demon. Kids have imaginary pals. It's no big deal.

Today I went to a movie and I tried to imagine Leonardo sitting next to me. The film was in wild 3-D – the sort of animation which would have disintegrated a novice movie goer – a tad over the top even for me. I had to look away from some of it. Queasiness should be renamed motion-picture sickness. The first silver screens would have wowed Leonardo well enough, but an Imax screen, surround sound, and objects hurled into his face, floating within reach, might actually cause physical harm. How could one ever explain such phenomena to a man born in the fifteenth-century?

There would be no possible way to prepare for such an onslaught of visual effects. Even the popcorn would be a miracle, and what would a 15th century palate make of Coca Cola?

I cherished being on a blind date, alone in the dark with Leonardo, in a world where the miracles of technology were mine to offer. Imagining him in the seat next to me was easy. Watching him would be as breathtaking as the film itself. I take bizarre comfort from pretending to be his personal tour guide. I'm such a kid.

I opened the balcony doors and the windows… humidity has left the building, and the scent of awakened grass is delightful. The cats are ecstatic, rolling on the nearest thing to outside they're allowed. There's too many ticks and fleas and teeth hiding in the foliage to make feline life safe or comfortable. I especially don't relish an infestation of parasites, since my entire cat colony prefers my bed to the dozens of their own.

I sing to amuse myself: Is it only 'cause I'm lonely they've blamed me for the Mona Lisa strangeness in my smile?

— Veritas Icona

   LISABETTA – A STOLEN GLANCE

chapter fifty-five

Family Snap

VICTORIA, BRITISH COLUMBIA
APRIL 19 – 2008

If it hadn't been for the umbrella or the storm or the wet dog, Lisabetta's story might still be a haunted sheet of paper, but the moment Veronica accepts the voice, she opens a floodgate of energy. Giving-up clears the mind. Surrender is like wiping an old lesson from a blackboard.

Jupiter and his lions crowd against her on the sofa. All four dolls are gathered into a group hug. A bedtime story awaits Jupiter's favorite book.

The room hums like a beehive. Lisabetta shouts "close your eyes and open the book."

When Veronica brushes aside the command, Jupiter waves Leo One's arms in her face and repeats Lisabetta's request. "The smiling lady says to please close your eyes and make a wish and open your book with the paintings. Leo One says please and thank you."

"I will to humor you, Sweet Pea. But let's not have so much of the smiling lady for a while, please and thank you."

"Can't help that," Jupiter replies holding Leo One's paws over his ears. "I made a promise."

The book opens to a page of bright colors, an absurdly stiff painting. Stiff impassive figures painted by a sculptor. Verrocchio's

'Tobias and the Angel' vibrates from the page. A boy, escorted by an angel wanders down a country road with his animated dog. The boy has been fishing. A shimmering trout hangs from a sling wrapped around the boy's finger. The angel is preoccupied with something in her hand.

"The angel is texting," Jupiter says. "*phew… the fish smells awful, but it's happy.*"

Lisabetta stands directly in front of Veronica and speaks in her normal voice. *"I was permitted to paint one of the embroidered sleeves. But you will see for yourself. I will take you there."*

"His leg must hurt," Jupiter says, pointing to the boy. "It's all wonky."

A sparkle catches at the right side of the page and the colors ripple as if underwater. Veronica covers her left eye with her hand, sure the customary aura will announce a migraine is on its way, but the painting is in focus. "The artist who painted this was ignorant of skeletal anatomy," she says. "Even the fingers look unnatural. The boy's bones are out of alignment. Look at his knee." He covers the tassel on Tobias' belt with his fingernail. "This makes me feel wonky, too."

A tall shape behind Jupiter shimmers like a net curtain caught in sunlight. "He's been in an accident," Jupiter says, massaging his knees and calves. He straightens the arms and legs of all four lion dolls.

Veronica stares defiantly into the curtain, choosing her words carefully. "I expect the fish is happy because it was painted by Leonardo." She frowns and looks away. Pico is a welcome distraction, crouching in the corner, hissing with his ears flattened. She encourages the cat to join them. "C'mon, Pico, she can't hurt you," she says. Obligingly, the shape dissipates and the cat's ears return to normal. He leaps onto Jupiter's knee.

To Jupiter's delight, Pico rubs his cheek on the corner of the book. "Did Leonardo have a cat?"

"His notebooks contain pages of cat drawings. We've studied them."

"There were cats on our farm. My brother loved all animals and birds. More than people."

Jupiter places his forehead against Pico's. "He was smart."

The 'shape' manifests in an adjacent armchair. *"He saw things the way you do. Things told him stories. And he was a wonderful storyteller."*

"And a house. Did he live in the forest like us?"

"We were born in the country. The country lived in us."

"Leonardo's backyard was wide open spaces, fields, hills, and distant mountains," Veronica says. "And he drew most things he saw. But…"

Jupiter looks up and touches his mother's mouth to interrupt. "He was a camera. You said he was a camera. Did he run out of film?"

She hesitates. "That's right. I *did* say that. I think perhaps Leonardo loved being outside so much that he beetled out his front door every morning and drew pictures of whatever fascinated him all day long, but he forgot to look back and sketch where he lived."

Jupiter giggles. "Like a beetle beetle beetle."

"Your mother is partly right," Lisabetta says to him. *"My brother escaped whenever he could and ran wild. But Leonardo never believed in looking back. He needed no reminders of a house that told a sad story."*

A shadow darkens Jupiter's mood. Looking back is full of sad stories. "My Dad is lonely," he says, singling out this historic tidbit to Leo Four, the faceless lion missing its tail, for a quick hug. His face brightens. "That's why there's hot chocolate."

A black and white photograph of my old home materializes on Veronica's computer monitor. Little has changed. The old cottage is a rustic cube of crumbling masonry, plain and unlovely. The contrast of light on bricks and dark shrubs is the same, and the reach of wild grasses still choke its threshold.

Veronica pours scalding tea in a cup and saucer bearing a classic Florentine pattern and allows the steam to rise in a facial. She breathes in her bergamot-scented tea like perfume. A green electronic glow tints her paperwork as the dim light from the computer screen flickers with my impatience. She's close now.

She rests her elbows on the desk and peers into the windows of the cottage. Desperate to see inside, her artist's mind brushes past the long skirts of the heavyset women in the photograph and wanders through the door left ajar. I wave hello like a crazy woman from behind a tree.

She's denied entry, scrolls down the text, and rests the pointer-device on her 'Mona Lisa' mouse-pad so that it covers my right eye. The pad is polished for optimum traction. Veronica straightens it parallel to the laptop. For a while the pleasure of tea is enough. Her eyes dust the objects on the mantelpiece. So many clues collected unconsciously for years. The word 'clue' triggers a picture of Leonardo's home in Amboise, 'Cloux'.

The ornaments of a prancing tin horse, the winged lion of Venice, and a Victorian butter-mold of a fork-tailed swallow in flight, glisten brighter. Her mind spirals around the core of a broken seashell and glints off the apex of a souvenir crystal pyramid from the Louvre.

To her right is a bookcase holding Leonardo's 'Treatise on Painting' and several volumes on sign language. She's made a collage of 'Mona Lisa' memorabilia: a postcard, two admission tickets to the Louvre, a novelty button that reads, 'I love Paris in the springtime', and three conjoined pieces from a miniature Mona Lisa jigsaw puzzle. I love the irony of my smile being an actual puzzle broken into fragments.

To her left is a dogeared thesaurus with the corner of a fifty-dollar bill poking from the top like a pressed flower. I cause it to flutter from the pages. It makes an imperceptible sound on the carpet, but Veronica sees it go. She retrieves it and pokes the money back, marking the wrong page. I make a fuss and shout 'look at the screen', but she clamps her hands over her ears and closes her eyes. I can't blame her. Father's are a painful reality for both of us. The money is an important sign she wants to forget.

She looks through the image of Campo Zeppi, circa 1908, captured one-hundred years to the day, in order for eternal synchronicity to register with poetic grace. Her eyes rest on the text below the photograph.

I sing to chastise her: "Many dreams have been brought to your doorstep. They just lie there, will they die there?"

"I … am … going … crazy," she says speaking slowly and deliberately to herself, the room, the drying dog, the violets, and to me. She taps the trees in the image. "I see you. Hiding, right there." Her astonishment is contained, *but Peyton sneezes from the waft of violet scent as I float by. She chuckles. "Well done, you. Hiding in plain sight... nice."*

Between sips of cold tea Veronica suppresses the muffled hysteria of a child awake too early on Christmas morning.

She used to hear me, but now she listens. I give her the year of my birth as 1458 and our work begins. There are two Lisas, I tell her. She types excitedly. A deft move opens a blank document file that balloons into a white window. She saves it as 'novel-Lisabetta-doc'. I have the pleasure of reading her working title emerge, safely centered on a fresh electronic page: 'Seconda Gioconda' – a novel by V. Lyons. It is enough for now. Bravo.

Veronica toasts me with fresh tea on her balcony, gazing over the panoramic rain forest of British Columbia. She inhales a sense of purpose on the awakening grass mixed with ozone. "I know you're here," she says. "Can I see you now?"

I answer, "all in good time, Cara. You have done well. Brava. Brava."

By April 2008, my anniversary year had already been ticking for three months. I knew instinctively that I had until December to achieve my goal. The day I followed my champions to the streets of Paris, I became Jupiter's surrogate mother as Veronica became mine. I had been awarded the prerequisite nine months to gestate, now my little poet must make my life rhyme by writing me to death in the remaining eight. I will need every moment to breach her resistance and save her son. One thing is clear. Mrs. Bently has to go.

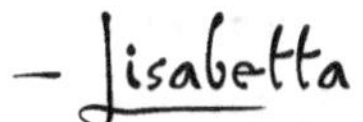

FROM THE DIARY OF VERONICA LYONS

- BURNOUT -
APRIL 20 – 2008 – 6 a.m.

Mrs. Bently has been with us five days. In two weeks we finalize a schedule. I can't remember not having a helper with Jupiter. I am allowing myself the luxury of feeling free. I am even free to indulge in feeling lost.

I sleep fitfully, and pace the balcony at 3 A.M. when my challenges have cooled sufficiently to be able to breathe. I feel that I've been playing with fire… hence the burnout and meltdown. I'm in spiritual shock. I long for peace, but I remember more of everything instead of less. There has been no special delivery of compassionate amnesia lovingly administered by hovering guardian angels. No Italian phantom can grant me asylum from guilt.

I wonder if my neighbors see me and report strange manifestations of 911 midnight activity in a house that's been empty for years. Have I haunted here for centuries? I've lost track of divine time.

We living ghosts are made of gossamer wind. We float and sigh, and nearby mortals shiver without knowing what has passed them by. We are the lovers of romance, dashed heroes, exhausted heroines and stillborn dreams.

But if one believes in reincarnation… then the waiting may be rewarded.

— Veritas Icona

FROM THE DIARY OF VERONICA LYONS

- MINOTAUR -
APRIL 22 – 2008 – 9 p.m.

I witness the spectacle of what used to be, by journeying through pages of text, highlighting with the frenzied glow of yellow ink as I go. I travel down side-word roads, and back-track to sniff out a warm trail, and pick up the labyrinth string trampled in the mud, missed from dizzy busy-ness.

The Minotaur is my guide. He is not stubborn… only persistent. I know he would surrender and turn his neck to Mithras for me, but I don't ask for sacrifice.

He is my consort to the sacred cow of Isis, and his lair is the crucible which burns away the chaff that surrounds me. All along I have been fearing his Apis form, never guessing he was tamed gentle from accepting he is the last of his kind. It is time to grab his horns, to spin and orbit a few far-distant world stars, before comet-ing myself back to the present day, reborn a Taurus baby-girl… priestess of the Serapeum.

I believe our ghostly intruder really is the 'Mona Lisa'. She's certainly Jupiter's Lizzie. She told him that her name is Lisabetta, and my Leonardo research confirms it. She is mentioned as an obscure throwaway in a government census. I will take steps to insure she is gone immediately. Right after Mrs. B... Religion mixed with a paranormal visitor is like a lit match and gasoline.

— Veritas Icona

FROM THE DIARY OF VERONICA LYONS

- MIDNIGHT PANCAKES -
APRIL 23 – 2008

In a waking dream, Lisabetta accuses me of being routine. She says I`m in danger of becoming predictable. That soon she won`t be able to tell me from a typical sleepwalker. I can`t let her think such a zombie exists under my skin. I tell her it's the work ethic kicking in and that it erases all other urges to create. She says to stop and refresh the page. She is learning computer-speak, and it made me laugh as well as making a lot of sense.

She gave me a pep-talk like a soccer coach. She commented the house is in need of a duster and mop. In spite of her enthusiasm, I finished my chapter before I attempted to score a goal in her game of search and reveal. She expects me to come out of hiding with her, but she`s right. I need to play and paint and dream regular dreams.

Two hours later, I challenged Lisabetta. I walked Peyton into a moonless country road with Jupiter. We ate midnight pancakes in the dining room off the best china. I decanted apple juice from a cardboard container into a glass Art Deco pitcher, and Jupiter was seriously impressed drinking from a wineglass.

The next day I said hello to an imperfect stranger in my bathroom mirror. I watered my parched house plants and pruned their dead dreams. I wore a peasant skirt and shook out the rugs, and I washed the bedroom floor as if I was under military orders. I see no evil, I hear no evil, I speak no evil but Lisabetta is the fourth monkey, so anything can happen.

— Veritas Icona

chapter fifty-six

Victorious Night Scribbles

WAKE-UP CALL
APRIL 29, 2008

Veronica's hand reaches out and turns off the dark with a tap on her bedside table. A sensitive magic lamp reveals the power of a human touch.

Pico lifts his head and blinks into the light. Nattie squirms. Veronica's hand fumbles for a pen and small coil notebook, and narrowly misses knocking over an owl-size statuette of Nike. These are her staples of writing. As her muse, I dictate at any hour. Her home and car are littered with spiral pads of all sizes. I remind her that her Latin name 'veritas icona'... means true face, and tell her once again how my face misses its name.

Veronica captures a couple of dream words on paper, and taps the table... thump... and the table turns-on the dark. The twenty-first century is a miracle.

Until we can speak openly, we communicate in key words too powerful to forget. Our night scribbles linger, teasing, demanding attention. Veronica chews them into translations that provoke questions I beg her to ask me.

— Lisabetta

From first…
APRIL 29, 2008

CAMPO ZEPPI, Tuscany / APRIL 29 – 1452

A young peasant woman heaves her tired body to the next task. She sets a basket with her newborn, two-weeks-old, under a shade tree and turns from her son towards the whinny of a grey pony. "Come Lezza. I have something for you," she says, and pulls a rosy apple from the pocket of her apron.

She misses the landing of a small kite on the blanket of her sleeping boy. It taps its tail on the baby's lips. Tap tap tap. *Are you awake?* the bird says, three times. A chubby hand reaches for it and clutches empty air and the ghost of a dreamed feather. Rather than cry, the infant blinks curiously at the space, that seconds before had been a pair of wings and an impertinent tail.

The sky which recalled the bird is a fractured triangle of dazzling blue, floating between two overhead branches. The branches interlocking fingers form a pattern of shimmering green spangles. Soon the tossing waves of a leafy sea hypnotize the child. He smiles, closes his eyes, and dreams he is Leonardo da Vinci.

NIGHT SCRIBBLE READS:
kite -- tail -- lips – birds

DADDY'S GIRL
MAY DAY, 2008
MAY 1, 1463 / A Dream of Campo Zeppi -

A stage set materializes from the balcony seat of a flimsy 2-dimensional cardboard pop-up theatre.

"Watch," Lisabetta says. "That's me down there."

A brown-faced peasant girl, five-years-old, waits center-stage on a cardboard floor. She kneels, surrounded by violets spread around her like a spell. She teases a ball of puppy-fluff with the stem of a flower. It barks ecstatically in a frenzy and rakes the violets into a small cloud behind it. The child's head lifts suddenly and her joyous expression evaporates. A man eclipses the sun. She squints up at his face.

Veronica feels the presence of cruelty. She reads defiance in the girl's eyes. The puppy chews at the flower unconcerned. Veronica sees the back of the man's grimy shirt. He lifts a dirt-encrusted boot towards the creature, and the child, anticipating the worst, throws herself in front of the dog.

The boot's trajectory collides mid-air with the girl's forehead. She is knocked off-balance – her neck whiplashed with pain. The man moves off snickering and the dazed girl rearranges the disturbed violets as if they will keep her safe.

A vicious bruise spreads across the child's temple and blood trickles into her left eye. The puppy licks it clean. The girl is too dizzy to stand. She leans on the puppy, pulling it into the curve of her arms like a pillow and curls into a ball. She looks like a child ready to be born. It is the last image Veronica remembers: a dazed girl and a reprieved dog viewed from above, inside a witchy circle of purple blossoms, getting smaller as she floats higher into the sun.

"There's no way I'm getting involved with this," Veronica says. "I was wrong to agree."

"Think about it for a few days," Lisabetta pleads.

"Absolutely not... no... no way. I refuse to tempt crazy. I've changed my mind. I will not entertain collaboration with a phantom, so please go." The effect of Veronica's last three words lacks the forcefulness she had intended.

"No matter," Lisabetta says. "I know someone you won't be able to dismiss."

NIGHT SCRIBBLE READS:

truth -- puppy -- violets -- 5 -- fear -- bully

… to last
MAY 2, 2008
MAY 2 – 1519 AMBOISE, France / The manor house of
'CLOUX'

Leonardo da Vinci sits at his open window, his mind a flutter of birds as he awaits death. When he hears the call of thunder behind him, he hesitates. No matter. He calls softly over his shoulder into the deepening shadows. "Lisa, is that you?"

Traces of Violet
MAY 2 – 2008
MAY 2 – 1519 – the Manor House of Cloux – Amboise

The hem of an emerald silk dress catches the light as it rustles across a carpet of Persian flowers towards a four-poster bed. The dress perches on a gilded armchair at the bedside. Graceful hands rest in the pose of the 'Mona Lisa' and wait.

Leonardo da Vinci, sixty-seven, hallucinates near death with his eyes closed. His long white hair splays out like a silver halo on a red velvet pillow bordered with rows of seed-pearls. The canopy sky above is blue velvet embroidered with gold stars. He opens his eyes and smiles. A green sleeve takes his hand. The scent of violets permeates Veronica's bedroom and follows her all day and into the business of controlled dreaming.

NIGHT SCRIBBLE READS:
deathbed -- violets -- silk -- loss – green sleeves – Mona Lisa

chapter fifty-seven

The Victory of Artemis

MAY 3 – 2008

The latest rescue cat arrives as fortuitously as the others – a discriminating feline, this one culled from a house fire, via the SPCA. The cat had been on one of her hunts when the flames expelled her from captivity and for a while she evaded the traps and the domestic embrace of a charity shelter. She has one life left.

The tabby is picky. She will know home when she smells it. For weeks she surveys the cul-de-sac network of Bear Mountain and scopes out the boy on Electric Street. They chat often. He tells her his name is Jupiter; she tells him hers is Nadia.

Nadia's coat is dapple grey and it reminds Jupiter of a nursery rhyme.

Nadia basks in Jupiter's voice with her eyes closed and listens to him recite: *'I had a little pony. I called him Dapple-grey. I lent him to a lady, to ride a mile away. She whipped him, she slashed him, she rode him through the mire. I would not lend my pony now, for all the lady's hire.'* Nadia is hooked.

There are two women at odds in Jupiter's house; Nadia studies them. She has a plan, but the goddess of the forest lures her into a savory bowl of delightfully fishy paste, left as bait. It's one of her leaner nights, and hunger is persuasive.

The cage door swings shut, and Lisabetta soothes the little creature. "Do not worry little one. Jupiter will help you." But when the van takes Nadia away she cries out. Lisabetta memorizes the number on the side of the vehicle.

Jupiter and Veronica formally adopt Nadia the next day.

Nadia tours the house, regal as you please, and claims her space. The tabby is starved for attention, but being a night huntress, she has managed to stay plump on the abundances of the wildwood.

Jupiter announces the cat's name is Nadia. Veronica looks up and to the right, and scans something invisible there. "That's a great name," she says. "It's an anagram. Both her names are."

By nightfall, Bear Mountain has weathered a freak snowfall, and Nadia has endured a bath and had her identity restored. Lisabetta is impressed and says so when she and Nadia share a moment under the moon. "It should be so easy, to have one's name respected," Lisabetta says, petting Nadia into a blur of soft tremors. "What's your secret?"

Nadia loves to chat. She tells Lisabetta why she's plump.

Nadia sharpens her claws on the nearest tree trunk. "Jupiter says this is your tree," she tells Lisabetta.

"He named it for me. Jupiter likes naming things," Lisabetta says.

Peyton accepts Nadia completely. Nattie will take time. Pico sniffs and plays possum. There's a feral scent about the new arrival which gives her authority, and alpha males aren't as dominant as their press. A familiar of Pan has presence enough to eclipse neutered power.

Nadia likes to play hide and seek. She's distracted by anything not tied down: a single Cheerio, Jupiter's triangle eraser, or a paper clip. Shiny things interrupt her cat thoughts. Batting them senseless under the furniture is a compelling career. Veronica indulges her; she knows that fire can make a girl crazy. Nadia deserves a second chance.

Trauma is everywhere for a cat with a cautious paw on the pulse of *humane* nature. Nadia is nocturnal as a ghost, compelled to sleep under the scent of a full moon. Captivity is a steep learning curve,

　　　　　　　　　　LISABETTA – A STOLEN GLANCE

but hunger wins out. Gift mice are laid at Veronica's bedroom door. The open air of the oak grove and the Lisa Tree calls, but the warm side of the cat flap is a world of pleasurable surrender. It's the place Nadia wants to birth her kittens. She knows they will be twins – a male and a female of Gemini power. Female cats learn early to submit to the males.

Nadia had spit at the old black tomcat before she surrendered, herself only a young girl, and becomes a mother at only eighteen and a half weeks-old.

FROM THE DIARY OF VERONICA LYONS

- THE SPIRIT OF CHRISTMAS: PAST & FUTURE -
MAY 8, 2008

Christmas tried to arrive early last week on the second of May, with its bells and baubles and an untimely gift. It was an out of season boon I ignored. The story arrived with complications. It scared me. Lisabetta's aura unnerves me. The last thing I need is to follow my mother down the slippery slope of mental illness. I decided to disregard the presence and paint... leave the writing thing be, but I have the feeling 'it / she' isn't going to leave me alone, and that my new life is only one out-of-control-event away. My poor son. I will call Uncle Oz if I don't feel stable soon.

My imagination is flying north and south at the same time. How I will ground myself remains a mystery and a must-ery. I had thought assembling thousands of words would do that. My must-story. I had been looking forward to a promise of literary stability – finally a peaceful writing nook. Seems I was wrong to wish for such an animal.

I will turn my Jupiter diaries into a sort of layman's guide to autism and polish my years of clinical observations with margins of emotional commentary. At least it will get me to the safer motion of an east-west keyboard and a left-to-right brain. Somehow, the ticking sound of the keyboard calms me. It's like a conversation with a trusted friend, and I think I am hooked on the fact I am in control of the text that comes. I can delete anything or change and rewrite. It's me talking into a neutral box, and after seeing my words spin out of my head onto a flat-screen I am free of a burdensome weight which has suppressed me.

There are different kinds of mates. Intellectual ones. Business ones. Teacher ones. So, is it greedy to expect an intellectual one to also fill the role of romantic lead? Having control is the only freedom a woman can have, apart from wealth. I want both. Then I can rule a subterranean world exactly how I want – lived apart from society, in luxurious reclusive freedom to purchase any environment I care to design. My own Mt. Olympus inhabited by goddess sisters and holy cats, and Jupiter and his trusty canine sidekick.

Zeus, Apollo and the rest of the toadies can be kept, boy toys – small action figures sealed in their original packaging on shelves in a dark room.

— Veritas Icona

NIGHT SCRIBBLE READS:
Nadia = Diana -- Diana = Artemis -- Artemis = art is me

*'Tobias & the Angel' a studio painting from
the studio of andrea verrocchio*

'Row row row your boat
Gently down the stream...
Merrily merrily merrily merrily
Life is but a dream.'

A Matter of Truth

VICTORIA – A STOLEN LILY PAD OF TIME
APRIL 24 – 2008

Veronica Lyons' arms refuse to cooperate when she gropes blindly to anchor her dream-space. Her urge to run freezes her to the moment; intense dreams always short-circuit the ability to flee or grasp or rationalize. She slumps to the floor asleep onstage like a puppet with its strings cut – obliged to watch a play or wake up. Behind her, a troupe of phantoms pays no attention to her decision. Beside her, stands her muse, Lisabetta. The images had seemed flawlessly natural until she woke up inside the dream and realized its scope and consequences. That's when she feels her grip on reality slipping and the ability to grasp onto something tangible becomes an act of survival. It feels like dying.

The studio of Andrea Verrocchio remains aligned to the business of art. A metal sphere under construction, eight feet in diameter, rests low to the ground in a cradle of sticks like a blank globe. Its unblemished surface awaits the undiscovered 'New World' and the land masses and oceans of the known world, soon to be caught in a lace net of invisible longitudes and latitudes. The metal workers have engineered a small hollow planet with an oculus like a Hobbit's front door.

Soon it will rise to crown the cupola of the Santa Maria del Fiore's dome – a floating gazebo, hooked on a spire – to become the default image of the Florentine skyline. The burnished orb, seen from below, as a copper pearl eclipsing the sun.

Veronica is familiar with the painting propped on a stand. It's closely attended by a slim teenager with long chestnut hair, standing in a room with the aura of a church: the easel an altar, and the young man before it – a devout artist deferring to an icon. He stares through the *'Tobias and the Angel'* panel – a slave to its voice.

It's a bright narrative of primary blues and reds and yellows: a boy's journey of compassionate intervention accompanied by his faithful dog and an enchanting fish strung onto a wooden handle. Veronica calls it the marionette fish. By her reckoning, the painting's many weaknesses serve to project a young whiz-kid's visions forward like gems sparkling from a handful of pebbles. The dog is missing. In its place is an outline of red chalk.

The young artist drums clean graceful fingers against his velvet sleeves and listens intently to the whimpers of a dog-sprite begging to be born.

The stunning youth in the spotless rose tunic, who stands absorbed in thought with arms folded, is the eighteen-year-old, Leonardo da Vinci.

The composition is an abrasive shape. Not Leonardo's choice. He prefers triangles. It sets him on edge, but he copes by isolating his two contributions. His eyes, once locked onto painting the scales of a single trout, now examine the space where a dog has decided to materialize. The artist is determined to experiment with the new technique of oils. Leonardo thinks it should stick to the tempura ground, but it's an oil and water story, and Veronica knows the little terrier will evaporate over time and become a ghost dog.

The conflicting styles of seven painters inflict discord to Leonardo's mind. There are too many flaws to correct: the angel's wings look too solid to flap. The apprentice, Bartolomeo, has copied a heavy wood and leather contraption made for a pageant, too literally. Fillepe has painted the tassel on Tobias's belt so that it flies free and tangles into a tree which destroys the illusion of distance, the most junior of Andrea's pupils has made puffball rocks made of cotton-wool, and the disturbing left leg of the boy, Tobias, twists back, painfully deformed, but these defects must be overlooked.

The most sensitive task of the day will be repairing the botched sky which must be diplomatically rescued from the blunder of the golden boy, Lorenzo's, weak hand. Without a decent sky, Leonardo's dog and fish will be further dishonored. One day he hopes to have a painting to himself. One day he will control the background and foreground and subdue the chaos in between.

Leonardo can do little to animate the stiff figures. Master Verrocchio is a sculptor first and a painter by necessity. His painted figures are creatures made of marble with claw-like affectations of twisted fingers who wear colorful clothes. Draperies of stone defy the wind and pin them to the earth, yet the angel, Raphael, come to Earth, makes no contact with the road at all.

The dog manifests effortlessly, and while Leonardo's brush is loaded with burnt sienna, he unconsciously adds a deft movement of color that softens the escaped curl at the Tobias's temple with a thin glaze of light. Leonardo smiles. This third involvement balances his others, now well-placed to shine with a satisfying degree of triangulation.

The sky is another matter. Leonardo has avoided it as a punishing task, but even his selective vision can no longer block the bungle of inept talent. The earth-tones on his palette are set aside for the shades of blues and yellows and violets he can make from the pure colors Lisabetta has prepared. He notes the precious lapis and Egyptian purple and steels himself to face Lorenzo's idea of a summer heaven, but fate intervenes.

chapter fifty-nine

*"I am her muse. She is my writer.
The story is ours."*
~ Lisabetta

Born Too Late

VICTORIA – A RAFT OF LILY PADS
APRIL 25 – 2008

Hanson's Art History textbook lies open on Veronica's knee. Jupiter and his lions are in bed. Leo four has pride of place in her son's arms. The other three are arranged at the foot of his bed.

The 'Tobias and the Angel' reproduction sends a blast of bright red and blue trickery from the page. It's the force of these primary colors that diverts the untrained eye to believing the painting is the work of a master painter. It's garish nature belies its glaring faults. It is, after all, the culmination of a group of junior apprentices in various stages of development with the patchy supervision of a more senior artist who has too much work on his hands to belabor the details. The studio is a busy factory. Commissions are late. Church dignitaries, focusing on religious iconography, will never notice anatomical discrepancies. Expediency is money. And novices have to fend for themselves.

Jupiter's fingers trace the fish and pet the ghost of an animated dog. "The angel has a cell phone," he says.

It's an absurdly static painting. Two lifeless figures painted by a master sculptor with architectural challenges on his mind. The angel's wings may as well be made of tinted concrete and stone clouds defy gravity, suspended in the sky by ropes as in a theatrical set. But for a little prancing dog, it's a stagnant scene set within a two-dimensional depth of field.

The contract had stipulated the main figures of the work, destined for public display, must be the hand of Master Verrocchio to justify the expense.

It is for similar reasons, that so many religious icons churned out in the *bottegas* of Florence, are sent into the world with ill-observed infants. The Christ-child is placed in the hands of men who rarely participate in childcare, let alone ones who are beguiled by the subtleties of their cuddly charm.

Andrea Verrocchio is as shrewd a businessman as his lawyer and neighbor, Ser Piero da Vinci. From the beginning of their foster arrangement, Piero had warned Andrea of his son's strange departures of consciousness and the singular bond between him and his younger sister, Lisabetta.

To Andrea's surprise, Lisabetta follows her half-brother to his studio with talent of her own. She handles Leonardo's moodiness which smooths the production line, and it has become advantageous to court Leonardo. Leonardo's talent is divine; he has the aura of grace about him when he loses himself in his work.

It's hardly surprising that Verrocchio will later defer to Leonardo when it comes to painting figures. The master's medium, being stone and marble, delivers hard-edged statue people whose heavy feet, incredibly, float above the ground. They clearly require pedestals betwixt their sandals and the earth, whereas Leonardo's excited white dog in the 'Tobias' trots effortlessly, leaving easily-imagined pawprints in the dust of the road. No-one cares when Leonardo takes the initiative, in a stolen moment, to practice on one sainted curl of Tobias' hair.

Veronica hyperventilates as her fingers pluck the surface of rough floorboards exploring the worn planks until she feels the sharp jab of a splinter. Dreams can be irritatingly lucid.

Lisabetta moves closer and suppresses her anger. "*Mia caro*, my dear, you are recovered?"

"Never."

"That is enough. Stop pretending to be a weak woman. You are not powerless. It is nonsense. My death is in your hands and we are moving too slow. This day is significant... important, yes? I think that you must see how it was, so I bring you here, and I cannot waste anymore time. I need you to keep your head. Please. Our work... my story and your chance will fail if you do not write every word of this."

Veronica waves towards Leonardo from her collapsed position. "No fair. You bring me here to see him... and all... all of this?"

"*Caro*, it was a surprise, and you are not so delicate. You must be stronger if we are to succeed. It is your freedom too. You want a new life, yes? You like my surprise, yes?"

"Yes, but ..."

"Look. I am over there. See? That is me. I am twelve. Do you see me? I offered to paint over Lorenzo's sky, but Leonardo said no. He wanted to do it." Lisabetta embraces the studio with outstretched arms – a human cross. Her body shimmers. She is hopelessly, fully there. "I bring you to this place for a reason," Lisabetta says. "This is the day I decided to become ... a little, as you call ... bitch? I look so innocent, no?" Lisabetta points to a confident figure making his way across the room. "There is my killer."

"Killer!"

"No, no ... a destroyer, yes? ... a bully."

Lorenzo di Credi, a dusky thirteen-year-old, prince of every-thing-Verrocchio, is on his way to alter the lives of a million people.

"He looks harmless," Veronica says.

Lisabetta makes a strangled sound in her throat. "He is about to eat me alive." She points to a far corner. "Over there is my Sandro."

"Please no, I can't take any more." Veronica looks back at Leonardo. "I've had enough."

"It is *not* enough," Lisabetta says. "It was *never* enough!"

"I should go."

"We are wasting energy. Come... I need you to remember this."

Lisabetta takes Veronica's hands, and pulls her to her feet. "You must see him as I do," she says, and propels her charge towards a tall man enveloped in light.

Fiery blue eyes stay locked on their work. Sandro Botticelli is safely blocked by subjective imagination. Veronica is captivated by a long tumble of auburn curls under a mauve cap. Long dark eyelashes flicker against his tanned cheeks as they follow his brush, and the pulse in his throat beats gently below. The stitching on the neck of his cotton shirt breathes the same rhythm – a straight line of peach thread against white fabric. Veronica feels dizzy from studying the nape of his neck.

Sandro turns towards the scent of feminine energy. His eyes darken as he stares through the two women. Botticelli's eyes, flash violet from the reflecting light. Veronica floats towards him, close enough to kiss, and a delicious itch is telegraphed to her remote body. The seduction is complete. Her form stirs above, moaning in a distant bed, the slave of an artist long-dead.

Lisabetta looks similarly drugged. Veronica thinks dream travelers must be co-dependent, like twins. She knows too much about twin-ship, and surely a muse is a potent reflection of one's psyche. "Yes, he is quite something." Veronica's words escape from her dry throat. Even dreamers get thirsty. The one thing Lisabetta has taught her since they first met a month ago, is that twins may be born six years apart.

Across the room, the younger Lisabetta mixes colors with blue fingers. She looks at Sandro with undisguised adulation and nearly upsets a jar of water. It wobbles against her sleeve and miraculously spins to a stop.

Lisabetta describes Sandro perfectly: "*Magnifico*, yes?"

"*Magnifico*, yes," Veronica agrees, and the scene disintegrates into thin red fog. Her sleeping body calls her as it arches with pleasure, but she wills herself to stay. No-one should eclipse the thrill of seeing a young Leonardo, but Sandro is a magnet and she is hardly pulled into his orbit; she runs there. Veronica's dream has a singular theme of organic adoration: the admiration of Veronica for two men, an artist in raptures over a section of painting, a young boy over a girl, and a besotted girl over a man twice her age.

A human drama unfolds. Magic pushes the ensuing argument into a blur. Lorenzo teases. The girl Lisabetta lashes out. Lorenzo flies into a rage. The event is sealed and the child Lisabetta has a strange look in her eyes. Lorenzo fades into the recesses of the studio. In retaliation, Leonardo dismisses Lorenzo's sky to history. The dog and fish will have to console each other. There will be other paintings. Sandro turns towards the disturbance. Behind him looms a backdrop of metaphorical white clouds that darken into a storm.

Botticelli's voice acts like smelling salts. "Come little sister," he calls to *his* Lisabetta. "I need your help. Do not mind him little one ... he is *insignificante.*"

Veronica's Lisabetta has vanished. She is inside her child self.

Veronica looks down, strangely jealous, and turns back towards an eighteen-year-old god.

Leonardo wipes the excess blue from his brush, dips it into red turpentine and the color swishes into mud. He selects a new dab of sienna and ochre and white – swirls them into warm brown, binds them together with a slick of oil, adds a tip of cooling black, and abandons the 'Tobias' to its botched sky. The sharp edge of an awkward cloud will forever prod the boy's head like a slow lightning bolt. Let it reflect the truth of the upstart's talent. Leonardo will attend to his dog and no more.

Veronica catches Sandro Botticelli teasing Lisabetta in a stolen moment. He lifts her blonde braid to his lips, kisses it slowly, and taps the end of it on her nose: "Little shadow, you should wear this down," he says as he wipes a small smudge of blue from Lisabetta's cheek. "*Caramia*, you have some sky on your cheek."

Leonardo engages his right-brain and enters his painting. To him, the studio disappears and he is alone with the faint outline of a dog in need of a body, waiting to emerge into a three-dimensional trickery of fluff. Leonardo waits until he feels the inner command to begin, and applies the first feathery brushstroke to the fur of a prancing mongrel. A cloud dog.

Sandro's laugh warms the room, Tobias's dog freshly glistens, the escaped wisp of Tobias's hair is combed with sunlight, and the delicate colors of Leonardo's iridescent fish have dried to a soft polish for over a month. Leonardo is barely eighteen. Lisabetta's nemesis, Lorenzo, is thirteen. Sandro is twenty-five. Veronica remains a young twenty-nine and now her muse has transformed from a shy twelve-year-old into a supple teenage coquette who has pinned Sandro into a corner, and he is exploring under her skirts.

Veronica ignores them by studying Leonardo. His breath rises and falls evenly. He is dreaming his dog into form, separate from her own trance and the other trances in the studio. The moment stuns her. "Don't let me wake up," Veronica calls out, but Lisabetta has not returned from her triumphant romp, and only a faint trace of her lingers where she once stood.

Veronica imagines being crushed into a corner against Sandro Botticelli, not giving a hot damn about the year 2008, and Lisabetta is shouting from the end of a long tunnel: "Write it for him as well as me."

Veronica sings lyrics to taunt Lisabetta: *"is this your way to hide a broken heart?"*

The morning threatens to part Veronica from Sandro, but she fights consciousness, latches on to his signature, and wills her way back to Florence without Lisabetta, to explore ghostly love in private.

Sandro is there, painting, and when he steals a glance at Veronica with an adoring smile, her life dissolves into the headiness of white sound. His energy absorbs hers, the world disappears, and Veronica Lyons, quite rationally, falls for a dream.

Lisabetta had been right to criticize. Veronica has been lax. She will have to apply herself. She made Lisabetta and Jupiter a promise, and now she's making strange assurances to Sandro, and for the first time since childhood there's power worth exploring.

Veronica and her muse bide on time-sensitive passports. She must fight for her own independence as much as Lisabetta's.

Finding Sandro was everything, but he belongs to both of them now, and he will have to choose.

PREVIEW of BOOK 2

'Lisabetta — a stolen smile'

chapter one

Time Pirates

JUNE 4 – 2008

For a time, in the year 1911, I was stored in a shabby box, locked in the dark hole of a closet. It was musty and hot. A stove belched dry heat beside me for two years. If my abductor had not been hungry enough to give me up, it's likely I would have rotted there until his death and been discarded in the smelly trunk with my companion newspapers, rags, and old boots. Rescue is an event which requires the grace of miraculous intervention, but my infamous vacation pushed me center stage. Fate is far more mysterious than a smile.

When I sipped the hemlock of fame it spat me out. I was grit in its wild teeth – a bitter lovechild expecting sugar.

Those claiming to be authorities, label my century a cultural renaissance, which gives it the air of a romantic party – a poetic notion incongruous with the violent shufflings of power that took precedence over human life. I've learned that historians err on the side of naivety and that time is a dishonorable editor. I do know that rebirths of civilizations are more painful than human birth and they take much longer. And I know what it's like to be ignored.

History only ever recorded me squeezed between two commas in a population census, and after all my climbing and dedication and discipline, I was still not a vital enough statistic to warrant a footnote in the memoirs of art. The irony is, Leonardo's 'Mona Lisa', the most famous portrait in the world, lost her identity while Lisa Giocondo, the spoiled 'principessa', became a household name with the wrong face... my face.

If time or the hand of man has not destroyed her, the original Lisa sleeps in the shadows, perhaps catalogued under an assumed name by a confused translator. She waits in the recesses of a museum warehouse or palace cubbyhole or a humble attic. She may be breathing underneath the facade of another skin in order to slip past covetous warlords, in which case, her disguise is a death mask. The world knows us too well without camouflage. It knows the slope of our shoulders and the curve of our folded hands, our long parted hair worn loose, the square of our neckline, our direct gaze, and our signature enigmatic smile.

In my time, artists were forbidden to sign their works, and there were female artists in almost every studio of Florence. All of us were daughters, wives, nieces or siblings of our male counterparts.

I was the half-sister of Andrea Verrocchio's star apprentice, Leonardo da Vinci.

I grew up as an invisible presence within the creative milieu of Florence and Milan, and Venice and Rome, which I suppose was only fitting because my beloved brother called me his little shadow. I was the silent updraft under his rising star so he could process his anguishes.

Leonardo was hardly the incandescent genius in amber the world has decided to immortalize. He lived and breathed quiet triumphs and weathered humiliating defeats. He lived a double life, riding a pendulum of erratic energy, equal parts outrageous exuberance and irrational despair.

While I had never managed to gain the Paris streets during my Louvre stay, I acquired an audio-visual understanding of the modern world that drifted through my 'still-life' every day, and I learned the English language, such as it could be gleaned from the limited conversations overheard within the sanctuary of museum hush. I referred to my visitors as the 'parade of forever' and thought of them as bloodsuckers consuming me. A true visitor would stay longer than three minutes, but they offered a harvest of entertaining facts and speculation. I grabbed hold of a few likely hosts every day, but they brushed me aside, and most of the remaining clock-time of visiting hours, I retreated into the wall behind me to contemplate my folly. I am fortunate that meditation affords me glimpses of a healthy Leonardo who patiently awaits my return, but even in death he's never idle. I don't know if he can observe civilization's advances. Whenever I see him he's wrapped in the serene embrace of our Tuscan hills with our dog, Rinato, too far away to hear me.

Sometimes I think he is, as he usually was, too involved in an idea to respond to me... the selective hearing of the possessed genius.

I'm a masterpiece in situ. I would even suggest that I am an investment in the machine of commerce. I've heard I'm a lucrative million dollar industry and that my portrait is priceless. And so, the consciousness of the sixteenth century spins its course while I wander a parallel existence of half-death and wait for synchronicity to save me from the shadow-lands between centuries.

My brother was widely known in the art world. Hardly revered during our many lean years and barely honored by a scatter of loyalties at the end. It was twentieth century spin-doctors who elevated Leonardo to a veritable god. Leonardo's professional reputation lacked responsibility and we navigated our peasant legacy of poverty by floating on debt and never staying too long in one place. We lived sparingly on a bland diet of random success and I'm not being metaphorical when I say, we often starved in a famine of our own making.

Women artists were of little consequence outside the sweatshops of paint and marble, and counted for nothing at all on the general map of social topography. We were child laborers and domestic slaves, and faced intensive periods of serial motherhood if we survived childbirth. Yet, we were also the alchemists who made beautiful children from our husband's shame and a many of us had the audacity to help turn raw minerals into the golden age of art.

Most studio panels were painted by several hands, each assigned according to the rules of creative worth. Senior artists painted the faces of the main figures: saints and the Christ-child, and the Madonna. Junior capabilities were calculated at a lower rate to placate the customers. We painted scenic backgrounds and the persistent swarms of hovering cherubs as well as draperies, hands, wings, and skies. This was how Leonardo began when he was twelve. He was given wings to paint and he couldn't have been happier.

Leonardo's childhood obsessions with flight caused his painted feathers to preen on the page... to flutter against the sticky surfaces of the wood panels and lift free of the paint. Leonardo studied live and dead flying creatures: birds, butterflies, bees, dragonflies, moths, flies, and bats. Each wing was a marvel. None were too insignificant to analyse.

Generally, customers believed what they were told, but in a demanding season, details were often executed by inferior hands. This was how Leonardo

          LISABETTA – A STOLEN GLANCE

won his break. A sensitive rendering of a fish caused a stir in the hierarchy of Verrocchio's domain, and when asked to add a dog beside a sandaled figure, my brother painted our pet mongrel. He rendered Rinato's coat with the same delicacy as a wisp of escaped hair on the main figure. Both ruffle in the breeze of a summer day. From there he was promoted to higher service and sweetened the contours of the mural's faces even when the senior assistants were idle. Leonardo painted movement and texture and air... and most of all, the divine breath called inspirito.

Arresting beauty and talent eclipse visual sightings of everyday sainthood. Leonardo had both. I was allowed to work beside him, grinding his colors and painting translucent clouds. My skills were quietly noted and even Sandro Botticelli asked for my help. As I said, skies were my specialty.

Only creative courage flaunts the rules of artistic order. My brother was one of these. Visual conventions were slight annoyances to be brushed aside, but Leonardo never did anything small. He swept away the dreary canons of art and started fresh. He surprised himself. He allowed every feral idea to evolve into its own story. He lived between the rules.

My brother was a born explorer, and if we had lived by the sea, no doubt he would have discovered the new world long before Captain Vespucci. As it was, Leonardo was surrounded by a different sea – a living sea of vegetation.

The grasses of Tuscany grew to the edge of our doorstep and the hills gifted him a place to hide and rest, and offered up their abundance of natural species: fauna, flora, and elemental. The countryside was a living entity – his home, his church, and his best friend. It was the safest place for Leonardo to talk with me while I awaited physical rebirth.

To summarize: my father, Antonio, was a kiln worker and a part-time soldier, and when he was away fighting in some local skirmish or distant war zone, I sneaked into the city to be Leonardo's assistant. I needed no excuses. I was in love with art and my brother's colleague, Sandro Botticelli.

Sandro was a striking contrast of copper hair and blue eyes. He had the confidence of a nature god and indeed he was one to me. I was ten when he first tousled my hair and told me I had the face of a ripe little Madonna. He teased that he would paint me, and that I may even be the one woman to supplant his obsession for Florence's darling, the Lady Simonetta. He left seductive hints for me to follow like breadcrumbs.

Sandro made every woman feel she was the only angel on his horizon. His horizons were always suffused with sexual honey, and I found intoxicating flashes of violet intimacy in his eyes. Leonardo was decidedly anti-Sandro for reasons I didn't yet understand, but Sandro continued to hold a dear place in my memory, and then later, much more.

First love is second to no other. Fantasies form a diamond within every young girl. Feminine potency polishes women into gems of cosmetic allure, but age dulls us into yesterday's jewels. We burn bright... zeniths of wild abandon and fall to earth spent like roman candles. We know our arc is complete when we become invisible to the least significant street courtesies. We see our decline in the reflection of common indifference. Such is the stretch of a woman's brief glory.

I knew Ginevra Benci well enough to be diplomatically civil the few times we met. We were not friends. Peasants and princesses do not mix. We were the oil and water of women, but more alike than either of us cared to admit.

Both of us were ambitious and extreme in our loyalties. I was loyal to Leonardo and Ginevra watched out for herself. Her biggest mistake was to underestimate me. She never understood that I could be a threat and she neglected to consider both high and lowborn women shared the same maternal instinct: that we are protective tigresses, and lionesses, and leopardesses... huntresses of transient beauty – cunning feline predators under our fated veneers of servitude.

Ginevra chose Sandro to paint her portrait, but he turned her down, and therein lies the crux of our collective problems. Leonardo was then chosen to paint her likeness by Master Andrea – a decision planted by Lorenzo. The contract came through Verrocchio's studio and it was my brother's first semi-independent work. The motto 'Virtutem Forma Decorat' (virtue adorns beauty) had been appropriated to purge Ginevra's soiled reputation and in case the message proved too subtle, in a fit of creative sarcasm, Leonardo emblazoned it in a formal crest, on the portrait's reverse side.

No painted likeness ever flattered the privileged as much as their own flowery self-descriptions. Portraits rarely show a true face, and without truth, beauty and virtue are rather superficial qualities. It's more honest to admit that any virtue worth having was twinned to wealth. Ginevra's family were rich. Verrocchio would have painted her under a thousand lies for the sake of profit. The business of art was his driving force.

Later, the title 'La Gioconda' was a clever name that took innocent root. My brother played with words like a cat plays with a piece of string – agile and quick, twisting suddenly into grace. He loved the double meanings of a phrase or title – the second joke under a first jest... the riddle above the pun... the visual clue inside a puzzle with a gentle sting in its tail, but in the years that followed his death, I became a shadow turned to stone.

I know that I blunt fame's teeth with my persistence. The pursuit of recognition serves no purpose other than vanity, but I want a lot of things: I want to return to the serenity of my skies – their simplicities of lavender and the blues of robin's eggs, and clouds suffused with light. I want to sit at the right hand of art and taste the fruits of eternity. I want to rest in peace.

Being ignored burns like acid, but the truth can expose the unfairness of history and remedy its indignities. Psychic varnish can leach off my skin. I'm tired. I want to have my real name whispered on Earth in the sanctuary of galleries and be written into the credits of Leonardo's life story.

My attachment to my portrait was not meant to last five-hundred years. I had thought I could join Leonardo any time. I was wrong. It's clear to me now that I created my present situation and that I was as trapped in the Louvre as I had felt in life. I have discovered that death is a continuation of purpose, so the anonymity I suffered in the fifteenth and sixteenth centuries, grew tenfold.

Being invisible is cruel. Being insubstantial is hell.

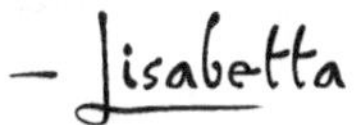

FROM THE DIARY OF VERONICA LYONS

- SLIPPERY SLOPE -
MAY 30, 2008

Maybe at the bottom of the slippery slope it's life re-birthing in the sludge and not the death we so often assume. Maybe death is a bright thing one ascends to where one's host ushers us in with companions and white light. Maybe it's an instant release with no residue, or perhaps a faint memory of what was suffered in the name of entertaining a muse.

I digest 'other's triumphs. It's only my personal story that's too hard to accept. I feel like the supporting character, an 'everywoman', who lives and breathes achieving no large thing. Small roles are left off the credits to float like the background static of soundtrack ghosts. How many hundreds of generations, born-once, did we miscast to find ourselves on a planet spinning in crisis? How many more will continue to read their lines as written? How many will throw a curve into the production, and call for a new script?

The burning between my shoulder blades from sitting hunched over a keyboard, reminds me that I am blood and bone, and that all forms of pain act as gatekeepers to block success.

Like attracts like, so how does one dis-spell the bad fairy's curse? Beasts of burden can also carry a jubilant messiah into an Emerald city. Pollyannas can still skin their knees.

The merry month of May's semi-invisibility is over.

This is the world I have made. It has locks, and bolts, and alarms. It has guardians, and moats, and spells against intruders. Ghostly males are as welcome as the ones playing easy to get.

— Veritas Icona

FROM THE DIARY OF VERONICA LYONS

- TERRITORIAL CLAIMS -
JUNE 4, 2008

Lisabetta led me through Mona Lisa's landscape. It was a confusing country of opposites: looking east there are stark mountains like shards of crystal. Cathedral-like with wild stalagmite pillars, where bears are limber enough to inhabit high caves and the desert plain below is populated with lions that roam over their yellow grasses. The rolling hills ramble to an ocean where Lisabetta's heaven waits as a faint light on the horizon – the aurora borealis of judgment. Lisabetta goes there to stare at her destination – her anticipated alternate destiny that beckons with freedom.

The living world is on her right. It flashes quietly – a receding thunderstorm with the muted grumbles of a distant battle. The 'other side' divides the picture plane in two.

Looking west, a chalk cliff gleams under a green blanket peppered with violets – a gentle pasture that slopes to a clear drop-off for the ornithopter launched by a griffin or two. And once I dreamed her a dragon that puffed sfumato breath across the vista and made her sigh.

Looking out, into the territory of the near dead – there is lush greenery and a red-brick manse embraced in the dewy emerald embrace of the Loire Valley. On the night of Leonardo's passing it had been encompassed by a malevolent ball of weather. An electrical storm – a tempest in a large French teacup. I witnessed Leonardo's bedroom window glowing like a square of fire and the Leonardo Tree as it exhaled bursts of sparks, it too was ready for death. The gargoyles stretched their wings on the pinnacles of each gable and frightened the ever-present birds ready to guide their champion home.

Trickeries of light polish the sky with undulating stripes of colors like the searchlights of an aerial circus. The small bridge to her left is the demarcation line that straddles failure and success. A trickle of the River Styx slips under it teeming with effervescent fish. We spend hours on its banks rearranging her clouds and pruning them into a menagerie of topiary clouds.

One can study the surface of the 'Mona Lisa' and imagine the rest. What you can't see are the marvels she and Leonardo have conjured. To me it's heaven, but Lisabetta insists no, it is the art behind art. I described it to her as a whimsical hologram. She didn't argue.

At dusk, the sky ballet begins with the finest display of fireworks imaginable: crimson showers of falling stars and firebrands flashing from gold to violet, and horned comets with forever tails that lash the air with flames. The smell of the wild moon, big as the planet Jupiter, floats on an ozone of smoky wind. And in the daylight we visit her formal sculpture gardens of angels and winged beasts where Pegasus and the Lion of Venice preen their stone feathers.

Lisabetta says she has created her personal heaven, far more grand than this.

— Veritas Icona

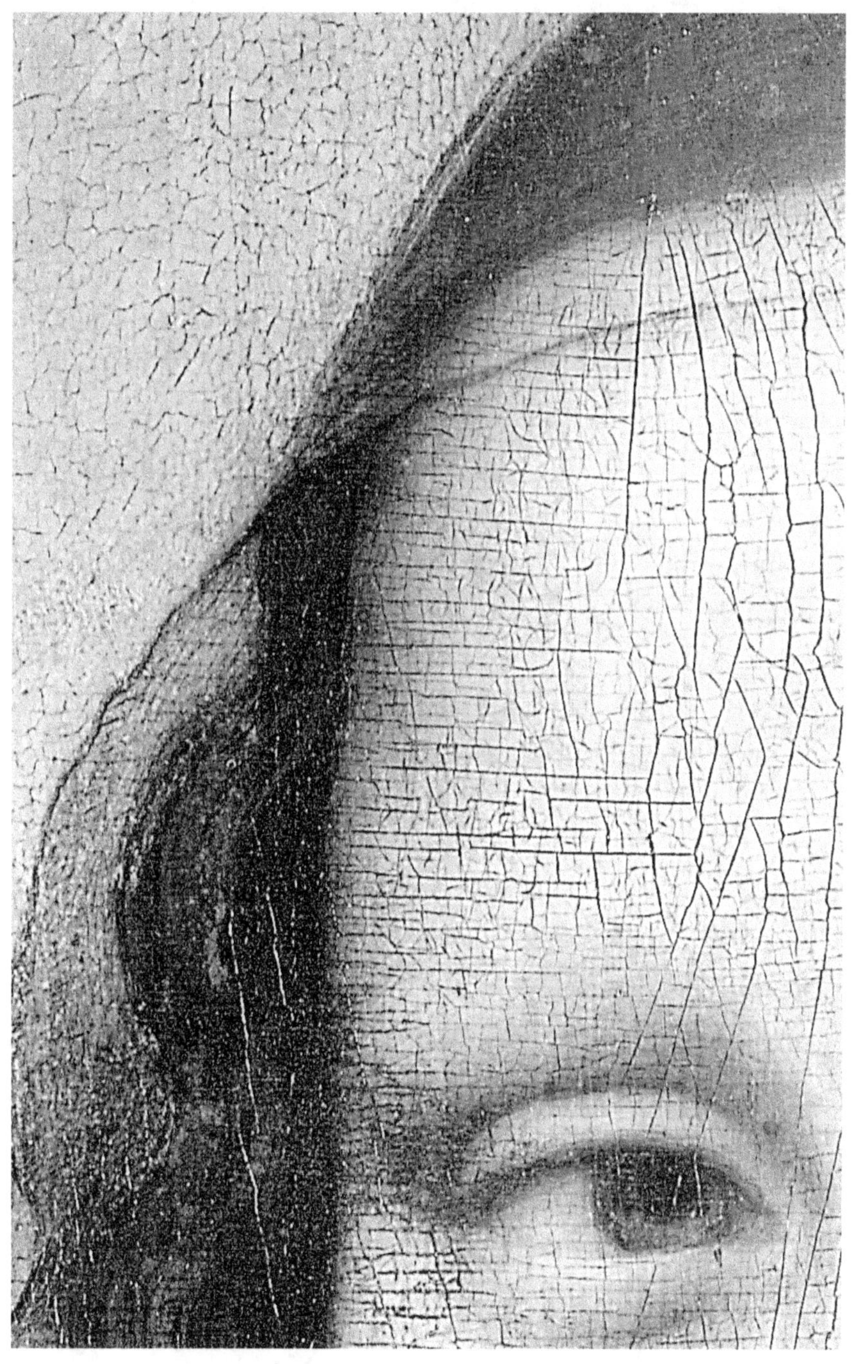

glossary

Apoplexy:	*a stroke*
Aslan:	*the magic lion from C.S. Lewis' Narnia series*
Bargello:	*the Florentine prison with fortified walls*
Bottega:	*studio*
Buchi Della Verita:	*the holes of truth*
Buongiorno:	*good morning*
Che cosa:	*what!*
Catamite:	*a boy kept by a man for sexual intercourse*
Campanile:	*bell tower*
Caro mia:	*my dear one*
Cecero:	*a swan*
Chiaroscuro:	*an object or figure in a painting emerging from deep shadow into subdued light*
Ciao:	*hello or goodbye*
Dimmi:	*tell me*
Ghirlandaio:	*an ornament worn in a woman's hair*
Gonfalonier:	*mayor*
Hypericum:	*St. John's Wort, a plant used in the treatment of hysteria and depression*
Ka:	*Egyptian term for the aspect of human consciousness which remains on earth as a replica of a deceased's body.*
La Vacca:	*the cow, nickname for the campanile bell which had a mournful, bovine sound*
Libricini:	*small books*

Loggia:	*veranda or terrace*
Melancholia:	*depression*
Niente:	*nothing*
Ornithopter:	*Leonardo's flying machine*
Ponte:	*a bridge*
Piazza:	*public square*
Predella:	*the decorated base of an altarpiece*
Putti:	*depictions of infant boys with wings who assist Eros/cupid and Erato, the muse of lyric and love poetry, in matters of profane love. *Cherubs are their counterparts who assist in divine love*
Quattrocento:	*the fifteenth-century of the Italian renaissance.*
Runcible:	*a nonsense word invented by Edward Lear*
Sfumato:	*literally, smoke — the distinctive soft hazy effect of the blended edges of wet oil paint*
Signoria:	*city council*
Stinche (the):	*the main prison in Florence. Derivative of the word, stench*
Tempera:	*water-based pigments mixed with egg yolk*
Tronie:	*a generic portrait of no particular individual*
Via:	*street*
Virtuem Forma Decorat:	*chastity adorns beauty*

art themes
Prevalent in Leonardo's World

Adorations:	*the birth of Jesus*
Annunciations:	*the virgin Mary's visitation from an angel, informing her she is with child.*
Ascensions:	*an image of the risen Christ*
Battles:	*political commentaries*
Davids:	*the biblical boy warrior – the weak overcoming powerful enemies*
Holy Families:	*groupings of any combinations of Jesus' relations*
Last Judgments:	*souls being judged to heaven or hell*
Last Suppers:	*Christ's last meal with his disciples*
Ledas:	*Leda is a Spartan princess, seduced by the god Jupiter, after he takes the form of a swan*
Martyrdoms:	*depictions of the deaths of saints*
Mother & Child:	*Mary with the infant Jesus*
Pietas:	*the Virgin Mary mourning over the dead body of Jesus*
St. Johns:	*John the Baptist, cousin of Jesus*
Transfigurations:	*a vision of the risen Jesus inside radiant light*

It is curious, that the definitive snapshot of Leonardo da Vinci is generally the magus with a long white beard, but what I find more compelling, is reaching back for the earlier Leonardo who was once a babe-in-arms crying for milk, a toddler who played in dangerous grasses without the protection of a playpen, and a mischievous boy with a pet dog.

Leonardo was also a sensitive teenager with adolescent challenges, a confused youth with an identity crisis, and a handsome young prodigy grappling with a relentless curiosity to understand the entire world as if it were a direct command from God. That he survived all of these stages amongst plague and violence is astonishing. Without these experiences our default Leonardo could not have been. And yet, 'Lisabetta' must begin with the elderly Leonardo, because it is a the moment of his death when she becomes ensnared and her story unfolds.

The end of creative lives are summarized by calendar highlights, but artists' works live on as random 'reincarnations'. It was the theft of the 'Mona Lisa' in 1911, which launched her to stardom. Until that time, the 'Mona Lisa' had been demoted to a relatively nondescript position within the art world. 'Mona Lisa's' celebrity revival (*after* her return) gave Leonardo's academic manuscripts their own rebirth. All eyes became focused on the miracle painting and its creator. The population was bombarded with all things Leonardo: exotica and trivia. His achievements were harvested from scholarly documentation and reborn to the common man. Society loves its cultural heroes.

The vast, Royal Collection of Leonardo's folios of drawings, were once set aside, and overlooked in a trunk for a hundred years. The universal 'Renaissance Man' image, formed into legend after the media triggered (and milked) the 'Mona Lisa' frenzy. For a while, the portrait of a Florentine lady was the kite, and Leonardo, its tail. The *tale* that grew into the modern Leonardo myth.

The works of the master painter, Sandro Botticelli, were similarly obscure outside Italy, unsung for centuries until the Pre-Raphaelites heralded his style, in the late eighteen-hundreds. It is these random acts of posthumous celebrity which change the biographical face of fame. For an artist, life after death, can be infinitely more rewarding than the hand-to-mouth careers they once lived.

Leonardo's sisters never figured in Giorgio Vasari's biography of Leonardo, and his mother, Caterina, was a speculative first-name-only, byline. Vasari's 'Lives of the Artists' was published a mere thirty years after Leonardo's death. It would have been easy to trace Leonardo's family from contemporary sources, but references to women disappear first, unimportant enough to document or research. Without old census records, Leonardo's half-brother and sisters, and cousins, would be entirely erased from the life of a great man, whose life was no doubt interwoven with theirs.

Leonardo glossed over his family too, unless he wrote about them in his missing papers. Leonardo trained as an artist and moved on, leaving his peasant years to memory. Alas, Caterina left no diary to celebrate her existence and her son's childhood.

For me, it is infinitely more rewarding, to imagine how the impressionable, young Leonardo, first harnessed his creative talents, rather than after he had become the benevolent, elderly master. Yes, Leonardo had survived the upheavals of his time, and likely, never 'lolled about' in the French countryside during his retirement, but the main energy of Leonardo's extraordinary legacy, are his early years of transformation, which modeled him into a force of science and art. A force which eventually earned him the honorary title: 'Renaissance Man'.

The romantic version of Leonardo da Vinci is a human bee, engineered against impossible odds, to defy gravity. He was seemingly born with a mission to sample knowledge, constantly lured from theory to theory before the nectar was gone, happily diverted by an insatiable appetite to document the world. Leonardo's brain was a multitasking hive for distilling, processing, and filing organic quests

– a slave to abstraction and distraction. Busy busy busy. He made art, but it was the sciences that were his academic honey.

I envisage the relentless sixty-seven-year-old Leonardo, an uncompromising charismatic genius, never quite tired enough to rest on his laurels.

I believe Leonardo would have loved to live forever, and of course he does, by way of his fame, but wouldn't it be amazing to show Leonardo the evolutions of flight and photography, or the umbrella and the fountain pen? In my historical fantasy, 'Lisabetta', we can imagine these things and more, through the posthumous insight of his sister.

For the first six years of his life, Leonardo was subjected to a rough peasant life surrounded by half-sisters and female cousins. His stepfather, Antonio Buti, a kiln worker and mercenary soldier, was known as the local tough guy. One may surmise the relationship with a stepson, forced on him in a business deal, would be less than nurturing. Antonio's marriage to Leonardo's mother, while she was pregnant with Piero da Vinci's child, was a purely financial arrangement. It appears that the ruling patriarch of the da Vinci clan, paid Antonio to take Caterina off their hands in order that his heir, Piero, was clear to marry another girl.

An indifferent grandfather, father, and stepfather were the primary male role models who influenced Leonardo, and it seems, instilled within him a sense of unworthiness that he struggled with all his life.

I have speculated, that Leonardo's intense work ethic may have been, in part, a form of compensation, trying to engage the love of the father who abandoned him.

Certainly, it's fair to assume that Leonardo experienced an ongoing drive to perform above the low expectations his biological father placed on him. Leonardo was kept on the periphery of the da Vinci compound as insurance – an heir by default should no other appear. And for twenty-four years, none did. The birth of Francesco da Vinci, Piero's first legitimate son, impacted dramatically on Leonardo's social position, and no doubt, his emotional health.

This is the point where Piero turned his back on his first-born son. Leonardo is rejected, ignored, and left to process his anguish and altered circumstances, alone. The push-pull years of early rejection and acceptance is a dynamic which could destabilize a vulnerable growing boy. A boy, perhaps already challenged, as the surviving records suggest that Leonardo may have suffered from the bipolar highs and lows of self-esteem, and possibly, high-functioning autism.

I premise that Leonardo was more than sensitive, and that he presented a rare form of genius savant – a creative-obsessive with a penchant for multi-level thinking and eccentric behavior. Leonardo's erratic work habits suggest he possessed a finite attention span. His projects were experimental breakthroughs, but Leonardo's temperament dictated that most of his major works of art would disintegrate or disappear.

I put forward, that Leonardo was not alone, and that he had a younger sister named Lisabetta who was strong enough to compensate for his weaknesses. Female artists during Leonardo's time worked in the art studios alongside their male relatives as unpaid assistants. They were an invisible workforce on the surface, but I theorize that they would still have possessed a formidable energy, natural to their own gender, more powerful perhaps, because they were overlooked and suppressed. There must have been individual women with equal, if not more talent, than their male counterparts.

Leonardo, farmed out to an artist friend of his father's at the age of twelve, was a star apprentice by the time he was thirteen. Andrea Verrocchio, his master teacher, ran one of the most successful art studios in Florence.

Verrocchio's busy studio would best be described as a factory, and it would be natural for Leonardo to sponsor an artistic sister into his world when she grew old enough to be of assistance. I have presupposed that Leonardo would have trained her on his visits to the homestead, and that by the time he was eighteen and a veteran apprentice for six years, that Lisabetta would be a proficient twelve-year-old artist.

I have never accepted that Leonardo's mother, Caterina, was a peasant, but that she and Piero were contemporaries of the same notary class. In my novel, I write them as childhood sweethearts, separated by the legalities of the day. The children of such families were betrothed, often from birth, and it is highly-credible that a mate chosen by a formality could clash later from a conflicting emotional attachment.

Antonio Buti was away for months at a time. Liaisons between young lovers living in close proximity would be tempting and relatively easy to arrange. Therefore I have given Leonardo a full-sister in addition to the daughters sired by Antonio.

Historical facts are glimpses of shadows. Here today… gone yesterday, but the historic record reveals that Leonardo had four half-sisters and one was named, Lisabetta. She was younger than Leonardo by six years. I have claimed Lisabetta to be the only sibling with the same parentage as Leonardo, and that they shared a natural bond greater than the rest of Leonardo's foster family.

Some children make it out of the social cocoon, whole. But a cocoon can be a womb or a tomb depending on the praise and criticism of others. For celebrities, then and now, fame or infamy is more mysterious than a curse or a smile, which explains the term: *there's no such thing as bad publicity*. History is, as history does.

Here now is my declaimer for naming Lisabetta's 'poetic sister', Veronica. I would have preferred to use a name other than my own, but in the end, iconography prevailed. A book about true faces, an iconic image, lost identities, and false names, demanded it.

The name Veronica is an anagram from the Latin translation: veritas (truth) and icon (image). My use of the name Veronica is purely a literary device. No other woman's name would serve the story of the true identity of the 'Mona Lisa', as well.

The face of the 'Mona Lisa' has the quality of a true portrait, and not a 'tronie' of an ideal woman-composite. Her likeness is the most famous iconic mystery to be trapped in the history of art.

'Mona Lisa' is in good company; the provenance of paintings is literally, a lost art. Even the attributed paintings, are often group efforts of master artists, senior assistants, and junior apprentices. Copies of paintings were made on a regular basis, with varying success. Admirers and followers mimicked a master's style. As Veronica Lyons says in the story, an attributed work is like a revolving door.

It is estimated that one third of Leonardo's manuscripts are presumed destroyed, but it is possible that a lost episode of Leonardo's extraordinary life, may emerge from the darkness like an artist's technique of chiaroscuro. Revelations are serendipitous by nature: time still hides some Leonardo surprises. The obscure margin note or dry official document, or a diary of a credible source, still hold wonders waiting to be revealed.

Leonardo is known to have kept the 'Mona Lisa' by his side until his death. I premise, that during the last eleven years of Leonardo's life: grief, denial, and declining physical and mental states, that the portrait of his beloved sister, Lisabetta, had become as real to Leonardo as she had been in life.

In 'Lisabetta', a work of fiction, a newly discovered cache of libricini (the small notebooks Leonardo carried) changes the art world, and Veronica Lyons' altered states represent the artistic awareness's of the broadest autism spectrum. Are they presentations of imagination, reincarnation or insanity? You decide. What-if Veronica Lyons isn't crazy, but madly inspired?

Art is a form of reincarnation: styles and themes progress similarly to a genealogical map, and no-one knows the flesh-and-blood or emotional dynamics of another's life. As for young Lisabetta, pining for her beloved older brother, couldn't she have grown up as a sister in need of escape from the drudgery of farm life to become one of the invisible female workers in Verrocchio's studio? Perhaps encouraged and trained by a talented big brother? A genius brother who needed to be grounded with committed support in order to shine as brightly as he did?

– V. Knox May 2, 2019

written on the 500th anniversary of Leonardo's death.

"When you want to confirm your personal power,
Tell a lie and watch it come true."
~ Veronica Lyons

Now Lost

The sfumato-like years between Leonardo's paintings become impossible to navigate. Francesco Giocondo had bought an original... a masterpiece, and Lisa Giocondo took her portrait with her when she retired to the convent of San Orsolo. Her daughter nuns were of a different opinion. Secular art and religious subjects were at odds. A portrait of their smiling mother defiled the solemn Holy Virgins and their sacrificial sons. It had to be stored, and once a painting goes underground, it leaves a cold trail.

Lisa's portrait is a window at best, a mirror at worst... a vanity to be concealed before God, in God's house, where brides of Christ wander on impressionable tiptoes. It is not considered true art. Sacred art depicts annunciations and resurrections and martyrdoms.

At Lisa Giocondo's death, her property is dispersed into the community. The functions of panel paintings are often reduced to table tops and doors, and manuscripts are left to attic mice and fungus in damp outbuildings.

There may have been no-one in the Giocondo line who cherished Lisa's portrait enough, to keep it above ground, or who bothered to claim the 'Gioconda' after Lisa's death. It is a 'now lost'. If it is still 'alive', then somewhere it illuminates a dark cupboard, abandoned, confiscated, and un-catalogued. If it lingers in a private collection, it's a clandestine one. The pose is the same as Lisabetta's. Easily recognizable. It will have the full touch of the master of course, and the dress is the same. The pose is a match. The second 'Lisa' was modeled on the first.

Lisa Giocondo lived to the age of seventy-one. Her two daughters were cloistered inside nunneries, apart from the world of art. Lisa lost her portrait, but 'saved-face' by gaining celebrity. Lisabetta lost her identity and gained immortality. While Lisabetta's face captures the King of France, Lisa's face hung on a private wall, safe from Salai and out of Melzi's protection. It was commissioned, temporarily held to ransom... and then it was purchased. It once belonged to Francesco Giocondo and his heirs. Now it belongs to time.

historical footnotes

Leonardo da Vinci had four half-sisters.

Lisabetta Buti was born sometime between 1458 and 1460. Leonardo was six in 1458. He lived with his mother, sisters, and stepfather, enduring a rough peasant lifestyle until the age of seven. He revered cats and horses and birds.

Historical evidence points to a separate version of the 'Mona Lisa', the painting Leonardo dubbed 'La Gioconda'. She will be recognized from the pillars of a loggia which frame her, and a pair of reportedly stunning eyebrows. Raphael went on to use Leonardo's revolutionary pose in several of his own works.

The portrait of Ginevra Benci has, in the distant past, been cropped. The lower third of the painting, containing her hands and what she holds, is lost. The painting surfaced in the 20th century, after being 'mislaid' under another mistaken identity for four-hundred-years. In 1480, four years after Leonardo painted her, the once celebrated Ginevra (Benci) Niccolini, age twenty-two, retired to the country. She was abandoned by her lover, Bernardo Bembo, who commissioned her portrait. Documents suggest she died alone, at the age of sixty-three, a childless, hypochondriac, widow, after living forty years in relative seclusion.

Leonardo left his signature on the first version of the 'Madonna of the Rocks' His collaborator artist, Ambrogio di Predis, had a deaf brother, Cristoforo, also an artist. From top to bottom, Mary, the angel and one of the babies sign the letters, L – D – V. Intentionally, either child can represent Christ or John the Baptist. Leonardo favored the underground cult of John the Baptist.

The 'bucha della verita', the 'holes of truth', were ballot boxes placed throughout Florence. Anyone could post an anonymous accusation against a fellow citizen.

In 1796, French troops used the Santa Maria delle Grazie, in Milan, as an armory, and later a prison. The soldiers thought it amusing to throw rocks at the 'Last Supper'. They climbed ladders and scratched out the apostles eyes. In 1943, during World War II, the church was severely damaged during a bombing raid. Several consequent restorations cover Leonardo's original work. What you see is what you get: an abused and befuddled, ersatz version of a da Vinci masterpiece.

In 1802, during the demolition of the church of St. Florentin, at Amboise, France, Leonardo's mortal remains were dug up and discarded.

Lisa Giocondo (1479-1551) was the mother of five children. Her two daughters, Camilla and Marietta, took holy orders and changed their names respectively to: Sister Beatrice and Sister Ludovico. Lisa's mortal remains fared a similar fate to Leonardo's. Her bones were raked from her grave in the foundations of the Sant' Orsola Convent when the building was renovated as an underground parkade for the local police station. In 1980, the rubble was dumped in a landfill outside Florence.

Salai had a violent end; he was killed in a street duel at the age of forty-four, in 1524, five years after Leonardo's death. Salai peddled his own copies of Leonardo's work as originals for the rest of his life. An inventory at his death lists a painting called the 'Mona Lisa'.

Lorenzo di Credi joined the followers of the fanatic monk Savonarola, called 'The Weepers', along with his colleague, Sandro Botticelli. Both burned works of art in 1497, during the 'Bonfires of the Vanities' and descended into lives of religious penitence. Lorenzo later inherited his lover Verrocchio's, studio.

Sandro Botticelli was reduced to wandering the streets of Florence peddling paintings of Madonnas, in his last years. He was buried at the feet of Simonetta (Cattaneo de Candia) Vespucci.

Leonardo's manuscripts, in the present Windsor Collection, were forgotten in a trunk for two hundred years and rediscovered in 1760, at Kensington palace.

There are at least nine known copies of the 'Mona Lisa' painted with the assistance of the master, by his apprentices... including the 'Nude Gioconda' (the 'Mona Vanna'), painted by Giangiacomo Caprotti, the spoiled child, gold-digger, thief, pimp, spy, and despot known as, Salai ('little devil'). He lived the life of a parasite, living off Leonardo, his gentle benefactor, for twenty nine years.

Although Leonardo only knew Francesco Melzi for the last twelve years of his life, he made him sole executor of his estate, and left his entire body of work to his care. Francesco (Cecco) was a diligent and loyal conservationist of Leonardo's legacy... or what was left of it after it was ransacked by Salai at the master's death. 'Cecco' recovered several of Leonardo's works from Salai's estate. Melzi's descendants treated Leonardo's estate with considerably less respect, and the collection was dispersed for profit or destroyed due to negligence. Two thirds of Leonardo's manuscripts are now lost. *Two lost volumes of bound sketches were found in 1967, misplaced in the stacks of a Spanish library.

Marie Corelli, 1855-1924, was an eccentric Victorian novelist – the illegitimate daughter of a doctor and a servant girl, and author of bodice-ripper/paranormal romances whose stories achieved a renaissance during the peak of occult New-Age soul-mate literature, in the sixties. Marie changed her name from MacKay to Corelli, and made a pretense of speaking Italian, borrowing the glamorous persona of an Italian aristocrat. Her desire for fame knew no bounds. Her novels were favored by Queen Victoria. Marie was a contemporary of the author Lewis Carroll.

'La Principessa' (the Princess) and the 'Salvator Mundi' (Saviour of the world) are two portraits which have been authenticated since the year 2008.

WHAT OTHER WORKS OF LEONARDO
MAY YET BE FOUND?

'The Leda and the Swan' last witnessed in 1519, in Amboise, France.

The fresco, 'The Battle of Anghiari's' lost location on one of the eight walls of the council hall of the Palazzo Vecchio, painted over, in 1560.

A finished portrait in oils of Isabella d'Este.

'The Madonna of the Yarnwinder with basket'.

Hundreds of stolen drawings cut from manuscripts. The missing two-thirds of Leonardo's notebooks and countless libricini.

A single fragment of the giant clay horse, twenty-seven feet high, which lay abandoned to the elements, scavengers, and vandals in the streets of Milan in 1493.

The mechanical lion made for the King of France, Francis I, in 1515.

The portrait of a certain Florentine silk merchant's lady: The Monna Lisa del Francesco Giocondo, titled 'La Gioconda', last documented sighting in the year, 1533.

And notations within contemporary documents: new facts, facts, facts.

REFERENCED WORKS OF ART
in THE COMPLETE SERIES

LEONARDO DA VINCI:

'The Mona Lisa'
'Portrait of Ginevra Benci' (front and back)
'The Last Supper'
'Madonna of the Rocks' (London version)
'Madonna of the Rocks' (Louvre version)
'St. John'
'Madonna and the Cat' (drawing)
'Vitruvian Man' (drawing)
'the pyramid parachute' Leonardo's invention (drawing)
the recently discovered 'Principessa' illustration on vellum and the
'Salvator Mundi'
the Battle of Anghiari mural is lost
the Leda and the Swan is lost
the portrait of Lisa Giocondo is lost

GIANGIACOMO CAPROTTI (SALAI):

'The Monna Vanna' (nude Gioconda)

THE STUDIO of ANDREA VERROCCHIO:

The 'Tobias and the Angel'
The Pistoia altarpiece
The orb for the Santa Maria del Fiore
The bronze statue of David

SANDRO BOTTICELLI:

'Mars and Venus'
'La Primavera'
'The Birth of Venus'
* the Diana is lost

SCULPTURES & MODELS:

Verrochio's bronze 'David'
Michelangelo's 'David'
Verrochio's 'Woman with the Flowers'
Leonardo's 'Angel of Gennaro'
*Leonardo's Giant Horse is lost
*Leonardo's Ornithopters are lost
*Leonardo's Mechanical Lion is lost, but there are modern reproductions
*The 'Nike of Samothrace' – the head, arms, and one wing are lost
Pietro Tacca's 'Il Porcellina' (The Market Boar)
*The original Hellenistic Antiquity 'Market Pig' is lost

historical fantasies

by V Knox/Veronica Knox

'ADORATION – Loving Botticelli' – *The romance between an art history professor and a five-hundred-year-old portrait leads from obsession to seduction.*

'I WAS THERE' – *a 'love poem' that explores the art of time travel in a lucid 15th century dreamscape.*

'WOO WOO – the Posthumous Love story of Miss Emily Carr' – *an eccentric artist decides to marry sixty-seven-years after her death.*

'THE INDIGO PEARL' – *an autistic girl with extrasensory abilities who converses with paintings and birds, falls in love with the portrait of boy.* *book one of two

'PEARL BY PEARL' – *the conclusion of 'the Indigo Pearl' AI = autistic intelligence… *'state of the art' time travel just became transcendental.*

'THE UNTHINKABLE SHOES' – *The spirit of a boy from the 'Titanic' remains earthbound as the invisible childhood friend of the girl he'd been destined to marry.*

'TWINTER the first portal' – *twelve-year-old telepathic twins discover their grandmother's haunted stately home, Bede Hall, nestled next to Hadrian's Wall in England, has a longstanding agenda with ancient Egypt, Pangea, and Mars.**book one of the time-slip 'Bede trilogy' for Y/A.

'TIME FALLS LIKE SNOW' *—teenage twins continue their adventure. Turning sixteen isn't going to be easy.*

'DISAPP<u>EARRIN</u>G TWICE' – *The girl in Vermeer's 'Girl With A Pearl Earring' disappears from her portrait.*

'TOMORROW AGAIN' – *book three of the 'Bede Series' for Y/A*

acknowledgments

I thank my lucky stars that life comes true in wilder ways than I can dream.

My book designer, Iryna Spica, who shapes all my books into better places to read.

Lisabetta Buti – a 'true face' historical footnote to her half-brother, Leonardo da Vinci

The hundreds of anonymous women who drove the visual arts forward during times that were less than nurturing.

And Leonardo… I wish I'd known you… and maybe I do a little.

My children, Sarah and David Guthman who inspire me to succeed.

And for all the times I neglected to thank my parents enough – a posthumous hug to my mother and father for their gift of time.

the author on her painted 'floorals'

Veronica Knox

A FEW WORDS ABOUT ME

I've lived in the Findhorn Community of Scotland and turned an abandoned Scottish church near Loch Ness into an art gallery with painted 'floorals'.

I write surreal fiction: **ART HISTORY DELIVERED IN GHOST STORIES** under the name V KNOX.

I love highly-visual, multi-layered stories that reconcile historical facts with imaginative fiction… and deliver big surprises. I explore the creative inner worlds of autistic savants and master artists, and in one case, the unknown child in the Titanic cemetery. I explore the discrepancies between reality and lucid dreams, fish the depths of the subconscious, the afterlife, and reincarnation, the anomalies of parallel lives and dimensions, and the classic psyche of 'the ghostly lover'. I write time-slip situations that defy the logic I firmly believe in.

Studying for a Fine Arts degree from the University of Alberta led me to develop an imaginative take on art history that led to other untapped avenues for stories.

Inanimate objects are rarely bereft of life? Paintings tell me juicy secrets.

Italian Renaissance paintings captivate me. Objects in a museum captivate me. A pair of baby shoes labeled 'from the Titanic' or painted portraits are frozen moments – snapshots of what was and more importantly, WHO was. I found a wealth of stories, hidden in plain sight.

WHAT IF two children aboard the Titanic were meant to marry? What if a master painting was attributed to the wrong artist? What if the 'Mona Lisa' was Leonardo da Vinci's kid sister? Renaissance paintings had to be 'signed' in covert ways. Who left their definitive 'I was here' imprints in code?

I love words, so I was particularly delighted to learn that I am a serious *pluviophile* – a lover of rain. I proudly attach this attribute to my profile. It makes perfect sense of an idiosyncrasy of mine, that although I continue to amass a collection of extremely cool eclectic umbrellas, I prefer to get wet in the rain. However, as a great part of the joy of rain is the sound it makes (and for which there is no greater pleasure than walking under a fabric dome) to receive its full sensory experience I have one umbrella I employ *after* I get wet. It is emblazoned with the face of the 'Mona Lisa'.

I remain intent on listening to the ethereal echoes from objects in museums and the voices of the Italian Renaissance – the artists as well as their anonymous subjects and companions. I grant them second chances to air their grievances, tell their stories, and together we set the dreariest history books on fire.

www.veronicaknox.com

www.ingramcontent.com/pod-product-compliance
Lightning Source LLC
Chambersburg PA
CBHW070608300726
48975CB00006B/1747